A Convenient Marriage

A Correspondence,

A Convenient Marriage

Jeevani Charika

hera

First published in the United Kingdom in 2019 by Hera

This edition published in 2020 by

Hera Books
28b Cricketfield Road
London, E5 8NS
United Kingdom

A CIP catalogue record for this book is available from the British Library.

Print ISBN 978 1 80032 161 8
Ebook ISBN 978 1 912973 18 7

Printed and bound in Great Britain by Clays Ltd, Elcograf S.p.A.

To Lokunanda

Chapter One

Chaya – Colombo, 1994

The day Chaya was due to leave Colombo, everyone came to visit. Aunts, uncles, cousins, friends. They arrived in noisy droves, bringing gifts that she couldn't take with her because there was no room left in her luggage.

In honour of the occasion, Amma had cleaned every inch of the house. Between them, Amma and Leela had prepared a feast. Party food was laid out on the table. In the kitchen, a full meal of several curries and rice was warming. A number of aunts had brought food with them too, attempting to ease the burden of entertaining.

There were people everywhere, laughing and talking. Everyone wanted to shake her hand and wish her luck. She was the one everyone loved, for once.

'A member of our family going to Oxford,' an uncle said. He himself had been the first in the family to go to university. 'On a scholarship, no less.' He patted her shoulder. 'Who would have thought it, huh? Our little Chaya!'

'I always said she'd go far,' said her sister's father-in-law. 'Didn't I? Always said that.'

'You'll do well,' said a cousin. 'Maybe get a first.'

'A first from Oxford, imagine that!' said another.

Chaya smiled and nodded. What else was there to say?

'You be careful in England, Chaya,' said an aunt, mopping her frowning forehead with a handkerchief. 'I hear it's very dangerous over there now.'

'Nonsense,' said the uncle. 'Oxford is a very civilised place.'

The aunt ignored him. 'And stay away from the white boys. They only have one thing on their minds.' She patted Chaya's hand. 'Remember you have to come back here,' she said, meaningfully. 'You don't want to be spoiled. You'll never find a husband if that happens.'

Chaya fought the urge to roll her eyes. She had no intention of losing her focus, but it was a waste of time explaining that to people. Her aunts never really believed her. They were more interested in finding her the right sort of husband than in making a difference to the world.

Keeping her smiled fixed, she looked around for means of escape. Her big sister Malini, who was listening politely to an elderly great aunt, caught her gaze. Malini gently excused herself and came over.

'I need to borrow Chaya for a minute,' she said and smoothly extracted Chaya from the throng. They hurried through the kitchen and out to the back, where it was quiet.

'Thanks.' Chaya sank onto one of the concrete steps that led down to the garden, where Amma tried to grow vegetables under the jackfruit tree. Leela, the home help, was hanging clothes on the line. She waved.

Chaya waved back. The washing line seemed to get less and less crowded these days. First Malini's bright and stylish clothes went when she got married, and now Chaya's sensible ones were going. All that were left were Amma's saris and Thatha's work clothes. Chaya sighed. The fact that she was leaving was finally hitting home. All this time, she had been so focused on the idea of the scholarship that she hadn't paused to consider what she was leaving behind.

Malini brushed some grit off the step and sat down next to her. She gave her a small smile that was pinched at the edges with sadness. 'Are you ready for your trip?' she said.

Chaya shrugged. 'I don't know. It still doesn't feel real.' She glanced up at her sister. 'You know what I mean? Until now, the exams, the scholarship applications, the interviews, all that was just a means to an end and now that I've got there... I don't know what happens next.'

'You go out there and shine,' said Malini. 'That's what happens next.'

Chaya stared at her feet. 'I'm scared,' she said, quietly.

Malini put an arm around her. Chaya leaned her head against her sister's shoulder.

'You're the cleverest, most determined person I know,' said Malini. 'Look at what you've achieved already. This is only another step. You'll be fine.'

'But what if I'm not good enough? What if it was a fluke that I got the scholarship?'

'It wasn't a fluke. You earned it.' Malini rested her cheek against Chaya's head. 'Take it one step at a time. I have absolutely no doubt that you will pass your degree and come back triumphant. It's what you do.'

One step at a time. It sounded so easy. Chaya sighed again. Maybe it *was* that easy. Malini had a point. She had made it this far and ... being clever was what she did best.

'Thanks.'

She felt Malini's cheek crease as she smiled. Her sister removed the arm from around her. 'I got you this.' She pulled something out of her pocket and handed it to Chaya. 'It's nothing much...'

It was a photo of the two of them, taken on the morning of Malini's wedding. They were laughing at something, the laughter bordering on hysteria as they tried not to cry. That's how she felt right now. Chaya's eyes filled with tears.

'It's not much,' said Malini again, her chin starting to wobble.

Chaya threw her arms around her sister, tears running down her face. Malini hugged her back. After a while, they disentangled themselves and sat side by side, both sniffing and wiping tears off their faces.

'You will write, won't you?' said Malini.

'Every day.'

'And tell me everything.'

'Of course.'

Malini took her hand. 'I'll miss you,' she said.

'Malini? Chaya?' Amma's voice came from inside the house. They got to their feet, both wiping away the last tears.

'There you are.' Amma bustled out of the kitchen. She had been holding her emotions in check, by concentrating on being the super hostess. 'Suri Nanda and her family have arrived, you should go say hello. Or goodbye...' she stopped and looked at the two of them. She sighed. 'My girls,' she said, putting a hand to each of their faces. 'My darling girls.' Tears glinted in her eyes. 'One married and the other going off to university abroad. I'm so proud.'

Marriage and education ... twin holy grails in her parents' eyes. Malini, by virtue of being beautiful, could get away with just one. Chaya, it seemed, would have to achieve both in order to be complete. She leaned in and gave her mother a hug. Irritating as it was, she wouldn't have it any other way.

–

Later, Chaya got into the car, checked her passport and tickets for the hundredth time, and looked at everyone who had gathered to wave her off. There was quite a crowd, some smiling, some crying, all wishing her well. To the side were Malini and her husband Ajith, standing too close to each other, like newlyweds do. Behind them, Leela was sobbing quietly into a towel. Amma and Thatha were in the car with her. Someone opened the gate and the car started out. Chaya waved and a host of hands waved enthusiastically back. All those people. Her family. All she had to do was make them proud.

How hard could that be?

Chapter Two

Gimhana – Birmingham, 1994

The music from the club was super cheesy and he was so drunk that he was actually singing along. He wouldn't be caught dead singing along to East 17 normally. Gimhana raised his arms above his head and did an elaborate Bollywood dance spin. Because he could. He came to a stop, overbalanced and stumbled. A strong arm grabbed him around the waist.

'Steady,' said a voice in his ear.

He looked down at the hand that was splayed against his side. Moving his gaze up, he found the eyes of that guy. The guy. They'd been catching each other's eye all evening. Sneaked glances, hastily lowered. 'Hello,' he said.

The guy smiled and didn't let go of his waist. 'You okay?' He had to shout in Gim's ear to be heard.

Gim relaxed and let his head rest against the other man's shoulder. He had looked inviting from a distance. Up close, he was delicious. 'I am now,' he said.

The guy laughed, but didn't move away. 'Drink?' he said.

This was the first time Gimhana had ventured out to this bar. It was known, apparently, for being gay-friendly. Seeing the mixture of couples around the place, that much was clear. He hadn't known it was possible to just *be* like this. To flirt and dance like everyone else did. They stood near the bar together, talking as best they could, Gim exaggerating his drunkenness to lean closer and his friend gently pushing him back, each touch lingering, until the moment when he slid his hand briefly into Gim's and said, 'Want to go somewhere?'

Gim nodded, finished off his drink and followed him.

Outside, the night air was a sobering slap in the face. 'I'm Gimhana,' he said. 'But everyone calls me Gim.'

'Nate.' They shook hands, oddly formal.

'My flatmate's away,' said Nate, looking sideways at him. An invitation.

Gim nodded. 'Okay.'

At that time of night there were knots of drunk people and a few policemen. Gim and Nate walked along, side by side, trying to look like there was nothing more between them than casual friendship. Nate told him he was a builder. Gim explained that he was a student. They were heading towards the bus stop a few streets away. They turned into the side road.

This street was less crowded. Deep shadows filled the recessed shop doorways. They got halfway down the road before they found one that was empty.

Nate's kiss was hot, urgent. Gim wrapped his arms around Nate and pulled him closer, kissing him with all the pent-up need of the past hour. He tasted of beer and peppermint. He reached under Nate's jacket and t-shirt and found warm, bare skin. Nate's breathing hitched at his touch.

Nate's kisses moved down to his neck.

'How far is it to yours?' Gim said.

Nate responded by moving his mouth back to his. It was wonderful, passionate. For a Sri Lankan boy who had realised long ago that he was different, it was almost unbelievable that he could have this. This touch. This kiss. This feeling.

The blow came from one side. It knocked them both, limbs tangled, into the door of the shop. His head hitting the door frame made Gimhana's ears ring. There was blood in his mouth. Nate was dragged, shouting, away from him. Gimhana staggered to his feet and felt the crunching pain as someone hit him in the stomach and then in the back. He fell. His knees crashed onto the cold concrete. He saw the next kick coming and lurched out of the way, just in time. He saw Nate push one of the attackers off. The man fell against the guy who was about to kick Gimhana again. Taking the opportunity, Gimhana scrambled to his feet and ran. 'You get that one. I'll take the other.' Feet pounded after him. One pursuer. More shouting. He hoped Nate had managed to run too. He could see the main road ahead.

'Help!' he shouted. His feet pounded, fear giving him speed he never knew he had. He burst into the street. People scattered around him. He looked around wildly for a policeman. There wasn't one. Two homeless people who had been looking through a bin came and stood beside him, looking past him. Gimhana turned. The man following him had stopped. Gim stared at him, not sure what to do. The guy had short cropped hair and what looked like a tattoo of a starburst climbing up his neck. He wore a snarl and, Gim knew from the pain in his side, heavy boots.

'Piss off home,' one of the homeless men growled. 'Leave the boy alone.'

Astonishingly, the guy turned and disappeared back down the side street.

Gimhana leaned forward and put his hands on his knees. His face was a mass of pain and he couldn't work out where the pain was exactly. His ribs hurt too and his hand, which had taken part of the first blow.

'You okay, sonny?' said one of the men who'd helped him. His breath was something foul and Gimhana felt the urgent need to be sick. He swallowed hard and nodded.

'You'll need to get that seen to,' the man said. He frowned. 'You got bus fare?'

Gimhana felt the pocket of his jeans. Miraculously, his wallet was still there. 'Yeah.' He was dimly aware that there were more people around now.

'Get to A&E, then. That bus goes there.' The man pointed.

'Thank you,' Gimhana said. 'Really. Thank you.'

The man patted him on the shoulder. 'Just do the same for someone else sometime.'

Gimhana limped away. He didn't catch the bus. Instead, he pulled up his hood and walked home, making sure he stayed in well-lit areas. He would report the attack in the morning. Then he would go and thank the homeless men properly. For now, all he wanted to do was to get back to his student house and clean himself up. The fact that there was no law against loving who he wanted to made no difference. Britain may be more amenable to people like him on the surface, but under the surface, things were exactly the same as they were at home.

Chapter Three

Chaya – London, 2005

Chaya couldn't concentrate. It was nearly time. The Geology department lecture theatre was only thirteen minutes away, twelve if the lift came quickly, which it would at this time of the evening. She glanced at the display on her computer screen. 18.50. The lecture started in ten minutes.

She shouldn't go. Really. All those times she'd stopped herself from typing his name into Google. All the techniques she'd learned to not think about him. All of those would have been wasted if she went.

She sighed and opened up her emails again. Her friend Sara had sent her a link to something funny, the rest were just work emails. There were three queries from students. About a hundred emails were marked unread because she hadn't had a chance to deal with them. Most of it was administrative nonsense anyway. Although, administrative nonsense needed to be done if she was to keep successfully getting grants.

She picked one marked 'urgent' and opened it. It was about the big European grant she was working on. Feedback and revisions. She groaned. This was important, though. The grant was big enough that if she got it, she could take her tiny group from two staff members and a student, to a decent size. She was hoping to get the application in before she went on holiday to Sri Lanka at the end of the month.

She managed three minutes of concentrating and jotting down notes about what to say in her reply before her eyes

9

dragged themselves back to the clock. Argh. She now had seven minutes to get there. She wouldn't be able to make it in time to the opening of the lecture, so may as well not bother, right? Right.

She drafted a reply email. At least she would be getting this done. Then she could pop into the lab, set up the bacterial cultures for tomorrow's experiment and go home early. Not that she knew what she'd do once she got home. There was a reason she rarely left work until ten p.m. This place, more than anywhere, had plenty to distract her from her own thoughts. It kept her busy and stopped her thinking about Noah and the wounds that had not quite healed over the years.

The trouble was, Noah was here. Thirteen minutes away, right now. He would be standing up to talk about the use of modern mapping techniques in the study of volcanic drift. When the monthly events email came through, she'd scrolled idly through it and his name had screamed out at her. She had deleted the email immediately, but she couldn't unsee it. She knew he was here.

It had been ten years and she could still remember everything about him. She had a sudden memory of him explaining his final year project to her; the way his voice came alive when he talked about his work. It was that passion that got him the PhD offer that took him to Canada. That passion would still be there. Unless he'd changed. She looked around at her cramped office, with its board covered in deadlines and proposals. You didn't stay in academia if you didn't love your topic. That passion was the only thing that made it worthwhile putting up with the rest of the crap.

It was 18.59 now. She reread the email she'd just drafted. Oh no. That would never do. She tried again, but her thoughts kept escaping and running back to a time when she was nineteen and stupid enough to fall in love. 19.01. Oh dammit. She had to know.

Chaya's footsteps echoed in the corridors of the Geology department. Everything seemed bigger and slightly eerie in the night-time lighting. The lecture had started fifteen minutes ago, so there was no one outside the lecture hall. She opened the door to the back of the lecture theatre and slipped in.

The lights were down. A video was playing. Colours moved across a map. Chaya took a seat at the back, in the seat with the worst view when the place was full. There wasn't a huge crowd now, though. There never was, despite the millions of emails that were sent out urging staff and students to attend lectures. That said, this turnout was respectable. Noah must be well known in his field. Of course, he would be. He was clever, her Noah.

She caught her train of thought just in time. He wasn't her Noah. He wasn't her anything. He was a guy that she used to know. Nothing more.

The video came to an end and the lights went back up. And there he was. He still had red-blond hair, cropped shorter now. Even from this distance, he looked a little older. The young face had firmed up, losing the softness that she'd never noticed back then. Protective walls she'd built around her heart cracked. She missed him, in spite of everything she told herself.

Coming to this had been a huge mistake. She wanted to leave, but she couldn't move. She watched him, suddenly too tired to pay attention to the words. He waved his arms around when he talked, in that way of his. He leaned forward towards the audience when he had a point to make. Each familiar gesture was a hammer blow to the walls that kept her feelings safe.

When the lecture came to an end, people asked questions. Noah answered them, self-assured as always. He made a joke, his voice lifting with a little laugh at the end. The sound was so familiar, so beloved, it stopped her breathing for a second.

People started to file out. Chaya knew she had to move, but she didn't. The crowd thinned. If she didn't leave now, he would spot her, lurking in the back. So she stood up. As she moved away from her seat she looked up. He was looking straight at her.

He frowned. 'Chaya?'

Trapped, she stopped and gave him a tiny wave.

'It is you,' he said. 'Hi.' He took a few steps towards her. His colleagues... no, his hosts, *her* colleagues, were looking at them curiously. She couldn't sneak out now, so she descended the steps to the front of the lecture theatre.

'Hi Noah.'

It was surreal, seeing him again. Chaya felt light-headed. She put a hand on one of the seat backs to steady herself.

'Er... Chaya and I knew each other at uni,' Noah said. He didn't meet her eyes when he said it. 'Knew each other' was probably the understatement of the century.

Chaya managed a smile. 'It's been... a long time,' she said. 'How are you?' Her voice sounded stiff and strange.

'I'm good,' he said, smiling warmly. 'How are you? You look great.' The tips of his ears started to turn pink.

She pulled herself together and tried to remain professional. She wanted to touch him, check he was real. She put her free hand in her pocket. 'I enjoyed your lecture,' she said. 'Very interesting.'

'And you work here, I take it?' he said. 'Still doing biochemistry?'

The door by the stage opened. A tall, beautiful woman came through, holding the hand of a little boy. It was clearly a late night for the kid, who stifled a yawn and leaned against his mother's side. Noah spotted them.

'Oh, hello darling.' He stepped towards her, away from Chaya. 'Er... Kath, this is Chaya, an old friend. Chaya, this is my wife Katherine and my son, Alex.'

Katherine smiled at her. 'Nice to meet you,' she said, polite, but clearly not interested. 'Noah, I'm going to take Alex back to the hotel. We'll see you later?' She sounded American ... no, not quite. Canadian? Well spoken and well groomed, she was exactly the sort of person Noah's diplomat attaché parents would have wanted him to be with. Much more acceptable than Chaya would ever have been.

Noah said, 'I'm going to dinner with some people from the department. I shouldn't be too late getting back.' He knelt down in front of the boy. 'How was the show?'

'It was great,' said the boy. 'Loud.'

'Tell me all about it tomorrow.' He kissed the boy on the head and stood up. 'See you later.' He kissed the wife too, a quick peck on the lips.

Chaya looked away. The others from the Geology department were shifting impatiently. 'I'd better get going too,' she said. 'It was good to see you again, Noah.'

'Yes,' he said. 'We should get back in touch. Catch up.' He sounded sincere. Clearly he had moved on and relegated his memories of her to somewhere where they didn't hurt. He held out his hand to shake hers.

She couldn't touch him. It would be too much to bear. 'Yes,' she said. 'I'll see you later.' She flashed what she hoped was a convincing smile and turned and fled.

She practically ran back to her office. There was a fist in her chest, a tight knot behind her sternum that was making it hard to breathe. She made it to her own department building before the pain hit. He had moved on. Of *course* he was married. Of *course* he'd changed. She walked along the empty corridor, head down, breathing fast. He had been pleased to see her. That just showed how far he'd moved on. She had thought that somehow he'd remained frozen in time as that boy who loved her. Of course he hadn't. Stupid, stupid Chaya.

The building seemed to lean in, darkening the edges of her vision. Her heart galloped and she could hear the blood roaring around her head. She put her hand on the wall next to her, fighting for breath. She was hot, then cold, in waves. The first time this happened, she'd thought she was going to die. Now she knew it would pass. She had to ride it out. Here in the deserted corridors of her work was as safe a place to be as any.

When it finally passed, she felt weak from the exertion. She pushed herself away from the wall. The worst of the panic attack was over, but the despair was not.

Breathe, breathe. She had to get back to the lab, away from the world. Don't stand there, move. Get it together Chaya. Go.

Instead of taking the lift, she took the stairs, forcing her legs to move. If she stopped, she might just fold over on the stairs and stay there. She had to keep moving. Her thighs started to burn. By the time she reached her floor, blood was pounding in her ears, and her throat and torso were a mass of pain again. Only this time, she was in control of it. She stopped at the lab door and leaned forward, her hands on her knees, breathing hard as the physical pain drowned out the emotional one.

When her pulse finally slowed and she could bear to breathe, she realised she was sweating underneath her winter clothing. She went into the office and shed some layers, then down to the toilets to splash her face with cold water. She dried her face using a scratchy paper towel and checked herself in the mirror. Under the harsh light, her face was pale under the brown, with hints of red where she'd rubbed it. Her hands trembled. She went back into her office and sat down, tucking her hands under her thighs until they stopped shaking.

Really, this couldn't go on. She really needed to get over it. Until recently, her work had been enough to keep her mind off the hollow left by Noah, but lately, it wasn't enough. Perhaps it was time to let someone else into her life. Someone to distract her and keep her busy. Perhaps she should get her parents to find her a husband, like they were always suggesting. She sighed again and went back up to the lab.

The lab was dark, lit only by the lights from the city outside. Machinery hummed, clicked and whirred; various control lights and displays winked. Chaya breathed in the familiar smells of agar, bacteria and chemicals. The tension in her shoulders dissolved a little. Regardless of whether the place was full of chatter and music, as it was during the week, or deserted as it was now, the lab soothed her. There was always something that needed to be done, something to claim her attention. It was more home to her than the bedsit was. If she were allowed to sleep here, she would.

Chaya flicked on the light switch. One by one, fluorescent strip lights came on, bathing everything in clinical white light. She shared the lab with another small research group – the space divided up, with the shared equipment in the middle. Her bench was the one at the far end of the room, the unsociable one that no one else wanted. Traditionally, it went to the most junior member of the lab, but Chaya preferred it. It gave her a secluded workspace. She could watch the movements and interactions of the rest of the lab from behind her palisade of reagent bottles, but the others couldn't see her unless they came round to her bay. She could interact with them when she had the energy or hide when she didn't.

Her lab coat was folded up on her stool, as always. She pulled it on and buttoned up. Without really looking, she grabbed a pair of fresh latex gloves with one hand, and flipped her lab diary open with the other. She always left herself a note on what to do next. Not that she needed reminding, it was just good practice.

Pulling on her gloves she read. 'Gels.' She nodded to herself.

Her lab technician had offered to leave her some ready-poured gels, but Chaya preferred to make things up fresh as she went along. Whilst the gel was setting, she prepared her samples. Her hands and eyes moved mechanically, measuring, pouring, pipetting, which left her mind free to wander.

Seeing Noah had been a shock. He seemed so normal. So settled. He had done exactly what he'd hoped to do. Unlike her.

Despite her initial ambition to work in the field of tropical medicine, she had ended up working on non-pathogenic bacteria instead. At the moment she was working on making recombinant proteins that she hoped would one day be useful in disease prevention.

She was still firmly an 'early career' academic. She was doing okay, but her attempts to progress hadn't exactly been a huge success. She had no social life to speak of, partly because she was always working, but also because all her friends were married and had kids now. Before the kids arrived, her friends Sara and Jay had let her tag along and hang out with them from time to time, but now that rarely happened. She made a note to call Sara to catch up. She could offer to do some babysitting.

She double checked her notes and set her pipette to the correct volume. She thought fleetingly of Noah's wife. How glamorous she looked! Perhaps she needed to rethink her own life a bit. All the dedication to her work was great, but maybe she needed to get out there a bit more. Go to more conferences, give more lectures about her work. Make an impression. Maybe that would help.

She could try and change her image. She wasn't getting any younger. Looking after herself a bit would probably make her look less like an oddball and more like professor material. Academia, as with everything, was about more than being good at your job.

Chaya smiled a thin smile. She was managing to talk herself into dramatic changes. The last time she'd done that, she'd broken herself. No. Thinking about *that* was not allowed. Not now, not ever. She shouldn't have gone to see Noah. It was a ridiculous thing to have done. She didn't have time to think about what might have been. She had work to do here.

She gave each of her samples a flick to mix the dye in, followed by a quick spin in the centrifuge to get them all to the bottom of the Eppendorf tubes, ready to be pipetted out.

A gentle shake showed that the gel was set and ready to load. She put it in the machine. Getting the tiny volume into the equally tiny well required Chaya to hold her perpetually moving hands still for seconds at a time. Each sample was the culmination of three or four days' work. Wastage was not permissible. Chaya bit her lower lip and concentrated, hands moving in concert. Gently, smoothly, keep steady. Pick up sample. Load. Pick up. Load.

Once her hands found their rhythm, her mind wandered again, skirting neatly round the issue of Noah and staying on this new idea of starting afresh. She had lost the knack of interacting with people. In the beginning, the effort of keeping up the appearance of normality and stamping down the panic was so great, that she'd tried to get through the day talking to as few people as she could manage. Over the years, this had become habit and she had retreated further and further into her work. She was careful not to be rude or unpleasant, just always busy. Too busy to go out. The others in the lab had stopped expecting her to go to anything social now.

She would have to brush up on her social skills; almost reinvent herself. Why not? She already did a good job of persuading people she was fine. All she needed to do was persuade them that she was enjoying herself as well. How hard could that be?

She loaded the last sample, put the lid carefully into place and set the gel running. It would run slowly overnight, stretching out the blue samples into their constituent parts so that by morning, the jumbled mess would be converted into beautiful clarity.

Chaya nodded to herself. Yes. Reinventing herself a bit felt like a positive thing to do. She glanced at the clock. But first, she had to respond to that email and revise her grant application.

Chapter Four

Chaya –Train to Oxford, 1995

The train drew away from the station and Chaya waved to the aunty who had come to drop her off. The aunty and her husband were her father's friends. Chaya stayed with them when college shut down for the Christmas holidays. It was unusual for her to go and visit them in term time, but after weeks of struggling, she'd let slip that she wasn't sleeping very well and her mother had insisted she take a break.

She had tried to relax, honestly, she had, but with an essay due on Monday and a practical write-up due the day after, she'd had to do some work, despite aunty's tutting. At least she was now extremely well fed.

Chaya settled back in her seat and closed her eyes. She seemed to permanently be in crisis mode these days. This was her second year and it was meant to be easier, but there was so much information being fired at her on a daily basis, she had to work constantly, just to keep up. At least she'd got the essay done. She opened her eyes again and picked up her bag. She should really read through it. She'd have to defend what she'd said when it came to tutorial time.

When she stuck her hand in the bag, her fingertips brushed the second-hand copy of *Little Women* that she'd optimistically packed, but not opened the whole weekend. Maybe she could read a bit. After all, her essay was done. Besides, she was travelling. Being in transit was a magical time when she wasn't fully tied to a place and the obligations that belonged there.

She carefully pulled the book out of her bag and removed the bookmark. Just a few pages.

When the train pulled into Birmingham New Street, Chaya looked up. It was raining. The train felt stuffy and smelled of wet coats, so it must have been raining for some time. Chaya shrugged and returned to her book where Beth was dying. She fell into the heartbreak of the March sisters. She forgot about the real world and read on, blinking every now and then to clear the tears.

'Excuse me?'

The voice made her jump. She looked up. A guy about her age, with hair plastered to his forehead from the rain, was standing by the empty seat next to her, his backpack hovering over it. 'Is this seat taken?'

She shook her head. A tear inconveniently detached itself from her eye and ran down her cheek.

The guy gave her a concerned look. He dropped into the seat. 'Are you alright?' he asked.

She wiped away the tear. 'Sorry. Yes, I'm fine. Just...' She gestured to the book. 'I just got to the sad bit.'

He smiled. 'Oh, right. That's okay then. I thought maybe I'd dripped on you.'

She gave him a small smile and opened the book again. He shuffled around, taking off his wet coat. The seats weren't exactly roomy and the shuffling was hard to ignore. She tried to shift away. The sleeve of the wet coat escaped from his grasp and smacked against her book.

'Oh no. I'm so sorry. Is the book okay?'

He looked genuinely worried. He stuffed his rolled-up coat down at his feet. 'I'm really sorry. If it's ruined, I'll buy you a new copy.'

'It's fine,' she said. 'It's a second-hand copy anyway.'

He nodded. 'A book that's been loved.'

What an odd thing to say. She looked at him properly then. He had reddish blond hair that was too long, blue eyes and freckles. He met her gaze and smiled. It was a smile that transformed him from nondescript, to someone enchanting. She couldn't help smiling back.

He offered her his hand to shake. 'I'm Noah,' he said.

She shouldn't talk to strangers. This was such a basic tenet of life. Anyway, people didn't talk to each other on trains. Never. So she wasn't sure what made her say 'I'm Chaya,' and shake his hand. She wasn't sure why she answered his next question and got into a conversation. She wasn't even sure when exactly she put the book down on her lap and forgot about it. It was a snap decision made almost subconsciously.

It was a decision that would change everything.

–

Reality reasserted itself when they arrived in Oxford and Noah offered to walk her to her shared house. It wasn't dark and there was no reason to accept his offer, really. She should say no. She didn't really know this guy, even though they'd spent two hours chatting about all manner of things. She knew he was reading Geology and that he was in the year above her. She knew which college he was in, which TV shows he watched and that he considered *Jo's Boys* to be a superior book to *Little Women* and was astounded that she hadn't read the full set. But really, she didn't know anything useful about him. So she should politely say no.

Except somehow, she didn't. He carried her bag for her, hooked on the handlebars of the bike he'd retrieved from station bike racks. It seemed like a ridiculously old-fashioned gesture, yet quite nice at the same time. When they got to the top of the street in Jericho, where she lived, she paused and said, 'This is me.'

He looked at the near identical row of front doors. 'Okay,' he said. 'Well, it was very nice to meet you, Chaya.'

'You too, Noah.' She swung her bag onto her shoulder and turned to go.

He shifted his weight. 'Um… would you… like to go out, some time?' He looked up at her through the hair that was now dry, but still falling into his eyes. 'Maybe to the cinema…' His ears started to go red. 'Or something.'

She had never been asked out before. Part of her was charmed. But no. Talking to a stranger on the train was bad enough. Letting him walk her home was probably worse. She didn't normally do these things. No. She had to end this now, before she did something really stupid.

'I'm sorry,' she said. 'I don't date.'

The hope left his face and she felt terrible.

'I see,' he said. 'I'm sorry. I… er… well anyway.' He turned his bike around. 'It was good to meet you. I'll see you around.'

Before she could say anything in response, he swung his leg over to mount the bike and pedalled away down the street.

Chaya turned and walked down the side street to her house, feeling oddly bereft.

When she reached her door, she looked back up towards the main street. She wasn't sure what she was hoping to see. Not Noah. But what she did see was her housemate Sara, practically running down the road towards her.

She unlocked the door, just as Sara got to the gate. 'Who,' said Sara, 'was that?'

Chaya sighed. Oh dear. She wasn't going to hear the end of this.

Chapter Five

Gimhana – London, 2004

'So, Jim,' said Barry. 'Have you got a girlfriend?'

They were in a bar, after work. Barry was one of the partners in the firm. Gim had realised some time ago that being competent at this job was all well and good but if he was going to get anywhere he had to be better than anyone else there. And he had to schmooze the partners. He didn't have the old school tie to help him make connections. Nor did he have an impressive alma mater. He needed people in power to notice him for all the right reasons and he needed them to like him enough that they saw past the colour of his skin.

He was a likeable guy, he knew that. He'd learned early on that people found it easier to like a person who was easy on the eye. So he worked on that too, until he had the grooming thing down pat. He knew how to flirt with people if he needed to, just enough to make them feel good. 'Attractive' was an appropriate word in every way.

Barry was still waiting for an answer, so Gim said, 'I'm in between relationships at the moment. You know how it is.' He laughed. 'I guess you could say work is my mistress.'

'Ah, and a saucy little minx she is too,' said Barry.

He had been working with Barry's team for about six months, assisting with the contracts and asset transfers of a complex merger. He'd done good work. He knew that.

Barry knew it too. In fact, he thought Barry was taking an interest in him, professionally speaking, giving him extra responsibility, providing the odd snippet of feedback. If he made this work, he would have someone who could mentor him and help him with his career.

'Being married to your work doesn't leave you much time for a social life,' said Gim, ruefully. Not that he wanted one, particularly. He'd learned his lesson at nineteen. A social life was something to be carried out carefully, quietly and, these days, infrequently. He was yet to meet someone he wanted to see more than twice. Work really did take up a lot of his time.

'Ah, you've got to be careful of that,' said Barry. 'At your age, you need to work hard, but you'll want to think about settling down soon. At least, if you want to stay in the firm.'

Gim raised his eyebrows.

'A man of a certain age,' said Barry, leaning forward, 'is better for having a wife and family. I know it's very modern these days to share parental responsibilities, but really, if you make it to partner, you can afford to marry someone who will stay at home. Or, if she's a career woman, you can hire a decent nanny to look after the kids.' He met Gimhana's eyes, his expression earnest. 'The senior partners, they're... old-fashioned in their outlook, if you see what I mean. They want a conventional sort of man, with a conventional sort of outlook to be part of the group. Not some young buck with strange ideas.' He looked down at his pint and lifted it slowly. 'You see what I'm saying?'

Not really. 'Were you a young buck once?' said Gimhana.

'Heh.' Barry pulled a face. 'Not for very long. I know when to give up. I got married young, not long after leaving university. By the time I made it to partner, the boys had already been born. The oldest was already in school. It gave us stability and flexibility and the wife was very happy. So... you could say it was the best thing that could have happened to me.'

'Was it, though?' He watched the other man carefully.

Barry looked at the ceiling for a few seconds. 'I think,' he said. 'That it was.' He transferred his gaze back to Gim's face. 'You see, Jim, you need to decide what you want. If it's the lonely bachelor life that allows you to work like a demon and rise to the top, then there are firms who would appreciate that. And starting afresh wouldn't be a bad thing for you... give you a chance to squash certain rumours.'

He didn't elaborate what the rumours could be. He didn't have to. Gim was careful about what he said and did, but people still suspected. Probably because he didn't date. On a day to day basis, he didn't care so long as it didn't affect his job. But if it did...

'So my advice to you, Jim, is to find a nice girl. Get married. Show them you're stable and steady.' Barry nodded, slowly. 'Yes. I like you. You're an excellent lawyer and a conscientious worker. You're a people person. The clients trust you, which goes a long way in this business.'

He had been waiting for an opening like this. 'Would you put in a good word for me,' he said, 'with the other partners?'

'Of course, of course. That goes without saying.' Barry smiled at him. 'I told you. I like you. Just get yourself sorted out.'

Right. Sorted out. Married. Gim nodded. 'I'll see what I can do.'

'Don't you people do arranged marriages? You could get one of those,' said Barry. 'I gather it's not as horrific as it sounds.'

He chose to ignore the 'you people'. It wasn't intended as an insult, although it certainly sounded like one.

'They're not forced marriages. It's more like a parent-organised dating service,' Gim said. He'd had this conversation before with many different people. 'All they do is introduce you to each other. Then, if you like each other, you meet a couple of times and... all being well, you get married.'

'Sounds efficient,' said Barry.

'It is, actually. Because your parents are vetting the people you meet, you bypass the whole "will my parents approve of this person" nonsense.' He smiled, as though he could ever reach the place where his parents would approve of his choices.

24

Barry chuckled. 'My parents didn't approve of my Rosie one bit. Especially when she got pregnant and we had to get married. But, as she rightly points out, she didn't get pregnant by herself.' He grinned happily. 'Never regretted it for a minute.' He looked at his watch and took a long drink. 'Speaking of Rosie, I should get back soon. I haven't seen much of her and the boys lately, what with all the stupid hours we've been working.' He drained his drink. 'It was good chatting to you, Jim. I'll see you at work tomorrow.'

'See you tomorrow, Barry.' He raised his hand in farewell. Once Barry had left, he leaned back in his seat and stared contemplatively into space. Since it was mid January, the bar wasn't as busy as it had been before Christmas. Without the Christmas decorations and the crowds, it looked a little forlorn. He stretched out his legs under the table and tweaked the trouser crease. For the first time in weeks, he didn't have to work late. He could go out, but he didn't really enjoy going clubbing. It was too tense. He was always expecting something terrible to happen. Besides, he was knackered. No, what he really wanted was a decent takeaway and a movie. He had a couple of DVDs from LoveFilm. He could watch those. He pulled out his phone to check his personal email. Hmm. He really needed to call his mother.

Someone approached the table. Gim looked up and saw one of the other people on Barry's team, Felicia. One of the bright young things that the company liked to bring in. He had been like that once. Full of optimism. He smiled at her.

'Mind if I join you?' she said. She was in her seat almost before he'd said yes. She sat sideways, with her shoulders angled slightly so that she had to twist a little to talk to him. It meant that if he wanted to, he could see down her top. He tried not to roll his eyes. Quite apart from not being his type, the kid was, what? Twenty-three?

'So, we're thinking of going to Chinatown and then on to a club. Want to come with us?' she said.

Gimhana looked at the group of young people near the bar and felt old at thirty-three. They were all so young and full of energy. At least being over thirty had one great advantage. 'You guys don't want an oldie like me cramping your style,' he said. 'You go ahead. I'm going to finish my pint and head home.'

Felicia's face fell. 'I guess your girlfriend will be looking forward to seeing you.'

He thought of his empty flat. His nice, cosy, non-judgemental flat. 'No girlfriend,' he said. 'But I do have a ton of laundry to sort.' He used a laundry service. His shirts would be waiting for him, neatly stacked on his bed. All he had to do was put it in the right cupboard.

'Don't you get lonely?' she said.

Gimhana admired her persistence. 'I'd be lying if I said I didn't,' he said. 'But today, I'm just completely wiped out after the week we've had. Thanks for asking me though. Maybe next time, huh?'

She made a sad face and left him to it.

They were still at the bar a few minutes later when he got up to leave. He gave them a friendly wave as he passed.

It was dark and cold outside, but it being London, there were people around. Gim dug his hands into his pockets and joined the flow. As he walked, he mulled over what Barry had said. Getting married was clearly the next thing he was supposed to do if he wanted to get on in his career. He could try and move firms. It was certainly an attractive option, but then he'd have to start again, earning trust, building credibility. These days there were firms which were far more open-minded than this one. But still. He was here. He could never be who he wanted to be, so maybe he could be what other people wanted him to be.

He got home to find his answerphone filled with a long rambling message from his mother. He listened to the monologue, smiling to himself. In the middle of it came the snippet, the real reason she'd been trying to get hold of him. 'I was talking to Mrs Rajasinghe, and she was telling me that they're looking for someone for their daughter. She lives in London. You could meet for a cup of tea and see how it goes.'

Gimhana stared at the phone, drumming his fingers against the table. Again with the wedding set-up. It was as though the world was pushing him towards looking for a wife. Could he do that?

He washed the smell of the pub off himself, put on jeans and a shirt and got himself a tumbler of whiskey. Could he cope with sharing his living space with someone? He looked round his flat. It was really just a place to keep his stuff and sleep in. He had no great attachment to it. He didn't even have a huge amount of stuff. He spent most of his time at work. His main indulgence was a big TV screen and a subscription to LoveFilm. He checked the two DVDs he had waiting for him. Neither of them appealed right now. Tonight he needed comfort viewing. He dug around in the bottom of his magazine drawer and found the old VHS tape he'd had transferred to DVD. *Jem and the Holograms.*

He put it in the player. If he had a wife, how different would it be? He guessed it would depend on the woman. He couldn't be a proper husband to a woman. He gave the matter some thought and shuddered. Nope. He took a gulp of whiskey before settling down on his sofa and pointing the remote at the telly.

The only way it would work would be if he found a nice lesbian who just wanted a marriage to hide behind in the same way he did. Gimhana liked women, in a general sense. He was comfortable in their presence. He'd even been known to flirt with them. It was fun. He never took it beyond a certain point, because, well, he wasn't actually interested.

He didn't know any suitable Sri Lankan women who were lesbians. Maybe there were some he didn't know about. Thinking about it, he didn't know any suitable single Sri Lankan women at all. Not ones he wasn't related to in some way.

His mother was getting upset that he kept refusing her offer of help. He could just go along with the meeting women thing.

Even if he did find someone to marry, the poor woman would want to have children. He took another sip. He couldn't very well ask his parents to find a lesbian for him to marry.

A burst of noise and the Jem logo came on the screen. Ah. Finally. He settled down to watch, the familiar cheerful rock music wrapping around him. See now, if he got married, how would he get his *Jem and the Holograms* fix? He couldn't see any women letting him indulge in that.

No, he was better off by himself.

Chapter Six

Chaya – Oxford, 1995

Although the sun was shining, the air was spiked with frost. Chaya trudged down the high street, satchel clutched to her chest. The cold nipped at her eyelids and the membranes of her nose. Despite this, she could appreciate that it was a beautiful day. Remnants of the previous week's snow clung to rooftops and window ledges. Everything was rimed with white.

She crossed the road and started walking alongside the long wall, aiming towards the university parks. If she had to walk home, she may as well take the scenic route. The tutorial had been brutal and she could do with something nice to take her mind off the scathing criticism of her essay. What didn't kill you made you stronger... but right now she was wondering what on earth she was doing here, pretending to be clever enough to keep up.

There was a squeal of brakes and she jumped instinctively out of the way. When she looked across to see if the cyclist was okay, he grinned at her. 'Hi Chaya.'

'Noah.' Her heart rose. She should be polite and distant, so that she didn't give him the wrong idea. Her head remembered this, but her face didn't. She beamed at him. 'How are you?'

'I'm fine thanks, you?'

'Just finished a tutorial. I'm heading back home.'

'I'll walk with you.' He pushed his bike and fell into step alongside her. 'So, how've you been?'

She glanced at him sideways. He had popped into her thoughts over the past few weeks, far more often than she'd liked. Thinking about him had been oddly exhilarating and seeing him again was making her feel fluttery and excited. Which was ridiculous.

They walked along in awkward silence for a few yards, when Noah suddenly said, 'I was thinking about writing to you.'

'Oh?'

'I knew which college you were at… and…' He cleared his throat. 'I've thought about you a lot.' He was looking straight ahead.

'That's nice,' she said and cringed at the blandness of her reply.

Another awkward silence. Chaya cast about for a topic of conversation, something that didn't take them anywhere contentious. 'It's a beautiful day,' she said. The weather was always a nice, neutral topic. 'The city looks like a postcard.'

'Yes. It does.' There was a hint of relief in his voice. 'Do you get snow in Sri Lanka?'

She shot him a glance. Was he being funny?

'I meant, in the hills. They're quite high mountains in the middle and I wondered…'

Ah. Okay. He'd taken the trouble to look it up. 'No,' she said. 'I don't think it snows, even up there.' She couldn't help but feel pleased that he'd looked stuff up about Sri Lanka.

'What do you miss most about home?' he said.

'That's easy! The sunshine.' She laughed and so did he. The sound condensed into a cloud around their heads. They walked on, leaving their laughter to dissipate in the air.

By now they were almost at the parks. Ordinarily, Chaya would have gone straight across but today, she followed Noah when he turned to the right to take the longer route. They walked past skeletons of trees and evergreens edged with frost.

'So, how come you decided to come here to study?' he said, as they walked along by the river. A lone goose paddled on the water. She noticed that he was careful to keep himself between her and the river. Keeping her safe from the goose, presumably. How thoughtful.

'Here as in England? Or here as in Oxford?'

'Either.'

'I won a scholarship,' she said, simply.

He looked at her sideways, his eyes wider than before. 'That's impressive.'

She supposed it was. It was a means to an end, though. She had applied for so many scholarships, if she hadn't won this one, she would have won something else. Less prestigious, but still good enough to get her closer to her goal. 'My family helped,' she said. When he continued looking quizzically at her, she added, 'I couldn't have done it without them.'

He nodded. 'They're very important to you, aren't they?' he said, carefully, as though filing the information away to think about.

'Of course. They're my family.'

If anything, he looked even more impressed than before. After a few seconds, he said, 'That's a lot of pressure.'

Was it? She had never stopped to think about it. If she was going to make a difference to the world, then this was what she had to do.

'How about you?' she asked. 'Have you got any brothers or sisters?' He hadn't mentioned any when they were chatting on the train.

He shook his head. 'Just me.' He looked away for a moment. Looking back, he said, 'It must be nice, having siblings.'

'It is.'

'You have a sister right? Is she younger than you?'

'Oh no. She's older. Not that you can tell.' She thought of Malini with her golden skin and movie star features. She was tall and delicate and had hair that behaved itself. If she were here, Noah would be too distracted by her to talk to Chaya, just like everyone else they'd ever met. 'She's the pretty one in the family.'

He smiled. 'I'm sure that's not true.'

'Oh it is. Everyone says so.'

'Which one are you then?'

'Me? I'm the sensible one.' Sensible Chaya. Dependable Chaya. The one who always did the right thing. Except she wasn't doing the right thing now. Her mother would explode if she knew that Chaya had been for an unchaperoned stroll with a guy. A white guy.

But she wasn't really doing anything wrong, was she? Just letting him walk along with her while she walked home. She'd already told him she didn't date.

They arrived at a pond at the far end of the park. It was covered in a thin layer of ice. She'd never come this way before and told him so.

'There are normally ducks here,' he said. He bent down and picked a pebble from the ground.

'Where are they now?' She looked around, seeking ducks in the undergrowth.

'Probably gone somewhere warmer.' He bounced the pebble in his hand. 'Here,' he said, taking aim towards the river. 'Watch this.'

He threw the pebble with a quick flick of the wrist. Chaya recognised the throw. Thatha used it to skip stones on the surface of the sea. Chaya and Malini had spent many a family holiday trying to copy it. She had never mastered it. Neither, it seemed, had Noah. The stone cracked the ice and went into the water.

'That wasn't supposed to happen.' He looked so crestfallen that Chaya had to swallow the laugh that rose in her throat.

'Try again?' she suggested.

He looked at her suspiciously as if checking if she was laughing at him and picked up another stone. His ears were going red. This time the stone skipped a couple of times, making a zinging sound as it ricocheted off the ice.

Chaya was enchanted. 'I've never seen that before.'

'It would have been more impressive if it had worked first time,' Noah said, glaring at the hole left by the earlier pebble.

Chaya couldn't stop the laugh escaping. She covered her mouth with her hand. 'I'm sorry,' she said. 'But you looked so cross.'

Noah grinned, a little sheepishly.

Chaya grinned back. In spite of the cold, her face felt warm.

—

They chatted easily as they walked the rest of the way back to the gates on Norham Gardens and crossed the roads towards Jericho. When they reached the place where they had to part ways, Noah said, 'I'm going for an ice cream, want to come with me?'

For a second, Chaya felt the pull of what might have been. But she shook her head. 'Look, Noah. I told you. I don't—'

His eyes met hers. 'I like you,' he said, simply. 'I really would like to see you again.'

She liked him too. If only she could allow herself to feel that … But she couldn't. There were things that just didn't fit into her world and dating was one of those things. It was so hard to explain. 'I'm sorry. I can't.'

She could tell him she wasn't interested in him in that way and it would be the end of this. But she would hurt him. Besides, it wasn't true. There was nothing she could say to make this better. So she looked away. 'It's complicated.'

Noah sighed. 'I guess it must be.' He put his cycle helmet back on. 'Still, you can't blame a guy for trying,' he said. 'I'll see you around, Chaya. Take care.'

'You too.'

She watched him cycle off and carried on walking, but now she was aware of a Noah-shaped absence in her world. She tried to untangle all the things he made her feel. She'd had crushes on people before, but it had all been at a distance; lukewarm and fleeting attractions to people she'd never actually got to know. Nothing visceral like this. She had butterflies in her stomach.

She'd assumed that was just a figure of speech, but it turned out it was a real feeling.

But she didn't have time for this. She was here to study. Her plan involved getting her degree, then focusing on prevention of tropical diseases for her PhD, so that she could do research that saved lives. She was going to be someone. A pioneering woman among all the male scientists you heard about at school. Someone who made a difference to the world. She owed it to everyone at home ... and to herself.

Oh, her parents wanted her to get married and have a conventional life. She would, eventually, but right now, it wasn't on her priority list. Her main task was to finish her degree with a 2.1 at least, so that she could go on to do a PhD. The degree was actually harder work than she'd anticipated. There was no room for distractions. So she had done the right thing, telling Noah she wasn't interested.

Her heart sank a little. Hadn't she?

Chapter Seven

Chaya – London, 2005

Chaya rang the doorbell to Sara's house. Her friend opened the door and Chaya stepped straight into her hug. She hadn't seen Sara for a few weeks. They usually tried to meet up at least once a month. Even though most of her social circle had disappeared off to live their separate lives, Sara and Jay had remained. In the absence of her real family, Sara and Jay were the next best thing.

When Sara released her, she handed over the bag containing a bottle of wine and a chocolate cake before taking off her coat. She followed Sara into the living room, which was a mess.

'Wine first? Or tea?' said Sara.

'You choose.' She looked at the Lego strewn across the floor and her fingers itched to tidy up.

'Wine,' Sara said, instantly. 'Lemme get some glasses.'

Chaya knelt on the floor and gathered the Lego into the box. 'Where are the boys?' she shouted over her shoulder. Sara had three sons, all under ten. If the boys were in the house, you knew about it.

'Jay's taken them to the grandparents. He's picking our dinner up on the way back.' Sara came back in with the glasses. 'Oh, you don't have to do that,' she said. 'Just leave it. I've learned to ignore it.'

'I don't mind.' She scooped up the various books and put them in the book drawer. She'd spent enough time hanging out here, helping Sara with the kids, that she knew exactly where everything went. Another quick round of picking up and the little cars and action toys were dumped into the right basket. 'There,' she said.

'Oh, you're a star.' Sara held out a glass to her.

Chaya took it and sank into a chair. There was still straightening out that could be done, but she had to stop. This wasn't her house.

'I'm knackered,' said Sara. She leaned back on the sofa, frowned and reached behind her. She pulled out a Wolverine figure from behind her and flicked it deftly into the toy basket. 'Who knew kids were so exhausting?'

Chaya looked at her friend. At university, Sara had been quirky and full of energy. She had worn odd grungy clothes and dyed her hair different colours. Now she had adopted the universal mum uniform of jeans and button-down shirts and looked shattered. Her hair was her natural brown most of the time. All that remained of the free spirit she one was, were the multiple piercings in her ears. And Jay, of course.

Chaya grinned. 'But you wouldn't change it for the world?' Sara always added that at the end, whenever she moaned about the kids.

Sara took a gulp of wine and waved her glass in agreement. She swallowed. 'They're so cute when they're asleep,' she said. 'Funny how you can love them more when they're not conscious.'

'That sounds... very wrong, somehow.' Chaya pushed a bunch of magazines into a tidy pile. Seeing Sara's glance, she said, 'Sorry. I'll stop now.'

'The only time this place looks tidy is when you've been,' said Sara. 'Remember that time when you got the boys to clean their rooms. I don't know how you did it.'

'Aunty magic.'

'So,' Sara said, settling back. 'What's new with you?'

Chaya cradled her glass and leaned forward. 'I... saw Noah a couple of days ago.' Now that a few days had passed, she could say it without residual panic. It still hurt, but not as much.

Sara almost choked on her wine. 'What?' she sat forward, turning to Chaya. 'When? Where?'

Chaya gave her a sideways glance. 'You forgot "who" and "why".' If she made light of it, maybe it wouldn't feel so bad.

Sara raised her eyebrows.

Chaya sighed. 'He was giving a talk at the uni. I went along to listen.' She shook her head. 'It was a stupid thing to have done.'

'And?'

She looked into her glass. 'He's married,' she said. 'They have a son.'

Sara put down her glass and wrapped her arms around Chaya. 'Oh, mate.' She gave her a hug. 'Are you okay?'

Chaya put her own glass down on the coffee table and leaned her head against her friend's shoulder. 'I don't know.' She sighed. 'I really need to move on, don't I?' she said. 'I had to focus on my career. I'm doing that. Maybe I should think about the other stuff too.'

Sara had been telling her that for years, but had the good grace not to point this out. 'Sounds sensible. What would you do?'

Chaya shrugged. 'Join… some… clubs?' she said. The sentence sounded unconvincing even to her.

'Uhuh.' Sara gave her another squeeze. 'Have you ever done clubs and societies?'

'Well no, but I could. Right?'

'You could join my book group.'

'The one you always complain about because they always choose big books that you can never finish in time?'

'That one. You can do the reading, because you *always* do the reading and then you can cover for me.' Sara grinned.

'Hmm.' She knew that Sara always did the reading too, even if she was too tired to recall any of it. Some things never changed.

'More seriously,' said Sara. 'What do you enjoy doing? Could you join one of the clubs at the uni—'

'I can't do stuff at the uni. My students might be there and that would be weird.'

'Okay… how about…' Sara thought some more.

'I was thinking, I might go home for a longer holiday,' Chaya said. She hadn't lived in Sri Lanka for over a decade, but it was still where she thought of as home. 'It'll be nice to get to know my niece and nephew a bit.' What she didn't say was that it would remind her of the whole point of giving up Noah. She had broken up with him for the sake of her career and her family. She may as well remind herself why.

Sara nodded. 'That's probably a good idea. You've been working so hard. You should take a proper holiday. Go learn to surf or something.' She nudged her gently. 'Who knows, you might meet someone.'

'Don't let my mother hear you say that,' said Chaya. 'She'll be lining up "suitable" men within minutes.'

'Would that be that such a bad thing?'

'I don't think I'm ready,' said Chaya. 'It's such a big thing. Give me time.'

Sara gave her a sharp look. It had been ten years since Noah. 'How much time do you need?'

Thankfully, the front door opened. Jay was home with several bags of Chinese food. Sara set Chaya the task of putting out plates, while a whispered conversation took place in the kitchen. Chaya knew Sara was telling her husband about Noah. This was confirmed when Jay came out of the kitchen and, without a word, gave Chaya a bear hug. Jay was a big man, tall and wide, but his hug was gentle. There was something about the size of him that made him seem more real than anything else around him. A solid, reassuring presence.

'Whatever you need us for, mate, we're here,' he said.

Chaya nodded. She knew that. They always had been.

'Do you want to talk about it?'

She shook her head. 'Not really. I mean, I appreciate Sara trying to find me a hobby, but...'

Jay rolled his eyes. 'I can imagine.'

'Hey.' Sara poked him in the back.

Jay pulled a face and Chaya laughed. This was why she came here. Sara and Jay were her role models for a relationship. If she were ever to have a marriage, this was what she wanted it too look like. Ha! *If* she got married. That wasn't likely.

Chapter Eight

Chaya – Colombo, 2005

The car reached the gate to the house and Thatha beeped the horn. Seconds later, Leela, the home help, came running down to the gate. She dragged the gates open and stood to the side to let them drive in. Chaya waved to her as they went past; she grinned her gap-toothed grin and waved shyly back.

Leela had been working for them since Chaya was about ten. Chaya could vaguely remember her turning up, a thin, tearful figure in a lungi cloth and blouse. She and Malini had stood in the corridor outside the kitchen, listening as Leela explained to their parents how she had left her husband because he hit her. Her parents were too old, she said, to support her and she needed a place to work and live. Chaya's parents had agreed to a trial period of six weeks. She had been with them ever since.

The car pulled into the shade of the carport. Chaya hopped out and looked around. A stretch of leafy green separated the gated walls from the front of the house. Over the years that she'd been away, the plants that made up the borders had spread out a bit – the various coloured roses, the bright yellow trumpet flowers, fat red hibiscus. Amma's lemon tree was so laden with yellow globes that its branches had been propped up to stop them breaking.

Closer to the house, providing shade to the veranda, were two frangipani trees. The garden and house met in the veranda, which had waist-high wooden lattice walls. The jasmine vines that they'd planted, one Malini's, the other Chaya's, now hid the main pillars entirely, making the roof look like it was growing out of the vines. She was surprised anew at how aggressively verdant plants in Sri Lanka looked, their leaves a dark green that you seldom saw in England.

The house was an L-shaped bungalow, with the bedrooms on a short corridor at one side, and a long living-dining room and kitchen on the other. The land sloped sharply down at the back, allowing a small room to be built as a basement to the kitchen. That was Leela's room, the coolest place in the house.

Having secured the gate, Leela came down to the car, still smiling broadly. She made an eloquent movement of the head that said how pleased she was to see Chaya.

'How are you, Leela?' Chaya said, in Singhalese.

'I'm well, baby,' she said, bowing her head slightly. Although Chaya and Malini were both adults now, Leela still called them 'baby'. Leela appraised her from top to toe, and said, 'Baby's lost weight.'

That meant that she would be spending the next three weeks trying to fatten her up. Again.

There was a cry of 'They're here!' and two small figures raced out to hug her. Chaya laughed and wrapped her arms around her niece and nephew. She bestowed hugs and kisses on tops of heads. Kapila, her nephew, was seven and still adorable. His big sister, Nayana, was ten. Chaya had come home when Nayana was born, despite it being in the middle of her undergrad studies. To her, Nayana would always be, on some level, the tiny baby that she had held in her arms and rocked to sleep. She was the only member of the family that Chaya had fully confessed to about Noah, and that was only because she was too tiny to understand any of it. Nayana was special.

But of course, she had to pretend she didn't have a favourite out of the two children. 'I've got some stuff for you in the bags,' she said. She had carefully got them the same number of presents.

Amma, Malini and her husband Ajith waited for her in the veranda. She went over and genuflected in front of her mother, who pulled her up and hugged her tightly. Chaya hugged her back, breathing in the familiar warmth of her. They held each other until the children got impatient for sweets and clamoured around them.

'Let me get my shoes off,' Chaya told the children. 'And I'll find the sweets I got for you.' They were in her handbag. She wasn't an amateur at this. You had to give the kids sweets before you got to talk to the adults.

With her shoes off, she stood still on the polished red floor. It felt cool. She savoured the feeling for a moment and then padded over to drop into a seat. The soles of her feet would turn red from the floor polish, but she didn't care.

She fished out the tubes of Smarties and handed them out, one to each child. 'Now go and play,' Malini said. 'Take the picnic mat with you if you're going to sit on the grass.'

The pair ran out into the garden. Malini could easily keep an eye on them from where she was.

'So,' said Amma, sitting down and fanning herself a little with the end of her sari. 'How is work?'

'It's okay,' Chaya said. 'I had a couple of papers published last year, so I'm getting there with that. I've just put in for a European grant. If that comes off, it would be great.'

From their glazed expressions, she could tell she'd lost them. 'It's good,' she said. 'Hard work, but rewarding.'

'So, you're not a professor yet?' said Ajith.

'It takes a long time,' she began. Seeing his grin, she stopped. She had told him all this before, he was just winding her up. 'So no,' she said. 'Not yet.'

The veranda often caught a cooling breeze from the garden. Thatha brought a standing fan in, making it even better. The drinks arrived and Chaya sipped her tea and watched her niece and nephew in the garden. It was nice to be home. Strange, in some ways, but still nice.

'So, how is London?' Thatha said.

She tried to tell them about her life in England. It wasn't exciting, the endless cycle of work and sleep, but the way Malini listened to her, you'd think it was impossibly exotic.

She was in the middle of telling them about the New Year fireworks, which she'd watched from the top of one of the science buildings, when someone banged on the gate. Out went Leela again and another car pulled up. Thatha's brother and his family spilled out. There followed a bit of a scrum as Chaya tried to genuflect at the feet of her aunt and uncle, they tried to kiss the top of her head, little cousins tried to kneel at the feet of all the various grown-ups and the adults exchanged salutations over all the genuflecting heads.

This melee happened every time her relatives met. It was a sign of respect that when you met an older relative, you bowed in front of them to receive their blessing. This practice was dying out now, but Chaya's family had always done it, so Chaya and Malini had learned to do it. Over the years they had refined the kneeling rigmarole down to a quick swoop that showed the necessary diffidence, but avoided having to actually get down very far.

Thatha and his brother looked very similar, but their wives could not have been more different. Amma wore her hair in a tight bun at the back of her head and wore saris or, at most, ankle-length skirts with smart, modest blouses. Chaya's aunt on the other hand, had a Princess Di haircut (still!) and tended to wear calf length skirts and high heels.

Ajith brought out more chairs from the dining room and the circle of people around Chaya expanded. She had to repeat what little news she had. It amazed her that people could think her life was glamorous. The fact that it was just work, home, then work again, never seemed acceptable.

Not long after, there was yet another clanging at the gate. This time it was a grown-up cousin, with her family. More chairs were sourced from the rest of the house. Soon the veranda was crammed with people.

Everyone ended up staying for dinner. Leela had cooked Chaya's favourite curries – devilled potatoes, pumpkin, beans and pork curry. They all ate together, eleven people crammed around the dining table designed to seat eight. Everyone was talking at once, sometimes in Singhalese, sometimes in English, mostly in a mix of both, changing from one language to the other mid sentence. Conversations flowed over, under and through one another.

Chaya nodded and joined in and laughed at the jokes, but as always, felt a little apart from the banter. Once, she had been a part of it, fitting easily into the flow, but ever since Noah, she had felt like she was something other. She could never fully relax, in case she said something that gave her away. Where once she had been open and free, now she had to make a conscious effort to blend in. Even though Noah was long gone, she still felt that distance and although she joined in the conversation, she wasn't fully part of it anymore. And that hurt.

Chapter Nine

Gimhana – London, 2005

Gimhana was furious. He managed to swallow his anger and make it out of the office. The firm had just announced the new senior associates. Three of them. He wasn't among them.

'Jim!' someone hurried after him.

Pah. Why did he expect them to give him his due? They couldn't even be bothered to learn his name properly.

'Jim, wait up.' Barry caught up with him.

Gim stabbed the button for the lift and breathed carefully through his nose. Barry was his friend, one of the people who supported him. Life was unfair. He didn't need to take it out on Barry. He let his breath out slowly, schooled his face into a neutral expression and turned. He was good at hiding what he was feeling. He'd had years of practice.

'Hi Barry. Off to celebrate?'

'Yes, I thought I might join the rest of them for a swift pint,' said Barry pleasantly.

The lift arrived and they stepped in. When the doors closed, Barry said, 'I'm sorry. It should have been you.'

It should have been. He put in the hours. He was good at his job. Better, in fact, than two of those people who had been promoted above him. He said nothing.

'It's not fair, I know,' said Barry. 'But remember what I told you last year. It's not just about the work. It's about fitting in, too. It's a very traditional place. If you want to make it here, you have to embrace that side of things. Old-fashioned family values.'

Old-fashioned. Gimhana nodded. A year ago, Barry had told him that if he wanted to get ahead, he needed to get married. It had seemed like too much of a leap then, but now...

The lift reached the bottom floor and they walked out together.

'Look,' said Barry quietly. 'If you want to leave, I can guarantee you a good reference.'

Gimhana took a swift glance around the main foyer. There was no one from the office around. 'And if I don't want to leave?' he said.

'Then you're going to have to... squash certain rumours,' said Barry. 'Get a girlfriend. Better yet, get married.'

He tried so hard to pass for straight. He was pretty sure he succeeded most of the time. He wondered if Barry knew.

As though anticipating his question, Barry said, 'You're a good-looking man. You seem to be permanently single and people talk,' he said. 'Your private life is your business, but if you want to get ahead in this particular firm...'

It was a good place to work. They had a great employee benefit package and very low staff turnover. There was a generally warm atmosphere. It was a great place to work, in fact, so long as you fitted in.

He sighed. 'Thanks Barry.'

Barry patted him on the shoulder. 'You're good,' he said. 'You deserve to be recognised.'

'Thanks.'

'So, you coming to the pub then?'

'I... can't. I have a dentist appointment. Pass my congrats on though, please.'

'Of course,' Barry said. 'Hope the dental appointment goes well.'

As he walked away, Gimhana's anger gave way to despair. He had hoped Barry was wrong, but he wasn't. It was an old-fashioned firm, in many ways. They were slowly opening up to people of different ethnic groups, mainly among the secretaries and support staff. The only non-white fee earners were Gimhana and another Londoner who was of Vietnamese descent. He had known all this when he took the job. At that time, he hadn't been in a position to refuse the offer. Now he was too invested to move on and start again.

He cursed under his breath. He was going to have to find a wife. He didn't want to, but it looked like he didn't have much choice. As he clattered down the steps to the underground, he reflected that it was a good job he was going to Sri Lanka soon. He could ask his mother to look out for someone for him. The thought brought with it a hint of a smile. His mother would love that.

Chapter Ten

Chaya – Colombo, 2005

After breakfast the next day, she wandered, barefoot, into the veranda and sat in a wicker chair.

As it was still morning, there was a hint of dew in the air. In a few hours, when the sun got to work, the world would be sweaty and airless and the plants would lie gasping in the heat, but for now, it was cool and pleasant.

A tin bell clanked. A cow was outside the gate, munching up the grass that grew on the roadside verge. From where she sat, she could see its tail swishing. She thought of Oxford, where everything was segregated; cars on the road, people on the pavement, cows penned into fields. Here, even in the suburbs, the cows wandered around, trimming the grass in public places and getting in the way of the motorists. It was utterly disorganised and elegant at the same time.

The bus rattled past in a cloud of dust and diesel smoke. The cow paused in its munching for a bit, then carried on, moving out of sight. Once the bus had passed, tranquillity returned. Chaya laid her head back against the wall and breathed in the smells of her childhood; cinnamon, garlic and onion frying in the kitchen, the trace smells of roses and frangipani, the hint of diesel, the sour undersmell of the roadside drain. She felt herself unfurling, spreading out to reach the rustling trees, the cawing birds and the vast, cloudless sky.

For the first time in what felt like forever, she could do... nothing. The tension in her shoulders eased, like knots untying.

She suddenly felt centred, as though she'd found the place where she fit best. This must be what it meant to feel at home. She wished she could bottle that feeling and take it back to England with her.

The sharp beep of a horn made her jump. She opened her eyes to see Leela running up to the gate with the keys. Malini drove her car in and parked in the car port, where Thatha's car usually was. She emerged from the car looking fresh and groomed, as though she hadn't just spent the morning shepherding children into school uniforms and fighting Colombo traffic to get them to school on time. Even in casual clothes – she was wearing jeans and a white cotton shirt – Malini looked like she was ready to be photographed. It had always been like that. Malini was the pretty one, Chaya was the clever one. These were their roles in the family.

Chaya waved, not bothering to get up. Malini dropped into a chair opposite her. 'How's the jet lag?'

'Been worse,' said Chaya. She tipped her head back and closed her eyes again.

Amma bustled in. 'Oh,' she said, stopping in the doorway. 'Look at the two of you. It's been so long since I've seen you both sitting in the veranda like that.'

The two sisters looked at each other and smiled.

'I'm so proud of you both,' Amma said. 'Malini has given me such wonderful grandchildren and Chaya is doing… such great things.'

Chaya shook her head, still smiling. Her mother still had no idea what she did.

'It's good to have you both together.' Amma joined them, moving a third chair, so that she could sit with them. 'So Chaya, do you have plans of things to do?'

'No,' said Chaya. 'I am going to relax. Read books. Eat stuff.' She smiled. She'd earned this break.

'I was thinking,' said Amma, 'it might be nice for us to go and have a facial and a hairstyling at the new salon I've found.'

Chaya frowned. Since when did Amma do pampering treatments? Hair cuts, yes, but *facials*?

'I've booked us all in for an appointment in two days' time,' Amma said. She gave Malini a pointed look.

Malini put her phone away. 'I'm really looking forward to it,' she said quickly.

Chaya didn't doubt that. Now that the children were in school, Malini did the odd bit of modelling. Having kids hadn't ruined her figure, it had just made it curvier. Amma often sent Chaya newspaper clippings of Malini looking wistfully into the distance in some designer sari blouse or salwar kameez set.

'You could do with a haircut,' Amma said, looking thoughtfully at Chaya. 'Perhaps you and Malini can go do some shopping afterwards. Get a nice outfit for the party. There are some really nice things in Odel.'

'That sounds like a great idea.' Malini's expression was a little too innocent. Amma, too, seemed a little on edge. Chaya looked from one to the other. They were up to something. She could tell.

'What's going on?' she said, glaring straight at Malini. She was the easier one to crack.

Malini looked at their mother meaningfully.

'What?' said Chaya, sitting up. 'Tell me.'

Amma rolled her eyes. 'Chaya, darling,' she said. 'You're thirty years old now. And we—'

Malini cleared her throat.

'I,' Amma corrected herself. 'I thought it would be nice if we introduced you to a few people. There's this young man, he's come over on holiday from Germany. He seems very—'

'No. Amma.' Her voice was too loud. She made an effort and lowered it. 'Don't try to set me up. We've been through this before. You know I don't want to get married.' Amma had tried to set up meetings with people who were in London before. She'd always found excuses to avoid them.

'But we're worried about you, darling. You are all alone over there, working so hard. Look at you. You're all skin and bones.

You're not looking after yourself and you're working too hard. You need to settle down, get married. This being on your own is bad for you.'

'I told you. I don't need to get married. I can manage perfectly well without a man.'

'Oh, but darling, you're thirty now. It will only get harder and harder to find a match for you. I don't want you to end up alone.' Her voice dropped as though just saying the words out loud were dangerous. 'A spinster.'

Chaya looked at Malini, who said, 'It's just an introduction, Chaya. What's the harm?'

'I don't believe this,' she said. 'You set me up.' But then she saw the anxiety in her mother's earnest expression. This was important to her. She glanced at Malini, who raised her eyebrows.

It was only an introduction. It wasn't worth arguing about it and ruining the whole of her holiday over it. 'Fine,' she said. 'I'll meet this guy. But don't expect too much. I don't need you to find me a husband. I'm doing just fine without one.'

The look they gave her told her that they thought otherwise.

'Well then, if that's settled. Let me make some phone calls.' Amma pushed herself to her feet. 'I am sure you'll like him, anyway. He seems very good. And if not, there are a few other options on my list.'

'Wait a minute, there's a list?' This was an ambush. Chaya glared at Malini, who had the grace to look embarrassed.

'Of course,' said Amma. 'I made a list, just in case you said yes.'

Chaya drew breath to protest, furious that they'd tripped her up like that.

'None of us is young anymore and Thatha's heart is weak,' said Amma. 'All I want is to see my two girls both settled while your Thatha and I are still alive.' She pressed a hand to her heart. 'When Chaya is married, then my job is done. I can die happy.'

Chaya sighed. How could she argue with that? When Amma had disappeared into the house, Chaya hissed to Malini, 'I can't believe you stitched me up like that.'

Malini shifted uncomfortably. 'I know you don't want the same things I did, but she does have a point, Chaya. You don't look well. You work too hard and… there's more to life than a career.'

'But it's my choice,' she said. 'And I choose to do something worthwhile with my life.'

Malini's mouth set into a hard line. Chaya winced. 'Sorry. I didn't mean to imply that raising a family isn't worthwhile. It really is. But it's not for me.' She smiled, trying to make amends. 'I'd be rubbish at it anyway.'

Malini shook her head. 'No, you wouldn't. You're really good with my two.'

'That's because they're not mine. I love them dearly, you know that. But I wouldn't want to be responsible for them full time.'

'Oh nonsense. No one is ever prepared for kids. The biological clock will kick in at some point.' Malini leaned forward. 'What are you so afraid of?'

Chaya stared out at the garden. What *was* she afraid of? She had given everything she had to her work. At first, she had wanted the career so that she could make her family proud of her, make her worthy in the way Malini seemed to be. And then her career had become the thing she wanted in its own right. She had given up Noah for a combination of family and ambition and if she slacked off now, it would have all been in vain. She needed to keep her focus. Noah had moved on, that chapter of her life was closed. Her career was all she had left.

'I'm not afraid,' she said.

Malini made a sceptical noise. 'Maybe just be open-minded. See where it takes you. You never know, you might like the guy.'

'Like him enough to marry him? I doubt it.'

'You're not looking for love, not immediately anyway. You just need someone you'd be comfortable being with. Love will grow,' said Malini. 'At least, it has for my friends who had arranged marriages.' She gave a small laugh. 'The arranged ones are doing a bit better than some of the love matches.'

Chaya looked over at her. 'Everything okay with you?'

Malini looked up. 'What? Oh, yes. Everything is fine. Ajith is… well, he's Ajith.' She gave that fond little smile that she always had when she talked about him. 'I meant a couple of my friends.'

Chaya nodded. She knew about those. Malini had told her in one of the many long emails she'd sent. Malini and Ajith were a textbook happy marriage. They seemed so close. 'How did you know?' she asked. 'When you met Ajith, how did you know he was the one for you?'

Malini laughed. 'It was so long ago, I can't remember. I suppose it was a gut feeling. I just knew.'

'Gut feeling,' said Chaya. That wasn't a helpful measure. 'Right.'

Chapter Eleven

Chaya – Colombo, 2005

Chaya had been back in Sri Lanka only two days and already the suitors were arriving. Amma had persuaded her to wear a sari for the meeting.

Amma came in. 'Aren't you ready yet?' she said. 'They'll be here any minute.'

Chaya looked at her watch. 'They're not due for another half an hour.'

'They might be early.' Amma tweaked the sleeves of Chaya's blouse so that it sat better on her shoulders.

'That's not going to happen. Is it?' Chaya jerked her shoulder. 'Sri Lankans are never early.'

Amma frowned. 'I hope you're going to behave in a more ladylike manner when they get here. You have to be charming and polite. Don't be too forward. Men don't want a woman who's too forward.' Amma picked up a brush and started fussing at Chaya's hair. 'And don't go on about your education too much. You don't want to intimidate him.'

Chaya closed her eyes. 'I don't really want a man who is intimidated by me.'

'No, no, of course not. But you can make an effort for the first time you meet. You know you never...'

'...get a second chance to make a first impression,' said Chaya. 'I know.'

'Amma,' said Malini, stepping in between them. 'Why don't you go and check that Leela has got everything in the kitchen. Chaya and I can manage the sari.'

Amma hesitated. 'Are you sure?'

'Yes,' both sisters said in unison.

When Amma had bustled out, Malini beckoned Chaya to stand in front of the mirror.

'Hold still, Chaya,' said Malini, pinning the sari into place at the shoulder and the hip. 'There. That's better.' She put her hands on her sister's shoulders and turned her towards the mirror. 'There.'

The sari was peacock-blue silk with a purple and green design on the border. Her hair had been carefully dried and styled. A pair of Malini's earrings dangled from her ears. She had make-up on. She looked elegant and composed, words she would never have applied to herself before.

Malini's face appeared next to her own. 'You look lovely, Nangi,' Malini said. Chaya looked sideways at her sister. Next to Malini, she couldn't help but look plain. Even after two children, Malini was still beautiful. Chaya could never compete. But then, she'd never tried.

Malini gave her shoulder a gentle squeeze. 'There's no need to be nervous,' she said. 'Let's hope he's the right one.'

Chaya sighed. 'What are the chances of that happening? Mr Right just turning up in my living room.'

'Stranger things have happened,' said Malini.

'I don't even know what I'm looking for,' said Chaya. 'So how can I know if I've found it?' She turned to face her sister. 'What am I looking for?'

Malini cocked her head to one side, thinking. 'Someone you can live with, I guess. Someone whose company you can bear day in day out.'

The metal gate clanked as someone rapped on it.

'They're here,' said Chaya. Her stomach dropped. A sense of dread settled on her.

Malini peered out of the window. 'Yes.' She came back. 'Don't worry,' she said. 'You'll be fine. I'm sure he's really nice.'

Chaya looked at her reflection again and patted her hair nervously. Perspiration was starting to bead on her upper lip.

She thought of the stranger that she was going to meet. If she liked him and he liked her, they would become… what? A couple? Or just married to each other. It wasn't the same thing. She had been half of a couple once. Could she ever be again? The darkness in her stirred and with it came a sense of something crucial. Her life was finely balanced on the outcome of the next few hours.

'I don't want to do this,' she said, turning away.

Malini laid a hand on her shoulder. 'Maybe not,' she conceded. 'But honestly, it will be fine.' She turned Chaya round to face her. 'You'll like him.'

'What if he doesn't like me?'

Malini laughed. 'He'd be an idiot not to like you. You're wonderful.'

There was a knock on the door. Malini said, 'Yes?'

Malini's husband Ajith popped his head round the door, looking slightly harassed. 'You ready?' He came into the room properly and took Malini's hand. 'You'll be fine,' he said to Chaya, making shooing motions with his free hand. 'Just be yourself.'

Chaya turned round and gave him her most withering look.

Ajith grinned. 'Okay then. Pretend you're someone interesting.'

Malini gave him a dig in the ribs. Chaya was too nervous to rise to the bait. She would have to get him back later. Malini and Ajith had said they were staying out of the encounter because they didn't want to overwhelm the poor guy and his family. Chaya knew that this wasn't true. They were staying away because whenever they were together, Malini's beauty completely overshadowed her sister. She was grateful.

Chaya looked at Malini and her husband, standing hand in hand, wishing her well. They looked comfortable together.

She thought of her lonely little bedsit and her lab bench hidden by bottles and gas cylinders. It would be nice to have companionship. In order to find it, she had to go out and meet this man. She took a deep breath, fixed a smile on her face and stepped out of the room.

—

Amma and Thatha had shown the visitors into the 'best' sitting room. They all stood up as Chaya approached. Amma came over to Chaya's side. 'This is my daughter, Chaya,' she said, taking her arm. Chaya wondered whether she should be walking in with her eyes downcast in order to look demure. The thought made her smile.

As they greeted each other, the man looked at her, his gaze sweeping from head to foot and back up again. Chaya found herself doing the same. He was thin and tall and looked pleasant enough.

When the introductions were done, she sat down next to Amma and started with her opening gambit. 'What do you do?'

'I'm a doctor,' he said.

'Oh, what sort?' said Chaya.

'Gastroenterologist,' he smiled. 'I gather you're a doctor too. What's your specialism?'

'Microbiology.'

'Oh, a proper doctor then!'

Chaya gave a little laugh. 'Hardly, I think proper doctors are the ones that treat proper patients.'

'What does it matter?' said Varuna's father. 'Both take about seven years to qualify for, right?'

'True,' said Chaya, nodding. So far so good.

'I hear you live in London,' said Varuna, 'I did my undergrad at King's'

'I love London,' Varuna's mother interrupted. 'It's so glamorous! Have you been?' she asked Amma.

'No, we never managed to visit England when Chaya was at Oxford,' said Amma, neatly slipping in Chaya's most saleable asset.

'Oh you must go! We went to Varuna's graduation. It was very exciting.'

Chaya hadn't even bothered to book her graduation, preferring instead to spend the time working. 'I haven't booked a ceremony yet,' she said. 'I'll have to organise that sometime soon.'

She wondered if Varuna realised how blatantly their mothers were showing off to each other. Seeing the glance he sent his mother, she decided she should try to like this guy.

–

A short while later, Amma suggested they go for a walk round the garden, in the hope that the change of scenery would make conversation flow.

'So,' Varuna said as they trailed round after their mothers, who were having a loud conversation about roses. 'Did you watch the cricket last week?'

Chaya shook her head ruefully. 'Don't really follow it, sorry.'

'Do you like art?'

'Not really.'

'Theatre?'

She had not paid attention to anything outside her work in years. 'Sorry.'

'Books?'

'Okay. I can do books,' she gave him a smile.

'Right ho, then. What's your favourite book?'

'*Little Women*,' she said, relieved. 'What's yours?'

He frowned. 'I read a lot of non fiction. Histories and war memoirs, mostly.'

They looked at each other. Neither said anything, but it was clear that this was a waste of time.

Chapter Twelve

Gimhana – Colombo, 2005

The woman Gimhana was being introduced to was lovely. It was awful. She had a sort of hopeful guilelessness about her that made him feel like a heel for wasting her time.

What made things worse was that she was quite clearly interested in him. As they sat near each other, drinking tea, she asked him questions and seemed to genuinely listen to his replies. Why had he agreed to do this? There was no way he could tie this nice girl to a marriage of convenience. How did he get out of this without too many people getting hurt?

The only thing he could do was to be uncharacteristically standoffish. His answers got shorter and more curt. He was as distant as he could be without being rude. His mother kept giving him puzzled glances.

By the time they left, the lady looked a little sad. Gimhana felt bad about that too. He had taken the poor woman's enthusiasm and trampled it into the ground. He had thought this pretending to be interested thing would be easy, but it really wasn't. He couldn't do this. He knew who he was. He could pretend to be someone else, but if he married this woman, she'd expect him to sleep with her. Maybe more than once. That idea made him feel queasy. He'd assumed that he'd be able to deal with deceiving someone to reach his own ends. It turned out he wasn't as ruthless as he'd thought.

'What was that all about?' his mother said, the minute they'd pulled out onto the road. 'Did you have to be rude to that poor girl?'

'I'm sorry, Amma,' said Gimhana. 'I don't think… she's not right for me.' He glared out of the windshield and concentrated on driving. He had learned to drive here, but coming back, the way people drove was always a shock. As much as he disliked it, he had agreed to drive when they went on these trips, partly because he could claim to be concentrating and delay awkward conversation a little. Clearly, not today.

'Really? What was wrong with her?' His mother leaned forward. She was sitting in the back, behind his father.

'She seemed very nice. They are a good family,' his father put in. 'I don't see what there is to object to.'

'I don't know. There's something…' Ugh. This was harder than he'd expected, largely because they were right. There was nothing wrong with her. He just couldn't go through with it.

'Well, you were so rude to her, I'm sure she's not interested in you now,' said his mother. She gave a little huff and settled back. 'I don't know why you asked us to find someone for you, if you were just going to find excuses for not liking any of them,' she grumbled.

Now was probably not the time to point out that she had been nagging him to find a wife for the past ten years. No. 'I'm sorry,' he said.

There was an annoyed silence for the rest of the journey. No one said a word until he stopped the car outside the gates to their house and beeped the horn for the servant boy to come and open them.

'Well, there's one more person to see,' Ammi said. 'Then I'm giving up. I despair.'

Gimhana said nothing. Ammi would come round and would be presenting women to him again in no time.

'At least we don't have to take time out to go visit them,' Ammi said. 'They'll be at the party next week.'

Chapter Thirteen

Chaya – Colombo, 2005

Chaya's holiday was nearly over and, despite her best efforts not to, she was thinking about work again. Malini came round after dropping the kids at school. When she came in, Chaya was sitting at the dining table making notes on a paper she was reviewing. Leela had left her a snack – a plate of pineapple slices under a cloth. Amma was on the phone gently telling another potential mother-in-law that Chaya wasn't interested.

Malini shook her head sadly. 'What was wrong with that one?' she whispered, dropping into a chair and mopping her face with her handkerchief. 'He seemed really nice.'

'You can't be serious! He agreed with everything everyone said!' Chaya whispered back. 'The man's a doormat.'

'God, you're fussy,' said Malini. She grabbed a slice of pineapple and bit into it, hand under her chin to catch the drips of juice.

'Well… maybe I am. I thought anyone "suitable" for Amma and Thatha would do… but honestly, I can't spend the rest of my life being bored silly by my husband!'

Malini chewed her fruit thoughtfully. 'That's fair enough,' she said. 'But can't you lower your standards a little?'

Chaya glowered at her.

'Okay. You can't.' Malini raised her hands in a gesture of surrender. 'Isn't there anyone you liked?'

Chaya thought for a moment. 'There was wotsisname, the doctor. He was nice. But we had nothing in common,' she said. 'Apart from that, no, nobody.'

At the other end of the living room, Amma put the phone down and sighed. 'He liked you,' she said, joining them at the table.

Chaya snorted. 'He wouldn't have the guts to dislike anyone.'

'This is turning out to be much harder than I thought.' Amma sighed and shook her head. 'I don't know, Chaya. You're so choosy. Maybe I'll never find a man for you.'

There was silence around the table. Chaya thought perhaps now would be a good time to put an end to the whole idea. She had met a few men since she'd arrived. At first she had been optimistic, feeling a flutter of anticipation before each meeting. Now, increasingly, she was giving up hope. Malini had said she should go with her gut feeling. She had felt nothing towards any of the men she'd met. Not even mild interest. The whole thing was a waste of time and it was getting on her nerves. She had better things to do. Like work.

'Maybe,' she said, 'we should call it a day and stop looking?'

Amma and Malini looked at each other. Amma sighed and pinched the bridge of her nose. 'I don't know. We shouldn't give up that easily.'

Chaya pulled a face. 'Not looking likely though, is it?'

Amma sighed again. 'Well, there are a few more on my list...'

'Oh Amma, I'm sick of it. All I've done since I got here is meet strangers. I really appreciate that you've tried, but don't you think we could stop now?'

Amma looked at her and shook her head. 'But we *have* to find you somebody.' Her voice rose at the end.

'Yes,' said Chaya gently. 'But you don't have to find him right away. Maybe we should just relax and enjoy my last week here. I can always come back next year and meet some others.'

'Hmm,' said Malini. 'Maybe she has a point. Maybe we're trying too hard.' She laid a hand on top of Amma's. 'Maybe we should see if we can find her someone who lives in England. We can talk to their family and see if we can arrange for them to meet in London.'

At the thought of the possibility of the search carrying on in England, Chaya suppressed a shudder. But Amma and Malini were trying so hard, it was important that she didn't obstruct them. Besides, it would be so much easier if they were in England already. Maybe that would work.

'I suppose I can ask Veena Aunty to keep an eye out...' said Amma, warming to the idea.

She looked so relieved, that Chaya had to smile. She would take the temporary reprieve for now and worry about the people in England later.

'So,' she said, pushing her advantage whilst she could. 'Does that mean we can relax now?'

'I suppose,' said Amma. 'Except for tomorrow night.'

'Tomorrow night?' said Chaya. 'What's happening tomorrow?'

'Mr and Mrs Wimalarathne's Silver Jubilee party, remember,' said Malini. 'We're all going.'

Chaya groaned. 'I'd forgotten about that.'

'Suri Nanda was going to introduce you to someone at the party,' said Amma. 'She seemed to think he was very nice.'

'Do I have to?' said Chaya. 'I doubt Suri Nanda's tastes are anything like mine.'

'Chaya, don't be rude,' said Amma. 'You should. It's not nice otherwise.'

'Besides,' said Malini, nudging her. 'Who knows, he might be the man of your dreams.'

Chapter Fourteen

Chaya – Oxford, 1995

It was raining. Chaya was meant to be reading papers about glucose oxidase, but she kept getting distracted. She watched the water trickle down the window and wondered what Noah was doing. She kept thinking she'd seen him and every time she realised she was mistaken, a hope she hadn't even been aware of having fluttered and died in her chest. It was like being haunted by someone who was still alive. It was infuriating.

She wondered where he was at that moment. Was he staring out of a window at this same rain?

'Chaya?' Sara's voice cut through her thoughts.

'Huh? What?' She turned back into the room. Compared to the dull wet outside, the room felt warm and cheerful. Sara was sitting at the small dining table, with a textbook in front of her. Jay was in his usual position, lying on the sofa with a book propped up on his belly. Even from opposite sides of the room they seemed joined by an invisible cord. There was a sense of ease and comfort about them. Chaya envied them their contentment.

Sara was looking at her expectantly. 'Well?' she said. 'What do you reckon?'

'Er...' Chaya looked at Jay for help. He raised his hands, indicating that she was on her own.

'You haven't been listening to a word I said,' said Sara.

'Um...'

Sara rolled her eyes and sighed. 'Jay and I are going to a party this evening. Would you like to come with us?' she said, enunciating each word with exaggerated care.

Chaya looked at Jay again. He peered over his book and said, 'It's a house party at Keith's. Should be good fun.'

She'd met Keith. He was a friend of Jay's. She pulled a face. 'I don't know...'

'Oh come on,' said Sara. 'You can't sit around moping all the time. It'll do you good. I'm sick of seeing you so miserable.'

Chaya looked at the photocopied research papers she was meant to be reading and felt guilty.

Jay sat up. 'Look mate,' he said, 'Sara's right. You have been bloody miserable these past few weeks. We're worried about you.'

She opened her mouth to argue, but realised they had a point. Ever since she'd turned Noah down for a second time, she'd been distracted and a bit down. Telling herself to stop being silly and get on with her work wasn't working. She couldn't concentrate anyway, so maybe going out would shake her out of her rut.

'Come to the party, Chaya, it'll do you good,' said Sara.

'It's better than sitting in your room by yourself on a Saturday night,' Jay added.

She looked from one to the other. Both faces radiated concern.

'But I won't know anyone.'

'You'll know us,' said Jay, flashing a huge grin. 'Who else could you possibly need to know?'

Chaya smiled. 'Okay.'

'Great,' said Sara. 'Trust me Chaya, you'll have a great time.'

'Yeah,' said Jay, disappearing behind his book again. 'You'd better, or you'll have to answer to Sara.'

Sara threw an eraser at him, grinning.

The party was in a townhouse near Iffley Road. They caught the bus up there and then ran, umbrellas held like shields, down the shiny wet side streets until they got to a house from which music and laughter were escaping into the night. The front yard was a mess of bicycles and assorted junk. Jay hammered on the door while Chaya and Sara tried to squeeze into the relative shelter of the porch. When the door opened they tumbled in.

Chaya had been to parties in people's college rooms before, but never to a house party. The place felt slightly damp and a pall of smoke hung around the ceiling. The girl who let them in told them to put their coats in one of the rooms upstairs and then tripped off to get more drink.

The stairs had been decorated with fairy lights, which twinkled in the haze. They went up, careful not to catch the frayed bits of the carpet and found a door with 'Cloak room' written on a piece of A4 pinned to it. Jay gathered up the coats and dumped them on the bed on top of all the others. They slid off and ended up in a heap on the floor.

There were people everywhere. Chaya followed Sara and Jay into the kitchen, resisting the urge to grab hold of Sara's arm for comfort. The kitchen table groaned with the weight of wine and vodka. Jay headed straight for the washing up bowl full of punch and started ladling it out into plastic cups. Chaya grabbed a cup and poured herself some orange juice.

'I've just poured you some punch,' said Jay, waving a cup of cloudy red liquid at her.

'I think I'll stick to juice,' she said.

'Hey, I'll have it.' Someone plucked it out of Jay's hand and wandered off.

Chaya followed Sara into the living room. She spotted the radiator and went towards it, hoping the heat would dry her jeans. Jay dragged Sara over to talk to someone. Chaya leaned against the radiator and looked around the room. People were lounging around, most chatting animatedly. Not far from her, a boy and a girl were deep in conversation, oblivious to everyone else in the room, their bodies angled towards each other. She looked away from them.

If she'd stayed in Sri Lanka, she would never have come to this sort of party. She would have had a carefully controlled social life, where she was always chaperoned. If she'd decided that she didn't want a social life and wanted to focus entirely on her studies, her family would have happily let her. In fact, they might even have encouraged her to do so while she was studying. The minute she finished, though, they'd rush out and try and find her a husband. The mismatch between their expectation that she should avoid men altogether before graduation but find someone to marry immediately after didn't seem to occur to them.

Chaya sighed. She understood Sara's theory that she needed to go out and mingle with people to become a fully rounded person, but right now it all seemed like so much hard work. All she really wanted to do was to stay at home and study... with the occasional break to daydream about what might have been if she'd felt free to see Noah again.

'Hello.' A guy in a loud green jumper came up to her. 'I saw you looked a bit lost, and I thought, "aha, a kindred spirit". I'm Rich. I live here.' He stuck a hand out.

She looked around for a polite means of escape, and saw none.

'So,' said Rich, taking her lack of reply as an invitation to join her by the radiator. 'What do you study?'

-

Inevitably, she was there for ages. At some point Rich started to tell her about his project on scanning electron microscopy. Chaya let her attention wander. Could she see Noah again? Did Sara have a point about having fun? Malini was always telling her to lighten up. Perhaps going on a date would be lightening up? Nothing serious. Just fun.

As Sara had pointed out, she was already distracted. Maybe spending some time with Noah would make her less distracted…

Oh. Rich was asking her something.

'Sorry?' she said. 'I didn't catch that… it's the noise in here.' As she said it, she realised it wasn't noisy anymore.

'I was going to get another drink. Can I get you a top up?' His face was all red and shiny, probably from leaning against the radiator for too long. She watched him take an unsteady step. Or maybe he'd just drunk too much.

'Oh yes, orange juice please.' She gave him her empty cup. He smiled broadly and picked his way out of the room.

Chaya looked round. While Rich had been talking, a subtle change had come over the room. Everything seemed a little more laconic. One couple had now given up all pretence of conversation and were attached to each other's faces. Sara and Jay were still there, talking to a girl with a pierced navel. Jay had his arm round Sara, and she was leaning into him, laughing. Chaya tried to get their attention, but they didn't notice. She suddenly felt very alone.

She had a few seconds before Rich came back. She really didn't want to spend any more time with him. She made for the door. When she got into the hall, she glimpsed a green jumper coming out of the kitchen, and ran up the stairs.

She stopped outside the 'cloakroom' and considered hiding in it. But what if it was Rich's room? If she went back downstairs, she was bound to get trapped again. Ugh. She hadn't even wanted to come to this stupid party in the first place. She could grab her coat and try to get out before Rich caught up with her.

That decided, she fished her jacket out of the pile on the floor. It was still wet. She put it over her arm and marched out. As she left the room she heard someone say '…coats in the room at the top of the stairs' and a familiar voice said, 'Thanks.'

She rounded the top of the stairs just as Noah started up them. He stopped. An enormous smile spread across his face. 'Hi,' he said.

'Hi.' All her anger evaporated. Her stomach fluttered. She had never been so happy to see anyone before.

He looked at the coat, over her arm. 'Are you leaving already?'

'Yes. I was thinking about it.' She wasn't so sure she wanted to now.

'Stay a bit,' he said. 'Please?'

She could stay, just a bit longer. Now that she had someone to talk to... She said, 'I could.'

His smile brightened. 'Tell you what.' He pushed his wet hair off his forehead. 'You grab a... er... stair and I'll get us a drink.'

She nodded, already torn. Was this the right thing to do? It felt right... but nothing had changed, really. It was still a bad idea.

Noah started to go back down the stairs, and then turned. 'Don't go away.'

Chaya leaned against the wall and tried to get her thoughts in order. She liked Noah. There was no escaping that. Letting herself spend time with him just meant lining up heartbreak for later. Her parents would never approve. If things got serious, she would have to choose between him and them. Besides, she really did have to focus. She had made so much fuss about her ambition to make a difference in the world. She couldn't let that be derailed by something as mundane as falling in love.

She was almost persuaded and had even descended a few steps when Rich reappeared, brandishing an orange juice.

'There you are,' he said, grinning. 'I thought I'd lost you.'

Oh no. 'I... just needed a bit of air.' She was glad she was still holding her coat.

'Oh it's too wet outside,' said Rich. 'We could go to my room and I can open a window for you if you like.' His smile was almost a leer. He came up the stairs. Chaya wished she could disappear into the wall behind her.

Just then, Noah came back. 'I got you juice...' His eyes took in Rich and then Chaya, pasted against the wall, then back to Rich. 'Oh, hello,' he said. He was still smiling, but his eyes had a hard glint to them. 'I'm Noah. I don't believe we've met.'

The two men stared at each other for a moment. 'This is a private party. Who do you know that lives here?' Rich snapped.

Noah's glance flicked to Chaya. She mouthed 'Keith'. He frowned. 'I'm a friend of a friend, you know how it is.' He smiled again. 'Anyway, it was nice to meet you. I haven't seen Chaya in ages, so, if you'll excuse us...'

Chaya smiled apologetically at Rich. He said, 'Right. Well. Okay,' and scurried back down the stairs, pausing at the bottom to glare at them.

Noah said, 'Are you alright?'

Chaya nodded. 'Yeah.'

'Do you want to leave?'

She shook her head and sank down on the stairs. There was no leaving him now. Her knight in soggy denim.

'Great.' He sat down beside her. The stairwell was narrow and his thigh touched hers. The skin on her leg tingled.

'Here.' He handed her the drink. 'Cheers.'

They tapped plastic cups together and Chaya laughed.

'Good party huh?' he said, taking a sip of his drink.

'I guess,' she said. 'I don't really know anyone here.'

'Me neither.'

She narrowed her eyes. 'So how come you're here then?'

He didn't say anything, but looked faintly guilty. Suspicion started to rise. Sara. She must have got in touch with him. 'Noah?'

'I heard on the grapevine...' He wasn't a very good liar.

'Sara told you, didn't she? No wonder she was so insistent that I come. She's too much.' She started to stand up.

Noah caught her arm. 'Chaya, please. I had to see you. I can't stop thinking about you. It's driving me nuts. I persuaded Sara to get you here. She didn't want to do it, so don't blame her.' He released her arm, but she sat back down again, held by his expression. 'Just explain it to me,' he said. 'Please.' His hair slid down over his eyes.

Without thinking, she reached over and pushed it out of the way.

–

It was difficult to have a meaningful conversation sitting on the stairs. They had to shuffle apart or stand up whenever anyone needed to go upstairs or down. Yet Chaya found the transient quality of the situation comforting. It was as though she were safe from the real world in stairway limbo. Noah seemed to sense this and didn't suggest they move.

'Have you got a boyfriend back home or something?' he asked, looking very worried.

'God, no! It's nothing like that.'

'Then what is it? Do you not like me in that way?'

She stared at him. Wasn't it obvious that she did like him very much? Sara had seen it straight away.

'I mean,' he continued, looking away, 'if that's it, then just say and I'll stop bothering you.'

She put a hand on his arm. 'No, no. The reason I can't see you is because...' She sighed. 'It's a cultural thing. I can't ever take you home to my family. We'd have to split up at some point and I ... why start something, when you know it has to end?'

He looked at her, not understanding. She sighed again and took her hand back.

She tried to explain to him about her family and how the way she was brought up meant she couldn't be with him.

He listened, head to one side. 'What about what you want? Doesn't that come into it?'

'It does come into it,' she said. 'Only, what I want has to fit within certain parameters. If you think about it, if I lived in Sri Lanka, most of the boys I met would be suitable.' She remembered the fuss over Malini's short-lived first relationship with Sumith the Unsuitable Boy and added, 'probably.'

'But I'm not,' he said. 'Because I'm...' He sought for a better word and gave up. 'White?'

'No.' It wasn't as simple as that. 'You could be the same colour as me, you could be from India, and it would be the same. You're not Sri Lankan. You're different to us. You have a different culture.' She felt a sense of *déjà vu*; she had given this same explanation to Sara countless times.

Someone wanted to go upstairs, so they had to shuffle apart to make room for them. When they moved back together Noah said, 'What do *you* want? You're not your family, you don't think like that.'

'No, but all that is part of who I am. If I let go of that, I wouldn't be me.'

He thought about that for a minute. 'You didn't answer my question,' he said eventually. He took her hand. 'What do you, Chaya, who's sitting on the stairs, want?'

She could see the fairy lights twinkling on-off, on-off, reflected in his eyes. She could also see the darker shadow of herself among them. She knew what she wanted, but also knew it wasn't going to end well. So how could she answer his question?

She chose not to. 'What is this? Some sort of charm offensive?'

He dropped his gaze to their hands, nestled together on his knee, then back up. He grinned. 'Is it working?'

How could she help but laugh? She didn't remove her hand from his. Noah gave it a squeeze. They both took that to be her answer.

Noah leaned forward and kissed her. It was the gentlest brush of lips, but she felt it in all of her body. He hesitated, lips millimetres from hers and this time it was she who closed the gap.

Kissing Noah was the most intense thing she had ever experienced. Sensations flooded through her, warming her up from inside and making her heart gallop. When he brought his hand up to gently cup her cheek, it felt as though there was electricity in his touch. She could have gone on kissing him for ever.

Chapter Fifteen

Chaya – Colombo, 2005

The party was in full swing when Chaya arrived. The great and the good of Colombo society were there in all their finery. Ladies in colourful saris flitted about like butterflies, bangles jangling. Men stood around, stubbornly wearing jackets in spite of the heat that followed them in from outside. The hall was large and the air conditioning stole away the smells of perfume and sweat.

Chaya followed Malini in, trying to make herself incon-spicuous behind the rest of the family. Malini was radiant in a pink and gold sari. The two children were neat and tidy in their best clothes. Malini had little Kapila firmly by the hand, whilst Nayana, very grown up at ten years old, was walking demurely next to Chaya.

Amma too was wearing a sari and her finest jewellery. She and Malini had done their best to persuade Chaya into her sari again, but Chaya had refused, reasoning that she was going to a party and should be able to wear what she liked. The man her aunt had lined up would realise she didn't always dress like that. So, Chaya wore a burgundy trouser suit that she knew flattered her.

As soon as Malini entered the hall, she was surrounded by a swarm of people. Chaya reached for her niece and nephew's hands and led them to a table with empty seats.

Chaya dumped her handbag on the chair next to her niece. 'Okay, you're in charge of saving seats for everyone,' said Chaya. 'Now then, what would you like to drink?'

'Coca Cola!' said Kapila.

'Can I have iced coffee?' said Nayana.

'No.'

Nayana sighed. 'It's not fair.'

Chaya smiled. 'Life seldom is, little one. Apart from iced coffee, what would you like?'

'Orange juice,' Nayana said, her lower lip starting to pout.

'Okay. Now you two be good. Don't move. I'll be right back.'

'Can I go play with the balloons?' said Kapila, spying a group of kids earnestly chasing a balloon.

'When I've come back, you can. For now, you need to behave,' said Chaya. She looked up in time to see Ajith and Thatha coming over. Ajith caught her eye and indicated that he'd take over.

'I'm just getting them drinks,' said Chaya as she passed him.

'Nayana's not allowed ice coffee,' said Ajith, automatically.

'I know.'

'I don't know what it is with kids and iced coffee. It makes them so hyper,' Ajith muttered.

'Think about it,' said Chaya, flashing a grin at him.

She was coming back, a glass in each hand, when an aunt, Suri Nanda, accosted her.

'Chaya *duwa*!' She looked her up and down. 'What are you wearing?'

'Hello Nanda.' She did a faint genuflection, careful not to spill the drinks she was holding. 'Sorry, I'm just taking these for the kids.'

Her aunt sucked her teeth and shook her head. 'How am I supposed to introduce you to a husband when you're dressed like a man? What will people say!'

'I'm hoping they'll say, "what a nice outfit Chaya's wearing. She looks lovely",' said Chaya, smiling sweetly.

Her aunt looked scandalised.

'I'm sorry, Nanda. It's a long story, all right. I have to get these drinks to the kids.' Chaya lifted up the glasses she was carrying to emphasise the point. 'Then I'll come right back to meet this man you've got lined up, okay?'

Suri Nanda looked round the room. 'I don't think he's here yet.'

'Okay, come find me when he is then.' Chaya beamed encouragingly at her aunt and manoeuvred past her.

Malini, Amma and Thatha were all seated by the time Chaya got back.

'You can sit next to me, Chaya Punchi,' said Nayana, patting the chair.

'Thanks.' Chaya slid into the seat. No sooner had she sat down when a voice rang out.

'Is that Chaya?'

Chaya got back to her feet and turned to greet one of Amma's Women's Institute friends. 'Hello Aunty,' she said, pulling a smile onto her face. She and Malini had known this lady for years. She was one of the many women who were not related to them that they called 'Aunty'.

The aunty gave her an air kiss on the cheek. 'Let's have a look at you.' She put her hands on Chaya's shoulders and scrutinised her. 'You've lost weight again, no?' she said, as though she was disappointed. She glanced at Chaya's legs and frowned at the trousers, but refrained from comment. 'How are you, darling?'

'I'm fine, Aunty.'

'How long are you back for this time?' The aunty pulled up a chair and sat down.

Chaya sank back into her chair. 'Only a few weeks.'

The aunty clicked her tongue. 'Is that all? You've been over there a long time now, no? When are you moving back for good?'

Smile, be gracious. 'I don't know, really. There aren't many jobs in my field over here.'

'You could always teach,' said the lady. She gave a little laugh. 'Unless there's another reason that's keeping you in London.' She winked. 'I can't believe you have been single all this time.'

Chaya forced her smile to keep steady. 'Well,' she said. 'I am.'

The lady laughed. Malini, who had been listening, came over. 'Hi Aunty, I haven't seen you in ages,' she said.

'Malini, how lovely to see you.' The lady leaned in and looked past Chaya. 'And these must be your children.' She wiggled her fingers in a wave. 'Hello darlings.'

The kids stared at her, both slurping their drinks. Malini gave them a frown and a nod. Obediently, they took the straws out of their mouths and chorused, 'Hello Aunty,' and went back to their drinks.

The lady gave a little laugh and turned back to Malini. Chaya took the opportunity to slip out of her seat. She gestured to Malini over the lady's head that she wouldn't be long and made a dash for it.

The soft drinks were at one end of the room, some way away from the bar. Chaya didn't often drink in front of her parents, but she suddenly wished she could have something stronger than fruit juice. She hesitated, weighing up the need for Dutch courage against the disapproval she'd face if she were seen drinking alcohol. While she stood vacillating, she caught sight of Suri Nanda approaching the table where the rest of the family were sitting, a determined look on her face. It could only mean that the man she had been intending to introduce to Chaya had arrived.

Chaya grabbed a fruit juice from the table and looked around for a place to hide. The hall was lacking in obvious hiding places, but dotted here and there were pillars festooned in balloons and ribbons. Chaya dived behind one of them. She leaned back against it, feeling a little silly. She was wondering what to do next when a man backed round the pillar and bumped into her. He jumped and swung round. Seeing her, he took a small step back.

'I'm sorry, I didn't realise this pillar was taken,' he said. He was slim, tall and very good-looking. He leaned backward and peered round the pillar into the hall. Chaya took the opportunity to look him and up and down. He was wearing an expensive-looking suit. Everything about him seemed impossibly well groomed. Even the fingers that were wrapped around the whiskey tumbler looked manicured.

She moved up. 'There's probably enough room for both of us.'

'Thanks,' he said, smiling at her. He had a nice smile, but it didn't sit well with the worry in his eyes. Chaya wondered whether it was just her own insincerity she was projecting, or whether he genuinely had something he was hiding. He took a sip from his drink. 'So,' he said, waving the tumbler, making the ice clink against the glass. 'Who are you hiding from?'

'My aunt,' said Chaya. 'She's got some man she wants to introduce me to.'

He grinned. 'What a coincidence. I'm hiding from my mother, who has some woman she wants me to meet.'

They stared at each other for a moment. 'I'm Gimhana,' he said, holding out his hand.

'Chaya.'

They shook hands.

Gimhana looked thoughtful. 'What's your last name?'

She told him.

'Well, it's not you I'm supposed to meet,' he said.

Chaya shrugged, feeling a slight twinge of disappointment. He seemed quite nice, if unsettlingly immaculate.

They were silent for a minute. 'What's that you're drinking?' he said, looking at her glass.

Chaya realised she had no idea. She tasted it. 'Passion fruit,' she said. 'I couldn't get to the bar.'

He nodded. 'You can have my whiskey, if you like. I can always get another one. You could add it to your glass and no one would know.'

'Whiskey and passion fruit?' said Chaya, pulling a face.

'Fair point,' he said.

'I don't normally drink,' said Chaya, feeling the need to explain.

He waved a hand. 'Say no more,' he said. 'I've been subjected to intensive bride-hunting since I got into the country. It's enough to drive anyone to drink.' He offered his glass. 'Go ahead. I haven't touched it.'

She shook her head. 'Where do you normally live, then?'

'London.'

'Whereabouts?'

'Finchley.'

'Really, I live in Camden,' said Chaya.

'Well we're practically neighbours, give or take a tube journey.'

Chaya wondered how one was supposed to progress with this sort of conversation. She wished she socialised more often.

Gimhana was clearly more used to networking. He moved onto the next question, seemingly without the slightest bit of awkwardness. 'What do you do?' he said, his head to one side as though she had all his attention.

'I'm a scientist. You?'

'I work in M&A,' he said. 'Sorry, mergers...'

'...and acquisitions, I know.'

There was a brief silence. 'I suppose I should check what the mater is up to.' Gimhana looked round the pillar. 'Damn,' he said. 'She's seen me.' He turned round to Chaya. 'I'd better go before I get you into trouble too.' He smiled. 'It was nice to meet you, Chaya from Camden.'

'You too, Gimhana from Finchley.'

He gave her a quick grin and stepped out saying, 'Ammi, there you are! I've been looking all over for you!'

Chaya leaned back against the pillar and smiled at his audacity.

The party progressed slowly. Chaya's aunt finally tracked her down and introduced her to a man who looked slightly embarrassed to be there. As soon as was reasonable, he and Chaya politely parted ways.

Dinner was announced and Chaya joined Malini with the kids at the queue. The food was served on a long buffet table with the food in hot tureens, so the smell of spices rose into the air. There was chicken floating in a fiery red gravy, pumpkins, fried okra, lentils, devilled potatoes, jackfruit, two types of fish and a selection of salads.

Two lines of people shuffled along on either side of the table, ladling out rice and various curries onto their plates. At one point Chaya looked up and saw that Gimhana was in the line opposite her. He raised his eyebrows in recognition. She gave him an answering nod and then looked away just in time to catch Malini staring. Chaya suppressed a smile.

'Who was that guy?' said Malini, as soon as they'd sat down to eat.

'What guy?' said Chaya, although she knew very well whom her sister meant.

Malini made an exasperated noise. 'The guy that smiled at you while you were getting dinner.'

'Oh, that guy,' said Chaya, not looking up from her plate.

Malini gave her a gentle kick under the table. 'Stop being annoying.'

'Ow. Okay, okay. I don't know him. I spoke to him for about two minutes earlier. His name is Gimhana. That's all I know. Really.'

Malini peered at Chaya to see if she was still teasing. Satisfied, she said, 'Gimhana,' in a thoughtful voice. 'Hmm. Was he nice?'

Chaya shrugged.

'Do you want me to ask around…?'

Chaya stopped eating and looked up. 'Please don't,' she said, suddenly feeling incredibly weary. 'Not now. I'd like to stop feeling like a window display, just this once.'

Malini nodded. 'Okay. Not right now.' She smiled at her sister and turned around to check on the kids.

Chapter Sixteen

Gimhana – Colombo, 2005

Gimhana was drunk. He knew he was. Quite apart from the fact that his face had that weird numbness that came when he'd had too much to drink, he was watching people dancing badly. It was terrible and wonderful at the same time.

He leaned back in an uncomfortable wooden dining chair. You had to love a Sri Lankan party. The DJ was old school. He'd started off with The Gypsies, then baila, and was now on to a selection of the cheesiest seventies and eighties pop. He'd be playing 'Under The Boardwalk' any minute now. They always played 'Under the Boardwalk'.

The dance floor was full of people dancing, regardless of age or ability. Tiny children jumped around, often holding hands with their adults. There were balloons underfoot. An intoxicated uncle with an exuberant dance style had cleared a sort of blast radius around him. There were a few married couples, laughing as they tried to hold onto each other. A group of teenaged boys were horsing around, arms around each other's shoulders.

He remembered those times. When life was simple. If something was unthinkable, you didn't think about it. Until you realised it wasn't unthinkable, really. A sudden memory flared. Of a hug that had morphed into something else. Of kisses stolen in hiding. The pain of being rejected and later, the very physical pain of being beaten up. He shook his head. No. Not thinking about that now. Not now, not ever.

He looked away, scanning the people at the periphery of the dance floor. People like him, who were watching, but not taking part. That girl was there. What was her name? Chaya from Camden. She was staring idly at some people dancing. A balloon escaped towards her. She batted it back to a little boy. She smiled. She had a small, tight smile, like she'd forgotten how to do it properly. Her mouth remembered, but the rest of her face wasn't really into it. Gimhana frowned. She was interesting, that girl. There was something about her that intrigued him. A sort of familiarity. He was used to the way women looked at him. But this girl had looked at him like she was assessing him. Weighing him up for something. There had been no interest in him... more in what he represented. Which was interesting. It occurred to him that it was how he sometimes looked at people while he figured out how best to get on their good side. Did she have a use for him? In which case, could she be the amenable lesbian he was looking for?

She must have sensed him looking at her, because she turned and caught his eye. She gave him a friendly nod and looked away again. See. Familiar, but distant. Interesting. Gimhana swirled the whiskey in his glass. The ice had all but disappeared.

Looking around again, he spotted his mother sitting at a table a short distance away, watching him with her lips pursed. Poor Ammi and her doomed quest to make her son get married like a 'normal' man. Perhaps he should go talk to that Chaya woman, just to see what happened. Ammi would have him married off to her before he got past the first sentence. But if his suspicion was right, that could work out perfectly.

He got up and ambled over. 'Not dancing, Chaya from Camden?'

She glanced at him and turned her attention back to the dance floor. 'Er, no. I can't dance,' she said. 'Besides, I'm watching my niece and nephew.'

Prickly. Gimhana swayed a little, and grabbed the back of a chair to steady himself. 'Cute kids,' he said.

Chaya nodded, but didn't bother turning to look at him. They watched the dancers for a while.

'So, Chaya from Camden,' said Gimhana. 'How was the man you had to meet?'

She shrugged. 'Nice enough.'

'But not your type?'

'Not really, no. How about the woman you had to meet?'

Gimhana waved a careless arm. 'Far too glamorous for little old me.'

She looked sideways at him, but didn't comment. Man, she was hard work. But there was something behind that cold façade. Something he recognised. He tried a different topic. 'Nice suit, by the way. I meant to mention it earlier, but you know, it wasn't appropriate.'

She looked surprised and then, miraculously, she smiled. 'Thanks,' she said. 'That's the first positive comment I've heard about it all evening.'

'Really? What's wrong with it?' He scrutinised her, leaning to look at the back too. 'It's very flattering.'

The corners of her mouth twitched. This time the smile was in her eyes, but not her mouth. 'Not respectable, apparently.'

This made him laugh. 'Ah, I see. Women wearing trousers. Yes. What will people say!' he leaned forward and added in a falsetto: 'You'll never find a husband dressed like that, young lady.' He winked.

Her gaze flicked up and down the length of him. Assessing, but not judging. She turned back to watch her niece and nephew again, but her shoulders were slightly less stiff. 'Exactly.'

He stopped laughing and looked down at himself to see what she had noticed. Without thinking he had put his hand on his hip. Camp. That's what she'd noted. He quickly dropped his hand and slowly lowered himself down in the chair he was using for support. She'd spotted that and not judged.

He studied her. She was pretty in a prim sort of a way and not objectionable. Okay, she was a little stiff, but he could tell that was just because she was uncomfortable. 'So, how come you're on the market? Divorced?'

That was the wrong question. Her shoulders tensed up again. 'Oh you know…' she said guardedly. 'Getting old and all that.'

He nodded. 'Parents leaning on you, huh?'

'A bit.' A balloon drifted towards her. She leaned forward to bat it away. 'How about you?'

'I've been concentrating on work and kinda let that side of things slip.' He sighed. 'My ammi's been on at me for years now. Finally she just told me she was going to start looking whether I like it or not.'

'I see. Is that okay with you?'

He gave the tiniest of shrugs. He took another swig of his drink. 'I'm not likely to find a woman on my own.' Had he just put a slight emphasis on the word woman? He had, hadn't he? Crap. Hopefully, she hadn't noticed. He looked at his glass. He should probably stop drinking now.

One of the children ran over and whispered something in Chaya's ear. 'Let's go,' she said. She stood up, holding the child's hand. 'Excuse us,' she said to Gimhana. 'You should probably get yourself a soft drink and sober up a bit,' she said, in an undertone as she passed him. 'Before you say something you regret.'

Bossy. Gimahana stared after her. She didn't turn round or check he'd heard. There was definitely something there. Gimhana looked down at his drink. She might be bossy, but she was also right. He should stop drinking. Before he let something slip.

He sighed and drained his glass.

Chapter Seventeen

Chaya – Colombo, 2005

The morning after the party, Chaya was late getting up, so she was still having breakfast when Malini showed up. Malini looked fresh and awake as though the late night had made no impression on her whatsoever. Chaya, on the other hand, had sore eyes and felt terrible.

'Morning!' Malini chirped, slipping into a chair.

'Is that Malini?' said Amma, emerging from the kitchen. 'Morning Duwa, have you eaten?'

Malini eyed Chaya's plate of mung beans, coconut and onion sambol. 'Yes, but I wouldn't mind a top-up if it's mung eta. I've only had one slice of bread that I ate whilst getting the kids ready.'

'Leela,' Amma called over her shoulder, 'bring a plate for Malini Baby.'

Amma turned back to her daughters. 'Where are the kids today?'

'Swimming lessons,' said Malini. 'Ajith is with them, so I can spend some time with Chaya.'

Chaya yawned and nodded. 'I'm grateful.'

Leela appeared with a plate and had a question for Amma, who sighed and followed her back into the kitchen.

'So,' said Malini, leaning over and washing her fingers in the bowl of water next to Chaya. 'What happened with that guy at the party? Gimhana. You were talking to him for ages.'

'Nothing happened. We talked a bit and then he went away.'

'Hmm,' said Malini, heaping some food onto her plate. 'So, what did he say?'

Chaya finished eating and washed her hand in the bowl, making the water smeary with oil and bits of coconut. She dried her hands on the napkin next to it. 'He thought your kids were cute.'

'Chaya!' Malini glared at her.

'Seriously, nothing interesting happened. He told me he works in London. We talked about how I would never find a man if I insisted on wearing trousers to parties and then he lurched off to get a drink. That was all. Really.' She reached for a mangosteen from the fruit bowl and squeezed it between her palms. She watched with satisfaction as the maroon skin split under the pressure of her hands, gaping to reveal the soft white flesh underneath.

Malini tilted her head and looked at her sister. 'What are you not telling me?'

Chaya scooped out a white segment of fruit and popped it in her mouth. She had liked him. Not sexually, just as a person. Something about him felt familiar. It was almost as though he was as lonely as she was. But her sister wouldn't understand that. She would get excited and think that Chaya fancied him. So she said nothing and merely looked blank.

Malini watched her a bit longer and finally said, 'I asked around about him.'

'Uhuh.' Chaya removed the seed and carefully deposited it on the edge of her plate.

'He's thirty-three.' Malini frowned as she tried to remember the information she'd gathered. 'He lives in London, works in banking or law or something like that. He's single. And apparently, he's very shy and he's been working too hard to have time to find a girlfriend – but that's according to his mother, so it doesn't mean it's true.'

'You talked to his *mother*?'

'Well, she came and found me, actually. She was after Amma, but ended up chatting to me instead. She wanted to know who you were and what you did. She seemed to think it was significant that he went up to you to chat.'

'I'm not surprised he's reluctant to talk to women if his mother's going to launch a full scale investigation every time he does. Anyway, he was drunk.'

Malini shrugged. 'The fact remains that you two seemed to get on quite well.'

'What's this?' said Amma, materialising behind Chaya.

Malini explained. Amma turned to Chaya, hope lighting up her face. 'Really? And did you like him?'

Chaya shrugged. 'I think you're making a fuss about nothing. The man had too much to drink. He was probably chatting to everyone he came across.'

Amma and Malini exchanged glances. 'He's available,' said Malini, meaningfully. 'He's been looking for a while, but hasn't found anyone yet.'

'Really?' said Amma. She turned to Chaya. 'Why didn't you tell me about this?'

'I didn't think it was important,' said Chaya, throwing up her hands. 'He's only looking because his mother is pressuring him. He's not really interested himself. It's a waste of time!'

'I gave his mother your number,' Malini said to Amma.

'What?!' said Chaya.

'Oh good,' said Amma. 'Well done, Malini.'

It was like she wasn't even there. 'Listen to me,' said Chaya. She couldn't tell them what she suspected 'I think he's got... something he's hiding. You know, something he's not telling his parents. Maybe he's got... someone already that they don't approve of?'

'No.' Malini shook her head. 'I didn't get that impression from his mother. She was genuinely concerned that he didn't meet women in London.'

The phone rang. Amma beamed. 'That could be them, now.' She bustled towards the phone. 'I'll get it.' Automatically, she patted her hair and checked her sari before she answered it. They'd had the phone for years, but she still couldn't bring herself to speak to someone if she wasn't 'presentable'.

Chaya sighed.

Malini frowned. 'Honestly Nangi, what is wrong with you?'

Chaya stood up. 'I'm going to go wash my hands.' She picked up her plate and the bowl of dirty water and went into the kitchen. As she washed her hands, she let the possibility that he might be interested creep in. He seemed nice, a little too fond of his drink, perhaps, but basically interesting. If he really was career-minded, he would appreciate her dedication to her work. He made her smile, which was something very few people managed these days. Despite his outward friendliness, he seemed to be hiding a part of himself away. That was probably the thing they recognised in each other – that sense of something hidden. Perhaps they had more in common than it seemed.

She wondered if he really was gay. There were other explanations for a good-looking man being single, but there was something in the way he'd said 'I'd never find a woman on my own' that had made her suspect. She thought about the way he'd assessed her trouser suit, with no interest in anything other than the suit itself. And the look he had given that group of boys on the dance floor – part sadness, part envy. But if he was gay, then why was he encouraging his mother to look for a wife for him? She understood that it wasn't an easy thing to admit, especially in Sri Lanka, but still, it seemed a bit extreme to want to get married in order to hide it. No. It had to be something else.

Perhaps, meeting him was a good idea.

Chaya returned from the kitchen just as Amma was hanging up. She and Malini both looked quizzically at their mother.

'That,' said Amma, pulling up a chair, 'was Mrs Herath.' She smiled. 'Gimhana's mother.'

'Ooh!' Malini reached over and poked Chaya in the arm. 'What did she want?'

'Apparently, Gimhana would like to meet Chaya again and talk to her,' said Amma dramatically. She looked at Chaya proudly, as though she had just produced a rabbit from a hat. 'They're coming to see us the day after tomorrow.'

Chaya said nothing.

'Well...?' said Malini. 'Say something. That's excellent, isn't it?'

'They seem a bit keen. Day after tomorrow...'

'He's going back to England. On the same day as you, in fact,' said Amma. 'We thought it was best to organise things as soon as possible.'

Amma and Malini were both still looking at her expectantly.

'I guess it would be nice to meet him when he's sober,' she said, cautiously. Gut feeling, Malini had said. Her gut feeling was that she liked him. She didn't fancy him, but there was something about him that chimed with her.

'Is that a yes?' said Malini, leaning forward.

'I guess.'

'Excellent.' Amma stood up. 'I'll go tell Leela. We must make a special effort.' She paused and put a hand to Chaya's face. 'Oh my *duwa*. I hope this is the man for you. I worry about you so much, you know. All alone in England.'

Chaya softened. She leaned her head into her mother's palm. 'I know, Amma. I know.' She decided she would do her best to like Gimhana, whatever her reservations. 'I hope he's the right one too.'

Chapter Eighteen

Chaya – Oxford, 1995

Having a boyfriend was an exhilarating experience. It was as though Noah made Chaya feel even more herself than before. They talked, a lot. He challenged her assumptions and made her think about things anew. He also made her deeply, heart-spinningly, happy.

But even in this state of happiness, Chaya knew she couldn't risk being spotted by another Sri Lankan. The diaspora was a giant network. There was always the risk of news getting back to her parents. Consequently, they rarely went out together in the daytime, and even when they did, she wouldn't hold Noah's hand. He humoured her, but didn't really understand. Amma always said that relationships required give and take, so at some point, she had to compromise on her vigilance. Going for ice cream was one such compromise.

The ice cream parlour had a vaguely hippy air about it and they made their own ice cream. Every time Chaya went in there she toyed with the idea of trying a new flavour. Each time, she ended up choosing chocolate.

'You really don't like trying new stuff, do you?' Noah said, handing her the tub of chocolate ice cream. He had bought himself a huge cone with two different flavours on it.

'I panic if I have too much choice,' she said. 'When I panic I withdraw to what I know.'

'And yet, you came out to study at one of the most challenging universities, on the other side of the world.'

'That's different. It's a means to an end. I'm going back,' she said.

He looked at her thoughtfully and nodded.

The shop was packed full of students and early tourists, so they headed for the University Parks. The days were warming up nicely and the flowers were out.

The parks were busy, full of joggers, dog walkers, picnickers and people out for a saunter in the sunshine. They set off across the grass, picking their way through groups of people. 'Do you remember when we came here last?' Noah said.

'Of course.' She ladled a spoonful of ice cream into her mouth. She should have got chocolate sauce added on top.

Noah chuckled. 'I can't believe I tried to impress you by skipping stones on the ice.'

'… Or failing to,' she grinned.

'I was so desperate to get to know you,' he said, his ears going pink. 'I was actually cycling in the opposite direction when I saw you that day. I did a u-turn to come and talk to you.'

'Really?' She looked sideways at him.

'Really.' He looked meaningfully back at her.

'Why?' The question escaped before she could stop it. She had often wondered. 'I mean, why me?'

He stopped and turned to face her. 'I can't really describe it. That first day, on the train, I felt like… like something clicked into place. Like I'd been missing something all my life and then suddenly I'd found it. Just like that.' He made a face. 'That sounds rubbish, doesn't it? Give me a couple of days and I'll try and think of something more poetic for you.' A puff of wind made his hair fall all over his eyes.

She laughed and smoothed his hair off his forehead for him.

'Thanks,' his eyes twinkled at her. 'So, what do you see in me then?'

While he was waiting for her to answer, his ice cream had trickled down his wrist. He brought his wrist up to his face and removed the drip from his hand with one long lick.

'Obviously,' said Chaya, 'I was bowled over by your impeccable table manners.'

'Cheek!' He swept at her with his free arm and grabbed her round the waist.

She instinctively wriggled to get out of his grasp. 'Noah,' she snapped. 'What if someone sees?'

He let go, surprised. 'Sorry,' he said. 'I forgot.'

She knew better than to reply straight away. The intensity of her panic had surprised her too. She stomped off across the grass. He followed quietly, like a confused puppy.

By the time they got within sight of the pond, which was now free of ice and full of ducks, Chaya's heart rate had slowed back down. They sat down in the tall grass and finished off their ice creams in silence.

'I'm sorry,' Noah said again. 'I didn't think.'

She sighed. 'That's okay. It must be hard for you, having to sneak around. It's not so bad for me. I'm used to it.'

'You are?' He brought his knees up and rested his arms on them.

'Oh yeah, my sister had a boyfriend once, when she was about seventeen. It was some boy from her evening A-level tuition class. They'd been smiling at each other across the classroom for months. But they never really got to talk to each other because our mother always dropped her off and came early to pick her up after class.'

She finished off the ice cream and twisted the tub, trying to get at the last drop. 'When I started going to the same evening school, my parents decided that we could chaperone each other. I was supposed to be sensible enough to make sure we both kept out of trouble.' That seemed like so long ago now.

'So, some days we would tell my parents that we were going shopping after class and we'd go meet with this guy in a tea shop. I would sit and read while they talked and held hands surreptitiously under the table.' She smiled at the memory of Malini, all starry-eyed. Chaya had rather liked Sumith, he was sweet and shy and totally besotted with Malini.

'So what happened?' said Noah.

'Someone who knew one of my aunts saw us. She told my aunt. My aunt told my mother...' She waved her hands to indicate the Colombo grape vine. 'My parents hit the roof. We were both grounded for weeks. Malini was in trouble for seeing the boy and I was in trouble for helping her.'

Noah frowned. 'Why were they so upset? It all sounds quite innocent.'

'It was,' she said. 'It's just that it wasn't the done thing. Apparently Sumith was not suitable. God, the rows at home were awful. It was horrible.' Amma had wrung her hands against her chest like a Bollywood matriarch, bemoaning how she could have given birth to such an ungrateful child. Malini had cried for days. Worse than all of that was the look on her father's face. He hadn't looked angry, they could have dealt with that, he just looked... hurt.

'Wow. Seems quite... extreme.'

Chaya shrugged. 'Not for a Sri Lankan parent,' she said.

Noah stared into space for a moment. 'What was wrong with him?'

'Sumith? He was low caste, I think.' Chaya frowned. 'I never really understood the relevance of that in this day and age.'

'Sounds like a Jane Austen novel,' he said.

She gave that some thought and nodded. 'Yes, I guess it does. In Colombo, your business is everyone else's business, a lot like the gossipy society in Austen's books. One important difference,' she said. 'Sri Lankans educate their daughters.'

'Clearly,' he smiled at her fondly. She smiled back.

He shifted position. 'So, what did your sister do?'

'She smuggled a note to him explaining why she couldn't see him again. She was miserable for weeks.' A sad Malini was difficult to imagine and even more difficult to watch. Chaya remembered desperately trying to cheer her up.

'She gave him up? Just like that?' he said. 'She must have been really scared of your parents.'

'Not scared, exactly.' Although that was part of it. 'It's also love. I don't think she realised that they'd react with so much feeling. They were angry, but more than that they were so...' She cast about for the correct word – upset? Betrayed? Disappointed? Distraught? In the end she settled for, '...distressed.' She shook her head, trying to dispel the images. 'I don't think either of us could handle hurting them like that.'

Of course, if they found out about Noah, it would be exactly the same. Or maybe worse, because they didn't expect it from her. She felt a sudden chill and shuddered.

Beside her, Noah was thoughtful for a long while. Chaya was suddenly struck by how differently Sara and Noah reacted to the same stories about her other life. Sara always erupted in a tirade about how backward the whole thing was, whilst Noah asked questions. This was important to her. It was her family they were discussing, after all.

Eventually, he said, 'I can't imagine what it must be like to be part of such a loving family.' There was real sadness in his voice.

That wasn't the reaction she had been expecting. She looked over at him. His eyes were focused on the middle distance.

'Why? What about your family?'

He rarely mentioned them. She had assumed that they called or wrote to him regularly like hers did.

'My parents are in the Middle East at the moment. They're diplomats, so we moved around a bit. I think I just got in their way. They couldn't wait to pack me off to boarding school.' His mouth stretched into a thin smile that didn't make it up to his eyes.

He looked so sad, she wanted more than anything to wrap her arms around him and tell him he was loved. But since they were in public, she settled for reaching for his hand and giving it a brief squeeze.

He gave her a smile, a proper one that did reach his eyes. 'So what happened to your sister? Did she find someone else?'

'Oh yeah. She met Ajith a year later, while she was waiting for her A-level results.' She didn't want to talk about this anymore. She wanted to find out more about Noah's family.

'What did your parents say to that?'

'Malini decided Ajith was The One pretty early on. So one evening, he came to visit and asked my parents if he could marry her.' It had been a more adult courtship. She could picture him sitting in the living room, hands clasped tightly together. 'My father nearly fainted with relief when they found out he was suitable!'

'Do you like him?'

'What, my brother-in-law?' She thought about Ajith; warm, funny, Ajith, who worshipped the ground Malini walked on. 'Yes, I like him. He's a thoroughly nice guy. And very sensible. Just what Malini needs.'

They sat in the grass for a while longer, cocooned in their own thoughts. She tried to steer the conversation back to Noah. He didn't talk about his life. She had already been aware of this, but now, for the first time, she could sense why. 'Was boarding school really horrible?' she said after a while.

Noah shrugged. 'It was okay. I kept a low profile, not too popular, not too shy. My father thought it would make a man of me. I think he's rather disappointed at the way I turned out.'

'Why?' She was genuinely baffled. As far as she was concerned, he couldn't have turned out any better.

'He doesn't approve of my wanting to be a geologist.' He pulled a blade of grass out of its sheath and started chewing on the tender base of it.

She watched the grass end going up and down. 'What's wrong with geology?'

'He wanted me to do economics or politics.' He took the blade of grass out of his mouth, pulled his chin in and puffed out his chest. His features changed. Scowl lines appeared on his forehead, and his eyes narrowed. Did his father actually look like that – an older, angrier version of Noah?

'A science degree is not necessarily a barrier nowadays, I suppose,' he boomed. 'Plenty of top businessmen have science degrees these days. No need to let your subject hold you back.'

He let out a deep whoosh of breath. His features relaxed and he was her Noah again. 'When my finals are over, I bet he'll line up a whole load of his contacts to offer me work experience to try and sway me over to the big bad world of business,' he said with a trace of bitterness still in his voice.

'When I finish my degree, my parents will try and line up people for me to get married to. Isn't it strange how much power our parents have over us?' She placed her hand on the grass next to his. 'Each in their own way.'

He stretched his little finger out and hooked it around hers. 'There's a difference with your parents,' he said. 'You love them.'

She was shocked. Was he saying that he didn't love his parents? 'Surely, you don't mean that.'

He thought about it, the blade of grass moved up and down. 'No, I suppose I don't. I just wish they'd stop trying to turn me into something I'm not.' He sighed.

Seeing him sad made her want to cry. She couldn't imagine what it must be like to not have your family behind you, ready to catch you if you fall. Poor Noah. 'If it's any consolation,' she said. 'I think you've turned out perfect.'

The smile he gave her made her feel warm from head to toe.

Chapter Nineteen

Gimhana – Colombo, 2005

'I must say,' Gimhana said, when they were shooed out to go for a walk around the garden, 'this bride-hunting is a great way to see people's gardens.'

'You're lucky, you get to see different gardens. The woman only gets to wander around her own garden.' Chaya sounded prickly, just as she had done at the party. It seemed to be her manner. She seemed to always be in motion, moving positions, fiddling with things. Highly strung, running on nerves.

Gimhana clicked his tongue in sympathy. 'I hadn't thought of that. How boring for you. Perhaps you should agree to one of the men, then you get to have a go at looking at their garden...'

Chaya's step faltered and she shot him a glance. Was that amusement?

He ran through what he'd just said. 'Not a euphemism,' he said.

'I see.' She gave him her tight little smile. So it was amusement, then. There was a sense of humour buried under that layer of defensiveness.

'I'll let you in on a secret,' she said. 'I'm not really interested in gardens.'

He was puzzled for a second. Was she trying to tell him something?

She caught his eye. 'Oh. Er... also not a euphemism.'

He laughed and she smiled back. He liked this woman.

Chaya was nice. In fact, her family were nice too. They seemed very keen and hopeful that Chaya and Gimhana would get on. Her mother had insinuated that she'd been looking for someone for Chaya for a while now. It was said jokingly, but he hadn't missed the glance Chaya had given her mother. He was still not sure what her angle was. Did she want to get married? Or was her mother pushing her into this?

He was starting to feel bad again. He'd thought that this whole marriage search would help him with his work. At work, you had to look after number one if you wanted to get ahead, but this wasn't just about work. It involved real people with real feelings. He actually liked Chaya. He could have been friends with her and he didn't like the idea of being a dick to her.

'Look, Chaya,' he said. 'I… I don't know how best to say this, but I don't think this is going to work out.'

She looked up and an emotion that might have been disappointment flitted across her face before she returned to her normal, slightly forbidding expression. Now, he felt worse.

'No?' she said.

'I mean, you're lovely. And your family are great. But I'm…' He shrugged. 'I'm sorry.'

She pressed her lips together and turned away. She took a leaf from a nearby croton bush and rubbed it between her fingers. 'Okay. Thanks for telling me.'

'It's nothing personal,' he continued. 'It's just that… I really don't think I can do this whole arranged marriage thing.' He was staring ahead, frowning. Up to now, he hadn't said anything to the women themselves when he turned them down. He always left it to Ammi. Was this what it felt like? He was an awful coward.

'I'm sorry,' he said, again.

'I understand,' said Chaya. Her voice was tight. 'Shouldn't you be saying all this to your mother?'

She sounded annoyed. He didn't blame her, really. He sighed. 'I know,' he said. 'You're right, of course. I'm just too… I don't want to hurt her feelings, you know.'

Chaya nodded. 'Hmm.'

They followed their mothers round to the rose plants. They didn't speak to each other again until it was time to say goodbye.

—

Afterwards, Chaya and her parents sat down to their usual cup of tea and discussion of how the meeting had gone.

'They're nice people,' said Thatha, nodding. 'What did you think of the boy, Chaya?'

'He's nice,' said Chaya, carefully. 'But I got the impression he's not very interested.'

'Really?' said Amma. 'You two seemed to get on really well. His mother seemed to think so too.'

Chaya thought about what Gimhana had said. She didn't want Amma to get her hopes up. It would make it that much more disappointing when the rejection finally came. 'Seriously, Amma. He said he didn't think it would work out...'

Amma wasn't listening. She helped herself to a slice of cake. 'You know,' she said, thoughtfully, 'from what Mrs Herath said, Gimhana might be flying back on the same flight as you. Maybe you could sit next to each other and really get to know each other by the time you get to London.'

Chaya sighed.

Chapter Twenty

Gimhana – Colombo, 2005

Gimhana glared out of the car window and felt bad. This was even worse than usual. The fact that two strangers who were meeting for the first time were unlikely to like each other enough to meet again was an understood risk with this marriage brokering business. His parents knew that and the parents of the girl knew that. He was always careful not to show any encouraging signs, even though he was naturally curious about people. This time was different. Although they were both clearly not interested in each other as sexual partners, there was something there. An understanding, almost. He had met her when they weren't weighed down with the huge expectation to get to know each other and they'd accidentally got on.

Once he'd worked out that Chaya wasn't looking for a convenient sham marriage, as he was, he had assumed that the meeting was something they both did to comfort their parents, but with no actual expectation from either of them. He'd been wrong. Chaya had been annoyed. He should have seen that coming. It wasn't so unexpected. What was unexpected was how disappointed that made him feel. Was he so lonely that the prospect of friendship was so precious?

Then there was the matter of his parents. They had clearly thought this was the end of their search. That they'd found a wife for their troublesome son. That was bad.

His mother was talking about how well she'd got on with Chaya's mother. 'And she says her daughter is very career-driven and shy and that's why she's still single.' She leaned forward and said, 'So, Gimhana…?'

The problem was, she'd seen him talking to Chaya at the party. She had assumed that there was a spark already. To Ammi, this meet up was a mere formality. It was like they'd bypassed the first date and jumped straight into a second one.

'I don't think so,' Gimhana said. He beeped the horn at a tuk tuk, leaning on it for an extra long blast.

'What?' She put a hand on the back of his seat and strained forward, as though trying to see his face. Since she was sitting directly behind him, she wouldn't be able to. She moved and tried to look at him through the rearview mirror instead. 'Why not? She seemed like a very nice girl.'

Why not? He ran through his usual lists of objections – they had nothing in common, they didn't really understand his ambition, they had unrealistic expectations about life in the UK… none of them worked. He could say something disparaging about Chaya herself, but that didn't seem right either. 'I don't think she wants to get married,' he said. 'I think she's only there because her parents are pressuring her.'

Her mother scoffed. 'That's not the impression I got. You are far too cynical.'

'Anyway, if that's the case, we'll find out. But aside from that, is there any objection?' said his father. There was an edge to his tone. He had been getting increasingly tense with each passing meeting. Did he suspect? Not for the first time, Gimhana wondered how his parents would take it if he just came out to them.

Ack. But he couldn't. They might hate him. 'I don't… I don't think we'd get on. She's too ambitious and work-obsessed.'

'But so are you. You'd get on perfectly,' said his mother.

'Two workaholics aren't a good idea in a marriage.'

In the tense silence that followed, his parents exchanged a glance. His father shook his head. 'This is ridiculous, Gimhana.

Are you actually interested in getting married or not? Every girl we've introduced you to, you have some objection about: not driven enough, too driven, too quiet, too loud. What is this, Putha? Have you any idea how much work we have had to do to arrange all this?'

'I'm sorry. I just—'

An army checkpoint loomed up ahead. His father cursed. For a second, Gimhana thought he was swearing at him, and was shocked, then realised they were being waved down. He slowed the car to a halt.

Looking out of the window, his eyes were level with the machine gun one of the soldiers was carrying. An older man leaned in at his window.

He lowered his window and the hot air rushed into the air-conditioned interior, bringing with it the smell of the muddy lake that lay on the far side of the road.

'ID please.'

Gimhana dug his Sri Lankan ID card out of his pocket. His parents did the same. He collected them all and handed them out through the window. The man's gaze locked on to Gimhana's. For a second he felt a trickle of fear. Homosexuality was still illegal here. If these guys knew, what would they do to him? Turn a blind eye? He thought of the beatings at school. Perhaps it depended on who was there to witness it. He tried not to hold his breath. And waited.

The man checked the ID cards, eyes flitting from each card to the faces in the car, and handed them back. He waved them on.

Nobody spoke for a few minutes. The war was in abeyance, but the checkpoints were a stark reminder that things weren't entirely safe.

Finally, his father said, 'I think we have to give up this search for a bride nonsense. Come back and talk to us when you know your own mind.'

His mother said, 'Oh no, we can't—'

'The boy is clearly not ready to settle down,' his father snapped.

He had to say something. 'It's true,' Gimhana said. 'I'm not fully ready. I'm hoping to become a partner in the firm and I'm putting in ridiculous hours. I don't know that I have the time to have a girlfriend. I barely have time to have friends.'

'But you're not getting any younger,' his mother wailed.

'I know, Ammi. I know. But it's not so bad for men, is it? We can wait another year or so and have another go.'

There was a grumbled assent from his mother and a sceptical harrumph from his father. Gimhana sighed. All he'd done was kick the can down the road a little bit. Unfortunately, that was all he could do.

Chapter Twenty-One

Gimhana – Colombo, 2005

Gimhana was a seasoned traveller by now. He knew to wear comfy jeans and layers. The airport in Colombo was air conditioned, but getting onto the plane involved a bus ride in the hot, damp air. He let the ground hostess check his ticket and passport and was shown into the departure lounge.

Looking around, he spotted Chaya. He'd known they'd be on the same flight. He had decided that he'd try to talk to her. He didn't know if she was gay or not, but she was the only woman who had come close to being a viable bride of convenience. If she was a lesbian, then... perhaps they could make this work.

She didn't see him approach. She seemed to be deeply engrossed in what she was doing. He stopped and watched her for a second. There was a stillness about her that wasn't normally there. She was working and work calmed her. He understood that. This, he thought, was the crux of what made him think they could be friends. Outwardly, they were as different as they could ever be, but inside... inside, they had a lot in common.

'Chaya,' he said.

She looked up, frowning. 'Oh,' she said. 'It's you. What do you want?'

He was taken aback at the strength of her animosity. 'Oh dear. What have I done to deserve that?'

She rolled her eyes. 'Have you any idea how much your mind games have upset my amma?' she demanded. 'I don't mind being messed around, but your mother was so convinced you were happy that *my* amma got her hopes up and… well. It's not fair.' She looked away.

He winced. 'Ah,' he said, 'I'm sorry. Really I am… Can I sit down?' Chaya sighed and indicated the seat next to her.

He sat down. 'I really am sorry, you know. I didn't mean to upset your mother. Mine was pretty annoyed with me too.'

Chaya gathered her papers together and didn't reply.

'I told her. You were right, I should have told her at the start.'

Chaya paused in her paper shuffling and looked at him, eyes narrow. 'Told her what, exactly?'

'That I wasn't really ready for all of this and that I was too engrossed in my work to think about marrying.'

'I see,' said Chaya, thoughtfully. 'Was that the truth?'

He met her eyes and knew that she was asking him a deeper question. Did she know? How did she know? Perhaps she *was* the friendly lesbian he'd been hoping to meet all along? But she would have said, or given some indication, wouldn't she? He looked away. Could he risk telling her?

Chaya put her papers in her bag and turned to him. 'I'm sorry, it's not my business. It's between you and your family.'

'No, no. It affected you. It gives you the right to tell me off… a little.' He gave her a small smile. 'But I think you might have to stop now, though.'

She hesitated, her face softening a little. 'Okay. Fair enough.'

They sat next to each other, staring into space for a moment. He had to know. He had to know. But how to ask without giving too much away?

'So,' he said. 'What happened with you? If you don't mind my asking. I got the impression you've got no more interest in actually getting married than I have.'

Chaya didn't look at him. 'I'm married to my work,' she said. 'I don't have time for someone else in my life.' She straightened the papers in her lap, even though they were already in a neat pile. She blinked rapidly.

Oh. Like that, was it? Heartbreak. Well, he knew how that felt too. He had moved on, but it seemed that maybe she hadn't.

'Who was she?' he said, softly. 'Someone who didn't love you back?' Chaya didn't respond. She screwed her eyes shut.

'Chaya,' said Gimhana gently. 'It takes one to know one, you know.'

She opened her eyes and looked at him. 'I'm not...' she dropped her voice so that only he could hear. 'I'm not gay.'

'Oh,' he said. 'I see.' He should have expected that, but he was still disappointed.

She nodded. His eyes met hers and he saw the desolation, the sadness. She had loved someone and lost him and never got over it. The prickliness, the constant sense of movement, those were all her ways of trying not to think about the pain, short-term coping mechanisms that had become so ingrained that she couldn't manage without them.

On an impulse, he put his hand over hers, gave it a quick squeeze and let it go. 'I'm sorry.'

Chaya froze. For a second she went completely still. Not even breathing.

An announcement crackled over the tannoy, informing them that the gate was opening for boarding. There was a general scrum as people tried to get to the gate before everyone else.

Chaya blinked. Gimhana gave her what he hoped was a reassuring smile. He leaned forward to pick up his bag.

'What about you?' she said, so quietly that he wasn't even sure he'd heard right. She hadn't moved to get her bags. She was sitting very straight, hands gripping the paperwork on her lap, looking straight at him. He had asked her a personal question, he owed her something back.

'Me?'

'Did he not love you back?' she said, quietly.

He held her gaze for a moment. 'No,' he said, levelly. 'He didn't.'

He'd expected something huge to happen, but nothing did. People continued to rush to the gate. Chaya remained seated.

She carefully put her paperwork into her satchel. Finally, she looked up. 'I'm sorry,' she said.

Her eyes met his and there was understanding there. Somehow, that was comforting.

'We should get to the gate,' she said, looking around. The seats around them were empty.

'Listen,' said Gimhana. 'We're not going to be sitting next to each other, so...' He pulled out his business card holder and extracted a card. 'Here's my card.' He found a pen and wrote down his mobile phone number on the back. 'Call me. Whenever you like. I think we could be friends.'

She took the card and handed him hers. 'Keep in touch, Gimhana.' Her eyes smiled at him. 'It's been nice meeting you.'

Chapter Twenty-Two

Chaya – Oxford, 1995

Chaya was on time for her meeting with Dr Goldworthy, but typically, her tutor wasn't ready for her. She sat on a shabby chair, whose faux leather had split from years of students sitting on it. The corridor housed eight tutors' offices, four on each side. In the middle of the corridor, there was a space that divided the rooms into two blocks of four. This space held the coffee machine, the sink, a rack of outdated magazines and the only window. A square of natural light fell just short of her legs. She stretched a leg towards it. The sunlight warmed her foot and made her think of home.

The door opened and Baz, her lab partner, came out. He shut the door behind him and grinned.

'How did you do?' she said.

'He says if I do a bit more work, I should be able to get my two-one.' Baz was clearly very pleased with himself.

'Well done.' She needed to get a two-one or a first, if she was going to be able to do a PhD. Baz rarely went to lectures and often borrowed her notes to copy. If he was going to get a two-one, she must be doing okay.

'Anyway, good luck.' He strode off down the corridor, his shoes squeaking on the lino.

Chaya got up from the uncomfortable chair and knocked.

'Yes.'

Dr Goldworthy was not what she'd expected from a tutor. He was in his late thirties with close-cropped brown hair.

In spite of his efforts to look smart, he always had a slightly bewildered air about him, as though he were a boy playing at being a grown-up. This impression of naivety was misleading, something that always became evident after a few minutes of his questioning.

'Ah, Chaya.' He looked up from the papers he was sorting. 'Sit down.'

Dr Goldworthy liked to hold his meetings sitting with his chair in front of his desk. The students had to sit on a saggy old sofa and balance their folders on their knees.

'Ah, here we are.' He pulled a sheaf of papers out of the mess on his desk and started leafing through them. 'Hmm,' he said, frowning.

She felt a stab of alarm. Frowning wasn't good.

He sat down. 'Well, Chaya,' he scanned the paper in front of him again before looking up. 'Is everything okay with you?'

Oh no, this wasn't a good sign either. 'Yes,' she said carefully. She nearly said 'sir', but stopped it just in time. He didn't like being called 'sir'.

'It's just that your reports this term have been…' He paused briefly to glance as the papers, 'Disappointing.'

'Disappointing?' Her heart got louder in her ears.

'Yes. Not up to your normal high standards. Have you been ill? Is everything okay at home?'

'No. Yes. I mean, I've not been ill and everything is okay at home. I went back to see my new niece, just before the start of term.' She'd only been back for two days. She had to focus. 'What do you mean disappointing?'

'Well,' he put his glasses back on and read a few out. 'Plant biochemistry: "has handed in work consistently, but that's the best that can be said – C." Metabolism: "Needs to improve – C plus" and for molecular biology, usually your best subject, B.'

As her tutor, Dr Goldworthy was supposed to look after her general welfare as well as her grades. He lowered the papers again and peered at her. 'Is there anything you want to talk about?'

She stared at him. There wasn't enough air in the room. The whole point of her being there, all her hard work, her scholarship, her years away from her family, the whole *point* was for her to get her degree. This could not be happening. She went to lectures. She did the work. What had gone wrong?

Dr Goldworthy sighed. 'If there's something going on in your life that's distracting you from your work, tell me and I might be able to help.' When she said nothing, he shook his head. 'You're going to have to work very hard if you're going to pull your grades up next year. At this rate all you'll manage is a two-two at best. I know you can do better than that.'

He paused and looked searchingly at her. 'Is the pressure getting to you?'

She stared blankly at him.

'If there is anything I can do to help, please ask. I'm always here,' he said.

'Yes sir.' She rose unsteadily to her feet. 'I… yes.'

Dr Goldworthy looked as though he would like to say something more, but took pity on her and handed her a set of notes. 'Your reading list for next week's tutorial,' he said. 'I'm sure if you find some of the more accessible text books and work hard over this term and the summer holidays, you'll be able to get yourself back up to speed.' He gave a smile.

'Yes sir. Thank you.' She let herself out, still not quite believing it. There was even less oxygen out here. She stumbled down the stairs, heart hammering, the walls leaning in so all she could focus on was putting one foot in front of the other. Her heartbeat was so fast that she sat down. Was she having a heart attack? There was no pain. She felt hot. Frightened, she thought about calling out, but her throat was tight. She sucked in a deep breath and let it out. And another. And another.

Eventually, her heart rate slowed down. Cold sweat broke out. When she was finally able to stand up, her legs shook.

She had to talk to her parents. They knew she was going to meet her tutor today. Her choices were to tell them the truth about her studies. Or lie.

Her breath hitched in her throat. She hated lying to her parents, but it was what she'd had to do for months. She never said anything directly untrue… she just conveniently left out the parts of her life that involved Noah. There was her life at home with her family and then there was Noah… and never the twain to meet. It worked, in a fashion, but it didn't stop her feeling terrible about it.

Every so often, she had wondered if she could tell her parents about Noah. After all, he was nice, clever, his parents were diplomats… but now there was this. The whole point of her parents keeping her away from boys during her school days was to stop her getting distracted from her studies. Her studies were the main reason she was here. Not Noah. She had let herself be distracted by Noah and look what had happened.

Eventually, she felt steady enough to walk home. All the way home, the horror of her falling grades went round and round her head.

Chapter Twenty-Three

Chaya – London, 2005

Chaya opened her eyes and instinctively knew it wasn't morning. Awake. At night. Oh no.

She stared at the darkness, her heart pounding already. It would only be a few more seconds before her mind dug up the past. Her shoulders twitched, making her breath hitch. Her lungs shrank to almost nothing. Outside the bedsit, thunder rolled.

Her breathing came in little puffs. Something terrible was coming. The dread gathered over her head to swallow her whole. She had no tears left to cry; she hadn't cried in nearly ten years, so all that was left was to fight. She had to get up and do something. It was either that, or give in and let the despair bury her.

It took everything she had to get up and turn on the light. It was just past midnight. Why was she awake? What could she do to distract herself? She looked round the room. The place was spotless. The dishes and sink were clean. The table was polished to a shine. Her heart was picking up speed. The fear welled up in her throat. The hopelessness would arrive any second now. She flicked the bed sheets straight. The distraction gave her a few seconds of reprieve.

Exercise helped. She could go for a run. She looked out of the window to see rain slamming into the brickwork opposite and running down the window. Lightning flashed. Chaya turned round. The room shrank. Blood roared in her ears. She stumbled across to her medicine cabinet and fumbled around for her beta blockers. She hated taking them and it was already too late, but still. She pulled the bottle out and stared at it. It was empty.

How? Then she remembered that she'd run out soon after she'd got back from Sri Lanka. That was nearly a month ago. She had meant to get a new supply, but she had forgotten. How could she have forgotten? It was on her list. She looked round the room again, searching for something to do to keep a lid on the attack. Suddenly, the crest of the wave hit and misery exploded on her. She folded down onto the floor and put her head in her hands.

She was transported back to her old college room, listening to Noah's footsteps moving away from her. Loss and loneliness coursed through her.

In the past she would have called Sara or Jay, but since they had kids, she didn't. Especially at night. They had enough on their plate without her being a burden to them.

Another wave of despair. Chaya whimpered. She had to move. With unbearable slowness, she raised her very heavy head. The pain was almost physical. If she'd been asked to put it on a scale of one to ten, she'd have said nine. But this hurt was worse than mere physical pain. It was there and not there at the same time. Uncontrollable. Maddening.

She had to do something, anything, to dull the ache. She drew up her knee, pulled up her pyjama leg and looked at her calf. The old scar had healed months ago, but the memory of it was still there, reminding her of that other way to release the pain. No. That is not an answer. It had been a mistake the first time. But the flood of relief when she saw the blood ooze out of the cut, that incisive moment when emotional pain was replaced with something physical; something she could stem, had been overwhelming. She knew it wasn't going to help, that when she was more herself, she would be ashamed of it. But right now, when everything was so bleak and in the face of the solid conviction that something terrible was going to happen if she let time carry on moving, she had to do something, *something,* to make it stop.

She got to her feet and reached for the kitchen drawer. In it lay her meagre cutlery collection and a small stack of takeaway leaflets. She moved past the big kitchen knife that she rarely used, to the small paring knife at the back, the one that she kept so sharp that it needed the little metal guard on it to prevent her accidentally cutting herself whilst getting a spoon. A rectangle of card rested just above the knife. She flicked it out of the way, but it fell back. A sharp corner dug into the back of her hand.

The small white card and the tiny jolt of pain derailed her line of thought. She stared at it, trying to remember what it was doing there. It was a business card. For Gimhana Herath. In a sudden moment of clarity she remembered Gimhana handing it to her before they parted ways at the airport. She had meant to call him, but with each passing week, it became more and more difficult to do, so she'd tucked it in with the leaflets, so she didn't have to look at it. She wasn't sure why she hadn't just thrown it away.

Gimhana. She could call Gimhana. He'd understand. She gripped the sides of the drawer to focus. Would he, though? Would he really know what it was like to wake up in the middle of the night and feel the awful weight of his life trying to crush him?

No. But it was better than the knife. He said he often worked late. He might be awake. She picked up the card, trapping it with her fingertips, so that the edges dug in. Sharp points of pain to keep her grounded.

She pulled her mobile phone out from where it was charging. A quick glance told her it was past midnight. Was it too late to call him? He was a complete stranger. She couldn't just call him out of the blue like that.

She put the phone back down, the tiny blue screen face up and found she couldn't leave it. She couldn't turn around.

She couldn't straighten up. She knew how to, but her body just wouldn't obey. It was getting harder to breathe. Her throat tightened. Her face felt like it was on fire.

She couldn't bear this. If she didn't do something to get help now, she might do something terrible.

Her hands shook as she typed in the numbers. If he was not there, she could always hang up without leaving a message. Do it. Anything to keep the panic at bay. He answered almost at once. 'Gimhana Herath.'

Chaya hesitated. She hadn't worked out what to say if he answered.

'Hello?' he said.

She had to squeeze the words out of her chest. 'It's Chaya.'

'Chaya? What's wrong?' He didn't sound annoyed. He sounded concerned.

'I... it...' What could she say? 'I woke up and I couldn't cope with being alone? I think I'm going to die?' She said nothing.

After a few seconds of silence, Gimhana said, 'Is everything okay?' He sounded calm. Unhurried. Somehow it helped.

'No.'

'Okay,' he said. 'Do you want me to come over?'

Just talking to him, hearing another voice, was helping. Her heartbeat was slowing down. She was starting to feel silly. The cold was creeping up through her toes. The residual heat in the thin cotton of her pyjamas had seeped away. Chaya shivered.

'Chaya,' he said again. 'Do you need some company?'

She should say no. Deal with this by herself. She tried, but all that came out was a strangled mewl.

'I'm coming over,' he said, firmly. 'What's your address?'

The minute he said it, something loosened in her. The vice around her chest seemed to lessen. She told him her address.

'I'll be there in half an hour.'

The feeling of relief was instant and incredible. 'Okay.' She felt the ache subside. 'Thank you.'

When she'd hung up, she clutched the phone to herself and sat still, remembering how to breathe.

By the time he arrived, the panic attack had mostly subsided. It was coming back in waves though. A flare of panic, followed by a period of calm. This, she could deal with. She dressed and warmed herself up. Why had she called Gimhana? She hardly knew the guy. She should have called Sara. Except Sara would have been asleep. She got precious little rest and Chaya would have felt awful for disturbing her. Anyway, calling a virtual stranger was sometimes easier than calling a friend whose opinion she cared about.

When she opened the door and saw him, rain-spattered and looking worried, she felt silly for getting him to come out in the storm. 'I'm so sorry,' she said, leaning against the open door to steady herself. 'I shouldn't have called you.'

He looked at her silently, studying her face carefully in the dim hallway light. 'No,' he said, slowly. 'I think you really should.'

Another flare of panic washed through her. Gimhana stepped forward and touched her elbow. It wasn't a full grip, but it was solid and oddly reassuring. As the panic subsided, she realised she was staring into his face. Her gaze finally made contact with his.

'I'm here,' he said, softly. 'You're not alone.'

Not alone. She hadn't realised how much she needed to hear that until he'd actually said it. She released the breath that had been pent up in her chest and gestured for him to come in. She closed the door and leaned against it, still a little shaky from the last flare up.

He stood in the middle of the room and looked around, taking in the bed, the sink, the tiny kitchen area.

'Nice place,' he said, shrugging off his wet coat. 'Very... snug.'

'Tiny, you mean,' she took his coat and umbrella and put them on the draining board. 'Can I get you some tea?' It was odd offering tea at this hour, but this wasn't a normal visit.

'That would be lovely,' he said, shaking water out of his hair. 'I haven't eaten, so I brought some food, hope you don't mind.'

Chaya shrugged. 'Why should I mind?' She didn't know what to say to him. She was glad he was there, but apart from that… what did you say in a situation like this?

'You can share it with me, if you like.' Gimhana gestured to the food.

'I… uh…' Had she eaten that evening? She couldn't remember. The food in his bag smelled amazing. 'I would like that,' she said. She hadn't intended to say that, but now she had, she knew it was the right thing. 'Thank you.'

Gimhana's shoulders relaxed. 'Thank goodness,' he said. 'My nurturing and comforting skills pretty much run out after the "give them food" option. You have no idea how glad I am that you said yes to food.'

He looked so genuinely relieved that it made her smile.

'That's better,' he said and smiled back.

–

She only had one chair, so they ended up sitting on the floor, with Gimhana's takeaway Chinese containers on the coffee table. They talked about what was in the news and the way Chinese food tasted so much better in Sri Lanka. They discussed politics, religion, the things they'd done at school. They discussed everything other than the reason he had come round. Chaya felt her insides untying. There was something comforting about him; a feeling that he understood living with pain. Even though they never discussed it, it was always there in the background, reminding them to be gentle with each other.

After several hours, Gimhana yawned. He looked at his watch. 'I should go home,' he said. 'I might be able to get a power nap in before I have to get up for work.'

'I guess so.' She didn't really want him to leave, but she knew he had to. She would be okay now. Even if she couldn't sleep, she could clean the flat until the smell of Chinese food and the smudges of muddy footprints were eradicated. That would take her until dawn, when she could go to the lab.

He leaned forward and put his elbows on the little table. 'Chaya, are you okay now?' he said, gently.

She was too embarrassed to meet his eye. 'Yes.'

'Listen,' he laid a hand on her arm. 'I know what it's like to be alone. Feel free to call me anytime you need me, okay?'

She looked up at his worried face. 'Thank you,' she said.

He smiled and gave her a theatrical wink. 'What are friends for?'

Chaya put her own hand over his and gave him a little smile, grateful that he wasn't going to make a big deal about it. He hadn't tried to force her to talk or insist she get help. He had just met her where he found her. It was as though he knew instinctively that all he needed to do was to be there. And it had been enough.

Chapter Twenty-Four

Gimhana – London, 2005

The next day, Gimhana couldn't concentrate. He could blame lack of sleep for part of it, but more than that, he was worried about Chaya. He hadn't known her very long and yet, when she had needed someone in the black of the night, it was him she'd chosen to call. That meant something. What was more, she had been right to call him. The moment he'd heard the panic in her voice, he had been on her side. He wasn't one of nature's givers. He couldn't be, when he had to fight so hard to get everything. But that raw fear in her voice and the look in her eyes when she'd opened the door had somehow touched him. He wanted to be sure she was okay.

The sensible thing would have been to not get involved. She had given him an excuse not to go, right from the start. He should have hung up, put it down to a narrow escape from weirdness and got on with his life. But he hadn't. Now he wanted to help.

Since he was completely out of his depth, he turned to the internet to see how he could help. A bit of searching brought up any number of quizzes about mental illness. Was Chaya suicidal? He had no idea. He hoped not. Was she likely to self harm? There was something in the way she had avoided looking at the knives in the cutlery drawer, deliberately reaching for the spoons the long way around, something in the way she'd looked faintly ashamed. So maybe, maybe not. Either way, he was glad he'd gone round. The idea that he had somehow stopped something terrible from happening frightened him.

Those big things aside, he spotted the nervous tics, the constant fidgeting. What did that mean? Some sort of undiagnosed ADHD or a form of anxiety?

He sighed and rubbed his eyes. All the internet search had done was give him a load of information and speculation with no real way of relating it to what he had seen. Really, the only thing he could usefully do was to persuade Chaya to get help from a professional.

He stood up. He needed more coffee. Today had been a hard day to get through. Half way out of his office, he paused. If it had been so hard for him, how must it have been for Chaya?

Coffee plan abandoned, he returned to his desk and called her.

'Chaya's lab.' She answered the phone on the second ring.

'Hi Chaya, it's Gimhana. I'm just phoning to see how you are.'

'Oh... I... er... fine. I'm fine.' Which was a lie if ever he'd heard one. Okay, so that was how she was going to play it. 'I'll be coming past where you work in an hour or so. I thought we could meet for a quick catch up.'

'I don't think—'

'I'm worried about you.'

She was quiet for a few seconds and he wondered if she was going to tell him not to bother. To his surprise, she didn't.

'I guess I owe you,' she said. 'I'll buy you a coffee. You must have been running on caffeine all day since I made you miss so much sleep.'

Gimhana relaxed a little. 'Sounds like a plan.'

They agreed a time and a place. As they were saying goodbye, Chaya said, 'I know we haven't known each other very long, but I'm... glad you came to see me last night. I think I might have done something very stupid if you hadn't.'

He had suspected, but it was a shock to hear her say it. 'Anytime,' he said. 'You can call me any time.'

'Thank you. You're a good friend.'

Gimhana hung up and felt glad. It was the first time he'd stepped out of his way to help someone and he rather liked the feeling of being a hero. He also liked being someone's friend.

Chapter Twenty-Five

Chaya – London, 2005

'I've got tickets to go and see an arthouse Japanese film called *Tampopo*,' said Gimhana. 'Want to come?'

No. The answer was no. But he looked so hopeful, she hesitated. They were walking round to the small park near her work. Gimhana had turned up and insisted that she get out for some air. This was the third time he'd done that and people in the lab were starting to raise eyebrows.

'Um,' she said. 'What's it about?'

'Noodles,' he said. 'And food in general. Look, I know it's niche, but that means there won't be so many people and it won't be as anxiety-provoking.'

The cinema didn't make her anxious. It made her sad. The only people she went to the cinema with these days were Sara and Sara's kids. The kids meant there was lots of distraction before and after the film, so that she didn't think about all the times she'd been to the theatre or films with Noah.

'I don't know...'

'Why not?' he said. They reached the park and Chaya kept walking without breaking pace.

'You can't hide from everyday things forever, Chaya. You're just giving them more power over you by tying yourself in knots trying to avoid them.' He easily kept pace with her.

She stopped walking and swung round to face him. 'Why do you care?'

For a second he looked annoyed, but his face softened. 'Because you're my friend,' he said. 'This is what friends do.'

Was it? Sara and Jay had done this sort of thing for her, back in the days before kids. Had it helped? It must have done, or she'd still be the broken mess she was after her breakdown. Maybe, Gimhana was right. She needed to stop wallowing and move on. Noah had. There was no point pretending there was any chance with him now.

'I… yes. Okay. Let's do the cinema thing,' she said, nodding to convince herself.

'Excellent,' he said. 'If it gets too much, we can leave. I don't think it'll come to that.' He smiled at her. 'Shall we continue on our walk?'

They started walking again. 'So, a film about noodles?' she said. 'Tell me more.'

—

The cinema wasn't full. Chaya gripped her popcorn and settled into her seat. Noah loved the cinema and theatre. Her own childhood had included rare occasions of both, but in the months that she was with Noah, she had been to see so many shows. She glanced across at Gimhana, who leaned towards her and whispered, 'okay?'

'I'm fine,' she whispered back.

He checked his watch. 'Still a few more minutes.'

She nodded.

'Chaya,' said Gimhana. 'Would you like to go out for dinner next Thursday? There's this place I went to with some clients about four months back. I'd like to go back and try the food without having to talk shop. It's always better with nice company. So will you come with me? My treat.'

She hesitated.

'It's my birthday,' he added sheepishly.

'So… you want to buy me dinner, as a treat… for your birthday?' She shook her head, frowning. By any standards, that was weird.

He smiled. 'Yes,' he said. 'I get to eat in nice restaurants all the time, but it's mostly with work. I'm on duty. I don't get to relax and enjoy the meal properly. So, for my birthday, I pick a restaurant I like and book myself a table. I usually eat alone. This year, I thought it would be fun to have company.'

Part of her was stunned that of all the people he could have chosen, he had picked to share his special dinner with her. Part of her was just sceptical. 'Why me? You know tons of people.'

His smile faded and he looked at her earnestly. 'I don't, though. Not people I can relax around.'

She frowned, but didn't reply.

The lights in the cinema dropped and the pointless curtain that they had in the front slid back. There was a general rustling as people settled in. The countdown came up on the screen.

'When I'm out with people,' Gimhana said, so quietly that she had to lean in to hear him, 'I have to be on my guard, all the time. If I'm out with white people I worry if I'm acting white enough. If I'm out with Sri Lankan friends, I worry if I'm acting brown enough. And all the time...' He lifted one shoulder in a shrug as though he didn't want to complete the sentence.

She understood. All the time, he had to check that he was acting straight enough. 'Oh,' she said.

'With you, I don't have to worry about any of that. You know who I am. I don't have to try to be anyone other than myself.'

'I see. I know what you mean.' She genuinely did. She had been pretending to be okay for so long, she had forgotten what it was like to actually be okay. With a jolt, she realised that she hadn't been quite as highly strung as usual that evening. Thinking about it, she seemed to have fewer bad days when he was around. She didn't need to pretend so much with Gim either. He had seen her at her worst and he was still here. The only other people she'd had that with were Sara and Jay. She nodded. 'That's nice.'

'Isn't it?' he said.

From off to the side, someone said 'shh.'

They both whispered 'sorry' in the direction of the voice and sank down in their seats. Chaya had to avoid looking at Gimhana, because she suddenly had the mad urge to laugh.

–

By the time they left the cinema, it had started to drizzle. When they got to Chaya's, she invited Gimhana in for coffee, safe in the knowledge that he wouldn't be after anything other than just coffee.

'Thank you for dragging me out,' she said, putting the kettle on and digging out the cafetiere. 'It's not a film I would have chosen to watch, but I enjoyed it.'

'Not many people have heard of it. Thank you for coming with me.' He hung his coat up carefully before sitting down on the edge of the bed. 'I take it you don't go out often?'

'No. Not unless it's a conference.' She leaned on the counter. 'Or Sara's harangued me into going on a date with someone she found.'

'Oh yes? Does she have good taste? Better than our parents, say?'

Chaya frowned. She'd never considered that before. 'Uh… they've all been nice guys,' she said. The kettle boiled and she poured. The smell of brewing coffee filled the room.

'But?'

'I don't know. I just… can't get interested. One guy tried to kiss me and it felt weird. I nearly panicked.' She sighed. 'I think I'm dead inside.'

Gimhana didn't say anything for a few minutes, while she carefully poured two black coffees. She handed one to him and sat down next to him.

'Why do you even go on these dates your friend sets up?' he asked.

That wasn't what she had been expecting. 'Because it's Sara. She worries about me. I... owe her.'

He was looking at her thoughtfully, waiting for her to continue.

'When... I...' she faltered.

He put his free hand on her shoulder. It was comforting. She had told him parts of what had happened, but talking about Noah was hard. Gimhana rarely pushed her to elaborate, so she had no idea how much he'd pieced together.

'When I had my ... breakdown,' she said. 'Sara was the one who came to find me. When I couldn't get out of bed, when my joints hurt so much and I had no energy, she and her boyfriend Jay, they were the ones who took me to see a doctor.'

'You've seen a doctor about it?' he said, thoughtfully. 'That's good.'

Chaya gave a snort. 'Yeah. He said that I was clearly under a lot of stress with my degree and not coping very well. And that young people do take break-ups very hard. And that the joint pain was psychosomatic and would go away when I "came out the other side of this heartbreak".'

'What? Didn't he offer counselling or any other help? That's outrageous.'

'Uhuh. He basically told me to pull myself together and get a lot of fresh air.' She knew now that she had been let down. At the time, however, when the despair was already overwhelming, she had believed him. She'd been convinced she was a freak for not dealing well with a simple break-up. Other people managed. She should too. She had to pull herself together.

She took a deep breath and carried on. 'I tried to bury myself in my studies. Which worked, a bit. It meant I had to drag myself out of bed and it distracted me from thinking about stuff. Sara tried to help me. She and Jay used to make sure I ate and went outside at least once a day.' But it had been an effort for her to do any of those things. When they weren't pushing her, all she'd wanted to do was collapse and cry. 'Then one day, I heard Sara crying and I realised how much of a burden I was to them. They had exams the next year too. So I started pretending that I was okay. Forcing myself to smile. That sort of thing.'

'Until you can't remember which bit is real and which bit is pretend?'

'Something like that.' She took a sip of coffee.

Gimhana frowned at his coffee. 'That's shocking,' he said. 'The doctor, I mean. That's awful. No wonder you struggled. You were… what… twenty?'

'Just.' She felt the darkness tugging at her. She didn't like to think about that time. She let out a shaky sigh.

Gimhana's hand squeezed her shoulder gently; reminding her that she wasn't alone.

'How about you?' she said. 'Surely, it's not all work and dinners for one.'

He laughed. 'I date… discreetly, you know. Hook-ups, really. No relationships as such. Never met anyone I wanted to date for more than a few weeks.'

'What happened?' When she'd met him, she'd recognised a kindred spirit. He'd had his heart broken too. 'There was someone special once, wasn't there?'

Gimhana put his mug down on the small table and leaned back, his arms behind his head. 'His name was Rukshan,' he said. 'He was in the year above me at school. He was… magnificent.' He sighed. 'Unfortunately, he was also not gay… or not ready to admit to it anyway.' He closed his eyes. 'I was an idiot and he found out how I felt. He laughed at me, which was bad enough. And then. He and his friends…' He cleared his throat. 'They waited for me after school and… uh…' He shook his head. 'I have scars.'

'Oh.' It was her turn to be a comfort. She wasn't sure how to do that, so she tried, 'I'm sorry.'

He looked at her through hooded eyes. 'Hmm,' he said, ruefully. 'At least they didn't report me to the police.'

'Was he your first love?'

Gimhana smiled. 'No. That would have been so much worse. The first... I met him on holiday. It was a short, but intense time.' His gaze focused on her and his smile faded. 'Ah. This guy, Noah... he was your first love?'

She didn't want to think about it. She took too big a gulp of coffee and grimaced from the pain.

'Ah,' said Gimhana. 'He was your first *everything*.'

She definitely didn't want to think about that. She shot him a warning glance.

'Oh. Right. Sorry,' he said. 'Nice Sri Lankan girls aren't supposed to sleep with men they're not married to.'

'Nice Sri Lankan boys aren't supposed to either.'

For a second, they stared at each other. Then Gimhana started to giggle. A few seconds later, so did Chaya.

Chapter Twenty-Six

Gimhana – London, 2005

The wrap-up meeting went extremely well. 'Well done, folks,' said Mr Thomas, the senior partner. 'You have an excellent team here, Barry.'

'All credit to Gimhana,' Barry said. 'Most of the work was his.'

'Indeed.' Mr Thomas eyed Gimhana. 'Not the first time you've excelled, I gather.'

'I do my best,' said Gimhana, smiling. 'My best is usually very good.'

Mr Thomas laughed. 'Tell me. Are you married?'

Taken aback at the bluntness of the question, Gimhana took a second to answer.

'I don't think you can ask him that,' said Barry. 'I'm sure there's a policy against that.'

'Why the hell not? He's not a woman! I can't ask women that, but man to man, it's fine,' said Mr Thomas.

Barry shook his head.

'Anyway, are you?'

'No,' said Gimhana. Barry gave him an 'I told you so' glance and looked away. Clearly this was a key factor in his promotion. He had worked too hard to let this chance get away. He blurted out, 'But I have a girlfriend.'

Mr Thomas nodded, as though he hadn't been expecting anything less. 'Will you be bringing her to the anniversary ball? I'm sure we'd all like to meet her. Wouldn't we, Barry?'

'Indeed.' Barry's eyebrows had risen.

'I... er... guess I could,' Gimhana said. He had a few days before they needed to confirm numbers, so technically, he really could. Even though he'd known her for months now, he hadn't considered inviting Chaya because taking her to his work do would make them look like a couple and they really were nothing more than friends. Regardless of what his mother, or hers, thought.

'Capital.' Mr Thomas got up. His PA, a smart and formidable lady called Jenna, knocked. 'You've got a lunch appointment next,' she informed Mr Thomas.

They left and Barry and Gimhana started gathering the files.

'I'm glad to see you took my advice,' Barry said, unhooking the laptop from the projector. 'Is this someone your parents set you up with?'

Gimhana gave up and let himself fall into the lie. It was easy enough to let people draw their own conclusions without directly lying. People tended to hear what they expected to hear. 'Sort of,' he said. 'They introduced us and we met up again once we got back to England. She's an academic.' He picked up the stack of files.

Barry looked at the door of the glass-walled conference room. 'Gimhana,' he said, in a low voice. 'Rather than email your RSVP, go and see Jenna directly. I happen to know that she's doing the seating plans tomorrow. If you ask her, I'm sure she can arrange for you to be sitting on the same table as Mr Thomas. He's the one you need to convince.'

Gimhana stared at him. Barry had once told him how when he'd started, he had been hampered by his working-class accent and that less able colleagues who'd been to the right sort of school were promoted over him. He'd had to do better work for longer to be noticed. He had made it his mission to redress the balance, by picking a few hard workers and championing them slowly so that they could rise up the ranks. 'Thank you, Barry,' he said. 'I'll do that.'

Barry gave him an approving nod. 'Good lad.'

Back in his office, Gimhana checked the time and dialled Chaya's number. One of the other people in the lab answered.

'She's in the lab downstairs,' she said. 'I'll just go get her.'

He put the phone on speaker and opened up his email. He was soon so absorbed in what he was doing that Chaya's voice, when it came on, made him jump.

'Oh. Hi,' he said. 'It's me, Gimhana.'

'What do you want?' Ah, Chaya. Never one for pleasantries. For a second he wondered how she'd cope with being at a party full of business types. But she was smart. He could trust her to pull out all the stops if she needed to.

'Just a sec, I'll just take you off speakerphone.' He did so and got up and shut the door to his office for good measure.

'Listen Chaya, I need a huge favour,' he was almost whispering. He reminded himself, just in time, not to look furtive by hunching over the phone. He sat back, trying to look like he was talking to a client.

'Sure, what is it?'

'I need you to come with me to a work party two weeks on Friday.'

'I can't. I'm going to the pictures with Sara and her boys that night. I promised her.'

Much as he loved Chaya, she could be so obsessed with routine. Gimhana tried again. 'Could you go to the cinema another day? Please, this is really important. Sara will understand, won't she?'

'I... suppose. Why is it so important?'

'You know I was telling you about the partnership... well there's a good chance that I might get it. Trouble is, the senior partner is a bit old-fashioned...' he trailed off.

'And?' said Chaya, a little impatiently.

'And I need you to pretend to be my girlfriend.'

'What?'

'I'm really sorry to ask you this, but the senior partners are always talking about how it's important that all the partners in the firm have solid families behind them and all that sort of thing. Then he asked me if I had a wife and I said no, but that I was seeing someone. He said I should bring my girlfriend along to the golden anniversary bash. So, please? Will you come?'

'Gim, is this a good idea?'

'Yes, it is. I've worked really hard. I deserve to be a partner. Please, Chaya, just for one evening. You're the only girl I know that I can ask.'

'Well, thank you,' said Chaya. The sarcasm in her voice wasn't lost on him. Normally, he would counter with a quip of his own, but this was too important to him.

'You know what I mean,' he said. 'Come on, Chaya. I've always been there for you.'

'Oh. All right,' she said. 'I'll cancel Sara.'

Gimhana let out a whoosh of breath. 'Great,' he said. 'Thank you so much.'

'That's okay,' she said. 'As you say, you're always there for me.'

He knew she was referring to the middle of the night mercy dashes he'd made when she was having a particularly low patch. He was getting to the point where he could spot the depressive episodes before they hit. Or rather, Chaya was. She'd tell him and often, he could help her avoid them, by distracting her from whatever was bothering her, if only for a few hours. It was hard work, but worth it, because non-depressed Chaya made him feel less alone. He felt a bit bad using it as a bargaining tool to get her to do this, but... needs must.

'Gim,' she said, her voice suddenly full of worry. 'What should I wear?'

Gimhana thought about it. It needed to be something eye-catching, so that people would remember her. 'Have you got a sari?'

'Yes, but I'm not sure how to get into it.'

'Tell you what, why don't I come round on Sunday and we'll see if we can get you into it. I'll bring lunch. How does that sound?'

'That sounds okay. I'll see you on Sunday.'

'Brilliant,' he said. 'Thanks again, Chaya. You're a real mate.'

He hung up, opened his office door again and sat back at his computer, staring at the screen. This partnership thing was so close now, he could almost feel it. He had met and schmoozed and impressed so many people. If Chaya was the missing piece of the puzzle, then so be it.

Chapter Twenty-Seven

Chaya – London, 2005

Chaya put off calling Sara for as long as possible. She would have to explain what she was doing instead and that was never going to be easy.

'Oh, what? We were looking forward to seeing you!' said Sara. 'What's so important that you can't come? You're not working again, are you?'

Chaya shifted her weight. The suspicious silence behind her told her that Trish, the lab technician, was eagerly hoovering up everything that was being said.

'I'm really sorry. I've… got to do someone a favour.'

Sara was quiet for a moment. Chaya could almost hear the cogs whirring.

'Would this someone happen to be your nice lawyer friend?' Sara said, after a moment.

'Yes.'

'So you're dumping me and the boys for a date with him?' There was mock indignation in her voice.

'No, not a date. It's difficult to explain.' Chaya tried to walk further away from Trish, but the telephone cord would not stretch any further. 'He's got a big company do and he needs someone to go with him.' She whispered into the receiver. 'I'm really sorry, Sara. I'll make it up to you. I'll babysit one evening and you and Jay can go out.'

'I'll hold you to that,' said Sara. 'So, things are getting serious with this guy? When are we going to meet him? Jay and I are both very curious to see who—' She stopped.

Chaya filled in the rest of the sentence in her head. *Who can compete with Noah.*

Sara cleared her throat. 'Who's won you over,' she finished weakly.

'I don't have time to talk about it right now,' said Chaya.

Sara sighed. 'Well, you have fun. But you have to come round and tell me all about it the day after. Otherwise, I will never forgive you.'

'Fine,' said Chaya.

There was a crash at the other end of the line. 'Oh bugger,' said Sara. 'I mean, bother. Listen Chaya, I'll speak to you later. You have a great time with this man of yours. Take care, okay?'

'Okay, bye.'

Chaya hung the phone back on the hook and walked out without looking at Trish. She sighed as she sat back in front of the paper she was writing. She wondered why she didn't just tell Sara and Trish that Gimhana was gay. It would be so simple, yet she didn't. She quietly kept his secret as though it were her own. She couldn't quite figure out why. Was she using him as a foil so that no one would pressure her to date? Perhaps she was. Or perhaps she just understood what a fragile thing a secret was.

–

Before Gimhana came round, Chaya cleaned the bedsit. She still felt awkward having a man in her room, so she went to the extra effort of rescuing her two cushions from under the bed and arranging them so that the bed looked more like a sofa. Gimhana was hardly a threat, but sometimes it felt like the Sri Lankan community had eyes and ears everywhere. Especially in London, where there were thousands of people, other Sri Lankans maintained a web of contact. She didn't want word to get home that Gimhana was visiting her flat.

Gimhana knew this too. He made an effort to be discreet. Chaya was grateful for their shared background that made so many explanations unnecessary. As she buzzed him into the building, she wondered where in the spectrum of acceptability him helping her put on a sari fell. Her mother would have a fit.

'Hi,' he breezed in, planting a kiss on her cheek as he passed. 'I've brought lunch.' He indicated the big bag slung over his shoulder. 'Eat now, or later?'

'Later,' said Chaya, concerned that she might not fit into her made to measure sari blouse once her stomach was full.

Gimhana was unpacking Tupperware boxes onto the little work surface that served as her kitchen. 'I've brought lamb curry, lentils, fried okra, pumpkin and biryani. All made by my own fair hands,' he said, opening the half sized fridge and kneeling in front of it. There was plenty of space in there for him to store the boxes.

'Jesus, Chaya, what do you live on? You only ever have milk and two pop tarts in there.'

Chaya shrugged. 'I don't have time to cook.'

'You have to eat, though.' His knee clicked as he stood back up. 'You'll waste away to nothing, if you're not careful.'

'Yes Mother.'

'What is this? Giving lip to your elders and betters? *Aney, Aney,*' he tutted at her with mock severity.

'Betters?' She muttered, shaking her head.

'Just elders then.' He strode over and sat on the bed. 'So then, Nangi, let's see about this sari.'

She had already taken out both her saris and draped them over her chair. The first was the teal one that she had worn for meetings with prospective husbands. The other was terracotta with little gold flecks and a border of red and gold leaves running all the way along one side of it.

Gimhana picked a corner of one and ran the fabric through his fingers. 'Nice,' he said. He put his head to one side and looked at the two swatches of fabric that looked loud and out of place in the grey room. 'I think the terracotta one,' he said. 'It'll complement your skin better than the other one.'

She had put the two sari blouses and underskirts on the chair. 'My amma and sister help me, normally.' She picked up the sari dejectedly. She knew the basics of how to wrap the material round her, but it was difficult to make it look tidy.

'Well, first we have to get you into the blouse and underskirt.' Gimhana stood up. 'I'll wait outside while you change.' He left, crossing the room in two strides.

Chaya locked the door after him and, feeling a little silly, changed out of her jeans and t-shirt into the incredibly snug blouse and cotton underskirt. The blouse was made from the same material as the sari and had the leaf motif on the sleeves. The underskirt was also in the same colour as the sari. It had no buttons or hooks to hold it in place, so she was obliged to secure it with a safety pin. The blouse did have hooks, but it took her a few minutes to get it safely closed.

There was a rumble of voices outside and she heard Gimhana explain to someone that he wasn't lost, he was just waiting for someone. Chaya waited until she heard footsteps depart down the stairs before she opened the door and let him back in.

'Let's see now,' said Gimhana, flicking the sari so that the six yards of material billowed out and floated gently down in a burnished pool on the floor. He beckoned her over. She obediently stood in front of him.

'How much do we need over your shoulder?' he said, draping it over her. When they'd worked out how much material should be allowed to trail behind her, he looped the other end of the sari once round her waist. Chaya noticed that his eyes were focused on the fabric and not her. She allowed herself to relax slightly.

'Okay,' he said. 'Hold it here.' While she held it at the place indicated, he deftly folded pleats into the fabric.

'Where did you learn to do that?' said Chaya, impressed at the way the folds fell neatly into line under his fingers.

'I used to watch my mother putting on her saris,' he said, not looking up from what he was doing. 'She used to let me help.' He looked around for a pin.

'Are you sure she doesn't know you're gay?' Chaya grabbed a box of safety pins from her desk and handed them to him.

One of the few advantages of living in a place so small was that nothing was very far away.

He shrugged. 'You know mothers. They don't see what they don't want to see.' He stuck a couple of pins in and secured the pleats. 'Okay, let's try this.'

She stood, her arms held away from her body whilst he wrapped the bottom half of her up in silk. She pinned the top part of the sari to her blouse whilst he tucked the fabric in at her waist.

'There,' he said, stepping back to admire his handiwork. 'Nothing to it, see.' He looked her up and down. 'You look fabulous.'

Chaya walked carefully over to the mirror, but she could only see her shoulders in it. She took it off its hook and gave it to Gimhana. He held the mirror for her, so that she could check for herself. The blouse was cut with a sweeping neckline, which showed off her slim neck whilst creating the illusion of a cleavage hidden under the swathe of material across her chest. The sari itself sat beautifully on her and he was right about the colour – the reds and golds gave her brown skin a warm glow. She nodded.

'You're good,' she said. 'I've never managed to set pleats on a sari. Ever.' He gave a little bow, making her chuckle.

'Can I get back into my jeans now?' she said, hitching the fabric up as it threatened to slide down her shoulder.

Gimhana rolled his eyes. 'Yes. Then we can eat, right?' He let himself out so that she could change.

–

Later, they sat on the floor, on either side of the coffee table, eating curry and rice with their hands. They discussed which films they wanted to see and Gimhana told her a Singhalese joke that made her laugh so unexpectedly that she nearly choked on a piece of lamb. He insisted she keep the leftovers, with strict instructions that she was to eat it all by Tuesday.

After he'd gone, Chaya folded away the saris and washed up the dinner plates. She reflected on her relationship with Gimhana. He was a good friend now. The fact that he was a man only ever came up if she was out in public with him. In private, she was comfortable with him. Almost as comfortable as she felt with Sara.

Gimhana was the first man since Noah to get beyond her defences, even in that small way. She shook her head, trying to get rid of the thought. After a few minutes, she threw open the window to get rid of the smell of spices and scrubbed the bedsit until it shone.

Chapter Twenty-Eight

Chaya – Oxford, 1995

Chaya had to call home. She'd been putting it off because of her conversation with her tutor. How could she tell her parents that she was failing? She waited until it was evening in Colombo, dug out her international phone card and called them.

The first thing Amma did was to give her an update about the baby. It seemed both baby and Malini were doing well.

'Do you want to speak to her?' Amma said.

'Malini? Oh yes please.'

'No, I meant the baby. We're looking after her for a bit so that Malini can have a sleep. Here,' Amma's voice moved away, cooing, 'talk to your aunty, baba.'

There was a snuffling noise on the phone.

'Hello?' said Chaya, awkwardly. How did one talk to a baby over the phone? 'Hello baby Nayana.'

More snuffling, possibly a little hiccup. She could almost feel the tiny person at the other end, listening ferociously. 'How are you?'

'Aww,' said Amma, her voice suddenly clear again. 'She likes you.'

'That's… great.' She drew breath and steeled herself. She had to tell them about her grades.

'Oh, Chaya, before I forget,' said Amma.

A distraction. Brilliant. 'Yes?'

'We've had someone approach us with a proposal…'

Alarm bells rang in her head. A proposal meant that someone had suggested a potential marriage match for her. They were trying to fix her up with someone who was 'suitable'.

'A proposal?' she said, trying to keep the dismay from her voice.

'Wait, wait, I'll put you on speaker, so Thatha can hear,' said Amma. 'How does this work?'

There was a beep and her father's voice said, 'Can you hear me?'

'Hello Thatha.'

'Anyway,' Amma jumped back in. 'This boy. He's a doctor, he's twenty-seven, educated in the US, sounds like a very nice boy.'

Chaya stared at the living room wall, trying to think of the correct response. She had known this would come, but she'd hoped they'd wait until after her studies were finished.

'Of course, he understands that nothing would be possible until after you've finished your degree,' Amma carried on. Her bangles jingled as she waved her hand. 'And he's fine with the idea of you going on to do a further degree.'

'But...'

'And we're aware that he is a bit too old for you.'

'Yes,' she clutched at the excuse, gratefully. 'Too old.'

'The thing is,' said Amma, 'we didn't want to turn him down without checking with you first.'

'I'm only nineteen!' It came out louder than she'd expected.

'Yes, yes, we know that,' said Amma, hurriedly. 'It's just that, now you're at Oxford, the offers are coming in really often. We can keep turning them away until you've finished your degree, if you want, but if there's someone really nice, you might want to consider it.'

She looked down at her hands. She couldn't tell them about what her tutor had said. Not now. She had to knuckle down and pull this back on track. Then there was Noah. She couldn't tell them about Noah, but she couldn't let them get their hopes up about getting her 'settled' either. She squeezed her eyes shut and opened them again. All she could do was get herself a few years' reprieve. Maybe this thing between her and Noah would fizzle out by then.

'I want to concentrate on my studies at the moment,' she said, softly. 'After my degree, I want to do a PhD. If possible, I'd like to stay at Oxford, or go to Cambridge or London for it. It will be a lot of work, I don't want to be distracted by marriage and babies and things.' She was distracted enough already. 'Also, I might find someone myself,' she added. 'I might meet a fellow student that I like. It would be much better.'

There was a tense silence on the phone. She heard a car horn beep somewhere in the distance. It was very strange being on speakerphone.

'Okay,' said Amma. 'We can understand that. That *would* be good.' She sighed. 'But be careful, Duwa, there are some terrible and sneaky men out there.'

Chaya smiled. 'Well, if they're after my money, they're in for a shock.'

Amma ignored that. 'And make sure whoever you meet is suitable. You know, Singhalese, Buddhist, ...'

Chaya held back a sigh. 'Yes.'

Amma said, 'I suppose we could live with someone lower caste, if they were well educated... but they'd have to be a doctor. At least.'

'Right.' She couldn't carry on like this. She had to say something. 'What if ... I met someone who wasn't Sri Lankan? How would you feel about that?'

'Oh, you won't though, will you?' said Amma, her voice quickening. 'You're a sensible girl.'

In the background, Thatha cleared his throat. He hadn't said anything so far.

'Hypothetically, I mean,' Chaya added, quickly.

The baby made a noise. She wished she could see what was going on. Her parents were probably exchanging one of those looks that spoke volumes to each other. She heard rustling and the jingle of bangles and Amma said, 'You talk to her.'

Chaya could hear the slap-slap of Amma's slippers as she walked away.

There was an awkward silence. Finally, Thatha said, 'Chaya. Is there something going on that we should know about?'

She was struggling to keep up with her workload, she had a boyfriend she couldn't talk about. There were a few things, yes. She didn't reply.

'Chaya,' he repeated, sternly. 'Answer me.'

She couldn't lie to him. She couldn't tell him the truth. 'It's… difficult,' she said.

'I see.' His voice sounded hard. 'Well, I did wonder. You're young and far away from home. It's understandable, I suppose. We should have expected it when we sent you. Although, I expected better from you.'

She didn't reply.

'I expect you to have grown out of these things when you finish your degree,' he said firmly. 'We didn't do all this to send you away for you to waste your time. Is that understood, Chaya?'

'Yes,' she muttered. She understood. He was saying 'have your fun, but when you come back to real life, you have to forget all about him'. It was an unexpected amount of leeway that wasn't normally given to a girl.

'I am trusting you not to do anything stupid.' She could tell from the tremor in his voice that he was angry, but trying to keep a lid on it. 'Understand?'

'Yes,' she said, even quieter than before.

'Okay.' In the background the baby started to cry. Thatha sighed. 'Was there anything else you wanted to tell us?'

'No,' said Chaya. 'I'll call you next week. Tell Malini I said hello.'

'Okay. We'll speak to you soon.'

She said her goodbyes and hung up. For several minutes, she sat and stared at the wall. Then she started to cry.

Chapter Twenty-Nine

Gimhana – London, 2005

Gimhana glanced across at Chaya. She was fidgeting in the taxi seat, tweaking the sari, checking the two bracelets on her arm, touching her hair. He knew how she felt. He was nervous too. Which was why he'd come prepared. He pulled a small hip flask out of his coat pocket and unscrewed the top.

'Here.' He offered it to her. 'It'll make you feel better.'

She frowned but took it and sniffed the top.

'Brandy,' he said. 'Dutch courage.'

She gave him a reproachful look. 'How much have you had already?'

He'd had a couple of glasses to get himself psyched up, but he knew not to get too tanked up before the party. He had to be on top of his game this evening. 'Don't worry about me,' he said. 'Go on. Have a swig.'

Chaya gave him another look and took a big sip. She pulled a face as the liquid went down. 'Are you sure this is a good idea, Gim? I'm not great with new people.'

'There's nothing to it,' he said. 'Just imagine it to be the truth and step into that reality.'

'Easy for you to say, you pretend to be someone you're not all the time.'

He laughed. 'The thing is, I've been playing the part so long, even I've forgotten which bits are real and which bits are made up.'

She still looked worried, so he said, 'We're friends, right? We go out together. So it's not a lie to say we're "going out", is it?'

She rolled her eyes. 'Oh, come on.' She looked at the flask in her hand and sighed. 'Okay. I'll try that. I hope I don't screw up and let you down.'

'You won't,' he said. 'I trust you.'

She gave a little snort, as though to say she didn't trust herself. 'Hope you're right.' She took another swig of the brandy and handed the flask back.

Gimhana grinned at her. Part of him was terrified for the same reasons she was. But another part of him was relishing the challenge.

Chapter Thirty

Chaya – London, 2005

The party was in a five-star hotel. Chaya's heels clicked on the marble as they strode through a mirrored hallway. She clung on to Gimhana's arm, concentrating on not falling over. They paused at the entrance. She looked up and caught sight of herself in the mirrors that lined the walls; a bright splash of russet against the austere décor. She looked nervously at Gimhana. He put his free hand over hers and gave her a reassuring smile.

The hall was enormous. The first thing Chaya noticed were the giant chandeliers that fragmented the light. The entrance was higher than the main floor, so that they had to descend a wide staircase to get to everyone else. This place was designed for someone to make a grand entrance. A few heads turned as they reached the last few steps. Not knowing whom she was supposed to smile at, Chaya avoided eye contact and looked at the floor.

White-jacketed waiters magically appeared, bearing champagne. Letting go of Gimhana's arm, she took a glass gratefully. She looked over at Gimhana, who was scanning the crowd.

'So who's who?' she whispered.

Before he could answer someone said, 'Jim!'

They both turned to see a man coming towards them. His face was flushed and shiny, and his hair was combed over to cover a bald patch. 'Jim, old chap! How are you?' He clapped Gimhana on the shoulder.

Gimhana caught Chaya's eye briefly and said, 'Russ, this is my... girlfriend, Chaya. Chaya, this is Russ. We used to share an office.'

Russ turned. Chaya held out her hand to be shaken. To her horror, Russ took it and raised it to his lips. 'Charmed,' he said, attempting to look into her eyes.

'Likewise,' said Chaya, retracting her hand and resisting the impulse to wipe it on her sari.

'I wish I could say I've heard all about you,' said Russ. 'But young Jim here has kept you very secret. Mind you, not that I blame him.' He gave Gimhana what was supposed to be a conspiratorial wink. 'Wanted to keep the lovely lady all to yourself, eh?'

Gimhana gave him a tight smile. 'You're right, of course.' He took Chaya's hand. 'Could you excuse us a moment? I should really introduce Chaya to a few people.' He led her gently away and Russ wandered off to gush over someone else.

'Friend of yours?' said Chaya, out of the corner of her mouth.

'Nope,' said Gimhana, out of the corner of his. 'He hates my guts.'

'Thought so.'

As they walked, Chaya looked around her. Most of the women were in cocktail dresses and lethal-looking stilettos. Silver lamé was in this season, by the looks of things. They looked like fish, weaving in between the men in black suits.

A glamorous young woman in a blue dress with a plunging neckline floated up to them. 'Gim! How lovely to see you,' she said, looking up at him and leaning forward. Gimhana leaned away slightly, his eyes wrinkling with amusement. Chaya suppressed a smile. This girl fancied him and had drunk too much to be subtle about it.

'Hi Felicia,' he said. 'Let me introduce my girlfriend, Chaya.'

'Hi,' said Felicia, giving Chaya an unconvincing smile and looking her up and down. 'That is such a fabulous outfit. Such beautiful colours! Did you get that from India?'

'Sri Lanka,' said Chaya and Gimhana in unison. They looked at each other and shared a grin. Felicia made a dismissive gesture with her hand.

'Yes,' said Chaya. 'I did, in fact, get it in Sri Lanka. I like your dress,' she added, as pleasantly as she could.

'Thanks,' said Felicia. 'It's Dolce & Gabbana.'

'Oh,' said Chaya. 'Right.'

Gimhana eased her away from Felicia.

'Let me guess,' Chaya whispered. 'She hates my guts.'

Gimhana grinned. 'Welcome to the world of corporate entertainment.'

–

Gimhana introduced Chaya to so many people that she couldn't remember them all. She got used to hearing Gimhana say 'my girlfriend'. More than one woman (and a few of the men) had given her the same appraising look as Felicia, but with considerably less venom. She knew they were curious about Gimhana's mysterious partner.

She looked sideways at him as he chatted to someone. They were seeing him the way she used to see him; a beautiful man sculpted in gold with sparkling black eyes and long eyelashes that had no business being on a man. They saw his easy confidence and cheerful smile and wondered how on earth he had stayed single for so long. No wonder they wanted to know what kind of woman had finally caught him. Tonight, she had to pretend to be that woman. That wasn't as hard as she'd thought it would be. She had never been the object of so much attention before. It was rather fun. She allowed herself a little smile.

When they finally sat down to eat, she found herself next to a large man with pepper-grey hair.

Gimhana introduced her to him. 'Chaya,' he said, 'this is Oliver Thomas, one of the partners in the firm. This is Chaya.' Although outwardly Gimhana seemed relaxed, Chaya could tell from the slight edge to his laugh and the angle at which he held his head that he was thrumming with tension.

They shook hands and Oliver introduced her to his wife, Beth, who was sitting on the other side of him. She was a short, plump lady whose hair was perfectly white. She gave Chaya a warm smile and complimented her on her sari.

'So, Chaya,' said Oliver, as the first course arrived. 'What do you do?'

'I'm a research scientist,' she said.

'Really, how fascinating. What do you work on?'

They chatted about science and the intricacies of turning ideas into successful businesses. Chaya hadn't needed to talk to anyone about her work in a non-academic setting for a long time. Neurones she hadn't exercised in a while woke up and started finding information for her. Much to her surprise, she was enjoying herself.

Eventually, Oliver's wife leaned across and said, 'Oliver, stop grilling the poor girl about her work!'

'It's very interesting,' Oliver protested.

'I don't mind,' said Chaya, nodding.

'Well, *I* want to know how you two met,' said Mrs Thomas, indicating Gimhana.

Chaya turned and looked at Gimhana in alarm. They hadn't cleared this part of the story. It hadn't occurred to her to ask what he had told people. Gimhana's eyes told her that he was thinking the same thing, but his expression remained affable and smiling.

She would have to answer before the silence became too awkward. 'We met... er... at a party,' said Chaya, turning back to Mrs Thomas, who was looking at her, expecting more information.

'I was hiding from my mum who was trying to introduce me to some girl she'd decided was right for me,' said Gimhana, from behind her.

Chaya relaxed and let him tell the story, broadly based on the truth, about how they had been expecting to meet other people and met each other instead. He made a performance of it, embellishing parts until everyone at the table was listening and laughing.

'Oh, what a sweet story,' said Mrs Thomas. 'Your mothers must have found it so funny when you finally got together.'

Chaya looked over her shoulder at Gimhana and their eyes met. 'Yes,' she said, turning back. 'They were very amused.'

Chapter Thirty-One

Gimhana – London, 2005

Gimhana was amazed. Chaya, after a few drinks, was spectacular. She was still a little reserved, but she chatted to people and answered questions and put up with the seemingly endless curiosity of his colleagues. More to the point, when she was required to lie, she did it effortlessly, sticking to the script they'd agreed on.

'She complements you nicely,' one of his colleagues said to him. 'She's quiet, where you're outgoing, but she's sharp and cutting where you're smooth. I can see why you make a good couple.'

That was the thing. They did make a good double act. He genuinely enjoyed her company. Since he'd started hanging out with her, he was rediscovering the things he did for fun – movies, books, the theatre, food. It was all so much better for having a friend to share it with. It turned out he loved having someone to cook for. He was his mother's son after all.

After those first few weeks, when he'd worried about her, they had fallen into an easy sort of friendship. Since they were both clear that they weren't going to be in a relationship, there was no pressure to be available. If they went to something together, it was because they both wanted to. He still worried about her, of course, but he rather liked having someone to worry about. For the first time, he realised just how isolated he'd become. His life revolved around work. He didn't really have a life outside of it. Until now. That was all due to Chaya.

At the end of the evening, they bundled themselves into a taxi. For a while, they sat slumped in their seats, neither of them speaking. The orange streetlights gently floated past as they joined the late night traffic.

Finally, Gimhana said, 'Thank you.'

Chaya turned away from the window. 'It was a pleasure. I enjoyed myself.'

'Really?' he said. 'I'm glad.' He was. She had done him a huge favour, so if she'd had fun doing it, that was only fair.

They looked at each other as the light slid over them, alternating orange and dark.

'I was a bit worried when they asked how we met,' said Chaya. 'I'm glad you told them the truth.'

'I didn't tell them anything beforehand,' said Gimhana. 'As far as they're concerned, you're the original mystery woman.' He smiled.

Chaya's smile faltered. 'Does that mean I'll have to do this more regularly?' she indicated her sari.

Gimhana nodded. 'Maybe. Would you mind? I'll try and make sure it's not very often. Maybe about once a year…'

Chaya shrugged. 'Sure. Like I said, I really didn't mind. It wasn't that difficult pretending to be your partner. After all, I spend enough time with you that I know you pretty well.' She yawned and settled further into her seat.

'Yes,' said Gimhana slowly. 'We do spend a lot of time together.'

Chaya closed her eyes. 'You know,' she said, sleepily. 'We make a great couple. It's a shame neither of us is interested.'

Gimhana didn't reply. They did make a good couple. Did they really have to be interested in each other sexually? He frowned and looked out of the window, an idea beginning to form.

Chapter Thirty-Two

Chaya – London, 2005

The morning after the party Chaya woke up expecting to feel the darkness towering above her. What greeted her instead was a colossal headache. She groaned and rolled out of bed. This is why she didn't drink more than one glass of wine. She staggered over to her medicine cabinet and clawed out an aspirin. Once the pill was safely gulped down, she crawled back into bed.

Chaya surfaced from sleep to an insistent buzzing. She was out of bed and standing in her slippers before she was awake enough to figure out what the noise was. It was the intercom from the bottom of the building.

She stabbed the reply button. 'Yes?'

'Hi. It's Gimhana. I've brought lunch.'

'Wha…? What time is it?'

'About midday.' He sounded far away and tinny through the microphone.

'Oh.' She pressed the button to let him in. 'Right.' She straightened up. She had a few minutes to make herself present-able. She dragged on a pair of jeans, t-shirt and jumper and was just staggering out to the toilet on the landing when Gimhana came bounding up the stairs.

'Morning,' he said.

She nodded and waved him into the room.

When she got back, he was sitting on the floor, unpacking food bags onto the coffee table. 'I brought you spicy chicken,' he said. 'It's from a place near my house. They make it nice and hot.' He upended a bag of chicken legs and thighs onto a plate.

'I haven't even cleaned my teeth yet,' said Chaya, rubbing her eyes with one hand and shutting the door with the other.

'You do that. I'll make coffee.'

Once she'd washed her face, she started to feel better. The smell of chicken and chips woke up her stomach and reminded her that she was hungry. Gimhana gave her a mug of coffee and sat down to eat. She sank down to the floor and joined him. Gimhana stretched his legs awkwardly to the side of the table. 'I wish you'd get some chairs,' he said.

'Uhuh, and where would I put them?' said Chaya, biting into a chip and feeling the hot starch melt into her mouth. 'I'm not exactly awash with space here.'

Gimhana looked around him, frowning, as though he were thinking.

'Sauce,' muttered Chaya, wondering if she had any ketchup.

Still frowning, Gimhana reached into his bag and pulled out a bottle of chilli sauce.

'Thanks,' said Chaya tipping some onto her plate. 'You read my mind.'

Gimhana gave her a guarded smile. Something was bothering him. Was it something to do with the night before? 'I thought last night went rather well, didn't you?' she said.

'I did,' he said. 'You were a hit.'

Chaya smiled. 'Good.' She ate in silence, relishing the fiery burn. She thanked whatever instinct it was that had led Gimhana to bring her protein and chillies, the best things to see off a hangover.

'Um... Chaya,' said Gimhana.

'Hmm?'

'Last night, when you said we made a good couple... did you mean it?'

She looked up. Where was this going? 'Yes, I suppose I did.'

He nodded. 'Do you think…' He was concentrating on his plate. 'Perhaps…' he looked up. 'We could be a couple?'

She stared at him. A suspicion of what he meant started to form in her aching head. Pretending to be his girlfriend for a party was one thing. Doing it long term was a different matter entirely. 'What are you talking about, Gim? You're gay.'

'I know that,' he shook his head impatiently. 'What I mean is, I need to find a wife, you need to find a husband. We get on really well. We'd both know what we were letting ourselves in for…'

'No!' said Chaya, appalled. 'That's a stupid idea.'

'No, actually, it's not,' said Gim. 'Think about it. You've been introduced to a number of blokes, right?'

'Yes, but…'

'How many of those did you like – as people, I mean, not potential husbands?'

She opened her mouth and shut it again. 'One or two,' she said.

'Did you think you could love any of those few?'

She shook her head. Her heart was no longer hers to give away. He knew that.

'See, you're not looking for an ideal partner, you're just looking for someone you don't hate. Someone you can see yourself spending evenings talking to, someone you can introduce to your friends.' He leaned forward. 'That's what I'm looking for too.'

'You,' said Chaya, 'are looking for a man.'

He shook his head impatiently. 'I can't *have* a man. It would break my parents' hearts.' He looked intently at her. 'I can't have the sort of relationship I want. You can't have the man you want. Why don't we just get together and get everyone off our backs?' He reached forward to take her hand. She frowned and his hand stopped millimetres away from hers.

'Come on, Chaya, think about it. You could have your career and you wouldn't have to pretend to love me. We get on well.

We could hang out, do stuff like we do now and everyone would think we were just like a normal couple.' He waved a hand to encompass the whole of her little bedsit. 'It'd be much better than living alone in this place for the rest of your life.'

Chaya moved back, away from him. 'I like it here. It's my place.' But it *was* lonely being all by herself. She shook her head. 'It's a big thing you're asking me to do, Gim. I'm not sure it's a good idea,' she said, getting to her feet.

'Your parents aren't going to stop, you know,' Gimhana said. 'They're going to keep nagging you and pushing suitable guys at you until you meet the perfect guy or they wear you down and you marry someone just to get them off your case.'

That first wasn't going to happen. When she fell for Noah, she fell completely. There would never be anyone else. But the second scenario? Her parents were important to her. Important enough that she gave up the love of her life to avoid hurting them. She could see a time when she stopped fighting and let Amma choose someone for her. The best she could hope for was someone she didn't mind spending time with. That being the case, why not marry someone who was her friend?

Gimhana leaned forward, earnestly. 'Think about it. All that you've done... giving up Noah. You did that to make your parents happy and they're not. Not yet anyway. They need you to get married, so that they are reassured that you're safe. You could give them that.'

That gave her pause. Not just because it was true, but because it was a low blow. She knew him well enough to know that he wasn't above being manipulative to get his own way. 'Don't try emotional blackmail on me,' she said.

His eyes widened, perhaps a little too much. 'I didn't mean it like that,' he said. 'But it is true.'

She raised her eyebrows at him.

Gimhana sighed and pushed himself away from the coffee table. 'Okay,' he said. 'I need to go into work, anyway.' He gathered up the leftover chips into a tidy bundle.

'It's the weekend.'

He shrugged. 'I have to put in the hours if I want to make it to partner.' He pulled on his coat. 'Getting married would make all the difference to my career. It wouldn't hurt yours either. And both your parents and mine would be happy. Please. Promise you'll at least consider it?'

Chaya's instinct was still to say no, but something made her hold back. She nodded, not looking at him. 'I'll think about it.'

'Thank you.' He stepped out into the corridor. 'I'll call you next week to talk about it. Bye.'

Chaya shut the door and leaned against it, listening to Gimhana's footsteps clattering down the stairs. For a moment, she stared unseeingly in front of her, torn between the flaws in the idea and the possibilities. She needed to think. She looked round the flat. She couldn't think there. She would clean the flat until it gleamed and then go to the lab.

–

Since it was Saturday the lab was empty. As soon as she entered the darkened rooms, Chaya felt better. She turned on the lights and watched the fluorescent tubes flicker on one by one. This was her real home. She pulled on her lab coat and gloves and flipped open her lab diary. After staring thoughtfully at her notes for a few minutes, she put a bottle of agar in the microwave. Her bacteria needed to be plated out. Doing that would give her the mental space she needed.

Chaya's hands moved of their own accord as she labelled and lined up agar plates next to the Bunsen burner. The mechanical action centred her, freeing her mind to think about Gimhana's suggestion. *Proposal,* she corrected herself. It was a proposal in the sense of a business proposal. Reluctantly, she acknowledged that what he'd said was true. It would be an elegant solution to both their problems. Why then, did she feel it was wrong?

She held a wire loop until it glowed white hot so the metal was cleansed by fire. The loop touched the agar and gave a satisfying hiss. She scraped a colony off the old plate and drew it across the surface of the new one. After a few days, the new plate would have bacteria thriving on it, each a copy of the original colony, with the same strengths and weaknesses, just drawn in a different pattern.

Perhaps she had secretly been hoping that she would meet someone who would cure her of Noah. Someone who could burn off the shadows that haunted her and make her new again; a new relationship that would thrive, proving to her that Noah wasn't her only chance of happiness. But that hadn't happened. It had been ten years and it still hurt as much as it always had. Noah, or the lack of him, was a fact of life now. In which case, Gimhana's suggestion made perfect sense. He knew about Noah and would be aware of the limits of her affection, which was not something she could expect from a conventional husband. They could get married and each have the life they wanted without the pressure to find a socially acceptable mate. She knew from her friends' experience that marriage gave you a sort of freedom. You were no longer under your parents' wing and suddenly you were your own little unit. Malini and Ajith, Sara and Jay; each couple a small team against the world.

It would be nice not to be alone. She thought about her evenings spent in the library or at work and the few hours she spent in the bedsit, trapped in her little life. It would be nice to have someone to come home to; someone to talk to about the happenings of the day. Except… she already had someone she could talk to. Gimhana.

He made her laugh and made her forget the absence inside her. With him, she felt… connected. Since he had entered her life, she was going out more. She hadn't had a panic attack in weeks and she was sleeping much better. She had even woken up that morning without the involuntary clench of panic that she'd come to accept as normal. Because of Gimhana's foodie tendencies, she was eating better too. He cared for her. He had been there for her when she was in crisis.

She paused, the inoculating loop in mid air. If she got married, she'd have to stop hanging out with Gimhana and spend time with the faceless husband instead. She would lose another friend.

Her stomach knotted. For a few seconds, she felt free-falling terror. That would be awful. There were so few people who understood her. The idea of having to turn away from them and share her carefully controlled life with a stranger was unthinkable. She shuddered. Her eyes focused back on her work, she put the loop back in the flame to re-sterilise it.

Maybe Gimhana's suggestion wasn't so crazy after all. She should at least consider it properly.

As far as Amma and Thatha were concerned, he was suitable – they already knew this. Their parents got along well. Her parents would be so happy.

She and Gimhana were both ambitious and tied to their careers. They both worked long hours and wouldn't demand the other stay in to pay them attention. In all ways but the obvious one, Gimhana was her perfect man. What did it matter that they would never be sexually attracted to each other?

Chaya started thinking about logistics. A conventional marriage was difficult enough to arrange, but this would require extra thought. It was best to be prepared in these matters or else one of them could get hurt.

She finished plating up and put the petri dishes away – the old bacteria in the cold room to stay as they were and the new plate in the warm cabinet to grow. Methodically, she tidied up. Since she didn't want to go home just yet, she went to the office and started making a list.

–

By the time Chaya got home, it was nearing midnight. She paused at the bottom of the stairs and felt the cold blow through the hallway. She shivered. Loneliness spread ahead of her. She couldn't go on like this for the rest of her life. A sudden vision of herself, alone in her bedsit in another ten years' time, flashed through her mind. That was almost as frightening as the idea of marrying a stranger. Slowly, she went upstairs to her bedsit and dialled Gimhana's work number.

When he answered, she said, 'It's me.'

'Hi.' He sounded like he was about to say something, but changed his mind. 'Um… how are you?'

Chaya took a deep breath and closed her eyes. 'I've thought about your suggestion,' she said. 'And the answer is yes. I'll marry you.'

There was silence at the other end of the line. Chaya let out her breath.

Gimhana cleared his throat. 'That's… brilliant. Really great.'

'Yes,' said Chaya, her eyes still shut.

'We… er… we should meet and discuss… things,' said Gimhana, sounding a little dazed.

'Yes,' said Chaya.

'I'll call you tomorrow and we'll sort out a time to meet?'

'That would be good.'

'Okay. I'll talk to you tomorrow then.'

'Okay.'

'Um… Chaya?' he said.

'Yes?'

'Thank you.'

Chaya nodded, even though he couldn't see her. 'Thank you too.'

Chapter Thirty-Three

Chaya – Oxford, 1995

Chaya took two mugs of tea upstairs to her room in the tiny student house that she shared with Sara. Noah was sitting at her desk, leafing through a student newspaper that he'd rescued from the waste paper basket. He was flicking through the pages too fast to be reading them; his mind was clearly somewhere else.

She put his tea down next to him. 'What's up?'

'Nothing,' he turned a page of the newspaper.

'Don't give me that.' She pulled herself up to sit on the table and nudged him with her knee. 'Something's bothering you. What is it?'

He sighed. 'I got offered a PhD place.' He was still looking at the paper.

'That's great news!' she said. 'Isn't it?'

'I'm going to turn it down.'

'What? Why?'

He looked up, his eyes finally meeting hers. 'It's in Canada.'

'Canada? With... wotsisname? The guy who gave a talk a few weeks ago? The one who liked your project?'

'Yes. He said he didn't need to interview me.' A faint trace of pride crept into his voice.

'And you're turning it down because...?'

He said nothing, just reached out and took her hand.

'Because of me?' she said.

He still said nothing.

'You can't do that!' It came out before she had a chance to consult her brain. 'That's your future.'

He squeezed her hand and smiled. 'I was rather hoping you'd be my future.' His eyes sparkled.

Chaya stared at him, lost for words. The only way she could reconcile being with him was to tell herself that it was just a temporary affair. It was a fact that lurked constantly in the background. She'd told him, right at the start. How could he think that a future together was possible? So much so that he was willing to compromise his education for it? A tiny part of her was thrilled that he loved her enough to choose her over his family and his education, but another, much bigger part of her realised that she couldn't do the same for him. 'I can't let you do that.'

His brow wrinkled. 'But… don't you want…?'

'Oh, Noah. I can't let you throw away an opportunity like this. You'll regret it later.' What she didn't say was *I can't be with you forever. When we split up, you'll need to have alternatives.*

'I might not,' he said. 'Besides, I don't want to leave you. If I lost you, I'd regret that even more.'

'If I wasn't here. All things being equal, you would take it. Right?'

He looked for a moment like he was going to protest, but then nodded, a little sheepishly.

'Then take it. If you don't, you'll be unhappy and I'll feel guilty. It's all very well making grand gestures, but this is the rest of your life we're talking about.' She was talking earnestly, advising him as though she knew what she was talking about.

His thumb rubbed the side of her hand, gently. She could almost hear him considering it. 'No,' he said, after a few minutes. 'I couldn't bear it.'

'Think about it some more,' she said. She wasn't sure she would be able to bear it either.

After Noah left that night, Chaya felt his revelation echoing round her head. Unable to concentrate on her studies, she went downstairs to find Sara, who was sitting in the living room, hand-painting a silver skull onto a skirt she'd bought in a charity shop.

'Can I talk to you about something? I need a sympathetic ear.'

She outlined her conversation with Noah.

Sara carefully put the lid back on her fabric paint. 'How do you feel about that?'

'I'm not sure, if I'm honest. On the one hand, I'm really happy for him… on the other hand… well, it means it's over, doesn't it?'

Sara looked at her for a long time before she replied. 'Does it have to mean it's over? Canada isn't outer space. There are ways you can keep in touch.'

There were. That wasn't the problem. 'When I… started this thing, when I decided to give me and Noah a chance, it was always on the understanding… no, the hope, that it was temporary. I can't take him home to meet my parents. I'm not sure his parents would be too happy about me either. We can't be together in the long term.'

'In which case,' said Sara. 'Perhaps this is a good place to end it? If you can't keep seeing each other for two different reasons…'

Tears welled up in Chaya's eyes. 'I was afraid you'd say that.' She shook her head. 'I can't.'

Sara put down her work and came over to perch on the arm of the chair Chaya was sitting in. 'Chaya, sweetheart. I'm so sorry.' She gathered her in a hug. 'You have a choice. You can either face up to your parents. Or lose Noah. You can't escape it any longer.'

Chaya sobbed into Sara's shoulder. 'I can't… won't upset my parents. I have to give him up and just thinking about it hurts. So much.'

Sara stroked her hair. 'I know. But, you know what, it won't always. You'll get over it and move on and meet someone else.'

'But what if I don't?' She sniffed and wiped her eyes. 'I know I'm… odd. I don't make friends easily and I'm not the easiest person to love. What if Noah is my only chance?'

'You're being a bit harsh on yourself,' said Sara. 'You're not difficult to love. We love you, Noah loves you and your family definitely love you.'

'And…' Chaya carried on. 'And I'm not doing so well with my studies. I'm headed for a two-two and that's not good enough. I know I'm not working as hard as I could because I'm spending so much time with Noah.'

'Oh Chaya. You should be having this conversation with Noah, don't you think? You can't let him think that there's a chance of you two staying together if there isn't.'

Chaya sniffed. 'I don't know what to do!'

'Honey, no one can choose this one for you.'

'My parents would be devastated,' Chaya said. 'I mean, they might get over it in time, but people around them will never let them forget. They'd be reminded in a hundred tiny ways that they didn't bring me up properly. And we wouldn't be welcome anywhere.'

'I don't know about that,' said Sara. 'Noah's family are diplomats. You'll be an Oxford grad by then… you might find you fit in better than you expect.'

'Not if I don't get a two-one. I'll be a thicko Oxford grad.'

Sara gave a little laugh. 'I'm not sure I follow that logic.'

Chaya ignored her. 'But I don't know if I can live without Noah.' She buried her face back in her friend's shoulder. 'I'm not sure I can.'

Sara hugged her tighter and said nothing.

–

In the days that followed she could see Noah watching her warily, as though he knew what she was thinking. One evening, when they were lying on her bed, side by side, reading, he asked, 'What are you going to do when you finish your course?'

'PhD.' She didn't even have to think about it. Life had always been mapped out – school, university, PhD, then get a job in research. Cure something. Make a difference to people's lives. She wasn't sure when the map had formed, but it was hardwired into her now.

Noah put his head to one side. 'Where?'

'I don't know yet. I have to get my grades up first.' She looked pointedly at the book that was in front of her.

He smiled. 'Maybe Canada?' He leaned in and gave her a little kiss. The one kiss became several, books forgotten. He rolled over and pulled her on top of him. He gazed at her for a long moment, his expression suddenly serious. His eyes looked darker blue than usual in her shadow. In them she could see a mixture of hope and fear.

'Chaya…' he began.

She put a finger to his lips and shook her head. 'No. Don't say it.'

If he pushed it now, she would have to make a decision. To choose between him and her family and she wasn't ready. Not yet.

'But… I've never felt this way about anyone before. I don't want to lose you, Chaya. Ever.'

'Please, Noah. Don't.'

He stared at her for a while, his lips moving occasionally as though he wanted to speak, but was stopping himself. Finally, he nodded. 'Okay.' He gently stroked her cheek. 'I understand.'

She buried her face in the hollow between his neck and shoulder and wondered if he really did.

Chapter Thirty-Four

Chaya – London, 2005

Chaya arrived early. She and Gimhana had picked one of the new gastro pubs halfway between his work and hers. Neutral ground, as Gimhana had put it. It was early evening and the place was still relatively quiet. She bought herself a Coke and found a table in a secluded corner, so that they could have some semblance of privacy. The last of the sunlight filtered in through the old-fashioned rippled glass in the window, casting a red glow that made the small nook look cosy. She took out her notebook with her list of discussion points jotted on it and was just getting comfortable when Gimhana arrived.

He waved to her as he ordered himself a drink. Dressed in a well-cut pinstriped suit and a long coat, he looked every inch the corporate lawyer that he was. Chaya thought about what she was wearing – jeans, t-shirt and jumper. She had a black jacket and a necklace hanging on a hook on her office door in case she needed to be smart, but generally, she didn't bother with them. Most of the time her clothes were hidden under a lab coat anyway. Perhaps, she reflected, as a lawyer's wife, she'd have to dress a little better. The thought was quite funny, really.

'Hello,' said Gimhana, placing a quick kiss on her cheek. He removed his coat and folded it neatly. 'How're you?'

'I'm okay.' Chaya smiled. 'You?'

'Pretty good.' He pulled up a chair and sat opposite her. 'Okay,' he said, pulling out a notebook with his scrawl on it. 'To business.'

Chaya took a deep breath. 'I've thought about your propos-
ition.' She fiddled with the edges of her own notebook.

'And?' He leaned forward, his elbows on the table. 'You
haven't changed your mind, have you?'

'The answer is still yes,' she said. 'Providing that we sort out
a few ground rules.'

Gimhana grinned. 'That's great.' He patted his notebook.
'Ground rules are a must. What did you have in mind?'

It was reassuring that they were both approaching this in
a business-like fashion. 'Firstly, we must appear to all intents
and purposes to be a normal married couple. Living together,
holidays, all that stuff.'

'Fine with me. I was thinking you could move into my
house. I've got three bedrooms, you can have one if you want…
or we can share.' His face twitched a little when he said this.

Chaya had given this some thought. 'I think having a room
each would be too difficult to hide. Especially, if people came
round unannounced. I think we should share the space, but we
don't need to actually sleep in the same room. Just keep our
stuff in it,' she said quickly.

Gimhana considered it. 'Okay. That sounds doable. If we
find it's too difficult sharing the space, we'll figure out an
alternative.'

'Okay.'

'That brings us to the obvious next problem,' he said. Then,
when she failed to respond, he added, 'Sex?'

'What about it?' said Chaya, taken aback. That was the one
area she'd thought she was clear on. 'I don't want to sleep with
you and you don't want to sleep with me…' she hesitated. 'Do
you?'

He laughed. 'No, that's not what I meant.'

She raised her eyebrows at him. She'd known he wasn't
attracted to her, but she hadn't expected it to be quite that risible
an idea.

He caught her expression and grimaced. 'Sorry, that was
insensitive of me. No. It's a given that we don't need to sleep

with each other. I meant seeing other people. How do you feel about that?'

Chaya frowned. 'I don't really care who you sleep with,' she said. She had thought about this a lot. While she seemed to have lost her libido along with her heart, Gimhana hadn't. This was an arrangement that had to work for both of them. There was no reason to force celibacy onto him. 'So long as no one else gets to hear about it. Not friends, not relatives, not me.'

Gimhana nodded. 'That's fair enough. You, of course, are free to do the same.'

Ha. Like that was likely. The only person she'd wanted to sleep with was Noah. Without him, she didn't care about sex.

Gimhana seemed to be thinking along the same lines. 'What if your Noah reappears?' he said.

Just hearing his name stabbed at her insides, making her feel as though she were somehow betraying him. They had split up ten years ago. He'd moved on and got married. It was time she did the same.

She looked down at her hands, which were tapping lightly against the side of her glass. 'That won't happen. We split up for a reason. That reason hasn't gone away.' She looked up and met his gaze. 'You don't have to worry about that.'

He looked into her eyes for a moment, as though trying to gauge the truth. 'Good,' he said, finally lowering his eyes. 'Shall we put that down as "no affairs"? We can hook up with whomever we like, but we can't keep seeing them on a regular basis.'

Chaya waved a dismissive hand. This wasn't something she was going to need to worry about. She wasn't going to have an affair and Gimhana was smart enough not to get caught. 'Fine.'

'Which brings us to kids. Do we want any?'

This was a difficult one. She had no craving for a child. It would only be a distraction from her work. Besides, the marriage she and Gimhana were planning wouldn't provide a suitable environment in which to bring up a child. 'I don't think so,' she said. 'Why? Do *you* want kids?'

'Not particularly,' he said. 'It's not been an option for me before... I'm not absolutely sure how I feel about it.' He tapped his notebook thoughtfully. 'And my mother will nag about grandchildren.'

They looked at each other. Her amma would nag about grandchildren too, but the idea of being responsible for a child filled her with cold dread. Chaya suddenly felt incredibly young and vulnerable. She couldn't believe that she was sitting in a pub, negotiating her future like this. This was not how things were supposed to happen. But her life wasn't like other people's. She was a broken person. She couldn't handle a normal life. This was the best solution for her. It would allow her to keep up her career and still have an acceptable life.

Gimhana looked like he was having problems handling it too. The realisation that he was struggling with this in much the same way as she was made her feel better.

'Shall we agree no kids?' she said, gently. 'And if one of us feels differently, we must talk honestly to the other one.'

He nodded, giving her a half smile. 'That sounds reasonable.'

'When our parents ask,' said Chaya. 'We can say that we tried and we can't.'

'If you're okay with that...'

Chaya shrugged.

'Okay,' Gimhana said.

They both looked down at their notebooks. As the implications of this conversation sank in, Chaya realised that her overwhelming feeling was relief, rather than regret. Relief was good. She must be doing the right thing.

'I've got work next,' she said. 'I want to carry on with my career. I'm not intending to be a housewife or anything.'

Gimhana grinned. 'I would have expected nothing less. I tend to work long hours if I'm in the middle of a project,' he said, 'Is that okay?'

'Fine by me. I tend to work late if I'm writing a paper.'

'Good.' He ticked something off his list. 'I would like you to come with me to the odd company event,' he said, looking up.

'I already do,' said Chaya, spreading her hands. 'So that's fine. So long as it's not every month or something ridiculous like that.'

'No. I'll make sure it's only sporadic.' He ticked it off his list.

She did the same. 'I travel to conferences a lot...'

'Not a problem. I travel a fair bit with work myself.'

Chaya looked down at her notes. Next on her list was the word 'money', which she had underlined twice.

Chaya cleared her throat. 'I... don't come with a dowry...'

Gimhana stared at her for a moment, then burst out laughing. 'Stop looking so worried. I don't care about a dowry! Whatever gave you that idea?'

'Well,' said Chaya. 'It's not just that. You earn a lot more than me. You own two houses. I'm an academic who's only just starting out. I don't make a whole lot.'

Gimhana shrugged. 'So?'

'I don't know, I just feel a little awkward. It seems a little unfair.'

Gimhana leaned forward and took her hand. 'Chaya, I know this is more like a business transaction than a marriage, but I would like us to have as normal a life as possible. I don't care about how much money you have. Okay?'

Chaya nodded and gave him a small smile, feeling rather silly for having brought it up. 'Okay.'

'Besides,' said Gimhana, leaning back. 'You're doing me a huge favour. It really helps my career to be married and... conventional.'

They chatted for a while longer, covering seemingly trivial topics that could expand into arguments later. It turned out that they both wanted exactly the same things from the marriage – freedom to carry on with their careers, social acceptability, companionship.

'Anything else?' Chaya said, when they'd come to the end of her list.

Gimhana looked uncomfortable.

'What?' said Chaya.

'I would like you to talk to someone about your... mental health. You're clearly depressed and anxious. You need to get some help.'

She stared at him. She hadn't expected that.

'Chaya, you don't have to hide it these days. I've been doing some research on the internet and there's lots of things you can do to help. Antidepressants are pretty effective and—'

'No,' she said. 'I can't... won't... take antidepressants.'

His frown deepened. 'But why not? You have an illness. It's a cure.'

'My brain...' She gestured, her fingers fluttering to her head. 'My brain is my best asset. I can't do anything that would mess with it.' Her feelings were controlled by her brain too, but she couldn't risk losing any of it. 'What if, by trying to fix how I feel, I lost my ability to think?'

'I'm pretty sure that's not how it works...'

'Isn't it? Are you sure about that?' she snapped. 'I'm a scientist. I read side effect logs.'

'But rare side effects.'

'I can't take the risk.'

He took a deep breath and let it out in an equally deep sigh. 'Okay. Not antidepressants then, but there must be something. Therapy, maybe. Counselling. Something.' He leaned forward and touched her hand. 'I worry about you. A lot. I don't want to have to worry about whether you're in one piece every time I come home.'

That was a fair point. Ever since she'd realised that her mental state was affecting Sara, she'd done her best to make sure that the only person affected by her episodes of despair had been her. Although she managed, she wasn't deluded enough to think that she was coping particularly well. Gimhana helped, just by his presence, but it wasn't right to make him feel responsible for her like that. A talking therapy could be an option. She was sceptical about how well that would work for her, but there wasn't any actual harm in trying, was there? 'Okay,' she said. 'I promise I will go and see the university counselling service.' She had a sudden thought. 'I'd like something from you in return.'

'What?'

'I want you to stop drinking.'

He grimaced and shook his head. 'Can't do that,' he said. 'It's very much part of the culture at work. I can't be the goody-goody teetotaller in the corner. No.'

'Well, cut down, then. You drink far too much.' She caught his gaze. 'I don't want to have to worry about whether you're in one piece every time you come home.'

He gave her a grudging smile. 'When you put it like that,' he said. 'Fine. I'll compromise. I will make a conscious effort to cut down on my drinking.'

'In that case,' said Chaya, smiling at him, 'I think we have a deal.'

They shook on it and then stared at each other for a moment, not sure what to say next. Gimhana reached across the table and gave Chaya's hand a squeeze. 'I think this is going to work, you know,' he said, grinning. 'I can think of worse people to spend the rest of my days with.'

Chaya smiled back. 'Thanks.' She raised her glass. 'Here's to "good enough".'

He clinked his drink against hers. 'To good enough.' He sipped and put his glass down, leaving a thin beer-moustache on his upper lip. Chaya pointed it out to him with a gesture.

'You know,' he said, taking a handkerchief out of his pocket, 'my cousins say that the proposal is almost more important than the wedding day for girls.'

'Is it?' said Chaya. She had stopped daydreaming about weddings years before. All her dreams involved Noah, and she couldn't allow herself to think about him.

'Apparently,' said Gimhana, grinning. 'So, this weekend, I'm taking you to a jeweller and you can choose whichever ring you want. And then I can propose to you properly.'

Chaya grinned back, feeling a sudden wave of affection for him. As far as a person to spend the rest of her life with went, she could do a lot worse.

Chapter Thirty-Five

Chaya – London, 2005

Amma was overjoyed when Chaya told her. 'Oh, that's wonderful news!' she said, her jewellery jingling as she bounced with excitement. 'I'm so happy. Oh, wait until I tell Janaki.'

'Janaki?' said Chaya. 'Who's Janaki?'

'Mrs Herath.' Amma clicked her tongue. 'Gimhana's mother.'

'I didn't know you were on first name terms with Gimhana's parents.'

'Oh, we kept in touch. We were so sure that you were perfect for each other. When I found out that you had met up again in London, I called her.' Amma laughed. 'You children forget how much a mother knows about you! We just knew you would get on, you see. It was just a matter of time until you two figured it out.'

The irony made Chaya smile. She could imagine the two mothers phoning each other up and comparing notes. As far as she was aware, Gimhana had only mentioned her to his parents in passing. They must have read a lot of meaning into a few casual statements. They had been right, on one level. She and Gimhana had been seeing a lot of each other. On another level, of course, they were completely wrong. She wondered whether it was fair to lie to her mother like this, through her actions as well as her words. Little white lies, she decided. Let her have her illusions. They protected her.

'Both my daughters will be married,' Amma continued. 'I'm so happy!'

Malini was similarly overjoyed. When she'd stopped shrieking in delight, she said, 'So, when's the wedding? Have you thought of a date yet?'

'Sometime mid November,' said Chaya. 'Amma is getting the horoscopes checked for dates.' All Buddhist weddings were dictated by auspicious moments, when the planets of both people aligned properly, to provide them with the best possible blessing. They also checked the horoscopes for compatibility. She and Gimhana were unlikely to be fully compatible, but everyone was so relieved to get the matter settled, that no one would worry too much about it.

'Are you coming over early?' said Malini. 'We'll have to go on a trip somewhere for a few days, just you and us and the kids. We can spend some quality time before you get married.'

'I'm getting married, not dying. I'll still be around to talk to you.'

'Yes, but it won't be the same, will it?' said Malini. 'Besides, there are things I should talk to you about.'

Chaya rolled her eyes. Her sister was probably intending to give her a lecture about the facts of life. Malini had been impossibly naïve in her teens, the idea that she was suddenly an expert amused Chaya.

'I know about sex, if that's what you mean,' said Chaya.

Malini drew breath slightly, as though shocked to hear her say it. After a moment's reflection, she said, 'Yes, I suppose you must do. You read a lot, I guess.'

'Yes,' said Chaya. She decided to ignore the suggestion that her knowledge came entirely from books. 'I seem to recall telling you about the mechanics of it when we were kids.'

'Oh yes,' said Malini. She giggled. 'I remember now. I didn't believe you at first.'

Chaya laughed. 'No, you didn't.'

Eventually, Malini stopped laughing and said, 'What happened to those kids, huh? We were so young and innocent.'

The laughter dropped away from Chaya's face. Those years seemed like a different life now. They had been full of hopes and dreams. They had been happy. Then real life had come along. Malini hadn't challenged the ideal of marriage and children. Chaya, on the other hand, had held bigger ambitions. Look where it had got her. Empty, broken-hearted and about to enter a sham marriage.

'Chaya? Are you still there?'

'Yes, I'm still here.' She sighed. 'I'd better go, actually. I've got to give a lecture tomorrow and I need to check the slides.'

'Okay.' Malini sounded disappointed. 'I'll speak to you soon. Congratulations again, Nangi. I'm so pleased for you. Gimhana seemed like a nice man. And he's very good-looking. He's a great catch.'

'Yes,' said Chaya. 'He is.'

–

When Gimhana told his mother, he had a full minute of her thanking gods and going on about karma before he could get another word in. He leaned back on the sofa and listened indulgently. She shouted the news out to his father. Gimhana had to move the phone away from his ear.

'Oh, darling, we're so pleased,' she said. 'I knew this would work out. Her mother thought so too.'

So she'd been in touch with Chaya's mother. Gimhana shook his head. He wasn't exactly surprised. He'd got used to the idea that whatever he let slip about his private life was being discussed by his mother and her friends. Humble-bragging about their children was an accepted practice in that set. It was one more reason to keep the truth from her.

'So, when do you want to get married? We can check for auspicious dates.'

'We thought November sometime?'

His mother clicked her tongue. 'That's a bit rushed.'

'Is it?' Given the pressure, he'd assumed they'd have wanted it done as quickly as possible.

'I suppose her parents are okay with that,' said his mother, thoughtfully. 'I mean, neither of you is exactly young. You'll want to get married and start your family sooner rather than later.'

He winced. He was genuinely torn whether to say anything about Chaya not wanting children. On balance, it was probably best not to mention it until after the wedding, when they could present it as a *fait accompli*. Neither of the mums would be happy, exactly, but they might be stoic about it. Maybe.

They chatted a bit more, Ammi talking, him agreeing or making non-committal noises as appropriate. It had been a long time since he'd heard his mother so happy. He hadn't fully appreciated how much his being single was grinding her down. He wondered if she might suspect the true reason for his resolute independence. If his getting married removed that lingering doubt, it wasn't surprising that she was so relieved.

'Oh, I'm so happy darling,' she said, when it was time to hang up. 'She's not the prettiest girl in the world, but she's very nice and I think you two make a good couple.' She sighed, a happy little 'aah'. 'You have made me so happy today.'

Gimhana hung up. He went into his kitchen and started cooking dinner for himself and realised that he was still smiling.

Chapter Thirty-Six

Chaya – London, 2005

On the day they were to go to Sara's, Gimhana turned up at Chaya's work still in his suit. 'Should I have changed, do you think?' he said as they walked from the underground station to Sara's house. 'I should have brought some jeans to work and got changed before I came out.'

'Don't worry about it,' said Chaya. 'Really, they won't mind.' She was dressed casually, but then again, she always was. Gimhana was the sort of guy who had to have the right clothes for each occasion. The idea of just showing up wearing whatever you had on was alien to him.

'Here, hold this a second.' He thrust a bottle of wine into her hands and undid his tie. He stuffed it into his coat pocket. 'There,' he said, taking the bottle back from her. 'That's better.'

'I don't understand why you're nervous,' said Chaya. 'It's not like you're meeting my parents.'

'I've already met your parents. That was different.' He ran a hand over his hair. 'These people... they know you on a different level. I'm worried they might see through us.'

'Gim, you've managed to convince everyone you've worked with that you're straight. You even convinced your boss that we were a couple at that party. You'll be fine.' She patted his arm and smiled at him, she hoped reassuringly.

She had had similar thoughts. Sara and Jay knew her – the anxiety-ridden, stress-driven her. Unlike her parents, who only saw what she wanted them to see, her friends saw all of it.

They might see through the marriage. On the other hand, they wanted to believe she'd moved on. Gimhana had told her that if people wanted to believe something was true, then persuading them that it was so, wasn't hard. She hoped he was right.

The fact that he was nervous worried her.

Sara let them in. 'Hi,' she said, brightly. Chaya could tell that she wanted to like him. That was good. That made it easier.

Chaya introduced him.

'Sara, I've heard a lot about you,' he said.

Sara gave Chaya a meaningful look. 'I wish I could say the same.'

Oh dear.

Sara ushered them into the living room where Jay was sliding the toy baskets into a line.

'Hello, trouble,' Jay said, grinning at Chaya as she came in. His attention moved to Gimhana. There was curiosity in his gaze, but not animosity. He gave her a quick hug.

'Er... Jay. This is Gimhana,' she said. 'My... fiancé.'

'Pleased to meet you,' said Jay, extending a hand.

'Hi.' Gimhana shook Jay's hand and looked him in the eye. Jay smiled. Gimhana's shoulders relaxed a fraction.

'Please Gimhana, take a seat.' Sara bustled. 'Can I get you a drink? Tea? Beer?'

'Please, call me Gim,' said Gimhana, sitting down. 'And tea would be great.' He caught Chaya's eye, as though to convey to her that he was keeping his promise about cutting down on the booze.

Chaya nodded.

'Right, tea,' said Sara. 'Same for you, Jay? Chaya, come help me a moment, will you?'

Sara had put the kettle on by the time Chaya joined her in the kitchen.

'I can't believe you haven't introduced him to us until now,' said Sara. 'You go on and on about him being just a friend and then suddenly you're engaged? What's all that about?'

'It just… sort of happened,' said Chaya. 'We really were just friends until a few weeks ago.'

'Hmmm,' Sara studied her face. 'Are you sure this is what you want? You're not just giving in to pressure from your family?'

'I'm sure,' said Chaya. 'I really like him. It took me a little while to realise how much. Luckily, he feels the same way.' She couldn't believe she was saying this stuff to Sara. Of all the people in her life, Sara was the one who had known the most about her, until now. Lying to Sara was harder than lying to her mother. But she had to do it. If this was going to work, nobody could know.

Sara said nothing. Her eyes searched Chaya's for a moment before she returned to her task.

'So,' said Chaya. 'What do you think?'

'He's perfect. What's the deal?' said Sara, rummaging in the cupboard for tea.

Fear struck Chaya in the chest. If Sara could see through them just like that, what hope did they have of this working? 'What?' she said. 'What do you mean?'

'Well,' said Sara, getting down some mugs. 'He's gorgeous, he's successful, he's charming. How did he manage to get this far without being snapped up? It's too convenient. There has to be a catch.'

Chaya felt her legs go wobbly with relief. She was glad Sara was too busy with the tea to see her face. She gave a little laugh. 'He's a workaholic, that's all,' she said. 'He wants to become a partner before he turns thirty-five so he works until all hours of the night. I've called him at one a.m. and he's still been at work.'

Sara leaned against the work surface and looked at Chaya. 'Sounds a bit like someone else I know,' she said. 'Are you sure you'll be able to leave your careers aside long enough to have a relationship?' She tilted her head.

'We've managed so far,' said Chaya. A friendship was still a relationship.

Sara smiled. 'I suppose you have.' She held out her arms. 'I'm sorry, I didn't mean to be snappy. I worry about you, that's all.'

'I know,' said Chaya, wrapping her arms round her friend and giving her a hug. 'I appreciate that.'

In the living room, she heard Jay laugh. He and Gimhana were clearly getting on okay. Chaya felt another wash of relief. She hadn't realised how important that would be to her.

Chapter Thirty-Seven

Chaya – Oxford, 1995

In the middle of the night, the phone rang. Chaya was out of bed almost before she was awake. She stumbled down the stairs, turning lights on as she went. Any phone call at this ungodly hour was likely to be for her. It was also bound to be bad news.

Her first thought was that something had happened to Malini's baby. When she picked up the phone and heard Malini's voice, for a split second, she was relieved.

'Chaya,' said Malini. 'It's Thatha.'

Her stomach dropped. 'What's happened?'

There was a small sob. 'He's had a heart attack. He's in hospital now.'

Slowly, Chaya lowered herself onto the sofa. 'Oh. How... how is he? Is he...?'

Malini sniffed. 'He's alive. Amma got him to hospital quite quickly. The doctor thinks he's been having small heart attacks for a few weeks now and he thought it was heartburn. Then he had a big one. They're keeping him in. He's in and out of consciousness. They said that if he has another one like that...'

She couldn't go on and stopped speaking. Chaya felt cold. Thatha could die.

She should be there with them. There was nothing she could do from over here. 'Are you okay?' she asked. With a small baby to look after, things couldn't be easy for Malini. 'You and the baby?'

'We're fine. Ajith brought us home and he's gone back to the hospital. He's going to come and get me again at visiting time.'

'I wish I was there.' Her weary brain clicked into action. Again, there was the feeling of the world conspiring against her. In the space of two weeks, her tutor had told her she needed to buck up, Noah had been offered his dream job in Canada and Thatha had guessed that she was seeing someone. She'd had three clear signals that she should give Noah up and she had ignored them. Was this how karma worked? Was it her fault? 'I'm so sorry,' she said.

In the background, the baby cried. 'I'd better go,' said Malini. 'I just thought I should tell you, just… in case.' She didn't have to say in case of what.

'Call me if—'

'I will. I promise.'

After Malini hung up, Chaya slowly lowered the phone. Sara and Jay had come downstairs and were watching her. Noah wasn't staying over that night.

'Are you okay?' said Sara.

'My dad's in hospital,' said Chaya. 'He's had a heart attack.'

'Oh, Chaya.' Sara wrapped her arms around her. 'Is he okay?' She shook her head.

'Oh, mate,' said Jay.

Chaya buried her face in Sara's shoulder. 'I think it's my fault,' she whispered.

'How can it possibly be your fault, you loony?' Sara rubbed her back.

She tried to explain, about how he'd found out she was seeing someone, how it must have been a shock … but what came out made no sense. Sara held her close and said, 'It's natural, at times like this, to blame yourself. It's not your fault though, honey. It sounds like your dad's had a weak heart for a while. There's no way it's your fault.'

'But if he was already fragile, what if I pushed him over the edge? I made him worried and angry and the stress…' Her eyes

filled with tears. And if she failed to get the degree she needed...
all this would have been in vain. She hugged her knees. Tears
escaped down her face.

Jay brought them tea and buttered toast.

'So what happens now?' Sara asked. She was sitting on the
floor, next to Chaya.

'I guess I wait until my sister phones back.' She looked up at
the clock and noticed that it was four a.m. 'You guys go back
to bed. I'll stay down here.'

Jay got to his feet. 'I'll go get your pillow and duvet. You
may as well get comfortable.'

When he'd gone. Sara knelt up and said, 'Are you sure you're
okay?'

Fresh tears came. 'Everything's going so wrong,' said Chaya.
'If I'd listened to my head and never seen Noah, none of this
would have happened.'

'Hey now,' said Sara gently. 'You know that's not true. You
and Noah, you're meant to be together. There's no link between
him and what happened to your dad.'

Chaya wasn't so sure.

As though reading her thoughts, Sara said, 'Karma doesn't
work like that. I'm sure it's not immediate.'

There was a clear link between her spending time with
Noah and her work slipping, though. She hadn't been concentrating on the one thing she was meant to be doing. She had
allowed herself to be distracted. Her family had put so much
into helping her follow her dreams and all they'd asked of her
was that she didn't do anything stupid, like dating a white guy,
and that she did her best with her studies. She had failed on
both counts. She was letting everyone down. Sara would never
understand that, so Chaya said nothing.

When the other two had gone she lay on the uncomfortable
couch, wrapped up in her duvet, the telephone an arm's length
away. If Noah had been there, he would have put his arms
around her and snuggled down, warm and solid against her.

But Noah was out with his friends from college that night, so he hadn't come over. Part of Chaya was glad of that. She struggled to hold thoughts of her parents and of Noah at the same time. The two worlds were too far apart.

The idea that she might have seen her father for the last time buffeted her every few minutes. *Please let him be okay.* He was resilient. He had to be. He was a constant presence in her life – firm, sometimes feared, much respected, always loved. She ran through all the gathas she knew. *Please let him be okay.* She would do anything to make sure of that.

If Thatha survived this, she would throw herself into her studies. She would split up with Noah. It was the only way to make this right. It would hurt ... but she was hurting now. It couldn't possibly hurt more than this.

The hours passed. Outside, the milk float whirred past. The birds sang. Life went on, while Chaya huddled on the couch, waiting for the phone to ring.

It wasn't until seven in the morning that the phone rang again. Chaya snatched it up by the second ring.

'Malini?'

'It's me.' It was Ajith.

Chaya's breath stopped. 'No. Is he...?'

'It's good news,' said Ajith quickly. 'He's awake. He's weak, but he's awake and he's talking to people. They're keeping him in to observe him, but the doctors seem pleased.'

Relief washed through her. 'Oh, thank god.'

'He'll have to take medication and eat carefully for the rest of his life,' Ajith said.

'But at least he'll have more life to be annoyed about that,' said Chaya.

'Exactly,' said Ajith.

Chaya let out a long breath. 'Thank you for telling me,' she said.

'We didn't want you to worry.'

International calls were expensive, so she said goodbye and let him go. She put the phone back at arm's length and flopped back against her pillow. Thank goodness. She closed her eyes. Now she had to make good on her promise.

Being with Noah had brought all this on. She had stayed with him because it felt so good, but no matter how much she wanted it to be the right thing to do, it wasn't ever going to be. It was affecting her parents' health and it was affecting her studies. How many more reasons did she need before she admitted that their relationship was doomed?

She sat up and rubbed her face. She hadn't slept properly for days now and her eyes were raw from crying. In a few hours, she would have to go to her nine a.m. pharmacology lecture. Not going wasn't an option; she hated missing lectures at the best of times, but now, after Dr Goldworthy's warning, it was going to be impossible. She had to knuckle down and get back on track. It wasn't going to be easy, but if there was one thing she knew about herself, it was that she would never shy away from something just because it was difficult.

After the lecture, she would break up with Noah.

She groaned and pushed the duvet off. Today was going to be a very bad day indeed.

Chapter Thirty-Eight

Chaya – Colombo, 2005

Chaya stood still, her arms held away from her sides as the dressmaker made changes to her wedding blouse. The final fitting was taking place in a back bedroom in the dressmaker's house. Through the open window sunlight and the noise from the road filtered in. There was no fan and Chaya could feel the sweat starting to bead on her back. She hoped she would be allowed out of the sari blouse before it stained. Things had moved fast since she and Gimhana discussed their future in the pub.

In the months leading up to the wedding, Amma and Malini had been on the phone more and more often. Thatha, through his contacts in the hotel industry, had secured a venue at relatively short notice. Chaya had assumed that the hotels would offer a standard package, but it turned out that there were a hundred small decisions to be made – menus, decorations, invitations, flowers, corsages, wedding cakes. Mostly, she relied on Malini's good taste.

In the meantime, the success of her grant application meant that work was going well, but she was even busier than before. She had returned to Sri Lanka at the start of November, leaving Trish and the PhD student with detailed instructions of what to do while she was away. She would be back well before the new members of her expanding lab started work in January. Gimhana was flying in next week, in good time for the wedding the week after. 'There,' said the dressmaker, in Singhalese. 'You can look in the mirror now, see if you like it.'

Chaya's eyes flicked to Amma, whose expression said everything was satisfactory. Chaya nodded and made her way to the full-length mirror that was fixed to the side of a wardrobe.

'Oh, wait a moment,' said the dressmaker. 'Shall we drape the sari on to see what it looks like?'

'Yes,' said Amma, fanning herself with a magazine. 'That's a good idea.' The dressmaker picked up the silk sari and unfolded it as though she was afraid it would dissolve. She draped the fabric loosely round Chaya's waist, setting the pleats deftly between her fingers. Chaya was suddenly reminded of Gimhana. What would Amma say if she knew? She turned her head away to hide her smile.

'There,' said the dressmaker, throwing the fabric over Chaya's shoulder. She gently turned Chaya round to face the mirror.

The sari was mostly ivory, with a profusion of tiny gold flowers, each with a sequin in the centre, embroidered along the bottom. A scattering of sequins further up made Chaya sparkle when she moved. The blouse, made of the same material, came down as far as her lower rib, leaving a strip of brown midriff peeping out in the midst of the ivory.

'Beautiful, no?' said the dressmaker.

Amma came over and stood next to her. 'My beautiful Duwa,' she said. 'Still so thin.' She reached over and touched Chaya's collarbone where it strained against her skin. 'You never did recover from that bout of laryngitis,' she said sadly.

For a moment, Chaya felt her heart sink. In the weeks after her split from Noah when Chaya couldn't muster the strength to phone home, Sara had called Amma and told her that Chaya had laryngitis. Suddenly, she felt insubstantial, standing there in her wedding sari, a hollow bride.

She moved slightly, watching the woman in the mirror turn. She was still too thin, she had to admit, but some of the jaggedness of her bones had eased, giving her an air of better health. Amma had put this down to happiness, but Chaya knew it had more to do with the regular meals that Gimhana made her eat. She now realised how much she had neglected herself. Gimhana, luckily, had taken it upon himself to look after her. He was good for her. She smiled at the thought. The woman in the mirror smiled back, some of the sallowness lifting from her face.

Amma let out a long breath. 'You look so beautiful.' She reached inside her blouse and fished out a handkerchief. 'I can't believe my baby is getting married,' she said, dabbing her eyes.

'Oh Amma,' said Chaya, rolling her eyes. 'You promised, no crying.'

Chapter Thirty-Nine

Chaya – Colombo, 2005

Chaya woke up in the night with a tightness in her throat. She lay in the darkness, staring up at the mosquito net. What was she *doing*? She was getting married in the morning. What if she was about to make a colossal mistake? Her heart raced and anxiety burned in her chest. It took her several minutes to force her breathing back into a regular rhythm. Around her, the house slept. It wasn't silent. It wasn't even fully dark. The standing fan whirred. Crickets chirped.

Quietly, Chaya slipped out from under the mosquito net that hung over the bed. She couldn't sleep, so she may as well do something useful. In the living room, she found the router, which had been turned off for the night, and turned it back on. The sound of the computer starting up sounded deafening in the night time quiet. While the machine booted up, she padded into the kitchen and made herself a Horlicks.

Eventually, when the computer had come to life, she logged into her university email account, feeling a little guilty. She and Gimhana had promised each other that they wouldn't check work emails until after their 'honeymoon'. The holiday was meant to be a proper break. What with the wedding preparations and the rush to get the paperwork set up for her new team to start work, she needed a holiday.

She skimmed through her inbox for anything important. An awful lot of emails had come in during the day or two since she'd last checked. There was nothing marked urgent. She resisted the urge to open one of them. She would be here all night. These emails never ended. As she logged off, the email count in her inbox went up. She shut it down before she was tempted to look.

She should go back to bed. She was getting married tomorrow.

Oh god. She was getting married tomorrow. Marrying Gimhana was either a brilliant idea or a terrible one and at this moment, she wasn't sure which it was. He needed this marriage. He was a good man and a good friend. Was she doing this just for him? She thought about how happy Amma and Thatha were. No, she was doing this for them too. And, if she was being brutally honest, for herself as well. She was choosing an easy option. She had no desire to fall in love with anyone. She'd done that once and had been forced to choose between him and her family. Given that situation, she would always choose her family. Wouldn't she?

She was about to turn the computer off, but she hesitated. One last time. After this, she would never look for Noah again. She put in, not his name, but the name of his wife. Noah didn't have a Facebook profile, but his wife Katherine did. An open one too. It contained endless pictures of her, Noah and their son. So many happy family pictures.

She found the profile and clicked on it, heading straight for the photos so that she could find a good one of Noah. Her favourite pictures were the ones where he wasn't posing, but looking more like himself – in the corner of a shot, smiling, or holding his son and laughing. She knew which ones because she'd found them before.

Looking at the photos made her feel faintly guilty. It was all very well justifying it to herself by saying that if Katherine wanted the pictures to be private, she should have locked her profile down, but from what she had heard, Facebook's privacy settings were prone to resetting themselves. Besides, who would want random strangers looking at pictures of them? Let alone random strangers who used to go out with their husband?

She kept being drawn to one photo in particular. It was Noah, slightly out of focus, laughing. There was something about the angle of his head, the way the light fell on his features, that punched straight into her every time. The sense of loss was palpable. She shouldn't do this. It wasn't fair on anyone, least of all her.

Slowly, she looked up and her gaze rested on the wedding flowers on the dining table. They had been lovingly set up resting in bowls of water, so that they would be perfect for her big day. It was just one of the many hundreds of little things her family had done. They were all so happy for her. This wedding was the right thing to do.

Gimhana had been at the house earlier that evening, laughing and joking with her cousins as they helped pack the favours. He fitted into her family like he was always meant to be there. Noah could never have done that. Even if her parents had accepted him, even if he had learned Singhalese, he would never fit in. He would always be obviously foreign to them.

Chaya sighed. She touched the screen and said a silent goodbye to Noah. He would always be the one that got away, but she need not dwell on it any more. She would get on.

She closed Facebook down and turned the computer off. Then the router. In the dark, she made her way back to her bed, crawled in and tucked the mosquito net in behind her. Whenever it came to a choice between her family and Noah, she would *always* choose her family. And by default, she also chose Gimhana.

Chapter Forty

Gimhana – Colombo, 2005

Gimhana's father was looking at his watch, counting down to the auspicious moment. At his signal, Gimhana stepped out of the house he'd grown up in and took the glass of water his mother offered him. He took a sip and passed it back to her, then genuflected, palms together, bending at the knees. His mother placed her hand on his head and blessed him.

He straightened up and then did the same at his father's feet. When he looked up, his mother was wiping her eyes.

On an impulse, he kissed her cheek. 'This is supposed to be a happy day, Ammi. No tears.'

She put her hand on his own cheek. 'My darling son,' she said. 'I'm so happy. I was starting to worry that this day wouldn't come. I'm so proud of you.'

'We both are,' said his father. 'Come now. It's time.' He put his arm out and patted Gimhana on his back, with pride in his expression. Suddenly, it was Gimhana's turn to blink back tears. This was all a lie. But it made his parents so happy, how could it be a bad thing?

He sat in the back of the car, just like he had done when he was a child. His parents chatted about the plans. Ammi occasionally fielded calls. 'I don't have much to worry about,' she said. 'It's Chaya's mother that has all the work. A son getting married is not like a daughter getting married, is it?'

'It's still a big deal,' said his father.

Gimhana wondered how Chaya was coping. Was she having second thoughts? He knew he wanted this marriage more than she did. It would give him a huge amount of freedom. He couldn't be who he really was, but this would give him the next best thing. At least Chaya knew. He had met gay men whose wives didn't know. Who had tried to fight who they were so hard that they'd got married and had children and lived under the pressure until one day they couldn't bear it. But equally, they couldn't bear being parted from their children. So they remained trapped with no escape from their lie. He didn't want that. He didn't want to hurt anyone. This way, he got to keep everyone happy. Including himself.

For him to be who he really was would be a risk. But for Chaya... there wasn't the same sort of pressure. Of course, she was expected to get married and all that, but she might have found someone she liked enough to have a conventional marriage with. What if she tired of the pretence?

But it wasn't just about that, was it? He knew Chaya well. Prickly, closed off, struggling to keep up with normal life, Chaya fought a battle against herself each day. He didn't know much about mental illness, but he knew distress when he saw it. That first night, when he'd sat on her floor, eating food and watching her carefully, he'd seen the raw pain and fear that she kept just underneath her skin. He had helped her, even though he wasn't sure how. He knew, because the woman who had let him in had been wild-eyed and skittish. The one he left behind had been calmer. Over the months of their friendship, she had changed. Not much, but enough. Perhaps that was what she would get from this arrangement. She found some comfort in his friendship.

He didn't have many friends left now. The ones in Sri Lanka had scattered around the world and they had grown apart. The ones in England... well there weren't any. He had colleagues from work, but no real friends. The only friend he had, the person he spent any amount of time with outside of work, was Chaya. He might not be marrying a girlfriend, but he was marrying a friend. Which had to be the next best thing.

Chapter Forty-One

Chaya – Oxford, 1995

Chaya sat on her bed and stared at the carrier bag on her desk. Outside, a bird was singing. It was a beautiful day. But inside, her room was small and it was closing in. She was going to break up with Noah and the pressure of it was crushing.

The bag was full of his things. Nothing big, but all significant: his P.G. Wodehouse books which she had meant to read over the summer; his spare hay fever pills; the custard creams that she bought only because he liked them; a photo Sara had taken of them after one formal hall dinner.

The photo was the hardest to part from. It was the only one of the two of them together. She could see it pressing against the side of the bag. She could make out Noah's hand, holding a wine glass and from there her mind recreated the whole of it – her wearing a long skirt she'd borrowed from Sara and her favourite top, him handsome in his suit, the way he was leaning towards her conspiratorially, her own bashful smile. She got off the bed, found another bag and double-bagged the stuff, like it was biohazard waste. Then she returned to sitting on the bed and waiting.

She jumped when Noah knocked on the door downstairs. She heard Jay let him in. There were a few seconds' chat and then he came up the steep stairs. After months of being together, his tread was as familiar to her as his voice. She was going to miss that. She drew a deep breath, gathered her strength for what she had to do, and opened the door.

'Hi,' he said, smiling cautiously. When he saw her face, the smile vanished.

'Are you okay? Jay told me about your dad.'

She let him in without saying anything and retreated to the other end of the room, which, given the size of it, wasn't that far away. He dropped his backpack and held out his arms. 'What's wrong Chaya? Is it delayed shock?'

She shook her head. 'No.' When she looked at him, she tried not to love him. It was impossible. But that was what she had to do. If she couldn't manage that, she would have to just love him and let him go anyway.

He took a step towards her. She took a step back, so her legs pressed against the bed.

'What's wrong?' His eyes searched her face, as though trying to work out how best to comfort her. He hadn't done anything wrong. It felt wrong to hurt him like this. But she had to.

She took a deep breath. 'I'm sorry Noah, this has to end. We can't go on seeing each other.'

His eyes widened. 'But why…? I don't understand.'

'We always knew this would have to come to an end at some point. I think that point is now. You can take your PhD offer in Canada. I can focus on getting through my exams next year. It's a natural place to end.'

He stared at her. 'I don't want to go to Canada. I want you.'

'This isn't about Canada,' she said. This had been so much easier when she was going over it in her head. More convincing. 'It's about this whole charade. We have no future together. We can't ever get married. We need to get on with things. Do things for ourselves. We've had some great times and now it's time to move on.'

'*Charade?*' he said. He looked hurt and bewildered as he stood there, looking at her through his adorable floppy hair.

'Not charade… You know what I mean.'

'But why? Why now? Why like this?'

Be strong, Chaya. Be strong. She had got further this time than the last time she'd tried to break up with him. That time she hadn't even made it as far as talking to him about it. But she'd always known that they didn't fit together, however much she wanted them to, and now her grades were slipping and her father had almost died… how many more clues did she need? 'Because… because I'm failing at my degree. And last night I thought I'd lost my dad. This… us… it was only meant to be a short term thing and it's time for it to end now. I can't afford to keep going like this. I can't hurt my family.' She shook her head. 'I just can't.'

Hope dawned on his face. 'You're in shock after all the drama last night,' he said, stepping towards her again. 'A lot happened in twenty-four hours. You need time to process it. You'll feel better tomorrow.'

She shook her head and backed away.

'Chaya, please. This is ridiculous … it's wrong. I love you.'

He told her that all the time. She didn't doubt for a moment that he meant it. She loved him too. But love wasn't everything. This kind of love, this heady, youthful abandon, it wouldn't stand up against the real world.

'No, it's not. I'm serious. I shouldn't have allowed us to start going out in the first place. I… It's been wonderful Noah, it really has, but it has to end now. Please don't make this any harder than it is.' She picked up the bag on the desk and held it out to him. 'I've packed up all your stuff. Here.'

Noah looked at the bag as though it had stung him.

'You mean it?' he said, not taking it.

She nodded. Tears welled up and spilled over onto her cheeks. When she looked back on it, she would think it was the tears that persuaded him.

His chin trembled. 'You were crying when I met you,' he said, softly.

She couldn't bring herself to look at him, and focused instead on her feet. Hesitantly, he put a warm hand against her cheek. She couldn't bear to pull away. 'Are you absolutely sure about this?' he said. 'If I leave now, I won't ever…' His voice disappeared.

Miserably, she nodded into his palm. This was what she had to do. She should have done it months ago.

She looked up and finally met his eyes. Her own pain was reflected in his. How could doing the right thing feel so terrible?

He took the bag from her and backed away. 'I love you,' he said. 'I'm not going to fight this. Because it's important to you. And because I love you.'

At the door he paused and looked at her one last time, giving her a chance to change her mind. It wasn't too late. Balanced on the razor edge of her decision, her resolve wavered. It would be so easy to give in, like she had done every single time she'd tried to do this in the past. To throw her arms around him and say she was wrong. But if she did that now, she would end up back here in a few months' time and it would hurt even more. This was her last chance to make things right.

So she said nothing.

He nodded. 'Okay. You know where to find me.' And left.

Her world narrowed and darkened at the edges. She listened to his footsteps going down the stairs. Each one taking him further away. With each step, the ties that bound her heart to his stretched thinner and thinner and thinner. His footsteps reached the bottom. There was a pause, a short conversation with Jay. Then, with terrible finality, the front door creaked shut.

There was a moment of numbness. She forgot how to breathe, how to think. The world took on an unreal aura. The roaring in her ears deafened her.

Jay thumped up the stairs. He pushed open the door. 'Chaya, what the hell—' He saw her face and stopped. His expression softened.

'Oh, mate,' he said, his voice full of sadness.

Everything holding her together gave way all at once. She collapsed just as Jay got to her.

Chapter Forty-Two

Chaya – Colombo, 2005

Walking into the hall felt like a dream. Chaya fought hard to focus. Maybe all brides felt like this on that surreal journey down the aisle, because when they walked back again, they would be subtly changed.

Traditional drummers and dancers preceded her. She barely registered the brown bodies dressed in red and white as she passed them. The drums were loud enough for her to feel them in her torso, mixing with her pulse.

People lined the path she was walking down, everyone craning their necks to catch the first glimpse of the bride. She stared blankly at the faces, barely recognising them. Her pulse quickened. The traditional seven necklaces sat on her chest; the fat clasp that held them all felt heavy on the back of her neck. She wondered briefly whether it was the drums or her heart that was speeding up. The space between her breasts prickled as cold sweat fought to break out from under the dusting of make-up. The world seemed to thin out and lose its colour. Her throat constricted. No, not now. She couldn't have a panic attack now. She tightened her grip on Thatha's arm. He placed a warm hand over hers and looked at her. She felt his stride falter, very slightly.

She continued walking, even though her legs felt like they didn't belong to her. Calm. Breathe, breathe, breathe. She didn't waste energy trying to smile. It was all she could do to keep looking ahead and walk.

Gimhana was standing by the poruwa, flanked by his parents. He was looking over his shoulder to say something to the best man, a cousin of his. As Chaya and her procession neared, he turned. His eyes met hers and Chaya glimpsed the same fear and loss reflecting back at her. She suddenly realised he was going through the same thought process she was. He was just better at hiding it. He understood. The thought itself calmed her. She had a sudden urge to go to him; he could comfort her and protect her. It was a good job they were getting married, really.

The bridal party walked slowly on, closing the gap between them. Gimhana blinked and broke the connection. Chaya continued to watch him. He took a deep breath. His shoulders straightened and his chin went up. When he caught Chaya's eye again, he gave her a tiny smile. It was almost as though he was saying, 'We're in this together. We'll make it. You and I.'

The bubble of pain that was building up in Chaya's chest burst. The relief was so sudden, she almost stumbled. Thatha's arm steadied her once more.

They reached their destination and stood either side of the poruwa. Chaya gave her groom the slightest of nods. Gimhana looked back at her and winked. At that moment the pact was sealed. They would carry this marriage off. It was going to work.

The Kapuwa, a wiry little man in red, looked at his watch and gave the signal. There was the slightest pressure from Thatha's hand and Chaya put her right foot forward and stepped onto the podium.

Chapter Forty-Three

Chaya – London, 2005

'Well, Mrs Herath,' said Gimhana. 'I don't need to carry you over the threshold, do I?'

Chaya laughed. 'I don't think that's necessary, do you?'

'Great. Don't want to take this too far, right?' He unlocked the door and hauled the suitcases in. The honeymoon holiday had done them both good. She had wanted to go somewhere warm, so that she could lounge around and read books for a few days. Gimhana had wanted somewhere with good food and art. So they'd ended up agreeing on Italy and a hotel with a bed big enough that they didn't feel they were sharing. It had been exactly what they'd needed.

They stood together in the hallway, suddenly awkward.

'So, what now?' said Chaya.

Gimhana gathered up the post that had piled up by the door. 'I don't know about you,' he said. 'But I'm itching to check my email.'

'Me too.'

'Well then.'

She smiled at him. 'I think this is going to work out,' she said.

Within minutes, they were both sitting at the dining table, cups of tea in hand, laptops open.

Chaya looked at the ring on her finger. They understood each other. Nothing needed to change as far as work went. This was why their marriage would work.

Her email inbox streamed to life. So many emails. She scanned through them, looking for anything that needed her immediate attention. Noah's name made her stop in her tracks.

What? Why was Noah emailing her?

She threw a quick glance at Gimhana. He was engrossed in his work. Her hand trembling a little, she opened the email.

It didn't say much.

Chaya. I'm in London for two weeks. Would you like to meet and catch up? Noah

She stared at it. What? *What??* Why was he emailing her? Why now? The date stamp caught her eye. He had emailed her in the small hours on the morning of her wedding. If she'd seen it then, would it have changed everything?

Opposite her, Gimhana was typing furiously. He must have felt her gaze, because he looked up. His eyes softened. 'Okay?' he said.

'Yes,' she said. 'All fine.'

No, she couldn't meet Noah for coffee. One of the things she'd said to Gimhana, when they'd started this mad plan, was that Noah was never coming back into her life. She closed the email down. But didn't delete it.

A few hours later, she opened it again and responded.

–

The next day, Chaya met Noah. He was waiting in the Geology department cafeteria, laptop open on the table in front of him. The sight of him made her feel light headed. Her pulse picked up. She went to the counter to buy a tea and took the opportunity to take a few deep breaths and get herself back under control. She could do this. She could.

When she went over to his table he looked up. 'Oh.' He swallowed. 'Um... hi.'

They shook hands. She let go too fast, because she didn't want him to feel her hand shaking. She sat down opposite him. He closed his laptop.

When he looked at her, his eyes were wide. For a second neither of them said anything.

'So,' she said, finally. 'Sorry I didn't get back to you before. I was in Sri Lanka. On holiday.'

'Yes, I saw your out of office. Good holiday?'

'Not bad.' She wrapped her hands around her cup and pressed her fingers again the hot porcelain. 'How come you're here?'

'I'm doing some collaborative research with some people here. We're correlating my geological movement research and their fish migration research to see if we can predict where the fish populations will be in the next ten years.'

She watched him talk, his eyes shining the way they did when he talked about work. She'd missed that so much. She'd missed him. She shouldn't have come to meet him. He was just being nice and trying to keep up a friendship. She wasn't sure she could do that. When he stopped talking, she dragged her thoughts back and said, 'Interesting.'

'It is.' He smiled. He looked tired, she noticed. He must have been working hard.

She forced herself to focus. 'How's your wife? And your son?'

He looked down at his hands. 'Ah… they're fine. But Katherine and I are… separated. We're getting divorced.'

She felt the world shift. This changed things. Chaya moved her cup in her hands and her new rings clinked against the porcelain. She blinked. Did it change things, really? She had had her chance with Noah before and she'd chosen her family and her studies over him. What was so different about now? She couldn't back out of her marriage, her family would be devastated. Gim would be furious. And her career… well, her career was here. He wasn't. It changed nothing.

'Oh no,' she said. To her surprise, she felt genuine sympathy. It couldn't be fun ending a marriage, especially with a child to think about. Poor Noah. 'How are you feeling?'

'A bit bruised, if I'm honest,' he said. 'It's not a huge surprise, but still. It's a bit of a kick to the ego, being dumped.'

They didn't make eye contact. They didn't have to. She knew they were thinking the same thing. Was that why he had got in touch with her? Fleetingly, she wondered what would happen if she told him the truth about her marriage. She could see other people, it was part of the deal ... but no affairs. There was no way she could be anywhere near Noah and not fall for him all over again. No affairs. A promise was a promise.

'I'm sorry to hear that,' she said. Drawing a deep breath she asked, 'Is that... why you got in touch?'

'Oh, no. It was only because I was coming anyway and I knew you worked here...' He looked up at her. 'Well, maybe,' he said. 'A bit.'

She held up her left hand, fingers spread out. His eyes focused on it. On the ring. Because she knew him, she saw the microexpressions that came before the smile: the disappointment, the anger, the sadness. Noah being the nice, polite guy that he was, would never press her into an awkward situation. So he smiled.

'You got married,' he said. 'Congratulations. That's fantastic.' If she didn't know better, she would have thought he was genuinely delighted.

'Just over two weeks ago.' She lowered her hand and twisted the ring on her finger.

Noah picked up his coffee. 'Someone suitable, I hope,' he said. The tone was jovial, but there was a hint of ice in it.

'Yes,' she said. 'And a genuinely good guy. We've been together for a while.' She and Gim had been friends for nearly a year. That counted as 'together'.

'That's good.' He took a contemplative sip of coffee. Something seemed to shift between them. He finally made eye contact. 'I'm glad you found someone who makes you happy.'

She nodded. She didn't trust herself to speak.

'He's a lucky man.'

His phone pinged as a message came in. He glanced at it, giving her a moment to pull herself together.

He turned the phone over. 'So,' he said. 'Apart from getting married, what else is new with you?'

It was a signal that the serious conversation was over. They made small talk for a bit, until it was an acceptable time to leave.

'It was nice to see you again and catch up,' Chaya said, for all the world as though they were nothing more than casual acquaintances. She was pleased that she managed to carry it off.

'I'll be popping back from time to time, I should think. As part of the collaboration, I mean,' he said.

A beat of silence. This was where one of them said they should meet up again. Neither of them did.

'Well,' he said. 'Good luck with… everything.'

'You too.' She studied him and saw the tiredness, the sadness in him. She wanted so badly to put her arms around him and make things better. It wasn't her place anymore. She scrunched her napkin up into her fist. 'It'll be okay, you know,' she said. 'You'll be okay.'

He met her gaze and smiled. 'Yes,' he said. 'I've survived worse.'

She felt it in her solar plexus, that blow to the emotions. He had survived. She hadn't. Until now.

'Bye, Noah.'

'Bye, Chaya.'

They shook hands. When she left the cafeteria, she paused at the door to look back. He was already back at his laptop. She knew he wouldn't call her again.

—

When Chaya got home, Gimhana was already in the kitchen, music playing in the background. She stood in the hallway and let the domesticity wash over her. This was what she got to come home to now. Company. Music. Good food. This wasn't a place to lay her head when she was too exhausted to be in the lab. This was actually a home.

'Hello,' Gimhana called out. 'I'm making carbonara.'

This was what normal was going to be like from now on. Chaya hung up her coat and smiled. 'Sounds delicious.'

She went into the warm kitchen. There was just enough room for her to get past Gimhana. The smell of frying bacon rose from the pan. He was standing by it, beating eggs.

'Good first day back?' he said, not taking his eyes off his work.

Saying goodbye to Noah was the right choice. She could make a future here. 'Yes, it was, thanks.' She grabbed the kettle. 'How about you?'

'All good,' said Gimhana. 'People from work bought us a set of wine glasses as a present. Very nice crystal ones.' He turned and gave her a huge smile. 'Dinner will be another five minutes. Can you throw together a salad?'

She smiled back. 'I think I can manage that.'

For once, she had made the right decision. Definitely.

Chapter Forty-Four

Chaya – London, 2012

It was only when Chaya got home that she remembered that Gimhana was away. She stood in the kitchen, car keys still in hand, frowning. He had told her, she knew he had. In fact it was in the shared calendar. She'd just forgotten in the excitement.

Ah, well. She shrugged off her coat and hung it up on its designated hook. It wasn't too late in the evening to call him. She didn't like calling him after what would be considered 'business dinner' hours when he was away. There were parts of his life that were none of her business. But it wasn't quite nine p.m. Still an acceptable time. She pulled out her phone, called him and put it on speakerphone so that she had her hands free.

'Hey.' Gimhana responded at the second ring. 'How did it go?'

'They liked the initial submission. They've asked us to submit a full application for the grant.' She grinned, even though he couldn't see her. The second European funding grant she had applied for followed on from the first and was much more prestigious. If she and the team landed it, it would be a huge boost to her ambition to land a professorship.

'That's fantastic!' He sounded genuinely pleased. She loved that he cared. 'Did they have any useful feedback?'

'Some,' she said. 'I can definitely tweak the full application to fit it in.' She opened the fridge door and looked in. There was a Tupperware container with a Post-it note stuck to the top. She tilted it. It said 'Pasta and sauce, Tuesday' on it. It was now Wednesday. 'Gim, is this leftover pasta still okay to eat?'

'You were supposed to take that for lunch yesterday,' he said, sounding put out.

'I forgot.'

'Did you eat lunch today?'

'I ... can't remember,' she said. Even though she knew she hadn't.

Gimhana clicked his tongue. 'You have to remember to eat.'

'I was busy.' She took the tub out of the fridge, opened the lid and sniffed. 'Smells okay.'

'It should be fine,' he said.

'So what are you up to?' She popped the lid off and put the food in the microwave.

'I've just ordered room service,' he said. 'I haven't decided what to do after that. I could do some work or pop down to the bar for a drink. Just one,' he added.

'Do both,' she said, getting a plate out of the neat stack. 'You've got time.' She had to trust him when he said he would stop at just one. In the years that they'd been married, she'd had no reason to doubt him. Gimhana seemed to be a man of his word, which was just as well, considering their arrangement.

'I guess I could,' he said. 'I hope you're not planning on working late tonight.'

She winced guiltily, because that was exactly what she'd planned to do.

'Chaya, you've been working all hours for the past couple of weeks. Take a night off and get some sleep.'

'Ha, like you can talk,' she said.

He laughed. 'I guess I can't argue with that.'

The microwave pinged.

'I'd better let you get on with your work,' said Chaya. 'I'll see you in a few days.'

'Okay. Well done on getting to the next stage of this grant, again.'

Once she'd hung up, Chaya grabbed a fork and nudged the drawer shut. The nice thing about Gimhana being away was that she didn't need to load the dishwasher. He liked to use as many pans as he could when he cooked. When he was away, she didn't cook. She just ate leftovers, or had toast for dinner. She looked at the Tupperware container, poised to tip the contents onto a plate and decided against it. Why dirty a plate? She put the plate back and ate her dinner straight from the tub. It was almost like being single again.

She wandered into the dining room and pulled up her laptop. It wasn't really like being single though, she had to admit. Their house was a much bigger home than her bedsit. She and Gimhana got on very well as friends. Getting married hadn't done her career as much good as it had done Gimhana's, but she was working on that. She smiled and popped a forkful of pasta into her mouth. The food was definitely better since she'd got married. She had space and comfort and, most importantly of all, companionship. Things could be worse.

Chapter Forty-Five

Gimhana – Manchester, (near Salford), 2012

Gimhana didn't bother going out for dinner. It was hardly worth it for himself. Instead, he had a sandwich in the hotel restaurant, reading his notes while he ate. He did a bit more work and went downstairs for a quick drink at the bar.

Despite it being midweek, the bar was busy. A group of people sat at one side, drinking and laughing. Gimhana took a bar stool at the other end of the bar. He didn't want to intrude. They clearly all knew each other.

The barman spotted him and came over. He was a good-looking guy, with close-cropped hair and a ready smile. He was dressed in the staff uniform of generic short-sleeved shirt and black trousers and still managed to look hot. Gimhana smiled and shut down that train of thought. Whilst he wasn't averse to company on these nights away, chatting up hotel barmen was not his sort of thing.

'What beers have you got?' He was doing quite well with his promise not to drink so much. It had been hard. The only way he could do it was to stop drinking whiskey. He could take or leave beer, so stopping after one was manageable. Whiskey, not so much.

He chose one at random from the list and watched the barman pull the pint for him. The muscles in his arms moved as he pulled the pump handle. Nice. Gimhana couldn't tell how old the man was. He looked young at first glance, but when he brought the pint over, Gimhana noticed the creases around his eyes and the set of his jaw. There was the tiniest hint of blond stubble on his cheeks, just begging to be touched. Not as young as he first appeared, perhaps.

The barman made eye contact and smiled. 'Will that be everything, sir?'

'For now, thank you...' he checked the name tag. 'Zack.'

'If there's anything else, just let me know.' More eye contact. Interesting.

Gimhana opened his paperback and started to read. Every so often, he glanced up to check out Zack. More often than not, he found Zack was watching him. He felt the thrill of attraction. He normally arranged his rendezvous through Gaydar where he could be completely clear about what he wanted. Random hook-ups were too risky; there was too much room for misunderstanding. While he knew Chaya didn't care who he slept with, she did care that he didn't get caught. He cared too.

He turned his attention to his paperback, fighting the urge to look up. When things quietened down, Zack brought a tray of glasses over.

'What're you reading?'

Gimhana showed him the cover. It was a crime novel, not even a very new one. 'You're new here, aren't you?' he said. 'I come to this hotel fairly regularly and I've not seen you before.' He'd have remembered.

'Yeah. I usually work at a different branch. Weekends, usually. But they were short-staffed and I needed the money.' Zack stretched to put the glasses on the high shelf, making his shirt pull tight against his body. 'So you come here on business then?' He bent down to pick up another box of glasses.

'Yes. I have a client who needs me to come up to their site once a month.' He tried not to stare. Even in the boring work trousers, there was no hiding that toned bum.

'What do you do?'

Gimhana hurriedly tried to look like he hadn't been ogling. 'Corporate law.'

'I'm a student,' said Zack.

He felt a curious drop somewhere in his chest. A student. A youngster. He'd looked too old. Gimhana tried to recalibrate his view. 'Oh yes? What are you studying?'

'Business and IT. I'm an app developer really, so the IT side is easy enough. It's the business side I'm really there for.'

Someone approached the bar. Zack said, 'Excuse me,' before heading off to serve the customer, which Gimhana thought was sweet.

Gimhana watched Zack walk over to his customer. He was cute and apparently interested. Gimhana reminded himself that he didn't do random hook-ups. He sneaked another glance at Zack. No matter how enticing the prospect. He should finish his pint and get himself out of there.

Zack returned. 'I couldn't help noticing you looking,' he said, quietly. 'I finish my shift and close up in half an hour. Would you like to… go for a drink?'

Gimhana was too surprised to reply for a second. He wanted to. Genuinely. But things were more complicated than that.

'That sounds tempting,' he said. 'But you're very young.'

'I'm not that young,' Zack said. 'I'm twenty-nine. Thirty in two weeks.' He gave a theatrical shudder.

'Oh that's not so bad.' He spoke before he'd thought it through. Oh, crap. That sounded keen.

'No?' Zack's eyes danced with laughter. The flare of attraction Gimhana felt at that moment made him forget how to breathe.

'Listen,' Zack leaned forward, wiping down the bar. 'I'm a mature student. I held down a job before I went back to uni. I'm not some fragile young thing fresh out of school. I work this job, keep up with my course and still work on my business…' His gaze locked on to Gimhana's. 'So I think I'm old enough to know what I want.'

Gimhana recovered his poise. 'You're… very direct.'

Zack shrugged. 'Life's too short.' He smiled. 'So…?'

Oh, what the hell. Just this once. 'Sure.'

He was rewarded with the most suggestive of grins. Zack went across to tell the others at the bar that it was nearly closing time. Gimhana finished his drink. He couldn't stand up right now without embarrassing himself.

'Will you be settling up now, sir?' said Zack. 'Or shall I charge it to your room?' The slightest rise of the eyebrow.

Gimhana nearly laughed out loud. He gave his room number. Zack said, 'thank you very much,' then added, 'thirty minutes,' in an undertone.

When Gimhana reached his room, he realised he was still grinning. He felt almost giddy, which was ridiculous. He was nearly forty, living a life that revolved around work and a housemate he called his wife. His life had been given over to functionality. Everything was practical. But half an hour of flirting with a hot young thing had made him feel a buzz like he hadn't felt in years.

He checked the room to make sure it was presentable. He was naturally organised, so it didn't take long to get everything tidied away. He checked the mini bar, then sat on the bed and waited.

The knock on the door was soft. He opened it to find Zack standing outside, wearing a leather jacket over his barman's uniform and looking insanely hot in it. Gimhana let him in and out of habit, checked the corridor.

'No one there,' said Zack. 'I checked. And I took the service lift. Relax. I can do discretion.'

Gimhana closed the door. Zack took his jacket off and laid it on the back of the chair in the corner of the room.

'Do you do this a lot?' He didn't know why he asked. He didn't really care about the answer at that moment. Now that Zack was here, standing only a few feet away, he could barely think straight for wanting him. All thoughts had followed the blood flow down to his groin.

Zack took a step closer. 'No,' he said. The faint stubble on his jaw caught the light.

Gimhana put his hands on Zack's sides and felt the hard body underneath. Zack smiled and reached up to caress his face, his palm rubbing along the side of Gimhana's neck. The warm touch made Gimhana's skin zing. He closed his eyes as Zack moved closer.

'You,' Zack murmured. 'Are gorgeous.'

Gimhana closed the gap and kissed him. He felt the responding kiss in every part of him. He knew at that moment that he was lost ... and he didn't care.

Chapter Forty-Six

Chaya – London, 2016

Chaya said goodbye to her sister and hung up. She had heard Gimhana come in whilst she was on the phone. She went into the kitchen to find him, frowning.

He was pulling things out the fridge to make dinner. It was Friday and he cooked on Friday nights. 'Hello,' he said. He glanced at her over his shoulder and paused. 'What's wrong? Is everything okay at home?' He closed the fridge door and turned to her, his hands full of tomatoes.

'Everyone's fine,' she said. 'But Malini had a strange suggestion.' She went to stand next to him.

'Oh yes?' He rinsed the tomatoes.

'She wants Nayana to come visit us. She and Ajith think it'll do her good.'

'That sounds nice.' He paused and looked at her. 'What's worrying you? Are you thinking you'll have to take time off to be their tour guide?'

'Well, there's that.' She was really busy at work. She needed to keep up the cycle of applying for grants and getting papers published, especially if she was going to apply for the professorship that would open up when the department's deputy head retired. Taking two weeks off to show her niece around wouldn't be ideal. 'Also, it's not "them", it's just her. They want to send her by herself.' She grabbed a knife and a chopping board.

He handed the tomatoes to her. 'Salad, please.' He got out his own knife and started cutting root ginger into fine slices. 'So?'

'I'd have to look after her,' she said. 'I'd be responsible for her.'

For a few minutes, he didn't say anything. They stood side by side, cutting up vegetables. Tomato salad was one of the few things that Chaya could reliably make. Gimhana had tried to teach her to cook, but he enjoyed it and she didn't, so now he did most of the cooking. Friday night was always curry night. She moved away slightly when he diced the onion, because the fumes made her eyes water.

'The other thing is, she'd be staying here. Just her and us. She'll be curious and … she might notice.'

Gimhana paused. 'Hmm…' he said. 'How long is she planning to come for?'

'Two weeks. Next summer.' Chaya threw the tomatoes in a bowl and added some coriander leaves on top. It was not a traditional salad, more a salsa, but it went well with Gimhana's chicken pilau and dahl, so who cared? 'Two weeks is a long time, Gim. She'll be in our pockets the whole time.'

'And she does look up to you,' he said. 'So she will be watching what you do. I see why you're worried.'

'I can't say no,' said Chaya. 'I said I'd check the diary for dates when we were both here. Just to buy us some time.'

Gimhana frowned and went back to his cooking. He added mustard seeds into the pot with hot oil and waited until they popped before adding the onion and curry leaves. The smell of frying onion filled the kitchen. She passed him the cinnamon sticks before he asked.

'I know we've had people come to stay before,' she said. 'But it's only been for a weekend and they're usually so busy sightseeing that they barely see the inside of the house.'

Gimhana put the lentil dahl on and pushed it to the back burner to simmer. He turned to her. 'I think,' he said. 'We should let her come. This...' he waved a hand to include the kitchen. 'This is pretty normal. Our life is pretty normal. I'll sleep in the master bedroom, like we do when we have guests and then it'll look just like any other couple's house. I don't think we have anything to worry about.' He smiled. 'I'm sure it'll be fine.'

She wasn't so sure. It must have shown in her face, because he put a hand on hers and said. 'It will all turn out for the best. Trust me.'

Chapter Forty-Seven

Gimhana – Manchester, 2012

Gimhana hesitated outside the pub. It wasn't somewhere he'd been before and he was wary. He passed for straight, but his past experience had made him nervous, plus he was also Asian. Besides, even in jeans and a jumper, his middle-class lawyer-ness was difficult to shake. It wasn't a problem in London, but here, who knew?

The misgivings he'd been feeling all week nagged at him.

His night with Zack all those weeks ago, was meant to have been a one-off. He remembered saying so on that first night, when he'd sat naked on the bed and watched Zack pull his clothes back on just before dawn. Zack had looked over his shoulder and said, 'That would be such a waste.'

'I ... can't. I can't do relationships. It's too much.'

Zack had moved across and pushed him back, pinning him under the weight of his gorgeous body. His kiss was searing. 'Too much?' he said. 'Are you sure?'

Gimhana shook his head and gently pushed him off. 'Pretty sure.'

The look of disappointment on Zack's face would have melted a heart of stone. But he couldn't see him again. Not because he didn't want to. 'If I see you again,' he said, slowly. 'I won't ever be able to stop. And I can't do commitment.'

Zack rolled his eyes. 'Seriously? Jesus. I'm not talking about getting married.'

Gimhana winced. Should he tell Zack he was already married? It was a sham marriage, but it would stop this conversation in its tracks. Somehow, he couldn't bring himself to do that.

Zack grabbed the hotel stationery and scribbled something on it. 'Well,' he said. 'In case you change your mind. You know where to find me.' He folded the paper and handed it to Gimhana. 'And don't worry. I won't try to find you. I'm not that needy.' He headed to the door.

'Zack...' Gimhana leapt off the bed and reached for him. 'What?'

'I'm sorry, okay?' He put his hand on his arm. 'I had the most amazing time with you. I'd like us to part on good terms.'

For a few seconds, Zack didn't respond. He looked sad and Gimhana felt terrible for hurting him. 'I'm sorry too,' Zack said, finally. 'I like you. I want to see you again. But you were clear about it from the start... so... yeah. It was fun.'

And then he'd left.

A few hours later, Gimhana, packing up, had put the note in the pocket of his bag. It would have been so easy to leave it behind; just throw it in the bin and walk away, but there was something about Zack. His normal encounters were always clear-cut. But with Zack it felt different. They had talked, lying in bed. Nothing too deep, but somehow full of meaning. So he had taken the number home. And a week ago, while making plans to go back to see the client, he'd texted him. He shouldn't have. But one drink couldn't hurt. It would be nice if he could make a friend.

It was getting dark when Gimhana reached the pub. He checked his phone in case of any last minute texts. No. This was still happening. He stamped down a last protest from his conscience and went in.

It was busy, considering it was mid week. Zack was standing at the bar. He waved Gimhana over.

'I got you a pint,' he said.

'Thanks.' He thought of that night, sitting at the bar, flirting quietly and felt a flutter low in his stomach.

He followed Zack to a table to the side of the bar and tried not to stare at his bum. Zack shrugged his jacket off and slung it over the chair. His t-shirt was snug against his toned chest and the jeans made it clear how muscular his thighs were. Gimhana gave an involuntary sigh.

'So,' said Zack. 'I told you we'd meet again.' He grinned, so sure of himself. It should have been off-putting, but it wasn't.

'Just for a drink,' said Gimhana.

'Right.'

When Gimhana held his gaze and said nothing, Zack sighed. 'Fine. If that's what you need.' He took a sip from his beer. 'So, how's it going?'

They fell into conversation, chatting about their respective work. Gimhana maintained a careful distance, making sure not to touch him. Zack told him about his app, the real reason for his interest in business and marketing. His final year project was relevant to his market research. His drive was impressive. Although Gimhana knew very little about apps, he knew a fair bit about investment contracts. As they got deeper into the discussion, he forgot his reserve.

The conversation moved on to music and art. Zack was horrified that Gimhana knew so little about music, while Gimhana pretended to be equally shocked by Zack's ambivalence to art. By the time a few hours had passed, they were laughing like old friends.

'I'd better get back,' said Gimhana. 'I should do some reading for my meeting tomorrow morning.'

Zack stretched, making his t-shirt pull tight against his sculpted chest. 'I'll walk back with you.'

Gimhana dragged his gaze away from Zack's chest and grabbed his jacket.

They walked back side by side, sticking to well lit streets, chatting quietly.

'So what changed?' said Zack. 'How come you called me?'

Gimhana looked straight ahead and answered, 'I couldn't stop thinking about you.'

'Hah,' said Zack. 'I have that effect on people.'

'Uhuh.'

'If it helps,' said Zack. 'I couldn't stop thinking about you either. It's like I know you ... like I always knew you. I just needed to find you again. If that makes any sense.'

Weirdly, it did. He hadn't expected to feel this way ever again.

'I know what you mean,' he said, miserably. 'I wish I could be with you.'

'And you can't ... why exactly?'

'I've told you why!' Except he hadn't been completely honest. He should tell him. He had a deal with Chaya. No affairs. Seeing Zack twice was probably okay. To see him any more than that would be pushing it. He could have the wife and the outward normality. Or he could have Zack.

He fell out of step with Zack, so that he could look at him. That body, those jeans, that confident strut. Oh, but he wanted to have Zack. He really, really wanted to.

Zack half turned and smiled at him. 'I told you. If it's that important to you, I can do discreet.'

But Zack was in Manchester. Chaya was in London. He was *good* at secrets. He'd tell Zack eventually, when he was ready. He'd understand. Probably. Gimhana looked him up and down. 'Really?'

Zack rolled his eyes. 'Yeah. So. Your place or mine?'

Gimhana laughed. Just like that, it was decided. They picked up the pace and carried on walking towards his hotel. This made him so happy it couldn't possibly be wrong.

Chapter Forty-Eight

Chaya – London, 2013

Chaya met Sara for dinner at a tapas restaurant that she and Gimhana had tried out a few months before. They ordered a bottle of red and stared at the menu.

'I don't know,' said Sara. 'I'm too tired to make decisions this evening. What's good?'

Chaya scrunched up her nose. 'I can't remember,' she said. 'The prawns were nice, I remember that.' She scanned the menu. 'There's a sharing platter here. Shall we just go for that?'

'Oh yes please! Let's do that.' Sara closed the menu. 'Done. Now then, let's get to the important stuff.'

'You first,' said Chaya. 'How is everyone?'

Sara told her what was new with her, Jay and the boys. 'Jay's just gone up a pay grade, so that's going to come in handy when the uni bills start coming in,' she said. 'So all in all, things are looking up. How about you?'

Chaya took out her phone. 'This went up today.' She pulled up a screenshot of the university's job alerts. 'It's internal applicants only at the moment.' She handed the phone to Sara.

'Professor? Nice. Are you going to go for it?'

'I think so. I've got a decent publication record and I've brought in a pretty big grant recently.'

'Brilliant. I'm glad. You've worked so hard, you deserve it.'

'The competition is going to be fairly stiff though,' Chaya said. 'And mostly men.'

'So?' said Sara. 'You've got to keep pushing, or the boundaries will never move. You're still going to apply, right?'

'Of course. You've got to be in it to win it, as Gimhana would say.'

Sara laughed. 'And how is he? We haven't seen him in ages.'

'Oh, busy. Always busy. He's up in Manchester at the moment. He's been working quite hard. I had to remind him to take a night off last month; it's usually the other way around.'

Sara took a sip of her wine and gave her a long look. 'Is everything going okay with him? Are you still happy?'

Chaya shrugged. 'Of course I am.'

Sara's gaze was serious. 'I'm glad,' she said. 'When you suddenly produced him and said you were going to get married, I was a little worried, but it seems to be working out. I'm pleased for you.' She smiled. 'I'm a little envious, to be honest. You guys have a remarkably ... laid-back existence.'

Sara knew her better than anyone. Lying to her never got any easier. 'Hardly laid-back,' Chaya said. 'One or the other of us is always running after some crisis at work.'

Her friend conceded that. 'Yes, but you still go out and do stuff. I can't remember the last time Jay and I did anything fun.'

'We don't have kids,' Chaya said. 'Which means our evenings are our own ... work permitting.'

'Oh yeah,' said Sara, wistfully. 'No regrets on that score?'

'No,' she said. 'I don't think I would make a very good parent anyway.'

'You're pretty good with my kids. They love you.'

'I can be the cool aunty. That, I'm good at.' She smiled. 'Speaking of which, my niece is coming to visit in a few months. I'll essentially be in loco parentis for two weeks. She's eighteen. It's terrifying.' The idea genuinely scared her. She tried to tell herself that, at nearly eighteen, Nayana was practically an adult, but when she thought about Malini at eighteen, she knew that adulthood was still years away. What if something happened? The very thought of it made her feel ill. 'So much could go wrong.'

'Or,' said Sara, 'nothing could go wrong.' She topped up the wine in both their glasses. 'You worry too much, Chaya. Have faith in your own ability. It'll be fine. You'll see.'

'Hmm,' said Chaya. 'I don't know. I have a bad feeling.'

Chapter Forty-Nine

Gimhana – Remote North Yorkshire, 2013

'I can see why you like this,' Zack said. He was reading a *Jem and the Holograms* annual. Gimhana sat next to him, idly sketching outfits for Jem. This was something he'd got into trouble for doing as a child. It was only since meeting Zack that he'd started again. He'd forgotten how much fun it was, making up designs that could be worn as conservative daywear and then changed to be something outrageous with a few adaptations. Given that the show was from the eighties, outrageous meant pretty much anything was allowed.

'Oh yes?'

'She's a serious, conservative girl on the one hand and a fabulous rock star on the other and she gets to keep the two identities separate. I can totally see how that would appeal.'

It was a fair assessment. Zack understood him in a way no one else did. 'That's true,' he said. 'Mostly though, I just liked the clothes. Even Rio gets some interesting things to wear, even if it is very eighties.'

They were in a holiday cottage in North Yorkshire. It was early summer, but not as warm as it could be. Chaya was away at a conference and Gimhana had taken the opportunity to take Zack for a weekend getaway.

Over the past year, he had met up with Zack every time he came up to Manchester. Thank goodness for his needy client. Although he still insisted on keeping a low profile, they had been out a few times, to places two blokes who were friends might conceivably go together; the cinema, the odd student bar. They sat a respectful distance apart. They never held hands. He was always careful that he and Zack didn't go up to his room together. He no longer stayed at his usual hotel, choosing different ones whenever he could. He'd told his secretary that he wanted to see the variety of places he could try on his budget. She had taken it to be some sort of weird bet he had with some of his colleagues and obliged.

Zack rested his chin on Gimhana's shoulder and looked at the sketches. 'Ever fancied making those and modelling them?'

Gimhana looked down at the drawings. 'No,' he said. 'I mean, I'd love to see them on someone, but I can't sew. I'm a lawyer. I wouldn't know where to start with this.'

'Oh, come on. Where's your entrepreneurial spirit?' said Zack.

'I don't think I've got one.' He closed the sketchpad and dropped it onto the coffee table. He turned round and kissed Zack. 'You're the entrepreneurial one in this relationship.'

He leaned back, resting his head against the back of the sofa, so that they were still entwined in each other's arms. He was warm and fed and happy. He didn't think he had ever been this relaxed in his life. He closed his eyes and sighed. This contentment couldn't last long. He should savour every last minute of it.

Zack kissed his cheek and snuggled against him. 'Do you believe in love at first sight?'

'Pardon?' he said.

'Love at first sight,' said Zack.

Gimhana opened his eyes and found Zack smiling up at him. Zack ran his fingers through Gimhana's hair. 'That night, in the bar. I saw you walk in and I knew. It was like you were meant for me. I saw you and everything in my world shifted into place.'

'Really? Wow.' Gimhana grinned. 'I saw you and thought you looked hot.'

'You have no romance in your soul.'

Gimhana chuckled. 'Yeah. That's why I've brought you here, to the cosiest, cutest little cottage in the middle of idyllic Yorkshire.'

'That's a good gesture, especially from a city boy like you,' said Zack. 'And to think, when we first met, you gave me all that crap about not being the sort to have a relationship. Look at us now, a year later and in love.'

They were, weren't they? Gimhana turned his head. That was the trouble. They had been seeing each other furtively for almost a year. He loved Zack. He adored Zack. But he couldn't be a proper partner to him. Not when he was lying to him.

'I was thinking,' said Zack. 'I'm coming to London to pitch to investors in a few weeks. We could meet up. I know you're busy at work, but at the weekend.'

'You know I can't do that,' Gimhana said. 'I told you.'

'Yes, but at the weekend...'

'Anyway, I have someone coming to visit. A relative. I'll be showing her around in the next few weeks. I can't just disappear.'

Zack pulled a face. 'When's she leaving, then? I'll come down again after she's gone.'

'Darling, I don't think it's a good idea.' Gimhana sat up. 'We've talked about this. I can't be that guy. I love you, but I can't.'

'Why do you do this to yourself?' said Zack. 'Who cares what people think?'

'I care.'

Zack made an exasperated noise.

'Excuse me a minute,' Gimhana said. He planted a kiss on Zack's nose and went to the bathroom. 'I'll be right back.'

In the tiny, twee bathroom, he sat on the edge of the bath and stared into space. He should never have started it. It would have been so easy – all he'd needed to do was not take Zack's number, scribbled on hotel notepaper. He could have just thrown it in the bin rather than tucking it into his suitcase. He could have just… not called. It would have been one glorious night and that would have been the end of it. But no. He had been unable to resist, he'd called him.

He buried his face in his hands. Now he was in too deep. He had let himself fall for Zack. He'd broken his agreement with Chaya. The only way he could get out of this fix was by hurting one or the other of them. He couldn't figure out what to do, so he carried on, spinning plates faster and faster, all the while, screwing himself further and further into the mire.

He had managed almost a year of keeping his lives separate. He didn't tell either one about the other. Weirdly, it was harder not mentioning Zack to Chaya than the other way around, because he thought about him all the time. When he was with Zack, no one else got a look in. All things being equal, he would choose Zack, every time. But Chaya was his stability. His ticket to social and professional acceptance. His best friend. He had asked her for this marriage as a favour. She had been his best friend and companion for six years. He couldn't abandon her now.

He flushed the toilet to keep up the pretence and washed his hands. This was the sort of thing he was having to do a lot. Little lies to cover up the big betrayals. Extra trips up to see the client. Secret dashes up north whenever Chaya was out of town. This was no way to live. He was having an affair without even really cheating on anyone. He pulled himself together and went back to the living room. 'Would you like a cuppa?'

Zack was looking at a mobile phone. Gimhana's phone. 'Who's Chaya?' he said.

'What?'

Zack turned the phone round. It was still locked, but a text had arrived and you could see the top line.

Train strike. Might not make it home
for dinner tomorrow.

'Who is he? Why is he having dinner with you tomorrow night?'

Scenarios flipped through Gimhana's mind. He could tell Zack, explain it all. Would he understand? Probably not. Maybe part of the truth.

'She,' he said. 'Chaya's a woman.'

'I've heard you talking to her before, a couple of times. You always answer when she phones. She texts you.' Zack's hand shook. He lowered the phone to his lap. 'Who is this woman to you?'

'She's my... housemate,' said Gimhana. 'My best friend. Really, she's my beard.'

'Your beard?'

'You know, goes to parties with me? Pretends to be my date.' *Wife*. Why didn't he just say wife? Because it sounded worse, that was why. Zack would get the wrong idea.

'I know what a beard is, dumbass. I'm just—' He stared down at the phone. 'Actually, no. I'm not surprised you've got one. You're so...'

Zack sighed and laid his head back on the sofa. For all his protestations, he still looked so vulnerable sometimes that it made Gimhana's heart ache. 'What's happening here, Gim?' he said, staring at the ceiling. 'Why are you so ashamed of me? We've been together nearly a year and I don't know anything about your life. I only see you in hotel rooms and bars, sneaking around, like I'm some sort of dirty secret. Am I just some sort of fuck toy to you? Because sometimes that's what I feel like.'

Gimhana stood in the middle of the room, lost for what to do. He had known this day would come. He had tried to make it clear that he could never be the boyfriend that Zack wanted. He could never be the guy that went to Pride with him or moved in with him. That just wasn't going to happen. Zack had said he was fine with that, but clearly, it wasn't enough any more.

'Oh, love,' Gimhana said. He took Zack's hand in his. 'I told you. I'm not out. I can't be. I have to keep you secret. It's—'

'But why? Why do you have to? I don't. You don't *have* to. You choose to.'

'You don't understand,' said Gimhana. He sighed. 'You know that scar on my back? How do you think I got it? I got beaten up when I was fifteen because some boys figured out I was gay. A year later, they broke one of my ribs. My parents thought I was being bullied because I was clever. So they moved me to a different school. When I moved here, to England, I thought it would be different. Guess what? It happened again. This time it was random people I didn't even know. I never saw the guy I was with again. You have no idea.'

'You think?' said Zack, bitterly. 'You think I haven't had any of that? The only difference between you and me is that I'm brave enough to be who I am.'

'Really? What happened when you told your parents? Did they throw you out? Disown you? What?'

'No. Yours might not either.'

Gimhana sighed and pushed himself up to his feet. 'You don't know anything about what it's like. The Sri Lankan diaspora… it's a small world. Anyone could know anyone here. If anyone got the slightest suspicion about us, it would be everywhere within a matter of days. And my parents aren't as open-minded and understanding as yours. No one in my family is.' He pinched his eyes shut and opened them again. The gulf between them suddenly seemed huge. 'You wouldn't understand.'

'But this Chaya would?'

'Oh, for heaven's sake. She's a friend. There's no need to get jealous. I'm not sleeping with her.' Which was true. He was only married to her on paper.

'So you say.'

'Oh grow up.' The minute he said it he wished he could take it back.

Zack drew a long, slow breath. His lips pressed together.

'I'm sorry,' said Gimhana. 'I didn't mean that.' He was only a few years older than Zack, but between Zack's student status and his own long, long years of working, he sometimes felt so much older.

'Yes, you did,' Zack said. 'It's always there, isn't it? You're the one who makes the rules and that's how you like it. I can't do that, Gim.' He shook his head. 'I think… I think I'd like you to take me back home now, please. Or to the nearest train station. I can make my way back from there.'

'Zack. Darling, don't be like that.'

Zack stood up and faced him. Tears glistened in his eyes. 'We both know this conversation has been a long time coming. You aren't willing to be seen with me. You're ashamed of me. I don't think I can carry on being in this… non relationship. You might be okay with hiding, but I'm not.'

Gimhana felt his throat closing in. 'Please, can we talk about this?' He reached for Zack's hand, but Zack backed away from him, shaking his head.

'There's nothing to talk about, Gim. Is there? You want me, but only in secret. Only on your terms and I'm worth more than that.'

Gimhana wanted to wail. To throw himself at Zack's feet and agree to everything, anything he wanted, but he couldn't. He had built too much of his life around the lies he was living. He couldn't afford to let all of it fall down. 'Yes,' he said quietly. 'You are.' He rubbed a hand over his face. 'Okay. Let's get our stuff. I'll take you home. It's the least I can do.'

Somehow he held it together while he crammed things back into his bags. They drove back in silence, Zack staring out of the window, occasionally sniffing. When he pulled up outside the nondescript terraced house with the overgrown garden in the suburbs, he realised this was the first time he'd seen the shared house Zack lived in. Zack felt he wasn't part of Gim's real life. He wasn't part of Zack's real life either.

Zack murmured his thanks, grabbed his bag out of the boot and walked up to the front door without looking back. Gimhana gripped the steering wheel so hard that his fingernails bit into the leather. Every neuron in his body was screaming at him to go after Zack and tell him he was wrong; that he could stay; that he could be the sort of man Zack needed him to be... But that would be a lie. Probably a bigger lie than any of the other lies he lived with. He had thought he'd known pain before, but that was nothing to the feelings clawing inside him right now. He watched until Zack let himself in and shut the door behind him.

He forced himself to blink back the tears and start the long, lonely drive back home.

Chapter Fifty

Gimhana – 2013, London

Gimhana slouched on the sofa, watching *Jem* on repeat. He took the empty plastic that had once been the top layer off his chocolate coated biscuit selection and started on the second layer. Since he'd come back home early, he had no plans, so there was nothing to stop him wallowing in his misery.

The conversation with Zack played over and over in his mind. He should have told him the truth. But Zack was all about being your authentic self. He would never understand why Gimhana needed to appear married. It wasn't like he'd got married and then come to the realisation he was gay. He'd known all along.

If he'd met Zack first, would it have changed anything? Much as he'd like to say it would, he knew it wasn't true. His work and his family were important to him. The only thing that would have changed is that he might have saved Chaya some pain. He'd truly messed up now.

He chose another biscuit. There was the sound of the front door opening. Shit. Chaya must be home earlier than expected. He scrambled to find the remote to turn *Jem* off. He fumbled it and it fell on the floor. He made a dive for it.

When Chaya came in, he was on his knees, biscuits strewn everywhere, with *Jem and the Holograms* still being Truly Outrageous in pink and yellow on screen. She took in the scene and looked first puzzled, then amused.

'Are you okay?' she said. She picked up the remote and paused the rock music.

'Um… yes,' he said, recovering as best he could. He picked up the biscuits that had fallen on the floor and stacked them up on the side plate he'd used for his sandwich earlier. 'Fine. You're back early.'

'They put some trains on, despite the strike,' she said. She sat on the arm of the sofa and pressed play. The cartoon started again. 'What are you watching?'

There was no way out of this. Gimhana sighed and sat back down. '*Jem and the Holograms.* It's a cartoon show from the eighties. It's about a rock band.'

'It looks familiar,' Chaya said. 'Some of the girls in school were into it. There were…' she gestured with her hands. 'Magazines… or annuals or something.'

'Annuals,' he said. 'And some comics.'

On screen, Jem's earrings flared and she turned back into Jerrica. For a few minutes they both watched. He didn't dare say anything. Although he and Chaya shared a home and a life, this was something he'd never shared with her. It was too personal. Too outside the norm. It was a thing he loved and took comfort in, which made it far too precious. Until now, the only person he'd shared it with was Zack, who had understood completely. Because Zack understood him like no one else did.

He waited. The episode ended. Chaya hit pause and handed the remote control back to him. 'I can see why you like it,' she said. 'It's got the secret double-life thing, which is essentially what you do. It's like Spiderman, but with more glamorous clothing. I can see the attraction.'

'You can?'

'Oh yes.' She stood up.

'And you don't think it's weird?'

She gave him an amused smile. 'Of course I think it's weird,' she said. 'But it clearly makes you happy, so who am I to judge?' She patted him on the shoulder. 'I'm guessing you've had a bad few days at work, if you need comforting. Just let me get sorted and you can tell me about it, huh?'

He nodded. After she left, he stared at the credits frozen on the screen. Chaya had said almost exactly the same thing as Zack had. She understood too, but in a different way. He turned the TV off. And she'd known that he was upset. He needed to think of a reason for him to be in such a state – one that sounded plausible and didn't involve the boyfriend he'd been hiding for months.

He was in a worse tangle than he'd thought.

Chapter Fifty-One

Chaya – London, 2013

Chaya stood at the foot of her bed and surveyed the room. The bed looked fine – neatly made up with Gimhana's pyjamas under one pillow and her own under the other. Satisfied, she turned round to check the rest of the room. The dressing table looked odd with Gimhana's things crowding out her face cream and hair brushes. They'd had to clear his stuff out of the guest room so that Nayana could have it for a fortnight. Since most of the wardrobe space in the master bedroom was taken up with her clothes, they'd had to move his suits into the study, in a brand new wardrobe.

Gimhana, who was now dressed for work, came in and picked up his hairbrush. He caught her anxious expression in the mirror. 'Relax,' he said. 'It all looks fine.'

He was taking Nayana's visit in his stride, or appeared to be, anyway. She had noticed that he wasn't his usual self sometimes though, lately, so perhaps he was worrying too. He was just so much better at hiding things than she was. 'Do you think she'll think it weird that your suits are all in the study? I mean, don't normal couples manage to squeeze everything into their bedroom?'

He opened a pot of Brylcreem and ran some through his hair. It always impressed her how he managed to stop short of making it look greasy. 'I don't think she'll find it strange. I have a lot of suits,' he said, patting a last stray lock into place. 'Besides, it's our house. We can keep my suits wherever we want.'

Chaya sat down on the bed, whatever drive it was that gave her strength, suddenly draining away. 'I suppose.' She rubbed her face with her palms.

Gimhana frowned into the mirror. 'You okay?' He turned and looked at her. 'What time did you go to bed last night?'

'This morning,' she corrected him. 'About two o'clock.'

'Again?' he said. 'Chaya.'

'I know, I know,' she said. 'But I've got everything together. I want to get my application in this morning, so that when Nayana gets here, I'm free to give her my attention.'

'That sounds sensible,' he said. 'But you need to get some sleep.'

'Tonight,' she said. 'Tonight, I'll sleep. Once my application is in and my niece has been safely collected.' She yawned.

'Make sure you do,' he said. He looked around the room. 'I think this looks great. All completely normal,' he said. 'The guest room looks good too. She's going to have a great time.' He came over and put his hands on her shoulders. 'Relax, okay. It'll all be fine.' He smiled his 'I'm here. I'll look after you' smile.

She nodded. 'I hope you're right.'

'Besides,' said Gimhana, straightening up. 'I reckon a lot of married people are too tired to sleep together anyway.' He grinned. 'Especially after seven years.'

Chaya managed a smile. 'Seven years. Isn't that when you get the itch and start sleeping with other people?'

He looked surprised, then laughed. 'Come on,' he said. 'Let's get breakfast.'

–

They sat opposite each other, the way they always did at mealtimes. It made it easier to talk. Over the years they'd split the territory of the table between them. Chaya's side had academic papers piled on it at one end. The other side had Gimhana's cooking and gardening magazines and the occasional file. Two Blackberry chargers sat side by side at the end.

'This is weird,' said Chaya. 'I can't believe I'm so nervous. It's only Nayana, for heaven's sake.'

Gimhana chewed thoughtfully before replying. 'I guess we haven't had anyone from home come to visit us before. It's easier when we go to them. Now we have to worry about how our lives have marked our environment.' His eyes roamed over the room. 'I don't think our house is that different to a normal one,' he said. 'I'm sure it'll all be fine.'

Chaya sighed.

'I can't believe Nayana's eighteen,' said Gimhana. 'I remember her when she was at our wedding. She was such a cute thing. How old was she?'

Chaya took a mouthful of cereal. She had bought the packet especially for Nayana's benefit. Normally, neither she nor Gimhana had breakfast at home. It had been a long time since she'd had cornflakes, she'd almost forgotten what they tasted like. For a moment it reminded her of being at university. She forced her mind back to the safer territory of the present. 'Ten, I think,' she said. She thought about it, calculating. 'Yes, about ten, nearly eleven.'

'Wow,' said Gimhana, shaking his head. 'She's quite the young lady now. It's so hard to imagine sometimes.'

'Yes,' said Chaya. 'It is.'

–

In his office, waiting for his computer to start up, Gimhana took out his phone and texted Zack again.

I miss you. Please, can we talk?

There was no response. There never was.

He sighed, put his phone back in his pocket and logged into his work inbox.

Chapter Fifty-Two

Chaya – London, 2013

A quick check on her Blackberry showed Chaya that the flight was on time. Not wanting to keep Nayana waiting, she left for the airport in plenty of time and ended up a good half hour too early. She ducked into the bathroom and checked herself in the mirror. Her hair was cut in a smart chin-length bob and sprayed into submission so that it looked sleek. She leaned forward and checked her make-up. Even with a decent amount of concealer, you could see the bags under her eyes. She had become quite adept at putting on subtle make-up now – a hint of eyeshadow, a touch of lip gloss, just enough to highlight what was good, without being obvious. Details were important. This was something she'd learnt from Gimhana; take care of the details and the big picture looked after itself.

A South Asian lady in a sari with a cardigan over it came and stood next to her. She looked tired and was probably at the end of a long journey. She looked sideways at Chaya in the mirror, appraising her. Next to this old lady, with her tired eyes and wispy salt and pepper hair, Chaya looked like a creature from another time. Chaya smiled and nodded to the lady and was given a bemused glare in return. She shrugged and went out into the foyer.

The arrivals board told her the plane had landed. It would still be a while before everyone made it through to the exits. She got herself a cup of coffee and joined the crowd of people who were drifting towards the arrivals gate. The flight came via the

Middle East, so the crowd was mostly Sri Lankans interspersed with Arab faces.

Chaya found a decent spot from which to watch. She carefully shielded her coffee against the jostling that was sure to start soon and fixed her eyes on the gate.

The last time she'd seen Nayana was when she went back for Thatha's funeral. She didn't like to think about it. Chaya and Malini, both torn with grief themselves, had had to practically carry Amma up to the crematorium. For a moment Chaya had a flash of remembrance; the dust rising from the sun-baked ground, the animal wails coming from Amma who was slumped, sobbing against her. It had been eight months, yet it seemed simultaneously like years and only days ago.

A small child walked into the side of her leg, breaking her from her reverie. She looked down. The little girl looked up at her with huge brown eyes, then gave her a gap-toothed smile, giggled, and ran back to her mother. Chaya looked up and caught the mother's eye. The woman mouthed 'sorry' and Chaya waved it away with another smile.

She returned to her coffee and contemplation. Nayana coming to stay had been Ajith's idea. When Nayana had expressed a desire to follow her grandfather's footsteps into the hotel industry, Ajith felt, with some justification, that after being sheltered from everything for so long, Nayana was too naïve for it. His solution was to send her to her aunt for a couple of weeks in the hope that the experience of travelling alone would be useful. It would also give her a chance to practise her English.

People started to trickle out of the exit, pushing trolleys towering with suitcases and boxes, some tied up with coconut rope. The press of people around Chaya got heavier. As more passengers came out, the semblance of order disintegrated. A child broke free from under the cordon and hurtled towards a man who left his trolley to swing his son up and kiss him. The boy was soon followed by his mother and brother and the family formed a tight little island in the middle of the flow of passengers. Soon the whole corridor was blocked with knots of people hugging, kissing cheeks and slapping each other on the back.

It took Chaya a few moments to spot Nayana. She was pushing a trolley with one suitcase and a backpack on it. For a moment Chaya was struck by how like her mother she looked. Nayana had Malini's fine features, but without the hint of roundness that had always bothered Malini. From Ajith, she had inherited height and hair that was thick and straight. She carried herself with that unconscious grace that teenagers have. Two boys who were following their parents gawped at her, but she didn't seem to notice.

Chaya waved, but Nayana didn't spot her in the crowd. She stood still, gripping her trolley and looking around, occasionally rising on tiptoe to see better. Chaya ducked under the now defunct cordon and weaved her way through the bodies until she was next to her niece.

'Nayana?' she said, touching her on the elbow.

Nayana jumped and turned round. 'Chaya Punchi!' She grinned and dropped into an awkward genuflection. Chaya acknowledged it with a light touch on her forehead. Suddenly, she didn't know what to say. Her niece was in her custody now, her responsibility. She didn't know how to look after a teenager. She smiled, a little self-consciously, and said, 'Shall we go?' in Singhalese. Reaching across, she took the trolley and set off at a determined pace, anxious to get herself and Nayana out of the crowded airport and into the relative calm of her house.

–

The next day, Chaya took Nayana on a whistlestop tour of London. They walked around all morning, taking photos of Nayana next to various monuments. Finally, they ducked into a café for a cup of tea and a slice of cake.

'I think that's most of the major places,' said Chaya, as she finished her coffee. 'Is there anywhere else you'd like to see?'

Nayana swirled her drink in its cup. She looked up. 'I'd quite like to see Westminster Bridge,' she said.

'Whatever for?'

'I want to see where Gimhana Bappa proposed to you.' Nayana smiled.

'Ah.' Chaya nodded. After they'd been to buy their engagement ring, she and Gimhana had ended up on Westminster Bridge. They'd stopped to look at the sunlight and tourists on the river and Gimhana had commented on what a romantic spot it would have been to propose. Never one to let a good idea go to waste, he had taken her back there the next night and formally presented her with the ring. It had been a cold and overcast night, but when the story was repeated to friends and family, the stars twinkled on the water and the moon was bright in the sky. The juxtaposition of reality and fiction amused Chaya; it was Gimhana all over. She smiled. 'Okay,' she said. 'Drink up and I'll take you there.'

They joined the flow of people walking across Westminster Bridge. A group of boys swaggered past. One of them winked at Nayana and blew her a kiss. Nayana looked at her aunt. 'Boys are the same everywhere,' she said, flushing slightly.

'Yes,' said Chaya. 'They are.'

They stopped at the middle of the bridge. 'Here we are,' Chaya leaned her elbows on the railing. 'Those are the Houses of Parliament.' She pointed. 'That thing over there is the London Eye.'

They stood there side by side, watching the light glint off the slow-moving water. A boatful of tourists slid down the river, a couple of them waved to the people on the bridge. Nayana waved back. People continued to flow behind them. Nayana gazed at the river, her eyes wide as she took it all in. Chaya looked at her niece and thought how beautiful she was. Barely eighteen, she was both adult and child at the same time. How did Malini cope with the burden of looking after something so precious and vulnerable? There was so much to protect her from. She resisted the urge to put an arm round the girl and shield her from the crowd. Was this what it was like to be a parent? She let her gaze slip down to the river. She was glad she and Gimhana had decided not to have children.

Nayana sighed. 'You're so lucky.'

'Pardon?'

'You... you've got a really cool life and you live in a really cool city. You've got the career you've always wanted, a nice house, great holidays...' She trailed off, suddenly looking embarrassed. Chaya stared at her. She and Gimhana had worked hard to portray the perfect life. She hadn't realised how well they'd succeeded.

After a few moments she said, 'Actually, a lot of it was down to hard work.' Nayana gave her a thoughtful look and then nodded as though conceding that perhaps hard work did come into the equation. Her eyes suddenly lit up. 'What about marrying Gimhana Bappa?' she said. 'Meeting the right man was luck, wasn't it?'

Chaya's lips tightened for a moment, then she managed a smile. 'Yes,' she said. 'That was a stroke of luck.'

—

They caught the bus back across town. As Nayana pressed her face against the window, drinking in the sights of everyday London, Chaya watched her niece and thought about how she'd held her as a toddler. Nayana was the only person in Sri Lanka she'd told about Noah, yet she would have no recollection of the secrets her aunt had whispered to her as she paced around the room, trying to soothe her to sleep. Chaya always found the fiction of her life hardest when it came to Nayana. Yet Nayana believed everything as true. She had no reason not to.

Chaya looked at her engagement ring and turned her hand so that it caught the light. Since her engagement to Gimhana, she'd half-heartedly been to counselling and whole-heartedly read countless self help books. She'd started taking care of how she looked, altered the way she moved, learned to be better at conversation. Even though she wasn't working any harder at work, she seemed to be having more success, and she put it down to her new, more sociable, persona. She felt almost in control of her mental health. Almost. She knew that she wasn't being herself, but somewhere along the line she'd forgotten what her real self was like. All she could do now was polish her new self until it shone.

Chapter Fifty-Three

Chaya – London, 2013

'I'm going to phone Amma. My amma, I mean. Your achchi,' said Chaya. 'Do you want to talk to her?'

They were back home from another day of sightseeing. Nayana was curled up in a chair looking at the day's photos on her digital camera. She looked up. 'Depends what mood she's in.' A sad smile flickered across her face. 'If she's normal, then maybe…'

Chaya nodded. She understood how Nayana felt.

Thatha's loss had hit Amma hard. Even though they'd known he had a weak heart for years, his sudden death still blindsided everyone. After the initial outburst of grief, Amma seemed to contract into herself, attempting to shut out the real world. Chaya, of all people, understood how she felt. She spent days and nights with Amma, talking to her, encouraging her to eat, trying to coax her out. Eventually, Amma resurfaced but she was not the person she once was. Some days she was 'normal', when she was hopelessly saddened by Thatha's absence, other days she forgot who people were, still other days she was para-noid and angry at the world. Malini had suggested that Amma move in with her, but Amma had refused, preferring instead to stay in the house where her late husband's presence echoed.

Chaya imagined the telephone ring bouncing off the walls and furniture in the living room. She wondered if Amma would answer it, or just leave it to ring. Leela was still there, but she was getting old too.

'Hello?' said Amma's familiar voice.

'Amma, it's me.'

There was a pause. 'Who is this?'

'It's Chaya.'

Another pause. 'Ah,' she said. 'Chaya. Of course. Sorry, Duwa, my mind was on something else.'

'How are you, Amma?' Chaya said, cautiously.

'Oh, I'm fine. How is England?'

Relief crept over Chaya. It sounded like Amma was having a good day. 'It's good,' she said. 'We've got Nayana visiting us.'

'That's nice,' said Amma absently. 'How is Gimhana Putha?'

'He's fine too. Working hard, you know how it is.'

'You must look after him. Make sure you cook him something nice when he gets home.'

Chaya suppressed a smile. 'I will.' She wondered if she should fetch Nayana. Amma seemed to be normal.

'Listen Duwa,' said Amma. 'I have to go. Your thatha is going to come home early today and we're going to the cinema.'

Chaya's heart sank. Not entirely normal then. Amma frequently retreated to a time just before Thatha's death. At least that way she was happy. 'Are you going to see anything nice?' Chaya said, carefully.

Amma named a Singhalese film that had been showing several years earlier. 'It's supposed to be very good. Now that you girls have gone, Thatha and I are trying to go out more.' She gave a girlish giggle. 'We went to the theatre last week.'

'Really? Was it fun?'

'Oh yes. It was fantastic. Now, I really have to go and get ready.'

'Okay Amma, you have a good time. I'll call you again next week.'

'Thunsaranai Chaya.'

Chaya put the phone down and closed her eyes. She pictured Amma, all dressed up and waiting for her husband who would never come.

Nayana popped her head round the door. Seeing that Chaya had hung up already, she raised her eyebrows. Chaya sighed and shook her head. Nayana sighed too and withdrew her head. Nayana had been very close to her grandmother and found her decline difficult to bear. Now Nayana avoided contact with her grandmother. Chaya wished she could do the same and remember her parents the way they had been before, but she knew that was impossible.

-

Later that evening, they had a ready meal for dinner. Normally, Gimhana cooked, but Nayana had wanted to try shepherd's pie, so Chaya had bought one.

'What do you think?' she said. 'Is it what you imagined?'

'It's nice,' said Nayana, taking a tentative mouthful. 'I expected a bit more... something.' She slowly took another tiny mouthful.

Chaya nodded. Without needing to be told, she knew why Nayana was playing with her food. 'There's a jar of katta sambal in the spice cupboard,' she said.

Nayana grinned. 'Thanks, I didn't want to be rude...' She stood up. Chaya waved her apology away. 'For these few weeks, this is your home, you should be able to just relax and be yourself.' She watched Nayana go into the kitchen. 'It's in the third cupboard from the left,' she said, even though the cupboards, shelves and jars were all individually labelled.

'Lunch was really expensive,' said Nayana, coming back to the table and dolloping a spoonful of chilli, onion and Maldive fish onto the side of her plate. 'Is everything so expensive in London?'

'Mostly,' said Chaya.

Nayana seemed to think about this. They ate in silence for a while. Suddenly, Nayana said, 'Can we go to Oxford one day?'

'Oxford?' Chaya went cold. It took some effort to keep her expression neutral. It was inevitable that she would have to take

Nayana to Oxford during her stay. She just wasn't sure how she would deal with it.

'Yeah, I can see your college, maybe watch some people rowing.'

'Erm... yes, of course.' Chaya looked at her plate. Why did she feel this wrench inside? She had been to Oxford before, for conferences and meetings. She had always maintained a professional detachment, preferring to move from train to taxi to venue, rather than amble through the city where memories might accost her at any point. 'Provided Gimhana Bappa is able to come.'

Nayana looked up at her. She was a smart girl, more like Ajith in the way her mind pounced on things, than Malini. She couldn't have failed to notice Chaya's reticence.

'Shall I ask him when he comes home?' Nayana said, her smile disarming.

—

Chaya was marking essays at the table by the time Gimhana got home. Nayana sat beside her, reading a guidebook to work out what she wanted to see the following day.

Gimhana had been made a partner in his firm soon after he got married. This didn't make any difference to the hours he worked. While Nayana was visiting he had promised to make an effort to come home early, but it was still nearly nine p.m. when he returned that night. The open-plan layout meant that they could see into the kitchen, past the counter that held the stove top.

'Hello ladies!' he said as he breezed straight into the kitchen. 'Have we had a good day?'

'Yes,' said Nayana, putting her finger in the book, so that she didn't lose her place. 'How about you?'

'Not bad,' said Gimhana.

'There's shepherd's pie in the fridge,' said Chaya, not looking up from her marking.

'Lovely.' He dished out a plate of it and put it in the microwave.

Nayana approached the worktop that divided the two rooms and leaned on it. 'Gimhana Bappa,' she said. 'Will you come with us to Oxford on Saturday?'

'Saturday?' said Gimhana, 'I've got a big project on at the moment. We're trying to land work with this venture capital group...'

Chaya looked up. The possibility of having to walk round Oxford without Gimhana for support was unthinkable. Her heart picked up speed. What if the memories got too much for her? What if she had a panic attack in front of Nayana? She tried to project to him the gravity of the situation.

His gaze met hers. For a moment, they stared at each other, communicating without words.

Finally, he said, 'I'm sure I can sort something out. I'll probably work late on Friday.' The microwave pinged. He picked up his plate and came to join Chaya at the table. 'Let's hope we have nice weather for it.'

Chaya gratefully extended a hand and touched his arm. He put his hand over hers and gave it a quick squeeze before settling down to eat.

'So, what sights did you see today?' he said, as he picked up his fork.

Nayana pulled out her camera and started to tell him about their day.

Chapter Fifty-Four

Chaya – Oxford, 2013

The outskirts of Oxford had changed over the years, but Chaya recognised the countryside as it slid past. The closer the train got to the station, the more her memories weighed on her. The last year she'd spent there, her final year, had been a weary exercise in study and despondency. The feeling of despair was still there, just waiting for her to step out onto the platform.

When the train pulled into Oxford, Gimhana sprang into action, storing his laptop in his backpack and taking the picnic basket down from the overhead shelf. He ushered Chaya and Nayana off the train, which was just as well, or Chaya wouldn't have got off. She let herself be hustled gently into the main station.

'Right,' Gimhana said, opening the map. 'I think we should go and see all the main sights first. Chaya can fill us in on any interesting facts as we go past.'

The world closed in. There was a knot in her chest, taking up room where her lungs should be. Chaya took a deep breath, trying to loosen up the anxiety before it got any bigger, as she had been taught by one of the counsellors she'd seen.

Gimhana nudged her shoulder with his. She looked up and met his gaze. His eyes gestured towards Nayana. Yes. Nayana. She had to focus on Nayana. She took a deep breath and tried to focus on the here and now.

'I want to see Chaya Punchi's college,' said Nayana.

'We can do that en route,' said Gimhana, pointing it out on the map. 'Okay, let's see now, we head off… that way. Is that right?'

Chaya nodded. They set off towards town. As they crossed the low bridge over the canal into Oxford proper, Gimhana offered her his arm. She slipped her hand through it, grateful for the support and the reminder of how far she'd moved on.

–

The weather brightened. It was almost as though the city itself had decided to make a special effort to welcome her back. Nayana appeared to have read everything she could get her hands on about Oxford and had a list of places she wanted to see, at the top of which was Chaya's old college.

'Has it changed much since you were here?' said Nayana.

Chaya looked around. The main quad looked the same as it had always done. Ivy clung to the stonework. Music and voices trickled down from the rooms above.

'No,' she said. 'The older parts of town don't usually change very much.'

Nayana photographed the windows that peeped through the greenery. 'Did you live in one of these rooms?'

'No, I never came up high enough on the room ballot. I lived in one of the newer buildings.' In her final year, she'd avoided halls and lived in a college house in Jericho with Sara and a few others. She remembered little of those rooms. Not the layout of the rooms, nor the colour of the walls. They had passed in an exhausted haze.

Curiously, she could remember every essay she'd written, every lecture, every hard-earned mote of knowledge.

'Is it far to where your room was?' said Nayana, still gaping at the quad.

'I'll show you if you like.' Chaya led them under the archway and through to the smaller quad flanked by stone buildings on two sides and a concrete monstrosity on the third.

'My room was...' said Chaya, counting the windows until she found the right one, 'that one. Third floor, second along.'

Nayana took a photo of it. Chaya knew it would be shown to the family. *And this is Chaya Punchi's room when she was a student.*

A girl wearing a dress over a pair of jeans was lying on the bench in the quad, reading. She looked up to give them that disdainful look that students reserved for tourists. Chaya remembered that look. She wondered if she'd ever used it herself. It seemed so strange that she should now be on the receiving end of it. This place had been hers for four years. Yet now, she was almost a stranger to it. It stayed the same, almost untouched by the ever-changing tide of students who, although dressed differently, were also, basically, the same. She wondered if, at this moment, there was a serious Sri Lankan girl in a college somewhere, falling in love with a man whom she was doomed to lose. She closed her eyes to dislodge the idea.

Seeing the places from her past through the eyes of her young niece, breathed on memories she'd tried hard to bury. At times, Chaya was unable to tell her anything about a place. The only things she could think of were along the lines of, 'Noah once bought me a rose from a wandering seller there,' or 'Noah used to lock his bike to that sign.' She felt the panic start to rise and did her best to control it, turning away from Nayana, so that she didn't see it. At these times, Gimhana would step in, smoothly reading extracts from the guidebook and directing Nayana's attention away. Chaya clung to his arm, no longer able to let go.

They walked round several colleges and ended up in the University Parks, sitting on the grass by the Rainbow Bridge. They had their lunch watching some children play poohsticks. Chaya sat with her back to the pond where Noah had once tried to skip stones to impress her. The hairs on the back of her neck stood to attention as the water seemed to call its presence to her.

Nayana lay back on her elbows and sighed. 'So, this was what your life was like, as a student,' she said.

'Not entirely,' said Chaya. 'I spent most of it in libraries, studying. That's what I was here to do.'

Nayana waved a hand. 'Still,' she said. 'You got to be here and hang out in this amazing city. That's just...' she swept out her arm to embrace the river, the ducks, the bridge and the parks, '...incredible.' She sighed and laid back. 'I wish I could have that!' she closed her eyes.

Chapter Fifty-Five

Gimhana – London, 2013

Back at home, Gimhana checked his phone for calls or emails while Chaya and Nayana were busy upstairs. He had sent Zack another long email apologising, but all he'd got back was a brief response: *I don't want to live in hiding.* Since then, nothing.

He stared at the last message and felt the emptiness gnawing inside him. He missed Zack more than he'd thought possible. He tried to tell himself that it was a blessing in disguise. His relationship with Zack had been risky at best. If Chaya found out, she'd be furious that he'd broken the rules he himself had helped set up. If Zack found out about Chaya being his wife, rather than his housemate… well, Zack deserved better than that.

For a second he indulged in the fantasy where he lived with Zack instead of Chaya. Could that ever happen? He thought of his parents and how they loved Chaya, even if she didn't give them the grandchild they so desperately wanted. They would never extend the same welcome to Zack. Ever.

It was for the best. Honestly. He put his phone in his pocket and sighed. If only he could believe that.

Chaya came past, carrying a basket of washing. He followed her into the kitchen and got down the Ovaltine. 'It's been a full day,' he said.

She looked up from where she was kneeling in front of the washing machine. 'It has. Thank you for being there.' Her eyes met his. 'I don't think I'd have managed without you.'

'I'm always here for you,' he said.

'I know,' she said. 'I'm grateful.' She sighed. 'I really am.' She sighed again. 'The next thing to deal with is Manchester.'

He nearly dropped the Ovaltine. 'What?'

'She's got a cousin, from Ajith's side, in Salford. She wants to go and see her, maybe stay overnight with her. I said I'd take her up and stay in the city, so that I can meet her and come back with her.'

Salford. Where Zack was. 'Can't you just put her on the direct train? Her cousin can meet her at the other end.'

Chaya stood up. 'I could. But I'd worry the whole time.'

'You'd worry the whole time anyway.' Never mind her, he'd worry the whole time. He couldn't go up there. What if they ran into Zack?

She sighed. 'I know it's silly, but I'd feel better knowing that I was able to get to her quickly if she needed me.' She frowned. 'Does that sound mad?'

'Yes,' he said. 'A bit. She's eighteen. She took a plane halfway across the world. She can cope with a train journey, surely.'

'I know, but I'd feel better…' She gave him a suspicious look. 'You don't need to come. We can go without you.'

He had to stop protesting or she'd know something was up. He needed to go and see his client at some point anyway. He had hoped to try and persuade Zack to meet with him, but it was clear that that wasn't going to happen. 'Let's all go,' he said. 'I'll have to work, but you can spend some time in Manchester. Maybe take in an art gallery or something.'

She grimaced. 'Actually, I was thinking I might go to the cinema. It'd be nice to sit in the dark and not have to be upbeat for a bit.'

He nodded. Yes. Hiding from the world. That would be so nice. He was tired. So, so tired of having to carry on – getting on with work, being a supportive friend to Chaya – while inside his heart was crumbling.

The stairs thumped as Nayana came downstairs. Gimhana asked her if she wanted a hot drink. He bent his head over the mugs, glad for the excuse to look away before Chaya saw through him.

Chapter Fifty-Six

Chaya – London, 2013

'What's that you're watching, Nayana?' said Chaya, perching on the arm of her niece's chair. Since the teenager had arrived, they spent more time in their living room than usual. Normally, Chaya and Gimhana would sit at the dining table, tapping away at their laptops in companionable silence.

'A programme about volcanoes.' Nayana shifted position to give Chaya more room and tucked her feet under her.

'Is it interesting?'

Nayana shrugged. 'It's okay. They had some spectacular aerial shots earlier.'

Chaya watched as a camera panned up the side of a mountain and the voiceover talked them through the formation of volcanic ridges. A bearded man, a geophysicist from California, according to the caption, came on and started talking earnestly about plate tectonics.

'I might join you in a minute,' said Chaya, standing up. 'Does anyone want a cup of tea?'

Gimhana, who was lying stretched out on the sofa reading a report, looked up. 'I'll have one, if you're making.'

'Nayana?'

'Can I have hot chocolate?'

'Sure.' Chaya slipped out into the kitchen.

Waiting for the kettle to boil, she got the tea things out of her well-ordered cupboards. On the whole, she felt Nayana's trip was going rather well. She, Nayana and Gimhana were getting along and her niece didn't seem to think there was anything odd about their life. She smiled to herself as she measured out the chocolate powder. Maybe Gimhana was right. They did look normal.

She took the tray of hot drinks into the living room. There were pictures of erupting deep-sea volcanoes and the voiceover was intoning an explanation. Chaya ignored the TV, concentrating on not spilling the drinks as she put them down on the table. She handed Nayana her hot chocolate, which the latter accepted without taking her eyes off the screen.

Chaya was in the act of passing Gimhana his tea, when a familiar voice cut through her saying 'On a geological time scale...' She knew that voice.

Noah?

Chaya spun round. There he was, on the screen, talking nervously to the camera, his eyes darting occasionally to look at someone off screen and then darting back again. His name appeared briefly underneath his left arm: 'Noah Burlescombe-West, University of Alberta.' He was seated on a rocky outcrop, the sea forming the background. As he warmed to his subject, he waved his arm in a sweeping motion.

Chaya felt the world close in. Everything disappeared; only her and the image of Noah remained.

A gust of wind blew Noah's hair, thinner now, but still red, into his eyes. He flicked it off his face with a gesture so familiar that Chaya thought her heart could break all over again. She backed away from the screen.

The picture changed to a computer simulation. As if she'd been released from a spell, sensations rushed back. Her pulse roared in her ears. The mug was burning into her fingertips. Hot tea had scalded the delicate webbing between forefinger and thumb. She felt the walls around her lean in. She turned and fled the room.

Suddenly, there was an arm round her. A hand extracted the mug from her and gently guided her to sit on the stairs.

Chaya was gasping for air. Her vision had taken on a fragmented quality. The atmosphere in the hallway was too thin to breathe. Everything pulsed. A brown paper bag appeared over her mouth and nose. Gimhana's voice said, 'Breathe slowly. Come on, there's a good girl.'

He held her next to him, stroking her hair. 'It's okay. I'm here.'

When her breath returned and the world swam back into focus, Chaya blinked. She was about to speak when she noticed Nayana, face taut with worry, standing next to her.

'What happened?' said Nayana.

'Migraine,' said Gimhana, quickly. 'It happens sometimes. They come on suddenly. She'll be okay. Come on darling, let's get to you bed.' He helped her to her feet and started to half-carry her up the stairs. 'She'll be fine with a couple of migraine pills. You finish watching your programme.'

Chapter Fifty-Seven

Gimhana – London, 2013

Gimhana ushered Chaya upstairs, gently. It had been a while since she'd been like this, but he still knew what to do. He guided her to sit on the bed. Her vision was probably still unstable. Her panic attacks almost always left her with residual visual effects.

'Vision okay?' he asked, taking her hand and checking the burn on it. Not too bad.

Chaya shook her head, still unable to speak properly. Her breathing was shallow.

'What happened?' Gimhana frowned to remember. 'Was it something on the telly?'

Chaya nodded.

'That guy on the TV. Was it someone you knew?'

Another nod.

'Was it... him?'

Chaya blew out her cheeks and blinked hard. Her breathing was getting less shallow now. She seemed to be forcing herself to breathe properly. Gimhana kept hold of her hand, knowing that she would start shaking in a minute. For a while, he said nothing. Finally, he said, 'You still think about him.' It wasn't a question.

She caught his eye. Of course she thought about him. She had been through the pain he was going through now. She'd done it when she was much younger and already under a huge amount of other stress and it had destroyed her. He was old now, and strong. If he'd felt this level of pain when he was twenty, whilst simultaneously trying to keep up with a punishing under-graduate curriculum, he would have crumbled too. 'I'm sorry,' he said.

'I try not to,' said Chaya. The trembling started. Her jaw clenched. He reached around her and pulled a pillow up for her to lean against.

'It's fine most of the time,' she said. She shuddered again. She let out a long breath and seemed to force herself still. 'I don't know why it's happening now.' She removed her hand from his and rubbed her eyes.

'It must have been the trip to Oxford and then this... each by itself would probably have been okay.' He watched her, worried. 'You've been working so hard preparing your submission for the prof job. I think maybe you over-stretched yourself.'

Chaya looked towards the door. 'I should get back down-stairs to Nayana.'

'No. You stay here. I'll tell her you're fine.' He paused at the door and looked at her. 'It's going to be fine,' he said.

Chaya gave a brief nod and let her head drop back against the pillows. Poor thing. Panic attacks always left her feeling drained. It had been a long time since she'd had a full-on attack like that. It was such a shame it had happened in front of Nayana.

He went downstairs to find Nayana sitting on the edge of the sofa, TV off, hot chocolate untouched. The poor child must have been really confused.

'She's okay now,' he said. 'It was just ... a migraine. It happens from time to time. We thought the medication—'

'It was some sort of attack, wasn't it?' said Nayana. 'Or a seizure.'

Wow. Okay. 'It was an anxiety attack. Not a seizure. I'm sorry, I wasn't meaning to mislead you. I thought perhaps you'd know more about migraines than panic attacks.'

Nayana gave him a disdainful look. Of course. Milliennials. They had the internet at their fingertips.

'Anyway,' he said. 'The main thing is, it's passed. She'll have a headache for a while now. So, I'm going to get her some of her sleeping pills and she'll be right as rain by the morning.'

The teenager looked at the floor and shifted uncomfortably.

'Nayana, is something wrong?' He perched on the arm of the chair opposite her. 'You can ask me anything, you know.'

Nayana fidgeted, looking far too young to be eighteen. 'It's just... is she ill?' Her voice dropped until it was barely audible. 'Mentally.'

Gimhana blinked. He knew what stigma mental illness carried. He had seen how stress forced colleagues to take time off and how badly it affected their careers. He had also seen the lengths Chaya went to hide the strain, because any kind of weakness on her part would affect her chances at work. There was more awareness now than a decade ago, but still, the stigma hadn't fully disappeared. People didn't know how to act around you if they knew you were depressed or anxious. If it was viewed so negatively here, he didn't dare imagine what it must be like in Sri Lanka. It would probably be viewed as badly as divorce or, heaven forbid, homosexuality.

'Mental illness is just like any other illness,' he said, in his best teacher's voice. 'You can take medication for it. Chaya was prone to anxiety, but isn't any more. Sometimes, when she's really tired, she has a relapse, but it's nothing to be scared of.' He stood up and patted Nayana's shoulder. 'She'll be fine in the morning. Why don't you go up and see her?'

He listened to her tread on the stairs. That was close. First the whole disaster that was the day in Oxford, where he'd had to distract Nayana while Chaya tried to hold herself together, and now this. Chaya tended to relapse under extreme strain. Neither of them had fully anticipated how much pressure would come with having someone living with them, even for a period as short as two weeks. There was no room to decompress.

Still. Only a few more days and they could relax. There was Manchester to deal with first.

Chapter Fifty-Eight

Gimhana – London, 2013

Gimhana packed a few files to take with him when he went to see his client while he was up north. Client meeting aside, he was intending to spend some time with Chaya. The idea of going to Manchester with Chaya was fraught with risk. There were too many memories of Zack and always the risk of running into someone he knew.

Manchester was to him what Oxford had been to Chaya. Only he didn't have a decade and a half of distance to soften the blow. He had faith that he could manage. He was made of sterner stuff than his wife. He was pretty sure he could deal with his feelings without anyone noticing. While Nayana was spending the day with her distant cousin, Gimhana and Chaya would be free to do whatever they liked.

Gimhana sighed and closed his briefcase. He missed Zack like crazy. It was as though something had been torn out of him and left a wound that wouldn't heal. He'd tried burying himself in his work, but it didn't help. Her niece being there was stressing Chaya out too, which made everything worse. Nayana couldn't have come to visit at a worse time. He and Chaya had worked so hard to build this illusion of a perfect life, it would be terrible if the cracks started to show while Nayana was there to see it.

'Are you okay?' Chaya asked Gimhana, the night before they set off for their trip up north. 'You seem … a little down.'

Alarm shot through him. He kept assuring her he was fine, but she must have seen through that. She was no stranger to pain. That was one of the things that held them together.

'Ah, it's just more stressful than I thought, you know.' He paused and listened. The shower was running in the bathroom. It was safe to talk about Nayana. 'Nayana being here. I keep expecting something to go wrong. It's hard being on high alert all the time.'

Chaya nodded. 'It is, isn't it?' she said. 'Ever since my panic attack, she keeps looking at me as though she expects me to shatter. I've told her I'm okay, but I can tell she's worried.' She sat on the bed, next to the suitcase she was packing. Everything was folded with excruciating precision. The more Chaya worried, the more precise she got with everything. Her hands twitched in her lap. She observed him, frowning. 'But it's more than that, bothering you. You seem… sad.'

He froze. Sad. Did that describe it? Not even close.

'Gimhana, is there something going on with you?' She said it quietly. She had never asked him about his private life before. It was understood that it was outside of the sphere that contained her. She leaned forward and touched his arm. 'Can I help?'

He shook his head. 'No. Nothing I can't handle.' He didn't meet her eye, but patted the hand that was resting on his. 'Don't worry, though. It's nothing that will get in the way of this…' He made a small gesture that encompassed the room, the house, their life. 'This, whatever it is we have.'

Chaya gave him a tight little smile. 'Nayana being here certainly makes you question things, huh?'

'Something like that,' he said. 'But we're doing okay. It's less than a week before she goes home. We'll manage until then.'

In the bathroom, the shower stopped.

Chaya nodded. 'Yes,' she said in a whisper. 'I love her dearly, but I can't wait for life to go back to normal.'

Gimhana managed a grin and went back to his reading. For him, life would never be normal again.

Chapter Fifty-Nine

Gimhana – London, 2013

They had spent the day in Manchester. Gimhana went to work, while Chaya took Nayana to meet her cousin. Despite his fear that something terrible would happen, much to Gimhana's relief, nothing did. He and Chaya even made it to the cinema, as they had planned, where they both nodded off during the film.

The next morning, they picked Nayana up and started the drive home. The teenager was quiet, unusually so. When Chaya asked how the evening had gone, she gave vague answers. More than once, Gimhana caught her looking at him, with a thoughtful and slightly angry expression on her face. It made him uneasy.

All the way home, he felt it. That quiet animosity towards him. Finally, when they got home, he couldn't take it anymore. When Chaya was out of the room, he said, 'You seem on edge, Nayana? Did something happen while you were with your cousin Chathuri?'

'It depends how you look at it,' said Nayana. Her hostility was no longer veiled. 'I went to the pub with Chathuri. There was a friend of hers there, who was trying to cheer up his friend, who had broken up with his boyfriend.'

Well, this was a weird conversation. Gimhana kept his expression neutral. 'Oh yes? Were you shocked ... by the gay man?'

'I wasn't shocked by the gay man,' she snapped. 'Oh, I know adults in Sri Lanka like to pretend it doesn't happen, but it's not the dark ages.'

'Right. Okay.' So the younger generation were less cosseted than the older one. That was progress.

Nayana's eyes were trained on him. 'He worked out that we were Sri Lankan and started telling us about his ex-boyfriend … who, it turns out, is also Sri Lankan.'

'I see.' Where was this conversation going? He mustn't panic and preempt trouble. His hands felt clammy.

'He said he was very private. But that his ex was a lawyer, older and a smooth-talker… and passed for straight.'

He made several mental leaps. Manchester. Gay man just broken up with his boyfriend. *Sri Lankan* boyfriend. Oh no. It must have been Zack. She must have met him.

He made sure he didn't react. She was watching him carefully. If she was trying to trick him into revealing something, she didn't know who she was dealing with. 'That's interesting, I suppose,' he said blandly.

'Oh come on,' she snapped. 'I know it's you.'

'That's a terrible accusation,' he snapped back. 'I'm going to pretend that you're just talking without thinking because you're tired. I don't want to hear any of this nonsense in front of your aunt.'

She opened her mouth. Teenagers. Why did they always have to argue?

He put up his hand to stop her. 'No,' he said. 'I'm offended. I will not have this.'

She still didn't back down. They glared at each other. Footsteps signalled that Chaya was coming back.

'Fine,' she said, suddenly, her voice very low. 'I'll keep quiet. But only because I know it's already over with him and I don't want to ruin things for Chaya Punchi.' She turned on her heel and marched into the house.

Gimhana waited until she was safely out of sight before slowly leaning against the wall. She knew. She knew and she knew she was right. Shit. Shit. Shit.

Now what happened? From what she'd said, she might not tell anyone. Maybe. Or perhaps she just wasn't going to tell Chaya. Either way, he was grateful for small mercies.

Could he try and brazen it out? Deny everything? Maybe there was enough doubt left in Nayana's mind to make her wonder if she'd missed something.

He would have to be extra nice to her for the last few days she was here.

He wondered how many other people Zack had talked to. He should have known not to talk to other Sri Lankans. Thank goodness he hadn't named him or he couldn't have denied it all. By rights he should be furious with Zack, but all the while, in the back of his mind, the idea that she'd seen Zack, that Zack had been upset enough to talk about him, buzzed. Zack missed him as much as he, Gimhana, missed Zack. Now that there was a connection between him and Gimhana's home life, he really could come clean and tell Zack the truth. Yes, it looked like it was over, but somehow, he felt worse about deceiving Zack than about deceiving Chaya. The least he could do was tell him the truth.

He got his phone out and sent a text.

Forgive me. Meet me for a drink next week? I have something to tell you. Please.

He didn't really expect an answer.

Chapter Sixty

Chaya – London, 2013

Chaya ushered her niece into the reception of Gimhana's office. The building had once been a house and it still had a Victorian vibe on the outside. Inside, it was modern and bright with a nod to its past in the carefully restored feature fireplaces. It had been five days since they got back from their trip up north and Nayana's visit was nearly over.

They hadn't seen much of Gimhana since coming back from Manchester. He had worked late most nights and tended to rush off early. If she didn't know better, she might have thought he was avoiding them. When she had suggested that they all go out for lunch on Nayana's last afternoon, he had been very reluctant to agree. In the end, she'd argued him down to at least go for coffee. She wasn't sure what had happened. Nayana too, was a little quieter than usual. When Chaya had asked her what was wrong, she'd merely said she was really tired. Chaya hoped that was all it was. It would be terrible if something had happened while Nayana was under her care.

The reception desk was in the first room on the left. Leaving Nayana to gawp at the paintings, Chaya went up to the receptionist. 'I'm here to see Mr Gimhana Herath. I'm his wife. He's expecting me.'

'Please take a seat,' she said, gesturing towards the sofas that were opposite. 'He's in a meeting. I'll let his secretary know you're here.'

Chaya sat down. Nayana came and sat next to her. There were several brochures on the table, they each picked one up.

'It's very nice in here,' Nayana said in a whisper.

'They used to be in the centre of London,' Chaya whispered back. 'They bought these premises to bolster that "old fashioned family service" atmosphere.'

'On brand,' said Nayana, approvingly.

Chaya smiled. Nayana seemed to notice these things. You could see her burgeoning interest in the hospitality industry showing itself. Branding. Key customer messaging. She threw these phrases around. Chaya didn't really have much time for that sort of thing. In her line of work you backed everything up with evidence and wrote it down as dispassionately as possible. All this stuff about persuasive copywriting was beyond her. She flipped through the brochure and started reading an article about one of the charities the company supported.

The receptionist said, 'I'm afraid Mr Herath is running a bit late. Can I get you a drink while you wait for him?'

'Oh, tea please,' said Chaya. Nayana ordered the same.

'Two teas. How do you take it?' She jotted it down. 'I'll be just a minute,' she said. But before she could leave, two men came in. One of them, an associate who Chaya had met at one of the office events, asked the receptionist to call a taxi for the other one. They shook hands and the associate left, leaving the younger man in the reception area.

The thing Chaya noticed wasn't the man, but Nayana's reaction to him. She startled, then looked quickly away. She pretended to read the brochure, with her hair hanging down, obscuring her face. Weird.

Chaya looked up to study the man. He was youngish, in his late twenties, maybe early thirties, and handsome, dressed in a smart-casual style that looked at odds with the old-fashioned law firm setting. He had a backpack slung over one shoulder and wore jeans, a shirt and a blazer. He looked slightly flushed. Did Nayana know this man? How?

She glanced back at her niece, who hadn't looked up. When she looked back at the young man, he spotted her looking and smiled. He had a charming smile. If Nayana did know this guy, it was no surprise that she was flustered by him. The man's gaze turned to Nayana. He gave a small frown and tilted his head.

'Excuse me?' he said, stepping forward, one hand slightly outstretched. 'I know you, don't I? You're Chathuri's friend?'

Nayana looked up, redness creeping over her face. 'Uh yeah. Hi.'

'I'm Zack. We met earlier in the week, remember? Up in Salford. In the pub.'

Nayana's eyes darted to Chaya and back to Zack. 'Oh. Yeah. I remember. Nice to see you again.'

'So, what are you doing here?' he asked her.

'This is my aunt,' she said. 'Chaya Punchi, this is Zack.' So far, so obvious.

Chaya nodded in greeting. 'Zack.' Who the hell was this? And why was he making Nayana so uncomfortable? Had something happened between them in Manchester? She watched the interaction through narrowed eyes.

'I just got some angel investment for my app,' Zack said, grinning. There was no awkwardness about him. He seemed entirely genuine. 'I've just signed the contract.' He gestured back towards the offices. 'You guys were right. I have to get on with my life and move on.' He rolled his eyes theatrically. 'I'm not going to let some man get me down.'

O-kay. Now Chaya was even more confused. Nayana kept looking at the door behind Zack.

Nayana cleared her throat. 'My *aunt* and I are here to see my *uncle*,' she said, putting some emphasis on the words 'aunt' and 'uncle'. She was clearly trying to tell him something. What?

Zack didn't seem to understand either. A small crease appeared on his forehead as he tried to work out what he was being told. What *was* he being told? What possible relevance could they have to him?

Zack's frown deepened. His gaze moved to Chaya's face. Something seemed to click. 'Oh,' he said. He looked back at

Nayana, who was making warning eyes at him. He took a small step back, his eyes wide.

'Nayana, what's going on?' said Chaya.

At that moment, the security door opened and the receptionist reappeared carrying a tray with two mugs of tea on it. Behind her came Gimhana.

Chapter Sixty-One

Gimhana – London, 2013

Gimhana stepped into the reception room, just as Zack whirled round. It was a scene from his nightmares. There they were: Zack, Chaya and Nayana. In the same room. The worst possible combination of people.

Zack's face paled. Nayana's had gone bright red. Chaya merely looked confused. Had Nayana told them? Gimhana felt the world stand still.

'Here's your tea Mrs Herath,' said the receptionist.

Zack turned his head. 'Mrs?' he said, faintly.

Chaya started to say something, but Zack was louder. 'So that's why. You. You... bastard!' Zack drew in a shaky breath, released it with an 'ugh!' and marched out of the office.

For a few seconds, Gimhana didn't know what to do. He looked at Chaya. She had gone very still. He knew that look. There would be trouble later.

And Zack. Zack was *here*. He was leaving. Emotions buffeted against each other. He was going to lose everything. What did he want? He could only salvage one relationship. Which was it to be?

'Zack.' He set off at a run. Outside, he looked down the street. Zack was already quite a way away. Gimhana ran after him.

'Zack! Wait.' All the running on the treadmill stood him in good stead. 'Zack!'

He caught up with him just as he got to an underground station. He grabbed his arm, forcing him to stop. 'Please,' he panted. 'We need to talk.'

'What is there to say?' said Zack. 'You lied to me.' He turned to glare at Gim and his eyes were full of tears. 'You cheated and you lied.'

'I didn't,' said Gim. 'Everything I told you was true. She is just a friend and a disguise.'

'You conveniently forgot about the part where you're married to her.'

'What difference does it make? I'm not sleeping with her.'

Zack shook his arm out of Gimhana's grip. He shook his head. 'I can't believe you think that's an excuse. You made a commitment to her. A *public* commitment you weren't willing to make to me. I'm just your tacky secret. How do you think that makes me feel?'

'I'm sorry. I'm really sorry. Please, come back. Let's talk. We can make this better.' He had no idea how, but he would. It was what he did. He found solutions.

Zack bit his lip and shook his head. His eyes brimmed with tears. 'No. We cannot. Nothing can make this better. I can't trust anything you say.'

'But Zack—'

'No,' he said. 'I don't want to talk to you. You disgust me. Leave me alone.' He turned and clattered down the steps.

'Listen—'

'Just leave me alone.'

Gimhana stared after him, watching him until he got swallowed up by the tunnel.

Chapter Sixty-Two

Chaya – London, 2013

Chaya shut her eyes. She had been dreading this for years. They had thought they could get away with this preposterous lie. They had thought they were so clever. Her house of cards was falling over. She saw, very clearly, the scandal that would follow. This was not the sort of thing that could be kept quiet. They would both be humiliated. Her mother would disown her. Malini, Ajith, Nayana, the other relatives, they would all stop speaking to her. She would lose everyone she loved.

Emotions bubbled inside her – fear for the future, regret about her lost life, sorrow that it was little unspoilt Nayana who had uncovered their dirty secret, anger at Gimhana for being so stupid as to get caught. She felt them building up like steam in her chest cavity, making it tighter and tighter until, all at once, something gave.

She opened her eyes. She felt numb, as though she were an impostor in her own body. There was a dull roar all around. She had given up Noah because she didn't want to lose her family. Now she'd lost them anyway. If things had been different, she would at least have had Noah.

Chaya slowly sat back down. The receptionist looked from aunt to niece and said, 'I'll just give you a moment.' She stepped out of the office and pulled the door gently shut behind her.

'Are you okay?' said Nayana, sitting back down beside Chaya. Her concern was sweet. She was clearly more worried about Chaya than about the revelation that her uncle was gay. But then, it seemed she already knew about Zack. How?

'You knew him,' said Chaya. 'How did you know him?' Had Gimhana brought that man to the house? Had he introduced Nayana to him one day when Chaya was somehow not there? How complicit was she in all of this?

'I met him in Manchester. We... went to the union bar and there was a group of people that Chathuri knew. One of them had dragged his housemate out to cheer him up after a break-up. That was Zack. He came over to talk to Chathuri and tell us about this Sri Lankan guy that he'd fallen in love with and how he had dumped him a few weeks ago... and, well, I didn't think anything of it until he said something about how he came up once a month to see clients... and then, the more he said, the more it sounded like Gimhana Bappa. So eventually, I asked about this guy's name. I didn't want to tell you,' she said. Her eyes filled up with tears. 'I thought it would be best if you were happy without knowing.' She wiped her eyes. 'I'm so sorry, Punchi. I'm so, so sorry.'

'Right,' said Chaya. 'So that man, Zack... was Gimhana's friend.'

'Boyfriend,' Nayana corrected her. 'I'm so sorry.'

'Boyfriend,' Chaya acknowledged. 'Whom he saw when he went to Manchester for work.' Well that explained a lot of things. The way he seemed to glow lately when he came back from Manchester. The way he seemed to want to tell her something, but held back. She'd assumed it was something to do with work, but of course, it could equally well have been about sex. She wasn't stupid. She knew that Gimhana satisfied his needs as and when he needed to. She didn't need to know any details, so she didn't ask. All she asked was that he was discreet, so that things looked perfect on the surface.

And now they didn't.

She could feel the horror building. It was coming towards her, a tidal wave of distress, but for now, it was far away. For now, she could be calm and do what she had to do. She drew a breath. 'I think,' she said, 'we should go home. Coffee is probably off the cards.' She stood up.

Nayana stood up too. She was looking at her with wide eyes. She looked frightened now. Chaya squared her shoulders. She felt curiously detached from all of it. It was as though the tsunami was sucking up all her feelings and piling them into the wall of pain that was coming. Later. She would feel it later.

She thanked the receptionist, who seemed mortified to have been involved at all, and left a message for Gimhana to say they'd decided to go home.

'Come, Nayana. Let's go home. We could grab something to take out if you like? What do you fancy?'

Nayana, looking worried, murmured, 'I don't mind.'

'Your flight is tomorrow,' said Chaya. 'We should probably pack and have an early night.'

'Yes, Chaya Punchi.'

Chapter Sixty-Three

Gimhana – London, 2013

Gimhana tramped back to the office. Zack was gone. He had been gone before, but this time it felt worse. Seeing the tears in his eyes had ripped something more out of Gimhana. Now he had to see what his duplicity had done to Chaya. Why was he such an idiot? He had hurt two people that he loved. Once this news got back to his parents, he would hurt them too. He reached the office and stared at the highly polished brass plate. Oh crap. The whole office probably knew by now. His career, his hard-won career was at risk too. The weight in his legs seemed to increase, as though someone had turned the gravity up a notch.

What could he do? First things first. They couldn't sack him. He hadn't done anything wrong and there were laws against discrimination. He was good at what he did and he brought in a lot of good clients. So the first thing to do was tough it out. He straightened his jacket and checked his tie was in place before striding in.

Tina was at the reception desk. 'Oh, Gim,' she said. 'Your wife said she was going home.'

Gimhana nodded, as though Tina hadn't witnessed his ex-boyfriend and his wife finding out about each other. 'Thanks Tina. I'll call her.'

Tina looked like she was about to say something else, but then closed her mouth. Gimhana hurried up to his office and shut himself in. His secretary, thankfully, had gone for lunch.

He checked his calendar. There was nothing that couldn't be moved. He really couldn't face talking to people today. Nor did he want to go home just yet. He could just get his head down and get some work done on the briefs that needed writing up instead.

Chapter Sixty-Four

Chaya – London, 2013

Chaya finished her sandwich. She and Nayana were sitting opposite each other at the dinner table. They'd been eating in silence. Nayana was watching her the way you watch a large spider that is far enough away for you to get on with your work, but still in vision and possibly a threat. Chaya sighed.

'Look, Nayana. I'm sorry you had to be involved in this mess. I'm going to have to talk to Gimhana and I don't want you to get caught in the middle of that.'

'Are you going to get a divorce?'

'I don't know.'

'But how can you not know? He cheated on you. With another man! How can you be so calm?'

This wasn't calm. This was anger and panic so strong that it had burned through normal and was holding her in emotional limbo. 'I'm not calm right now,' she said. 'I'm trying to keep everything in place until I know you're safe. Then... then I'll deal with Gimhana. Although, I really don't know how.'

Right on cue, her phone rang. She checked. Gimhana again. She dismissed the call.

'What are you going to do?' said Nayana. 'My flight isn't until early tomorrow.'

Chaya looked at the ceiling. She could feel herself unravelling, gently fizzing at the edges like an aspirin dropped in water. It would get worse. For now, she had to hold on.

Nayana's attitude suggested that things had changed over the last ten years. If Gimhana could break their deal, then she could too. The world was a different place now. It wouldn't care so much about what she did. But she had to consider Gimhana in this too. She couldn't do that while she was worrying about Nayana as well. 'I think,' she said, slowly, 'I think we should get packed and take you to the airport. We'll book into the airport hotel for tonight, that way there isn't such a rush to get you to check in at three a.m.' She had a thought. Was there any way they could contain this? Limit the damage a little bit... 'I don't suppose I can persuade you not to tell your amma?' she said.

Nayana looked affronted. 'Of course I won't tell,' she said. 'But you're not going to carry on like nothing's happened, are you?' She looked appalled at the idea.

'No,' Chaya said. 'But I don't know what I am going to do yet. It's been a bit of a shock.'

Nayana considered this. 'Yes. I can see that.'

'I need some time to iron out how I feel and work out what to do. Do you understand?' She leaned forward, looking into Nayana's eyes. 'It will take me a while.'

'But you can't stay with him,' said Nayana.

Couldn't she? Did she even want to? She didn't know the answer to any of that. Chaya sighed. 'Life is complicated, little one,' she said.

Nayana stared at her. 'Oh Punchi,' she said. 'You still love him, don't you?'

That response made her head spin. She shook her head. 'It's complicated, okay?'

Nayana sighed. 'Yes. Okay. I understand. I won't tell anyone.'

Chaya nodded and stood up. 'Thank you.' She gathered their plates and put them in the dishwasher in the kitchen. 'Shall we meet back here in an hour?'

Chapter Sixty-Five

Gimhana – London, 2013

Gimhana knocked on the door of Mr Thomas's office, his heart a lead lump in his chest. How typical that this debacle should happen on a day when Barry wasn't in the office. At the deep 'come in', he entered. Mr Thomas was sitting behind a desk with another senior partner. Neither of them smiled.

'Gimhana,' said Mr Thomas. 'Sit, please.'

He sat in a chair opposite the desk. It was like an interview. He took a deep breath and forced a smile.

Mr Thomas said, 'We've heard about a certain situation in the reception area earlier. What do you have to say for yourself?'

'There was a slight... misunderstanding between myself, my wife and another party,' said Gimhana. 'A lack of communication, if you like. I will get it sorted out.'

'You know that we expect you to keep your personal life outside of this office.'

'Of course.' He angled his head. 'I apologise.'

'We are a family firm,' said Mr Thomas. 'With family values at the core. There is no room here for scandal involving infidelity and... homosexuality.'

What? For a second he couldn't believe he'd just heard that. He glanced at the other partner, who had the grace to look away.

'Is this a disciplinary discussion?' Gimhana asked.

When Mr Thomas didn't answer, he added, 'Because you need to have someone here from HR, if so.'

'Nonsense,' said Mr Thomas. 'This is just a friendly discussion about not creating a scene in the office. Think of the clients.'

'There were no clients in reception at the time. It does not affect the clients in any way.'

Mr Thomas harrumphed. 'Word gets round, young man. Just be aware of the values of this firm.'

He pressed his lips together to stop a retort from coming out. He knew what this meant. He would now be slowly excluded from things. Mr Thomas couldn't sack him for being gay or bi, there were limits to where even a prejudiced old man would go, but he could make life very difficult for Gimhana.

'Will that be all?' he said, quietly.

The two men on the other side of the desk looked at each other. 'Yes,' said the other man, firmly. 'That will be all.'

Gimhana nodded, stood up, straightened his jacket and left. His time here was limited. He needed to start looking for a new job. Jump before he was pushed.

–

Gimhana left the office at five, something he hadn't done in years. He had finally given up and told his secretary that he would be working from home for the rest of the day. She had given him a look full of sympathy and said, 'Good luck.'

He had dropped his guard long enough to say thank you.

The house was quiet when he got there. He checked the coats and realised that Chaya's coat was gone. So was Nayana's. He wondered if they had gone out somewhere. He took out his phone and called Chaya again. She cut him off mid ring. Again.

'I'm worried about you,' he said to her answerphone. 'I know you don't want to talk to me right now, just tell me that you and Nayana are okay.'

He went upstairs and peered first into Chaya's room and then into Nayana's. Nayana's bags were gone. Chaya must have taken her to the airport early.

Gimhana prowled through the house. His home. The home he'd made with Chaya. He noted the little details and remembered how they had made the place their own. The argument about the side table which was now so much a part of life that he no longer noticed it. The negotiations about where the baking trays should be stored. The afternoon spent working out which pictures should go on which walls. These were all things couples did and he'd done them by default with Chaya. Although he told himself that he looked after her and she needed him, it hit him now that he needed her too. It wasn't just socially. She had stopped him from disappearing into his work, helped him moderate his drinking. He enjoyed her company. She genuinely was his best friend.

But Zack. He wanted to do all those things with Zack. To argue about furniture and bicker over which pictures went where. To put up with beige bedding because it wasn't worth questioning his taste. To just be with him.

Was it possible that he loved them both? In very different ways? Yes, he decided. It was entirely possible. And now he'd lost them both anyway.

One of the things that he'd done when he got married was stop drinking whiskey, his drink of choice on dark days. He had stopped drinking it, but he always kept a bottle of single malt in the garage. It was his reminder of how far he'd come. He retraced his steps to the garage and rummaged around until he found it. He took it back inside. When he opened the bottle, the smell greeted him like an old friend. He pulled out his phone and dialled first Zack, then Chaya. Both cut him off. He put the phone down on the table, sighed, and poured himself a measure.

Chapter Sixty-Six

Chaya – London, 2013

Chaya gave Nayana a hug. 'I'm sorry your holiday ended up so wrong,' she said.

'Are you going to be okay?' said Nayana. She looked bleary-eyed and kept stifling yawns. It was just after three in the morning and she had just checked in for her five-thirty a.m. flight.

'Of course I'm going to be okay,' Chaya said. She didn't believe that, but it was what Nayana needed to hear. 'I'm made of stern stuff. I've been through worse.' That, at least, was true. This didn't hurt. Not yet.

'I'm so sorry. I wish there was something I could have done.'

'There isn't. It's just one of those things. The only person who could have done anything about it was Gimhana.' She handed Nayana the bag she'd been carrying for her.

'Have you spoken to him?' Nayana hitched the bag onto her shoulder. Even in the last few days, she seemed to have grown. Or perhaps just grown up.

'Not yet. I will though. Hopefully, by then I'll be calm enough not to kill him.' She smiled to take the sting out of her words. 'Now go. You'll have time to get a drink and something to eat before they call your flight.'

Nayana bent her knees and pressed her palms together. Not a full genuflection, but an attempt. Chaya placed her hand on her niece's forehead in blessing. 'Thunsaranai.'

She watched Nayana go through the departure gates, waving until the last minute. When the girl had disappeared from view, she let the fixed smile drop from her face. She checked her watch. It was too early to go to work.

She stared blankly at the departure board, watching the display flow and change. It took her a few seconds to realise she was staring at details of a flight to Canada. Where Noah lived. She read the details, turned her head and spotted the sales desk not far away. Could she? It was so tempting; she felt that tug at the base of her ribs, where her heart was. But she couldn't. Not before she spoke to Gimhana. She was still furious with him, but she couldn't avoid talking to him for much longer. Like it or not, her life and his were inextricably linked.

Did she want to face Gimhana now? Would he even be home? Maybe he'd caught up with his lover and disappeared off into the night with him?

A snarl escaped her. How could Gimhana be so careless? The one thing she'd asked for was discretion. She drew herself up to her full height. Well. Standing here wasn't going to achieve anything. She may as well go home.

—

Chaya ran up the path to the house, the rain pattering on her coat. The landing light was on, but the rest of the house was in darkness. Gimhana must have come home at some point. He would be in bed by now. Was she angry enough to wake him and shout at him? No. She was tired. She hadn't slept and the night was almost gone.

This disaster would still be a disaster in the morning. Quietly, she hung up her coat. She stood for a moment in the hall, breathing in the familiar smells of the house; the smell of wood polish, a trace of curry and hint of Gimhana's aftershave. This was the smell of success and delusion. The smell of the life they'd built. It was the sort of life that everyone looking in thought was perfect. The illusion had been so good, she had fallen for it herself. Now it had been stripped from within. The truth shone through the varnish, highlighting the cracks.

She felt the need to do a quick tour of the house. To check that it hadn't all somehow crumbled away. She crept into the kitchen.

'You should have called,' a voice said out of the darkness.

She yelped and flicked on the light. Gimhana was sitting at the table, a tumbler of whiskey in one hand, an almost empty bottle next to it.

'I was worried about you,' he said.

Her eyes flicked from the whiskey to his face. 'You've been drinking.' It was an accusation.

He looked down at his glass, as though surprised to see it there. 'So I have.' When they agreed to get married, he had promised to cut down his drinking. He had done so, to a large extent. At least she thought he had. She wasn't sure anymore. What else had he lied about? How stupid she had been to think that someone who was so good at deception wouldn't fool her too.

'I haven't drunk very much,' he said, as though reading her thoughts. 'I started this bottle... oooh... hours ago.'

'It's four a.m.' All her strength left her. She needed a shower. She wanted a hug. She wanted her friend, not this man who lied and drank too much and sat around in dark kitchens. She shook her head. 'I can't do this right now,' she said. 'I'm going to bed.'

As she turned around to leave, he said, 'I'm sorry, Chaya. I'm really, really sorry.'

She looked over her shoulder to see his pleading expression. He was giving her that look, the one that always seemed to get him out of trouble. 'We'll talk about it in the morning,' she said, firmly.

'You didn't want to do it in the first place and I talked you into it,' he said. 'I let you down.' He sounded drunk and maudlin now.

She didn't have the time or energy to deal with this crap, but... 'You did. All you had to do was be discreet. That was all you had to do.' She leaned against the worktop. 'How long were you seeing this boy?'

'Man,' he said, slurring. 'He's a man.'

'Whatever. How long?'

He shrugged. 'A year. Bit less.'

'The poor guy. At least I knew what I was signing up to.'

Gimhana didn't look up. He topped up his glass.

She looked at her husband, sprawled in his seat, looking like he was the one who had been hurt. She recalled with sudden clarity, the shock on the young man's face. He'd had no idea. Gimhana had lied to him as thoroughly as he'd lied to the world. 'I don't know who you are anymore,' she said. She turned away. 'I can't talk to you right now. We'll talk tomorrow when you're sober.'

'Chaya—'

'I said, we'll talk about it in the morning.' She made her way to the stairs.

'I'll make it up to you,' he called after her. 'I will. I promise.'

Chaya sighed. Another promise. Great. She knew how good he was at keeping those.

Chapter Sixty-Seven

Chaya – London, 2013

They met for lunch. Chaya had left mid morning for work. After a few hours of sleep, she was still angry, but not as much as before. She didn't want to have this conversation at home, so when a croaky Gimhana called her in the afternoon, she'd agreed to meet him for a late lunch. When he kissed her cheek in greeting, she caught herself breathing in to see if she could smell alcohol on his breath. It was something she hadn't done in years.

It turned out he had a plan.

'Is Nayana going to tell anyone?' he said.

'I don't know.' She really didn't. 'I asked her to give me some time to work it out… but…' She shrugged.

'We could go to Sri Lanka and brazen it out.' Gimhana poked at the ice cubes in his glass of cola. 'Even if she says something, if we turn up, as a couple, acting normally, people will start to question whether the gossip is true…'

'She's only a kid. She might crack under the pressure,' Chaya said.

'Yes, but she's a teenage girl. It'd be her word against ours.'

Chaya gave him her best withering look. 'You think calling my niece a liar is

going to help?'

He pursed his lips. 'If only you hadn't just turned up at work like that,' he said.

'If only you hadn't just shacked up with a boy.'

'He's a mature student. He's thirty years old.'

'You're nearly forty.'

He looked up and studied her, as though he was seeing her properly for the first time. 'Touché,' he said, inclining his head. 'But I am allowed to see people. It's part of the deal.'

'The deal,' said Chaya, through gritted teeth, 'was that you could sleep with whomever you wanted, so long as you were ultra careful and no one ever found out. Not. Even. Me.'

He looked like he was going to argue. She raised her eyebrows. He looked down at his glass again.

They sat together in silence for a while. Gimhana didn't look good. There were shadows under his eyes and the corners of his mouth were turned down. His guard was down. Her anger ebbed away a little. She was one of the few people who was allowed to see him like this. Normally, his vulnerabilities were tucked away, hidden behind his smile and dazzle. He frowned and tapped a finger on the side of his glass.

She thought about all the things she knew about him. She knew his favourite restaurants, his favourite actor, which books he'd read until the spines disintegrated, which ones he'd bought for show. She knew which shampoo he used, that he tweezered out the grey hairs at his temples and that he could happily evict spiders but was freaked out by bees. She even knew about his *Jem and the Holograms* fandom. All these were things that you got to know from living together. He had become a good friend. She had been comfortable with him. Happy, even. Did she really want to lose that?

The waitress appeared with two plates of food. Gimhana looked up, the mask already back in place.

'Would you like some parmesan?' the waitress said. Gimhana gave her his most dazzling smile and said no. The waitress looked from him to Chaya and back again. They got this a lot, the look of puzzlement as people wondered what such a plain woman could have that would attract such a handsome man. Chaya smiled at the waitress, who bid them 'Buon appetito,' and rushed off.

She returned her attention to Gimhana. He looked up and met her gaze. 'I'm sorry, Chaya,' he said, carefully. 'I didn't mean to hurt you.'

'I know.'

He looked away again. 'I messed up our arrangement. I'm not sure how to make it better again. The only thing I can offer is a divorce... If that's what you want.'

Angry as she was, she didn't know what to say to that. This scandal was worse for him than for her. She was just the injured wife. Homosexuality was illegal in Sri Lanka. If word got out, no one would say anything to his face, but it would upset his family greatly. It would impact his family, friends, and maybe even his work. He was offering to release her and take the scandal upon himself. She also knew that, angry or not, she couldn't let him do that. He was her friend.

She sighed. 'What's done is done. What do we do about it?'

Gimhana didn't ask her what she meant or if she was sure. He sat taller, flicked open his napkin and put it on his lap. 'What we need,' he said, 'is a plan.' He picked up a forkful and raised it to his mouth. 'And preferably,' he said, pausing before taking a bite, 'a plan B.'

Chaya felt something loosen in her chest. This was better than feeling angry and helpless. This felt purposeful. She and Gimhana, facing the world together. 'A plan,' she said, picking up her own fork. 'Okay. What options have we got?'

–

There was a period of quiet for a few days. Chaya felt like she was holding her breath. In the meantime, she got an interview date for the professorship. She handled the stress in the usual way, by throwing herself into the preparation for it. She was sitting at the table, looking over what she'd said in the application when the phone rang. It came up as an international number. Who could that be?

'Hello,' she said, cautiously.

'I'm so sorry, Punchi,' Nayana said, hoarsely. 'Amma knows.' She sniffed.

Chaya sat back in her seat. Nayana had clearly been crying. 'Tell me what happened,' she said.

'You know what Amma's like. She felt something was wrong and she kept asking me and asking me and finally, I cracked and told her. She told Thatha... I'm so sorry. I tried to keep your secret, but she was so...'

'I understand,' said Chaya, her voice calm, even though she felt tension pulsing through her. 'Malini can be very... persuasive... if she thinks you're hiding something.'

'What are you going to do?' said Nayana.

'I'm not sure. Let me have a think,' she said.

'Thatha says I shouldn't talk to you,' said Nayana. 'He can't say that. You're my aunty. We... argued.'

Chaya sighed. Oh dear.

'Thanks for letting me know,' she said. 'I'll see what I can do. And Nayana?'

'Yes?'

'Don't beat yourself up about it. It was bound to come out some time or other.'

Nayana sniffed. 'I'm so, so sorry.'

'Don't worry about it,' she said. 'Gimhana and I have been planning for this eventuality.'

'You're... staying with him?' Nayana said. 'After what he did?'

Chaya rubbed her eyes. 'It's a complicated situation, okay,' she said. 'Listen, darling, I have to go. I have an interview the day after next and I need to carry on preparing. You look after yourself, okay? I'll talk to your mother and see if I can smooth things out a bit.'

She hung up and sent Gimhana a text.

Malini knows.

He replied almost instantly.

> Your interview comes first. Then let's
> go to plan A.

Chapter Sixty-Eight

Chaya – London, 2013

The plan they came up with was simple. They would go back to Sri Lanka immediately after her interview and assess the damage. Just the fact that they'd shown up together would help quash some of the rumours. If they could persuade Chaya's family to keep the story quiet before rumours got out that they were splitting up, all would be well. It wasn't as huge a disaster as it had first seemed.

The first major hurdle was finding somewhere to stay. Normally, when they went to Sri Lanka they stayed with Malini and Ajith some of the time and with Gimhana's parents for the rest. To do otherwise would raise suspicion. Once the annual leave and flights were booked, Chaya phoned Malini to let her know. Malini greeted the news with silence. Chaya braced herself.

After a few seconds, Malini said, 'Where will you stay?'

'I was… we were… hoping to stay in your spare room.' She almost added 'like we always do' but stopped herself.

'I see,' Malini said, slowly. 'Just a minute, I'll have to check with Ajith.' There was a muffled conversation. After what sounded like a disagreement, Ajith came on the phone.

'Chaya,' he said. 'Malini tells me you're coming to visit.' His tone was clipped. Not at all like usual.

'Yes. We were wondering about staying with you.'

'I don't think that's a very good idea under the circumstances.'

'But—'

'It's not you. You're welcome here any time,' he said. In the background Malini called out 'no matter what'. 'It's Gimhana,' Ajith continued.

'Gimhana?' Did they sympathise with her and feel Gimhana had treated her badly? Which, in fairness, he had.

'You have to understand,' said Ajith. 'We have a son.'

She shouldn't have been shocked. She lived in England, where people didn't say such things – not out loud anyway – but such sensitivity wasn't common in Sri Lanka. Another part of her understood the fears of people who had never had to confront their prejudices before. The knowledge of Gimhana's sexuality would be difficult for them to handle, especially given that he was married to her and living a lie. She could try explaining that being homosexual and a sexual predator weren't the same thing, but her brother-in-law was unlikely to move on that point. As far as Ajith and Malini were concerned, the brother-in-law they had known and liked was gone, replaced by a stranger that they didn't recognise.

'You don't have to worry,' she said. 'He's not...' Not what? Predatory? Harmful? Contagious? 'He's not like that,' she said, weakly. 'He's the same guy he always was.' She had lived with the man for seven years, she should know. 'But,' she continued, 'I do understand. Can I come and see Malini and the children – without Gimhana? Is that okay?' There was no point fighting it. Not yet.

Ajith sighed, a strange sound to rush down a telephone line. 'Yes, of course,' he said, sounding relieved. 'Here, I'll pass you back to Malini.'

Chaya spoke to Malini for a few minutes, an awkward, stilted conversation. Chaya could tell that her sister felt bad about what was happening. But she could also sense her confusion. She couldn't understand why Chaya was still holding on to the shell of her marriage. If Chaya was being completely honest, she wasn't entirely sure herself.

'I'll call you when I get there,' she said.

'Yes,' said Malini, sounding stiff and not like her sister at all. 'I will see you soon.'

'See you. Take care.'

Once she'd hung up, Chaya looked up at Gimhana, who had been sitting at the other side of the table, listening.

'I take it that's a no,' he said.

She nodded.

'They're afraid I'll corrupt the kiddies?' he said, with a sad smile.

Again, she nodded. There was no point sugar-coating it. They both knew how it was.

He shrugged. 'It's what I expected,' he said. 'People are scared of what they don't understand.'

'What do we do now?' she said.

'I'm not sure my mother can really deal with extra guests now,' he said. 'We'll stay in a hotel.'

Chapter Sixty-Nine

Chaya – Colombo, 2013

The hotel room was luxurious. And why not? They could afford it. When they went on holiday to anywhere other than Sri Lanka, they stayed in luxury hotels. In Sri Lanka, they always stayed at someone's house.

Chaya stood in the air-conditioned room looking out at the sun-baked beach and felt like a stranger in her own country. Outside, the sun shone. Trees moved in the salt breeze. Hotel staff, dressed in starched uniforms, scurried around. Tourists lounged, looking red and ungainly. Frangipani flowers glowed white against dark green leaves. Inside the room, it was cold. Everything was spotless and perfectly arranged, as though the room were a showpiece that was never really meant to be lived in. She was looking at the world from inside a glass box. She had built layers of insulation around herself so that this world couldn't touch her and now it felt as though she could no longer touch it.

Gimhana came over and put his hands on her shoulders, making her jump. 'Okay then, Nangi,' he said. 'Time to put the plan into action. Where do you want to start?'

The plan was simple. Talk to each party and minimise the damage. 'You should go see your ammi,' she said. 'I'll see if I can catch up with Malini.'

–

Malini suggested they met at an ice cream parlour, the same one they'd loved years ago. Chaya's tuk tuk dropped her off at the foot of the polished red steps. She walked up the steps slowly, noting how it had changed. The colonial grandeur of the place had faded even further. The potted plants were still there, covered in a thin layer of road dust. Sunshine could be unforgiving in what it revealed.

A guard opened the door for her with a smile. The cool, conditioned air immediately made her feel better. Two ladies, with shopping bags cluttered around their feet, were tucking into ice cream sundaes and chatting. Neither one bothered to look at up at Chaya. The feeling of being on high alert faded a little.

A bored-looking young waiter who had been leaning against the counter reading a newspaper, bounded up with a laminated menu almost before she'd had a chance to sit down.

She ordered an iced coffee with an ice cream float and settled down to wait. There was something sad about the place. It was still spotless, but everything seemed dated and slightly worse for wear. The chrome on the bar had bald spots where years of customer elbows had rubbed the plate away. The metalwork on the tables had been repainted too many times and blobs of paint filled in the more intricate bits of the design. It seemed that this was no longer a trendy place to go. The world had moved on, leaving the venerable old ice cream parlour gathering dust. Maybe Colombo had moved on in other ways, too. She could hope.

Malini turned up late, as always. She wafted in, looking elegant in her linen skirt, floaty white blouse and sunglasses. She stepped inside, removed her sunglasses and looked around, waiting for her eyes to adjust. Chaya waved and stood up, uncertain of how she would be received.

She need not have worried. Malini came over and hugged her. Relief brought tears to Chaya's eyes. She squeezed her sister back. Malini released her and stepped back, letting her hands slide down to take hold of Chaya's. 'Nangi, how are you?'

'I'm…' She remembered the plan. Brazen it out. 'I'm okay, actually.'

Malini shook her head. 'But how can you be? You and Gimhana… Nangi, he lied to you. All these years. How can you be so calm?'

How could she unpack that one? 'Let's sit down,' Chaya suggested. When they were seated, she asked, 'How's Nayana?'

She was genuinely concerned about her niece. Nayana was an intrinsic part of this fiasco and Chaya knew, from growing up in Colombo herself, that children, even teenagers, were protected from a great many things there. Sex education hadn't really existed when she was a child. There wasn't any reason to think that things had changed. While Nayana had seemed okay when she'd last seen her, she had no idea of knowing how she really was, once the shock wore off.

Malini's shoulders stiffened slightly. 'She's okay.'

'How… what does she think?'

Malini shot her a quick glance and then looked away. 'She thinks you should leave him, of course.'

Chaya nodded. Of course.

'She says you shouldn't stay with him because he cheated on you.' Malini frowned and fiddled with a bracelet. 'She seems to find it irrelevant who he cheated on you with.' She looked mystified by this.

That was a surprise. Chaya thought back to what Nayana had said to her on the evening, before her flight out. It occurred to her that her niece had been incensed by Gimhana's infidelity, but had shown sympathy towards the boy… man… towards Zack.

Clearly, times and attitudes were changing. But had they changed enough? Nayana's moral code was clear: if he cheated on you, you threw him out. It must be nice to live in a world where everything was so well defined.

'Can I see her?'

Malini hesitated. 'Ajith…' she started to say, and trailed off. She didn't need to finish her sentence. Ajith would want to keep Nayana away from them until everything was resolved.

'Does she hate me?' Chaya said. Nayana wouldn't disobey her father directly, but if she really wanted to talk to her, she could call or email. She hadn't.

'No,' Malini said. 'Of course she doesn't hate you. She's worried about you and thinks you're slightly mad, but she doesn't hate you.'

The waiter returned with Malini's drink on a tray. Malini smiled at him gratefully and moved her arm so that he could put the glass down in front of her. She stirred it delicately, her bracelets clinking. The sound reminded Chaya of Amma. She sighed and picked up her own drink.

Malini avoided eye contact by looking down as she sucked her drink up through the straw. She still looked beautiful, but was no longer young. Tiny wrinkles were gathering around her eyes and her face had lost that glow that Chaya had envied so much when they were younger. Her hair was still black, but it was less luscious than it used to be. They were middle-aged women now. Chaya had been trying to grow old with dignity. Fat chance of that now.

'Why did you do it, Chaya?' said Malini, so suddenly that it made Chaya jump.

Her tone was accusatory, as though it was Chaya who had done something wrong.

'Didn't you know about him?' Malini continued. 'You must have realised…' She cast about for the right words, but failed to find them. 'You must have suspected.'

For a moment Chaya thought about pretending that she didn't know what Malini was talking about. Malini studied her as she hesitated, looking for clues in her expression. She would know in an instant if she lied. 'I knew,' she said.

'Before or after you married him?'

Chaya realised what her answer would mean. If she lied, Gimhana would be ruined. If she told the truth… her sister would think less of her. Ah, but that boat had already sailed. 'Both,' she whispered.

'Why then? Why did you marry him?' Malini frowned. 'I don't understand this.'

Chaya sighed again and squeezed her eyes shut. How could she explain such complicated reasons succinctly? 'I needed a husband. He needed a wife. Neither of us was looking for anything more than companionship. It seemed… sensible at the time.' She opened her eyes to see her sister's reaction.

'But…' Malini moved her hands in the air, unable to articulate her sentiments. 'I don't understand,' she said. 'You seemed so happy.'

'We were. We had a deal.' Until he got careless and broke it.

Malini's frown deepened, as she digested the information. 'What are you going to do now? You have to get…' she dropped her voice. 'A divorce?'

Chaya shrugged. If there had been a way to put things back the way they were, she would have taken it. But the illusion of their marriage was broken. Now, all they could do was damage limitation.

'But you can't stay married to him! Not now that you know.' For a moment, Malini seemed to forget her awkwardness and grabbed her sister's hand. Chaya stared at her. Malini would never be able to understand what it was like to be desolate. To be so desperately lonely that you'd need physical pain to make yourself feel better. She had never been alone in her life. There had always been someone there – Chaya, Amma, Ajith, the kids – someone to reflect her charmed life back at her.

'Why not?' Chaya demanded, louder than she'd intended.

'But you don't love him,' Malini said, as though that was all there was to it. 'You can't have a marriage without love.'

The laugh that escaped from Chaya was not a familiar one. It tasted sour as it left her mouth. 'It's easy for you, with your film star looks and your perfect husband and your kids that look like a TV commercial. You've always been surrounded by adoration. *Everyone* loves you.' She pulled her hand out from under Malini's. 'You have no idea what it's like to be the plain one that has to shout to be heard.' Her eyes started to fill with tears. She blinked them away impatiently.

'All I wanted,' she said, forcing the words past her constricted throat, 'all I ever wanted, was for them to look at me the way they looked at you. They were so proud of you. You were everything a daughter should be. But me,' She waved a hand to indicate herself. 'I was the boring one. The only way I could get noticed was to work so bloody hard and I still didn't get recognised. It's not fair.' She smacked her palm on the table, making the iced coffee slop over the side of the glass. The icy liquid on her skin calmed her. 'Not fair,' she muttered, and used the napkin to dry her hand.

Malini was staring, her eyes wide and her mouth slightly open. Even now, she looked like a movie star. Slowly, she reached across the table for Chaya's hand again. 'I had no idea,' she said softly. 'I had no idea that you felt like this.'

Chaya sniffed and looked away.

'Chaya,' Malini said. 'Chaya, look at me.' For a moment, she sounded just like Amma used to. Chaya's head automatically turned towards her.

Malini squeezed Chaya's hand. 'Really?' she said. 'Is that why you did all this? Made up a romance and married Gimhana? Did you think you had to do that to make us proud?'

She didn't reply.

'But Chaya, you didn't have to do that. We were so proud of you anyway.' She sighed. 'And you're wrong, you know. It wasn't easy for me. Next to you, I always felt so... stupid.'

Chaya frowned. 'Stupid?'

She gave a small shrug. 'All I could do was look pretty and marry well. No one thought I was clever enough to get a good job and have a career and be able to talk to anyone about anything, like you do. All I can talk about is kids and homes.' She smiled, a little sadly. 'I don't mind, it's enough, but sometimes I wonder if I could have been more.'

Chaya didn't say anything. She had always been bright and articulate. But she never would have thought anyone would want to trade beauty for that.

'I was lucky,' Malini continued. 'I met Ajith. He's a wonderful man.' She looked down at her wedding ring and smiled fondly at it. 'Without him and the kids, I'd be nobody.' She looked up at me. 'But you,' she said. 'Without Gimhana, you're still someone. You can do things and live a life that's totally independent. You have no idea what an inspiration you are to people.'

For a moment, they were both quiet. Malini's hand was still on Chaya's. They looked at each other for a long time. Finally, Malini said, 'Of course, now I'm getting old, too. I don't get to be pretty forever.'

'Yeah well,' Chaya said. 'Some clever people can do really stupid things.'

Malini squeezed her hand again. 'I'm sorry, Nangi,' she said. 'I had no idea.'

'Nor did I,' Chaya said, squeezing back.

They drank their coffees and talked about Amma and how things were going.

'We weren't going to tell her,' said Malini. 'But she was there when Nayana came home...'

Chaya winced. She had hoped that Amma would be spared any knowledge of the imminent scandal. If she and Gimhana managed to contain it, Amma would never have needed to know.

'How did she take it?'

This time it was Malini that winced. 'I'm not sure she understood completely,' she said. 'But she thinks you've left Gimhana.' She paused and made a face. 'At least she thought that last week. By now, depending on how her days have been, who knows?'

Oh great. 'I'm going to see her tomorrow,' said Chaya. 'I guess I'll find out.'

'Do you want me to come with you?'

Chaya shook her head. 'No. I'll be with Gimhana.'

Malini's eyes narrowed. 'So you're going to pretend it's all okay? Really?'

'It *is* okay. Nothing's really changed for us...' As she said it, she realised it wasn't true. Things had changed, but they'd decided not to let it affect the status quo. Not really the same thing at all.

Suddenly, Malini's mobile phone beeped. She looked at it. 'That's my alarm,' she said. 'I have to go and pick Kapila up and take him to cricket.'

'Oh.' She didn't want her to leave. They were only just getting things patched up.

Malini stood up and hesitated. She dropped a quick kiss on Chaya's cheek. 'Listen,' she said earnestly. 'No one hates you.' She smiled. 'We're all just... confused.'

Chaya stood too.

Malini suddenly leaned forward and gave her a quick hug. 'You're my baby sister. The clever one that kept me out of trouble. How could I hate you?'

Chaya wrapped her arms around her big sister and whispered, 'Thank you.'

Chapter Seventy

Gimhana – Colombo, 2013

Gimhana was lounging on the bed, doing some work on his laptop while they waited until it was time to go. Today's task was to go and see Chaya's mother. There wasn't much point being early.

Chaya paced past, she stopped to look out of the window, tapped the glass lightly with her fingertips and then moved on. She was in full fidget mode, vibrating with tension. She hadn't been this bad in years. He recognised the signs. If she carried on like this, she would be a mess, in physical pain, by the end of the day.

He saved his document and moved the laptop off his thighs. 'Chaya.'

She stopped, almost still. 'Mm?'

'Relax, okay. Breathe. It's going to be fine.'

She gave him an exasperated glare. 'It's all very well for you to say. It's not your mother.'

'It will be fine. If she's having a good day, she'll have forgotten that there was any sort of scandal in the offing and she'll be really happy to see us.' He knew her mother had a soft spot for him. He was, in her eyes, the charming and handsome man who made her awkward daughter happy. She'd made no secret of the fact that she had almost given up hope of seeing Chaya married and 'settled' when Gimhana came along. The fact that they didn't have children was a source of much disapproval, but she'd given up nagging them about that now.

Chaya scowled. 'That's not a *good* day though, is it? That's a bad day.' She drummed her fingers on the edge of the table next to her. 'She'll only remember on a different day and hate me all over again.'

He considered that. His mother-in-law's memory problems baffled him. Second-guessing it was like trying to tie down fog. 'I suppose,' he said, carefully. 'But even if we explain everything, there's no guarantee she'll remember any of it.'

Chaya sighed and pushed her hands through her hair. 'I know!' She looked at her hands, tutted and grabbed a hairbrush. 'There isn't any good way to get this sorted out.' She started brushing her hair in short, anxious flicks.

'Chaya.' Gimhana put his hands on her shoulders. 'Perhaps you should take some of your anxiety medicine?'

She glared at him in the mirror.

Okay then. Maybe not.

'It's going to be a difficult day,' he said. 'At least do some breathing exercises?'

Her glare softened. She lowered the hairbrush. 'You're right. I'm sorry.'

Gimhana smiled. 'Don't worry.'

Chaya closed her eyes and breathed in, counting under her breath. After a few breaths, he saw her shoulders drop, not completely, but a little. It was a start. He felt his own shoulders relax a bit. Chaya was never very good at protecting herself from stress. Without him to help her, how would she cope?

Chapter Seventy-One

Chaya – Colombo, 2013

Chaya peered through the grille of the gate at the house. The garden was missing Thatha. Someone had cut the grass, but without Thatha's careful pruning, the rose bushes spilled fading petals onto the lawn. The jasmine vines had shot out errant branches that criss-crossed the openings in the veranda. The house looked like it was besieged by vegetation. A heaviness settled on Chaya's heart.

The gate was padlocked, so she banged on it to get someone's attention. It was mid afternoon, but the sun was trapped behind thick clouds. The air was close and sticky, making everything seem damp and breathless. Sweat beaded on her upper lip. She wiped it off with a hanky. Gimhana had wisely stayed in the car, with the air conditioning on.

After a few minutes, Leela arrived, limping slightly with her arthritis. She looked suspiciously through the grille and spotted Chaya.

'Chaya baby,' she said, her crumpled features moving into a smile. 'Just a minute.' It took her a moment to remove the padlock. Chaya helped her open the gate. While they waited for Gimhana to drive through, Chaya looked at the garden, sadly.

'She keeps saying he'll come back and do it,' said Leela, coming to stand next to her. 'She cries when I try to do anything.'

Leela had shrunk in the past year. Amma's moods were clearly taking their toll on her.

'How is she?' Chaya asked.

'She's having a nap,' said Leela. 'She was having a good day.' She paused and brushed a bead of perspiration off her face. 'At least, she was until she went to sleep. We'll have to see what she's like when she wakes up.'

Chaya put a hand on Leela's shoulder and was surprised at how insubstantial she felt. Leela, like her parents, had been a solid presence in her childhood. Now she too was fading away. 'It's good of you,' she said. 'Staying on to look after her. I know it's not easy.'

Leela looked at the house and shrugged. 'She and sir were like second parents to me,' she said. 'This is my home too. I have nowhere else to go.'

Not knowing what to say, Chaya smiled. Gimhana got out of the car.

The sound of the car door shutting seemed to spur Leela into action. 'Come in, come in,' she said, rushing down the drive. 'I'll get Nona up.'

'Hello Leela,' said Gimhana, beaming at her.

'Gimhana sir,' she replied, barely looking at him. Normally, she adored him. 'I'll bring tea,' she said, disappearing into the house.

Chaya followed her in. Without the light that normally poured in from the veranda, the sitting room looked gloomy. Chaya ran a finger over the coffee table and found a thin layer of dust. Clearly, Leela and Amma weren't able to keep the house the way it used to be.

One of the windows had its shutters closed against the sun. She went over and opened it. The sunlight that came in was weak from passing through rain clouds. It cast a dull light on the collection of framed photographs that Amma kept on top of the display cabinet. Chaya paused to look at them. There were wedding photos; Malini's and hers. Her graduation photographs, undergrad and postgrad. There were photos of her niece and nephew at various ages. Right at the front was a photo, taken about three years before, of Amma, Thatha, Malini and Chaya, posing near the jasmine-covered veranda. Malini and Chaya were perched on either side of Amma's chair. Behind them stood Thatha, a hand on the shoulder of each daughter, his face glowing with pride. It was taken the day before Chaya left Sri Lanka after a holiday. It was the last time that she'd seen him alive.

'Who is it?' Amma's voice came from behind her.

She spun round. 'Amma,' she began, but her words dried up. She had known what to expect, but it was still a shock. Amma's hair, now totally white, was escaping from its bun. She was still neatly wrapped in a sari, but her blouse was too big for her. Her collarbones stood out and her neck sagged with wrinkles. There were dark circles around her eyes. She had aged ten years in less than twelve months. Her face was etched with a permanent sadness.

When she recognised Chaya, she frowned. 'Oh,' she said. 'It's you, Chaya.' She put her hands on her hips. 'What,' she said, as though speaking to a naughty child, 'is this I hear about you leaving your husband?'

'Amma...' Chaya stepped forward, one arm outstretched towards her.

'I can't believe I raised such a child!' Amma clasped her hands to her chest, like a heroine in a Bollywood film. Her fingers seemed to claw into the hollows between ligaments. 'What is wrong with you, child? We spent so long finding you someone to marry. Now you leave your husband to run off with another man? Didn't I teach you any values?'

Chaya stared, confused. When Malini said that Amma might have the wrong idea, she hadn't been exaggerating. How did she get out of this?

Amma raised her hands, imploring to the sky. 'What did I do wrong?' she cried. 'Aney!' She gripped her hair and started pulling at it. 'Aney!'

She had been nervous about seeing Amma, but this was worse than anything she'd expected. She opened her mouth, but no sound came out. She stepped forward, not sure what she could do to help.

Leela limped in from the kitchen, alerted by Amma's shouting. 'What's going on?' Gimhana appeared in the doorway.

Amma stopped wailing and stared, her rant completely derailed at the sight of him. Her hands slowly came away from her head. Gimhana smiled as though nothing untoward were happening. 'Ayubowan Amma.' He genuflected in front of her.

Still staring, Amma automatically laid a hand on his head, blessing him. 'Thunsaranai,' she muttered.

Gimhana stood up again and beamed at her. 'What has my wife done to upset you?' he said, coming over to Chaya and putting his arm around her.

Amma's gaze flew from his face to Chaya's. She looked back at Gimhana, looking thoroughly confused. 'But...' she said. 'She... She left you. Didn't she?'

Gimhana laughed. 'Really Amma, does that look likely to you?' He removed his arm from round Chaya and went over to her. 'Perhaps you should sit down.' He helped her into a chair. 'As you can see, Chaya and I are very much together.' He waved an arm in Chaya's direction. 'Maybe you had a bad dream and that's what you're remembering.'

Watching, Chaya was torn between relief and outrage at what Gimhana was doing. He was diffusing a very painful situation, but he was doing so by manipulating Amma's fragile grasp of reality. She heard a small sound and glanced across to see Leela standing there with her mouth open, staring at Gimhana. Amma might be fooled, but Leela wasn't.

Amma looked at the floor and shook her head. 'Perhaps...' she said unsteadily. 'Perhaps you're correct, Putha.' Having decided that this was right, she looked up. 'Chaya Duwa. Forgive me.' She held a hand out, in a placatory gesture. 'How are you?'

'I'm fine, Amma.' If this was how things had to be done, she may as well go along with it. She went and knelt by her mother's chair.

Amma put her hand to Chaya's cheek. 'You look thin,' she said. 'Are you eating enough?'

Chaya's throat constricted so that all that came out was a whisper. 'I'm eating enough.'

Amma looked at Leela, who was still staring. 'Leela,' Amma said. 'Bring some tea.'

Leela jumped. 'Yes, Nona.' She bowed her head, shot another glance at Gimhana, and limped off to the kitchen.

Amma watched her go and shook her head. 'Poor Leela,' she said. 'She's getting a bit forgetful now. She's getting old, you see.' She smiled. 'I guess we all are.'

Chaya nodded, not trusting herself to speak.

Amma touched Chaya's shoulder. 'I'm sorry about before,' she said. 'I get... confused, sometimes.' She smiled. 'Your Thatha is very patient with me, he's always helping me with things.'

Tears filled Chaya's eyes. Thatha had been dead for nearly a year now.

Amma looked alarmed. 'Why are you crying?' she said. 'Is something wrong? Are you ill?'

Rubbing the tears away, Chaya shook her head. 'No, I'm not ill.' She moved forward and hugged her mother, gently, so that her bones didn't creak. 'I'm just... so glad to see you.'

Amma patted her back and kissed the top of her head. 'I'm happy to see you too, my Duwa.'

Leela came in with tea and smacked it down on the table with a clatter. She left, glaring pointedly at Gimhana, who pretended not to notice.

Amma frowned. 'She hasn't poured the tea,' she said, looking at the tray. 'And there are no biscuits.' She clicked her tongue. 'I don't know what's got into Leela today.' She looked towards the kitchen. 'Leela,' she called.

'It's okay,' Chaya said. 'I'll pour it.'

They drank their tea and made small talk. Afterwards, Chaya took the tea things into the kitchen, where Leela was slowly chopping vegetables. She looked up when Chaya came in. 'Is it true?' she said.

Chaya put the tray by the sink and picked up the wash cloth. 'What?'

'Malini baby said… it wasn't you who left for another man, was it?'

Chaya didn't look up. She carefully washed a cup. Leela had known her all her life. She would spot a lie if she faced her. 'No one has left anyone,' she said, keeping her focus on the washing up.

Leela sighed. 'Baby, I hope you know what you're doing. Because secrets never stay hidden. Once a corner is seen, the rest will be dragged out sooner or later.'

The concern in her voice wrung something out of Chaya's heart. These were the people she loved. In trying to keep them happy, she had created a lie so big that it could hurt them even more. Suddenly, the plan she and Gimhana had come up with didn't seem such a great idea anymore. She carefully put another cup upside down on the draining board. It slipped and clattered back into the sink. She fished it out and checked it for cracks.

'Be careful,' said Leela quietly.

They both knew it wasn't the cup she talking about.

Chapter Seventy-Two

Gimhana – Colombo, 2013

When they got back to the hotel, Gimhana washed his face and changed his shirt. The humidity had made him sticky. The air was so close, it was bound to rain soon.

He came back into the room to find Chaya staring out of the window, fingers drumming lightly against her thigh. She was still tense. This trip was difficult for them both, but Chaya was struggling more than he was. Which was ridiculous because he was the one with the most to lose. All she had to do was play the deceived innocent and she'd be relatively unscathed. He, on the other hand, would face all kinds of stigma, potentially even violence, who knew? Back at home... Back at home, Chaya's job would be completely unaffected whereas his would be made difficult. Oh, there was a non-discrimination policy, of course. But there were ways, weren't there? After all, did he want to be that guy? The one who made trouble by complaining? It was hard enough being the brown one among the partners. He didn't want the burden of being the gay one, too. His search for alternative employment was going slowly and there was no guarantee he'd find anything better. No, he had to make this work.

He joined her at the window.

They had a sea view. The sky looked thunderous and the steely grey ocean had been whipped up into frothy waves. Trees waved as the breeze picked up. Everything outside seemed to be in motion. Inside the room, everything felt very still.

'I thought that went rather well,' he said.

Chaya didn't turn around. 'Only because you made her think she was going crazy.'

Oh, what? 'She's confused anyway,' said Gimhana. 'I only made her happy. Where's the harm in that?'

Chaya stared out of the window for a moment before replying. 'It just didn't seem right.'

'Well, I didn't see you rushing in to stop me,' said Gimhana. 'We agreed on this plan, remember?' He turned away and went to the safe to retrieve his laptop. He had taken time off work for 'personal reasons', but he couldn't afford to give the firm grounds to accuse him of slacking off. 'I think,' he said, turning the device on, 'we're doing rather well with our plan. We might just be able to get away with it.'

'We've been getting away with it for years,' Chaya muttered. Abruptly, she turned away from the window. 'I'm going for a walk,' she said. 'I need to think.' That didn't sound good.

'Shall I come?'

'No. I need some space. To think.'

He tried to assess how keyed up she really was. Perhaps going for a walk would do her good, let her vent some of that nervous energy that was fizzling beneath the surface. 'Don't go too far,' he said. 'It looks like rain.'

Chapter Seventy-Three

Chaya – Colombo, 2013

The hotel was built on a promontory that stuck out into the Indian Ocean. It meant that the seaward side of the hotel had access to beaches and rock pools on either side of the headland. Chaya walked down some steps, onto the beach. Overhead, the sky had lowered so that it was almost skimming the top of the hotel. She passed the beach restaurant where a few hardy diners were still sitting at the tables, sheltered by the coconut thatch umbrellas. The beach itself was deserted because of the angry sea and the taste of rain in the air.

Chaya looked at the frothing waves and headed, instead, for the rocks. They started suddenly, sprouting black boulders out of the sand and climbing up from the beach towards the towers of the hotel. At the lower end, the seawater sprayed in the air as the surf shattered against granite. She scrambled, sandals skittering over the slick surface. The wind had picked up and was whipping the coconut trees in a violent dance. Above her, she could see the balconies of the hotel. Somewhere up there was her room, where Gimhana would be working. From outside, on the rocks, the hotel seemed like a mirage. A thing from another world where nothing was what it claimed to be.

A fat drop of rain landed on her head. She climbed further, higher, but closer to the hotel. Globs of water started to fall, faster and faster. She climbed, half blinded by the water that ran down her face, higher still, until she reached the top. From her slippery perch, she shaded her eyes to get her bearings. Ahead was a short drop that ended in a fringe of frangipani trees in the hotel garden. Perfect white garden furniture glistened in the rain.

Behind her the sea boomed as the first wave of the storm crashed against the rocks. She turned round to face it. The ocean, usually flat and blue, was a boiling, ugly thing. It was as though the face of serene perfection had been lifted and she was seeing it as it really was.

It reminded her of her life. All she'd wanted was for her family to be proud of her. She had done everything, *everything* in her power to give them that. She had worked hard, studied long hours, taken every opportunity. She had given up anything that she thought would distract her. She had given up the love of her life. And she had broken herself.

She thought of her Thatha, who had died believing she had a perfect life. She remembered him talking about his daughters – Malini, the pretty one with the perfect family, and Chaya, the clever one who was a lecturer and married to a successful lawyer. She remembered the way he'd glowed when he said it. 'My girls. They've both done well.' He had been proud of her. Lightning streaked across the sky. Water ran down her hair and clothes. She looked at the sea and flinched at the crash of thunder. Thatha had been proud. She smiled, grimly. One out of three wasn't bad.

Chapter Seventy-Four

Gimhana – Colombo, 2013

Gimhana was completely absorbed in his work when someone knocked. He muttered a curse under his breath and went over to open the door. A man in a hotel staff uniform stood there, looking profoundly uncomfortable.

'Yes?' He hadn't ordered room service.

'Sir, your wife,' said the man urgently.

For the first time, he realised how long Chaya had been gone. 'What about my wife?'

'She's on the rocks. We're afraid she might…'

Thunder crashed outside. Gimhana shoved his feet into shoes and followed the man out.

He shouldn't have let her go out. She'd been weirdly quiet on the way back and she wasn't taking her anxiety medicine. There was no way of knowing how bad she was feeling. He should have paid more attention.

They got to the garden and pushed past a small knot of people. The man pointed. This part of the gardens ended with a rocky outcrop. Normally, it was a picturesque feature against the gentle blue sea. Now it was a rain-slicked hulk of black against the thunderous grey. Standing at the highest point, hands clasped in front of her, was Chaya.

'Oh. Shit.'

Chapter Seventy-Five

Chaya – Colombo, 2013

By now the storm was in full swing. The wind lashed more rain at Chaya, almost pulling her off her perch. She put her head back and stared into the rain, watching the drops fall from far, far above. Her ears were full of the sound of water. Playing in the monsoon. She had always loved to do that. She held out her arms and let it all wash over her.

Water drenched her, weighing down her clothes. Warm rain ran down her arms and back, washing away the lies she'd told to everyone and to herself. She had lived her life trying to twist herself to fit other people's dreams. It hadn't been a bad life. She'd been very convincing. She'd even convinced herself that it was what she wanted.

Now that the illusion was destroyed, she finally saw what she had lost in the process. Her eyes streamed with tears and monsoon. She didn't want to pretend any more. She couldn't change the past, but she could start afresh on the future. There didn't need to be a drumroll or cymbals. She could make just little changes. It didn't matter what they were, so long as they were based on what she really wanted. But what did she really want? Did she even know anymore? She thought about what Malini had said. Without Gimhana, was she really still somebody? Everything in her career, she had built herself. She had stood up for her work, even in the combative environment of academia. She had earned her place. So, yes, she was still somebody. It would be harder if he wasn't with her, but she'd cope.

And Noah? For seventeen years she'd thought that the one thing missing in her life was Noah. In a flash of understanding, she saw her nervous breakdown in a new light. It wasn't heartbreak caused by her split up with Noah. It had been a breakdown caused by the combination of that with everything else. She had been an undergraduate at one of the most punishing and stressful universities in the world and struggling to keep up. She was far away from home and trying to navigate between homesickness and independence. On top of all of that, she had been in a relationship she had to keep secret. The pressure had been too much and she'd buckled. Breaking up with Noah had only been the last straw.

She pushed her hair away from her eyes. Everything that she had been certain of was now gone. She should have been petrified, but she felt oddly calm. She was never calm. The panic was bound to come in a bit. But for now...

Voices came out of the roar of the rain. Someone was calling her name. Frowning, she turned and looked behind her. Gimhana was scrambling up the rocks from the garden. He looked up and stretched out a hand. 'Don't move!' he shouted. 'I'm coming for you. Don't move.'

She stared at him, so dramatic with his white shirt plastered to him in the rain. He found a safe place to stand and reached his arms out to her. 'Take my hand,' he said, blinking to keep the water out of his eyes.

Chaya hesitated. She didn't want to leave this rock, where things made sense. Gimhana moved his hand, his eyes frantic with fear. Fear of what? Lightning flashed again and she realised he was frightened for her. He was probably right to be. She sat down on the rain-slicked rock, reached down and put her hand in his. His fingers clamped round hers and he pulled her off the rock. She fell and collided with him, almost sending them both down into the frangipani trees.

Over Gimhana's shoulder, she could see a small knot of hotel staff standing at the doorway, carrying large umbrellas and towels. They didn't step out into the rain, but stood there watching. Behind them some hotel guests had stopped too. Everyone enjoyed a moment of drama.

Gimhana held her tight against him. 'It's okay,' he said in her ear. 'I've got you now. Let's get down slowly.' He sounded like a character in a soap opera.

Chaya looked at his earnest face. Then she began to laugh.

–

Afterwards, she sat on the bed, legs curled under her. Her hair was wrapped in a towel. She undid it and rubbed it over her hair. Outside, the storm still raged.

Gimhana came out of the bathroom, now in dry clothes. He stopped at the foot of the bed and looked at her, head cocked to one side. 'How're you feeling?'

She studied him right back. He was a good friend. He had supported her through difficult times and helped her find ways to cope when things got too much. Had she ever loved him? Maybe, in her own way, she had.

'Chaya?' he said, worry lacing his voice. He sat on the end of the bed.

'Gim,' she said, carefully. 'I want a divorce.'

He stared at her for a moment, frowning. 'Oh dear, I think you're in some sort of delayed shock.'

The last person who had said that to her was Noah. The memory resurfaced. Her stomach twisted. She accepted the pain with only the smallest flinch.

'No,' she said. 'I mean it.'

'But the plan is working,' he said. He moved up the bed until he was sitting next to her. 'We can sort this out and go back to the way things were.'

'Things will never be the way they were before, Gim. It's too late for that.'

'Is this because of what happened with your amma?'

'Not really,' she said. 'Well, not entirely.' She sighed. 'I'm tired, Gim. I'm tired of trying to be what people expect me to be. Tired of lying. I'm just... so tired. I've had enough. I think we've come to a point where we can't sustain this any longer.'

'You're serious?'

She nodded. Very slowly, he nodded too. 'I see.'

He looked away, rubbing his neck. She watched him, feeling his sorrow. He had more to lose than she did.

'I'm sorry,' she said. 'I know it's more important for you than it is for me.'

He made a noise, but didn't disagree.

'Your work... will that be okay?'

He sighed. 'I don't know. You know what the firm is like.'

She did. It was a stifling place to work, with the small cadre of equity partners holding so much power. Gimhana had been made a salaried partner several years ago, but further progress still eluded him. It wasn't that he didn't do the work or bring in the money. 'I've wondered for some time,' she said, quietly, 'whether you should try to move. Your loyalty to the firm isn't really being rewarded and... times have changed. Other firms might have changed with them.'

'I've been thinking about that too,' he said. He turned his head, resting it lightly against the headboard so that he was looking at her. 'Perhaps this is an opportunity?'

'Perhaps.'

'Let's think about this,' he said, his forehead wrinkling the way it did when he was working on something complicated. 'If we get divorced, how does it affect you?'

She shrugged. 'I'll probably have to find somewhere to live...'

He waved that aside. 'We'll deal with money later. I mean, in terms of life.'

Without waiting for a reply, he carried on. 'Your family will think you've chucked me because of what happened with Zack. I'm guessing they'll keep that quiet because of the stigma. So my family will think…' he frowned. 'Mine will think that I chucked you.'

'Stigma all round,' said Chaya.

'We're never going to escape that. Even if we stay together, people are going to be weird about it.' By 'people' he meant family. He had a point. 'Will you be okay, on your own?'

'I have lived on my own before, you know.'

He rolled his eyes. 'I meant the other stuff. The mental health stuff.' He sat up and put a hand on her arm. 'Earlier today, I genuinely thought you were going to… you know.'

'I'm not suicidal, if that's what you mean.' She felt a little offended that he thought so.

'But—'

She sighed. He had a point. 'But I do need help.' She glanced sideways at him. 'Not drugs, but some other therapy again. You're right. I've been in denial for far too long. I need to go to these sessions and give them a chance.'

The look of relief on his face was wonderful to see. 'I'll still be around, if you need me,' he said. 'It's not like we're never going to see each other.'

This was what she would miss. His friendship had been a solid rock that she could brace herself against. She had been a panic-ridden mess when she'd first met him. It was his company that had eased her out of despair and taught her how to talk to people again. She had been wrong before. It wasn't him that had the most to lose by their separation. It was her.

'I'll be okay,' she said.

He studied her face. 'Yes,' he said, finally. 'I think you will be.'

She felt a stab of alarm at the idea, but it didn't escalate into full blown panic. Something had changed.

'So,' Gimhana said, going back to his original train of thought. 'My family will think I left you for reasons unknown, which is fine. Yours will think you dumped me.'

She nodded. 'Also fine.'

'And that just leaves you and me.'

'I'm sure we can split up in a nice, civilised way.'

'I'm sure we can.' He gave her a big smile. 'Thank you,' he said.

'For what?'

'For seven years of fake married life. I've enjoyed it.'

She laughed. 'Funnily enough,' she said. 'So have I.'

He put his arm out so that she could lay her head on his shoulder. 'We made a good team,' he said.

'Yes,' she said. In their own ways they had saved each other, making each other's lives so much more free. She would miss him. 'Yes, we did.'

They sat there next to each other for a while, two warm bodies in the over-chilled room. After some time, Gimhana moved. 'I need whiskey,' he said, standing up and brushing his clothes straight.

Chaya started to protest, but then realised she no longer had the right to monitor his drinking.

'Come on,' he offered her a hand up. 'I'll buy you a celebratory drink.'

She took his hand and he hauled her to her feet. 'What's to celebrate? We're getting a divorce.'

'Exactly,' he said. 'Which means it's time for Plan B.'

'Plan B?' She said, grabbing her handbag and following him out. 'What's plan B?'

'I don't know yet.' He grinned. 'But I'm sure I'll think of something.'

Chapter Seventy-Six

Gimhana – Colombo, 2013

Gimhana felt fuzzy. He swirled his latest whiskey around and listened to the sound of ice clinking against the glass.

Next to him, Chaya ordered another bowl of chili cashew nuts. They had been sitting together at the bar, reminiscing for a few hours now. Anyone looking at them would have thought they were a couple. No one stared or whispered or made them feel unwelcome. Things would never be like this if he brought someone he genuinely loved to visit his home country. Someone like Zack. He sighed and took a small sip of his drink.

Chaya nudged him. 'Zack?' she said. How did she do that? For someone who was so stiff and awkward talking to people, she could be remarkably prescient.

'What are you going to do about him?' she said, when he didn't reply.

'I don't know. I've tried calling him, tried calling his house-mates, I even tried social media.' He suppressed a shudder. 'He doesn't want to talk to me.'

'Understandably, he's upset,' she said. She poked at her drink with her straw. 'How about if I talk to him?'

'What? How would that help?'

She shrugged. 'Once we start divorce proceedings, I could tell him that we're splitting up and about the whole marriage of convenience thing. He might believe it, coming from me.'

Hope flared unreasonably in his chest. He should know better than to hope. These things rarely worked out the way one envisaged. 'Do you think it would make a difference?'

'I don't know. It's worth a shot.' She nodded her thanks to the barman who brought her a bowl of fresh cashews. 'We all make stupid mistakes. If you have a chance to fix them, then you should try everything.' She picked up a handful of nuts. 'Better to regret something you have done than something you haven't done.' She popped the cashews into her mouth.

'That's nonsense,' he said. 'It's better not to regret anything.'

She didn't reply.

But she was right. He had the opportunity, however small, to try and make things right. He could only try. He ran her comment through his mind again and realised that she was talking about herself as much as about him.

'What about you? Are you going to contact Noah? Find out if he's still married?'

She took her time before replying, chewing her mouthful of cashews and staring into the middle distance. He waited.

Finally, she said, 'He's not married anymore. At least, not to his first wife.'

She had clearly known this a while. 'Oh,' he said. 'When did that happen?'

'Around the time we got married.' She toyed with a cashew nut, rolling in her fingers. 'He... uh... met me for a coffee. To catch up.'

'Chaya, why didn't you say anything?'

'What was there to say, Gim? We'd just got married. I couldn't un-marry you and go off with him. Besides, he lives in Canada. I live in England. It would be bonkers.'

'But you don't have to live in England,' he said. 'I'm sure they need microbiologists in Canada too.'

She gave him a sideways look. 'But if I get this professor-ship...'

He knew she deserved it, but a small treacherous voice said she wouldn't get it because her main competition was a noisy white man. He couldn't say that to her. 'I'm not saying everything will fall into place,' he said. 'But it's worth thinking about, isn't it?'

She looked thoughtful. He saw hope rise and fall in her expression and felt guilty for making her think about it. 'I think I closed that door fairly conclusively seven years ago,' she said. 'He wanted to stay in touch. I said no.'

'Oh.' Had she given up a chance to be with the one that got away, just because she'd made a promise to him? Now he felt even worse about breaking their deal. 'I didn't realise that you gave him up again... for me.'

She smiled, a small, bitter smile. 'I didn't do it for you,' she said. And frowned. 'Well, not entirely for you, anyway. I did it for my family.' She rolled her eyes upward. 'For all the good it's done me.'

'God, Chaya, I'm so sorry.'

She nudged him gently. 'You weren't to know. We had a plan. It could have worked.'

They both stared thoughtfully at their drinks, contemplating what might have been.

'Could have been a beautiful thing,' said Gimhana, finally.

'Yeah. Shame it didn't work out.' She raised her glass. 'To failed marriages,' she said.

He clinked his glass against hers. 'To failed marriages.'

Chapter Seventy-Seven

Chaya – Colombo, 2013

Chaya couldn't sleep. Gimhana was snoring in his side of the bed. She picked up her laptop and tiptoed out to the balcony. One thing she wouldn't miss would be sharing her space with him. She'd never felt vulnerable sharing a bed with him, they had no sexual interest in one another, but it was always annoying. She liked her own space. She thought Gimhana probably did too. She didn't understand how proper married couples shared a bedroom night after night without wanting to kill each other.

The night was warm and clear after the storm. The half moon was bright enough to dot silver highlights on the sea. Chaya sat on one of the chairs on the balcony and checked her emails.

There was nothing urgent. She fired off a few short messages and exited the mail app.

Gimhana's comment about Noah nagged at her. She opened Google and put in his name. There he was. She scrolled past articles and profiles. He had a Facebook profile that was private.

She closed down that search and ran a search of his ex-wife. Skimming through the pictures, she saw that Katherine had remarried. There was Noah and Alex at the wedding. Noah, without a partner. That was from two years ago.

That didn't mean he was single. But... but...

She looked over the balcony wall at the tranquil sea. A few hours ago, it had been a frothing, seething nightmare and now it was calm. So much had changed, so fast. In times like this, in times of change, every chance was worth reaching out for.

She opened her laptop again and started looking at flights to Canada.

Chapter Seventy-Eight

Gimhana – Colombo, 2013

Once he'd seen Chaya off, Gimhana returned to their room and stared out to sea. Silently, he wished her luck. Her quest had only the smallest chance of success. Even if this Noah guy was still single, would he still be interested in the girl who dumped him seventeen years ago? He sighed. Poor Chaya was going to be crushed. She said she needed to know for sure. He could understand that.

If there was any way that he could get Zack back, then he'd take it. Admittedly he and Zack had only split up a few weeks ago, which was quite different to seventeen years.

He turned back and looked at the room. He could try and reschedule his flight, or he could just hang out here, working for a couple of extra days. What was there to go home to? The house. Work. He may as well stay where he could get a decent kotthu roti when he wanted one.

He was going to start applying for new jobs. He could update his CV while he was here, maybe even register with a few head-hunting firms. But before that, there was something he needed to do. He'd told Chaya he would think about it, but he knew she was right. It was well beyond time to make some changes.

Chaya had made the decision to stop pretending and be who she really was. She was a determined sort, once she set her mind to something. She never made promises she couldn't keep. Even if things went wrong with Noah, she would carry on with her mission to reclaim herself. Maybe it was time he did the same?

He got out his phone, called his mother and told her he was coming round.

–

His parents' house was once surrounded by fields, but now it was a largish house, behind a high wall, surrounded by other smaller houses. One of the servants let him in. The approach to the house was past a small grove of coconut trees. He breathed in the familiar smell of home.

His ammi limped up to the front door. She had fallen a few months ago and it was taking her a long time to heal. Worse than the injury was the damage it had done to her confidence. Where before she had been formidable, she had suddenly become old.

'Hello Putha.' She looked behind him. 'Where is Chaya?'

'I… need to talk to you and Thathi about something. It involves Chaya.'

'Are you expecting a baby?' Her face lit up. She put a hand out to steady herself.

'No.'

Just like that, the light dimmed. He felt bad. Once she heard what he had to say, it would dim even further.

He offered her his arm and they went inside. Thathi appeared from the bedroom, hastily buttoning up a shirt over the cotton vest he normally wore when he was at home. 'Oh,' he said. 'No Chaya.' He looked down at his shirt, as though wondering whether to bother, then carried on buttoning it.

They sat down and one of the servants brought Gimhana a glass of iced water.

'So, what did you have to talk to us about?' his ammi said.

He took a deep breath to steel himself. He knew that what he was going to say would hurt them. 'The first thing,' he said, 'is that Chaya and I are getting a divorce.'

There was a shocked silence at this. His parents looked at each other. His mother placed a hand against her heart.

'Why?' she said, her voice radiating disbelief.

'There… er … was someone else.'

Ammi gasped. 'Oh my,' she said.

His father scowled and harrumphed.

'Well,' said Ammi. 'I would never have thought that Chaya would be the sort of woman to go off with another man.'

'She wasn't,' said Gimhana. 'I was.'

His parents stared at him. For the longest time, no one spoke.

'All those years of rejecting woman after woman after woman,' his mother said. 'And now you want two? Who is this woman you thought was better than your wife?'

He felt cold and sweaty. He had to do this. Even if he never met anyone like Zack again, he owed it to himself to be real. 'Not a woman,' he said. 'A man. I'm gay.'

This silence was different. Whereas before the silence had been shocked and questioning, this was darker, angrier. His father muttered something that sounded like 'I knew it'. He got up and walked out of the room.

'Thathi,' Gimhana called after him. But his father didn't stop.

He looked at his mother. She was staring at the floor, thinking. He could almost feel her looking back at all the signs she'd ignored, all the lies she'd told herself.

'Ammi,' said Gimhana. 'I'm still the same person.'

'I think,' she said, her voice very quiet, 'that you should go.'

'But Ammi, just because—'

She turned her head away. 'Please go.'

He had been expecting this, but it still hurt. He stood up slowly. 'I'm leaving in a couple of days,' he said. 'I'll come and see you again before I go.'

She still didn't look at him. He stood up slowly and walked out of the room. He paused at the door. 'Ammi,' he said. 'I'll call you.'

Finally, she looked up. Her eyes were full of tears. 'Yes,' she said.

He wanted to say more, but she'd turned away again. No more conversation. At least she had agreed to speak to him on the phone. She hadn't turned him away completely. That was a small comfort.

He let himself out and strode back to the road, fighting back tears. He should have done this while Chaya was still around. Right now he felt untethered from the world. No Chaya, no Zack, no parents. He was utterly alone.

He hailed down a tuk tuk and gave the address of the hotel. Once he got back, even though it was still daytime, he headed for the bar. Today was not an easy day to get through. He was going to drink. A lot.

Chapter Seventy-Nine

Chaya – Canada, 2013

Chaya looked up at the imposing university building and felt a rush of fear. She hadn't thought this through. She hadn't emailed ahead, like she should have done. It was almost as though she'd been subtly sabotaging this trip the whole way – giving herself excuses for it to fail. Now she was standing outside the building where Noah worked. She couldn't very well turn back.

She climbed the steps, carrying her backpack with her. Since she'd come straight from Sri Lanka, she only had a few items of suitable clothing with her. She'd left most of her tropical summer stuff with Gimhana to take home. It had seemed a good idea at the time, but now it seemed like just another way in which she hadn't planned this properly.

The reception was a window that looked into a busy office. She gave them Noah's name and her maiden name, which, thankfully, was still her professional name.

'Is he expecting you?' the lady asked.

'Um. No. I was… in the area.'

She fidgeted while she waited for the woman to call his office. What if he was busy? What if he wasn't and he didn't want to see her anyway? What if he hated her for the pain she'd caused him? Or worse, what if he'd forgotten her altogether? After all, she had rejected him twice. Why on earth hadn't she emailed and made contact before she came?

The woman hung up and came back to the window. 'I'm afraid Dr Burlescombe-West isn't in today. We can leave him a note to say you came by.'

'Yes. Please.' She gave her phone number, thanked the woman and walked back out. She wasn't sure what she was feeling. Was it disappointment or relief? Or both? Mostly though, she was feeling tired. She really needed to find a hotel and get some sleep. Once she was rested, she could have a proper think about the mess she was in.

She started back down the long flight of steps, her feet feeling like they were encased in lead. She was so wrapped up in her thoughts that she didn't notice the man and boy who were heading towards her until they were only a few yards away.

The sight of Noah struck her like an arrow in the chest. He was talking to the boy and hadn't noticed her.

As the boy talked, he gesticulated his arms and briefly, ran his hand over his forehead, unconsciously mirroring Noah's gesture.

Now that he was actually in front of her, she wasn't sure she could go through with this. Hesitation made her falter and almost fall down the steps. The movement caught his attention. 'Are you alright?' He put out a hand, as though to catch her.

She steadied herself and nodded.

'Chaya?'

Her eyes met the familiar blue of his and her mind went blank. They stared at each other for a long moment. Her heart buffeted against her ribs like it wanted to be let out. She couldn't think of a single thing to say. What do you say to the love of your life after seventeen years?

'What are you doing here?' His accent was a curious mixture of English and Canadian.

She looked over his shoulder. His son was standing just behind him, head to one side, watching them. Oh goodness, she hadn't thought this through. But she was here now. She took a deep breath and summoned up her best professional manner. 'I was in the area and thought…' Pathetic. She had spent most of the last decade lying, why was it so hard to lie now? 'I thought it would be nice to catch up.'

Emotions flitted over his face before settling on a half smile. 'It's been a long time,' he said. 'It's nice to see you.'

She didn't respond. She didn't know what to say. At least he wasn't being hostile. He couldn't hate her all that much.

Her silence made things awkward. The tips of his ears started to go red. He was embarrassed. But why? She smiled, trying to make things better.

'So… er… are you here on business?' he said. 'Or… um… holiday?'

'Business,' she lied. Telling him the real reason she'd come seemed like a very, very bad idea right now. 'But since I was here, I thought I'd look you up. To see if…' she cast about for an end of the sentence. 'To see if you were still available,' simply wasn't an option. 'To see if you still worked here. You know. As you say, it's been a long time.'

Noah's eyes skittered around as he tried to think of something to say. Silence stretched painfully taut.

'Dad?'

They'd both forgotten about the boy.

Noah cleared his throat. 'Alex. So… er… Let me introduce you.' Noah put his arm round the boy's shoulders. 'This is Alex. My son. Alex, this is Chaya…'

'We met once, when you were really little.' She held out her hand to Alex, who shook it. He was almost as tall as Noah and had the same eyes. Close up, Chaya could see he had dark curls peering from underneath his cap. He got his hair from his mother.

'Chaya is an old friend of mine,' said Noah. 'We haven't seen each other in… too many years.'

Alex nodded. 'Nice to meet you,' he said, his voice oscillating. She took him to be about twelve or thirteen years old. He looked at Noah. 'So, Dad. You need to get those papers from your office.'

Noah was still looking at Chaya, frowning a little. 'Oh, that's not so important. They can wait.'

Alex rolled his eyes. 'O-kay. About that ice cream…?'

'Oh yeah,' said Noah. 'We were about to go and get some ice cream.' He gave Chaya a polite smile that didn't have the same warmth as before. 'How about… er … maybe you'd like to come with us, Chaya? You don't mind do you, Alex?'

Alex shrugged.

'Ice cream would be lovely,' Chaya said. 'I'd love to join you.'

–

As he drove to the ice cream shop, Noah talked – pointing out places of interest, telling her about restaurants she should definitely visit if she had the time. All three of them knew he was babbling, but he didn't seem able to stop himself.

Alex seemed mortified with embarrassment for his father. After some time, he intervened. 'How long are you here for, Chaya?' he said, twisting round in his seat to look at her.

'I'm not really sure,' she said. Damn, why hadn't she worked out her cover story in advance? She improvised frantically. 'Depends how long my work takes me. Probably about a fortnight, I should think.'

An awkward silence descended in the car, until Noah turned off to the ice cream parlour with an over bright, 'Here we are.'

As they walked from the car park to the building, Alex said, 'So, where do you guys know each other from?'

'University,' said Noah. He glanced at Chaya. The answer was so hopelessly inadequate to cover what they had been to each other. What they weren't anymore.

Alex looked at Noah and then at her. He frowned. His eyes widened, then narrowed. He knew who she was. She felt strangely pleased that Noah had talked about her.

The ice cream parlour had a rural feel to it. Ice creams in myriad colours and flavours were lined up along a long counter. A board proudly announced that they made their own ice cream and listed all the different flavours. She stared, bewildered by choice. Alex reeled off what he wanted and how he wanted it. Noah turned to her. "Chaya?'

She stared at the board and frowned. How could she possibly choose one out of all those flavours? She had a sudden memory of staring at the menu of another ice cream parlour many years and many miles away. She looked at Noah. His mouth twitched. Her choice had always defaulted to the most obvious one.

'Chocolate,' they said in unison.

'Some things never change, I guess,' said Noah. There was warmth in his voice.

'Guess not,' she said.

Ice creams in hand, they followed Alex, who led them to a small booth that seated four. He slid into a seat and Chaya shuffled in opposite him. Noah hesitated a moment, then sat beside Alex.

'So, you're here for work?' said Alex. He seemed stiff and hostile now, no longer the disinterested teenager he had been before.

'Yes. I'm here to discuss a collaboration with one of my colleagues.' The lies were coming more easily now.

'What's their name?' said Noah. 'I know a few people in the biology department.'

She forced a laugh. 'I don't really want to talk about work right now, if that's okay. It's been a few years, Noah, why don't you tell me what's happened in your life?'

'Let's see,' said Noah, his eyes lifting up as he lined up his thoughts. 'Nothing too exciting, really. Since we last spoke, I've just been here, doing the same old stuff. That project we did with your university – we had a paper published in *Nature: Geoscience*.'

Chaya was suitably impressed. 'Nice.'

Alex rolled his eyes.

'How about you?' said Noah.

'Well,' Chaya said. 'Similar, really.' She looked at her hand. The rings were still on it. Was it too early to remove them?

She opened her mouth to say, 'I'm getting a divorce', but realised that wouldn't even begin to cover the complexity of their arrangement. 'That's it, really,' she finished. 'I've applied for a professorship, but I'm not holding out much hope.'

Alex was staring at her now, his eyes flashing. 'What does your husband do? Is he a scientist too?'

She had just taken a mouthful of ice cream. She shook her head.

'Commercial lawyer,' said Noah, absent-mindedly ladling some ice cream into his mouth.

Alex and Chaya both looked at him. Noah stopped, spoon in his mouth. The tips of his ears started to go red again.

'How did you know that?' Chaya said.

Noah shrugged. 'Grapevine, you know how it is.'

'Grapevine?'

'I met Jay, quite by coincidence, some time back.' He wouldn't meet her eyes. Seventeen years and she could still tell when he was being shifty.

'I see.' Her mind whirred. He had been looking for information about her. She thought about all the times she had typed his name into Google. Had he done the same with hers? Did that mean that there was some hope? How could she find out?

She got her chance when Noah said, 'Sounds like it all worked out perfectly for you.'

'Not really,' she said. 'It's complicated.'

Noah looked up and finally met her gaze. His expression guarded.

Alex said, 'How did you meet your husband?' He seemed very defensive. She wasn't sure why.

Chaya tore her gaze away from Noah's and gave a polite laugh; the one that she used when talking to Gimhana's colleagues. 'It's a boring story, I'm afraid. We met in a very Sri Lankan way.'

Noah was looking down at what was left of his ice cream. He looked up. 'Excuse me,' he said. 'I'll be back in a moment.'

He slipped out of his seat and walked away, his shoulders were sloping inwards, as though he were fighting the urge to curl up into himself.

–

Alex watched until his father was out of earshot and then moved across until he was directly opposite Chaya. She watched him, apprehensive.

'Look, lady,' he said, leaning forward. 'I don't know why you're here, but you have to leave my dad alone.'

'Pardon?'

'I know who you are. You broke his heart when you dumped him, you know. It took him years to get over it. In fact, you're part of the reason Mum and Dad split up.' He glared at her, daring her to deny it.

How could that be? She'd had nothing to do with Noah's divorce. 'Alex…'

'I'm not going to let you hurt him again. He's been through a lot in the past few years, he doesn't need you using him as some sort of…' He cast about for an appropriate word. 'Some sort of rebound cushion,' he said, finally. His eyes glittered, so blue, just like his father's.

'It's not like that, at all.' Wasn't it? Wasn't that exactly what she was doing? Running away from Gimhana, back to Noah? She wanted to tell him it hadn't been easy for her either. That she'd married a man whom she didn't love. She'd built a shell of lies around herself and now the shell had cracked. But how could she explain that to anyone, let alone a teenager who thought he was protecting his father? Who would believe her anyway? She wasn't sure she believed herself, most of the time. So, instead she said, 'Alex, I would never want to hurt Noah. Honestly, the last thing in the world that I want to do is to cause him any pain.'

He looked beaten for a moment. 'Just… leave my dad alone,' he said. 'Please.'

She looked at him and saw the lines of Noah's face in his. She couldn't promise him that. She'd already ruined her life once by promising to stay away from Noah. 'I didn't mean to hurt him, Alex. I would never do that. Okay?'

He looked like he was going to say something, but Noah returned and he clamped his mouth shut and shuffled over to his end of the booth again.

–

She spent an hour with Noah and Alex. Alex didn't leave them alone together for a moment, not even when his mobile phone rang. He was watching her.

Suddenly, Chaya felt tired. The events of the previous days were catching up with her. She needed space to think. She couldn't do that when Noah was around. She asked him if he minded dropping her off at a hotel.

'Where are you staying?' he said.

Another thing she hadn't thought through. She had seen a sign for a Best Western as they'd been driving around, so she told him that. He drove her there and offered to walk her, with her small bag, into reception. Alex started to get out as well, but Noah stopped him. 'You wait here for me, Alex. I shan't be long.'

They walked up to the entrance, side-by-side and stopped under the overhead canopy. She didn't want him to come in and realise that she'd lied about having a room booked. This suddenly seemed very important. What was happening to her? Had she run away from one set of lies only to weave another?

'So, er, thanks for the afternoon,' she said. 'It was really nice to see you and meet Alex.'

They both turned to look at the car. She could just about make out Alex, slouched in his seat, glowering.

'Although I don't think he likes me very much,' she said.

'I'm sorry about that,' said Noah. 'I don't know what's got into him. He's normally such a friendly boy.' He shook his head. 'I've never known him to be so sullen.'

Chaya forced a smile. 'Maybe he resents me gate-crashing your father son time.'

'That sort of thing's never bothered him before. He used to love it when Jess joined us.'

'Jess?'

Noah flushed. 'This lady I was seeing for a while. It was some time ago,' he added quickly.

Chaya nodded. 'Oh well, who knows what goes through teenagers' minds?' she said, thinking suddenly of Nayana.

Noah nodded. There was an awkward silence, neither of them sure what to say next. Noah cleared his throat. 'It was nice to see you again,' he said.

'Likewise.' She had to think of a way to see him again. The whole point of coming there was to talk to him. 'Would... er... you be up for meeting again before I leave?'

'Sure. We could do dinner...' he stopped. 'Nothing fancy, just dinner and a drink somewhere... catch up properly?'

Her heart leapt as she had a sudden sense of history repeating itself. 'That would be nice.'

'I have some time, tomorrow evening?' she said. The sooner she worked out where she was going with this, the better.

'Works for me. I'll pick you up at eight from here?'

She nodded. 'Sounds lovely.'

'Great.'

They stared at each other for a moment longer. His very presence pulled at her, luring her closer. She'd known that she'd never stopped loving him, but she hadn't expected the feelings to be so strong. She'd spent all afternoon fighting the urge to slip her hand into his, to brush the hair out of his eyes, to sit next to him so that their thighs touched – all those things she'd taken for granted when they were going out. But they were strangers again now and that sort of thing wasn't allowed. How did people manage to stay in touch with their exes? It was too hard. A moment's lapse would be all it took to open a floodgate.

'I'd better go in,' she said, although she really, really didn't want to.

'Yes,' he said.

She made a half move towards the door.

'Oh, hang on, I'll give you my phone number, in case you need to contact me... if you're running late tomorrow, or something.' He pulled his wallet out of his back pocket and extracted a small card. He found a pen in another pocket and, using his knee as a table, scribbled his mobile number on the back. 'Call me anytime. If you need anything at all. Okay?'

'Okay.'

'So, I guess I'll see you tomorrow night, then.'

For an awkward moment she wondered whether a hug or a kiss on the cheek was appropriate. In the end, they shook hands, his warm hands closing over hers. His touch was so familiar, it sent a thrill up her arm. She hadn't been expecting that. Clearly, he felt it too. He held her hand a fraction longer than was necessary. It took all her will power to extract her hand from his.

Chapter Eighty

Chaya – Canada, 2013

The next day, Chaya took a taxi to a shop where she could buy some cheap clothing. That evening she dressed with care. She looked at the finished product – tidy hair, carefully applied make-up. She'd chosen a simple pair of slacks and a cotton shirt that looked more expensive than it really was. The jacket was smart and fit her well. It made the rest of it come together to make an outfit. Details. Gimhana had trained her well.

Standing sideways on, she examined her figure. Since getting married, she had eaten better and got out more, so she was no longer skin and bones, but was still far from podgy. She eyed her chest and stomach. She knew she looked smart. For the first time in years, she wondered if she could look sexy.

She rarely thought about sexual satisfaction. It was as though she'd locked that part of her away along with her heartbreak. It was the only way she could function: focus on her work; get through a day, then another, then another. Once she met Gimhana, things had improved. She'd remembered how to enjoy life a bit, but always, there were limits. What if those limits were permanent? She thought of the little frisson she'd felt when Noah shook her hand. What if they weren't?

She looked at her hands. They were clammy. This was new. She washed them.

She felt as though she was about to go on stage, not go out to dinner. In fact, she wasn't sure if she'd be able to eat anything. The tightness in her throat and chest had been there all day. If she wasn't careful, she'd have a full-blown panic attack before she even got to see Noah. She closed her eyes and took deep breaths, trying to force open the knot above her diaphragm. She was going to tell Noah what had happened. She had made a mistake all those years ago, letting him go. If there was anything she could do to undo that, she would do it. Things may not work out. They were both different people now. It was a risk she had to take.

Her wedding and engagement rings were still on her fingers. She tried to ease them off, she even tried putting soap on her skin to slide them off, but it seemed her fingers had moulded to their presence. Besides, there would be a pale line where they had shielded her skin from the sun. Their absence would only make them more obvious.

She was still fiddling with her rings when the phone rang. It was reception, calling to say she had a visitor. She told them she'd be right there, took one last look in the mirror and flew downstairs to see him.

'Wow,' Noah said, when she arrived downstairs. 'You scrub up nice.'

Warmth rose in her face. 'Thanks.' They both hesitated a moment before dropping kisses millimetres from each other's cheeks. Noah held the door open as they headed out.

He took her to a bustling restaurant full of families and big groups. It was a nice, safe choice that made it clear that this was not a date. They were given a table against one wall of the restaurant. The only chance of privacy was the hope that no one would hear what they were saying above the general ruckus. But it didn't matter. They fell straight back into a comfortable pattern of conversation, as though the intervening years had been just a few weeks.

They shared gossip about mutual friends, compared life in Canada to life in England, discussed how their careers were going. They talked about everything other than the thing that was on Chaya's mind.

Noah seemed to have decided to treat her like an old friend and nothing more, so he was relaxed and friendly. He still maintained a polite distance, as befitted someone meeting an ex. She was a married woman, and certain boundaries applied. He was a gentleman and respected that. She knew all this without having to be told and loved him all the more for it.

For her part, it was obvious that her feelings for him hadn't changed. It was as though she'd packed them away so carefully, that they'd been put into stasis, ready to come back to life when she let them, even after all these years. Every familiar gesture and facial expression was a little explosion of recognition.

They sat opposite each other, careful not to touch each other, even accidentally. Every atom in her body screamed to reach forward and make contact, just for a moment. She clutched her cutlery and picked at her food, trying to keep her composure.

'So,' said Noah, stirring cream into his coffee. 'What are your plans for your stay here?'

For a second, Chaya thought about returning to her subterfuge of the evening before and claiming work appointments. No. Enough lies. The sole reason she was in Canada was to find him. Now that she had, it was silly to pretend otherwise.

She cleared her throat. 'Actually,' she said. 'I wasn't entirely honest with you yesterday...'

He raised his eyebrows. They disappeared into his hair. She clasped her hands together to avoid reaching out to touch his face.

'I'm... not really here for work.'

He waited for her to go on, holding his spoon mid stir. His face was carefully neutral.

'I... er...' She looked down. 'I've left my husband. Or rather, we're leaving each other.' She looked up to see his reaction.

For a moment his eyes shone, then the mask of neutrality returned. 'Really?' His voice wavered a moment and steadied. 'What happened?'

Good question. What could she say to him? 'It's a long story.'

Noah crossed his arms and leaned back. 'Try me,' he said. He couldn't have looked more defensive

Where should she begin? She closed her eyes. 'Well… you know all the criteria I had, for a person who was suitable to marry?'

He gave a small laugh. 'How could I forget?' Was there a trace of bitterness in his voice?

'Well, one of the things that wasn't on the list, was "heterosexual".' She opened her eyes.

Noah's forehead furrowed while he worked it out. 'You mean he left you for a man?' His expression was one of sympathy now.

'Worse,' she said. 'My niece found out about it and eventually everyone found out.'

'Your niece?' His frown deepened. 'Okay, now I'm confused.' He beckoned the waitress over and requested more tea and coffee. When she had gone, he said, 'Now. Tell me from the beginning.'

She told him: about Gimhana; about their arrangement; about how they'd fooled everyone for seven years; about that day in Gimhana's office. Finally, she told him about how she was finally leaving the empty life she'd created and trying to right the mistakes she'd made. To her own surprise, a tear meandered down her cheek. She quickly brushed it away with the back of her hand.

Noah leaned forward. 'So, that day when you told me you'd got married…'

She nodded. 'That was to Gimhana. A fake marriage. I could have seen you again, but I had promised "no affairs" and I thought… I just couldn't see how it could have worked.'

Emotions flitted across his face. For a moment, he looked like he was going to reach for her hand. He hesitated, curled his fingers into a fist and tucked it back close to him. 'Why did you come here?'

'Letting you go was the biggest mistake I ever made. I was so young, Noah. I was failing at my studies, my dad had a heart attack, and I felt it was my fault somehow...' She raised her hands, in a gesture of confusion. 'I wanted, more than anything, to make my family proud. But everything was going wrong and I thought splitting up with you would make it right again. It didn't. I got things back on track, but I lost too much in the process.'

He stared at her, his expression a mixture of sympathy, puzzlement and... something else. Could it be hope? Wishful thinking. She could see just how bad it must have looked. She had left her husband and come back to find the jilted lover from aeons ago. Hoping for... reconciliation? It made her look crazy. This was a terrible idea.

Noah's expression had settled on neutral, but his body language hadn't. His arms were crossed over his chest again and he was leaning back, away from her.

'I shouldn't have come,' she said. 'I'm sorry. You've got a life of your own. I have no right...'

'Hey,' Noah interrupted. 'Don't be like that.' He gave her a small smile that didn't quite make it to his eyes. 'It's a bit of a surprise, that's all. I'm not sure quite how to handle it.'

She gave him a grateful smile back, then remembered, too late, the problem with nice English boys – they were always polite, even when they had to carve themselves up inside to manage it. You could never be sure what they really felt.

Noah looked away. Chaya could feel the slow burn of his thoughts as politeness and hurt battled against each other. She picked up her tea, letting the heat from the cup warm her fingertips and wishing it were hotter. There was nothing she could say that would ease the situation now. It was all up to Noah.

He looked up. 'I think I should take you home,' he said.
'Noah...'

He put up his hand. 'No, Chaya. Don't.' He leaned forward, his voice dropping to a whisper. 'Seventeen years, Chaya. That's how long it's been. You dumped me *seventeen years* ago and when we met in London, you made it very clear you'd moved on. And now… you're back. I don't know how to deal with this.' He sighed and pinched the bridge of his nose. 'I mean… what is it you want?'

At last, a question she knew the answer to. Given the circumstances, it would have been wiser not to say anything, but she owed him the truth. Feeling wretched, she said, 'You.' She sighed. 'I want you.'

He opened his mouth to answer, then shook his head. Raising an arm, he caught the eye of the waitress and asked for the bill. Neither of them said anything until they were in the car. She stared out of the window, feelings churning inside her like indigestion. Oddly, there was no panic. There would be pain and tears later, but for now, she could keep them at bay. This was progress, of sorts.

'You know,' Noah said suddenly. 'Alex warned me about this. He told me you were here for me and I told him not to be silly. I should have listened to him.' He shook his head. 'I can't believe I should have taken advice from my thirteen-year-old son!'

Chaya said, 'Well, teenagers do know everything.'

Noah glanced at her. The tension lightened.

She stared at his hands on the steering wheel and yearned to touch them. She cast about for a subject to talk about. 'So… are your parents still working in the Middle East?'

'Yes. I keep suggesting they go somewhere less dangerous, but they insist that nothing is going to stop them. They're in Riyadh at the moment, so it could be worse.' He paused. 'How about your family?'

'My father died last year.'

He turned to look at her. 'Shit, really?' He looked back at the road. 'I'm so sorry to hear that. It must have been awful for you.'

Chaya shrugged. 'Yes. Pretty awful.'

'How's your mum coping?'

'Could be better.'

There was silence for a moment. Was he thinking about how she'd been torn between loving him and loving her family? She'd thought that by making him walk away, she could stop loving him. She had been so wrong.

In the hotel car park, Noah stopped the car and turned out the lights. He turned to her. 'I'm sorry about back at the restaurant. I'm just… not sure how to handle this.'

Chaya unbuckled her seat belt. 'I understand. Really, I do. I'd have been the same in your place. I'm sorry I just walked back into your life and made a mess of things. I don't know what I was thinking.' She smiled, trying to look braver than she felt.

He nodded. The light was behind him and she couldn't see his face.

'Okay then.' She opened the door.

'I'll walk you to the door,' he said, diving out of the car.

They walked slowly, unspoken conversation hanging heavy between them. When they got to the foyer, they faced each other. All she wanted to do was throw her arms around him and kiss him. But he'd rejected her once already.

So she held out her hand. 'I guess I'll be seeing you.'

They shook hands. 'Yes. Goodbye.'

'Let's hope it doesn't take another seven years, eh?' She tried to smile, to make light of it.

He didn't reply. He squeezed her hand and let it drop. 'Bye,' he said.

'Bye.' She turned round and walked into the hotel. When she looked back over her shoulder, she could see him walking out of the building, his shoulders slumped and his head down. Poor Noah. What had she done?

Back in her room, the emotion finally hit. Everything was destroyed. Her life with Gimhana, any hope of a life with Noah. All gone. The last seven years had been a disaster. She tried to tell herself that she hadn't lost anything more than she'd already lost by coming here, but that wasn't true. Before, she'd had hope, however faint, that Noah might still love her. But his reaction told her otherwise. It was too late for them now.

Chaya buried her face in her hands and cried for the years she'd wasted, for opportunities lost, for the woman she could have been, but wasn't.

Chapter Eighty-One

Chaya – Canada, 2013

She must have fallen asleep crying, because she woke up in the small hours of the morning, curled up on her bed, her eyes sore and her face taut from dried tears. She felt strangely calm. She washed her face, got into her pyjamas and lay in bed, one arm tucked under her head, and considered what had happened as dispassionately as she could. If she was methodical about this, she could work out a way to get through it. She had survived worse.

She loved Noah. There was no doubt about that anymore. Underneath all that resentment, he probably loved her too. But he had made it clear that he didn't want to just pick things up where they'd left off, and it was unfair of her to expect that of him. She had to let him go.

Turning on the light, she checked the time. It would be afternoon in Sri Lanka by now. Today was the day Gimhana had been planning to go home. She phoned him. His phone was off. He must have boarded the plane already.

'I'm coming home,' she said to his answerphone.

–

Once her flight was booked, Chaya took out the piece of paper with Noah's number scrawled on it. The writing was lumpy and uneven because he'd used his knee as a writing surface. She stared at it, debating whether to call or not. On the one hand, he had told her he wasn't interested. It would be common courtesy to leave him alone now. On the other hand, what else did she have to lose?

She had to psych herself up to make the call. The phone rang and rang. Finally, the answerphone kicked in. A young voice, probably Alex's, said 'This is Noah's answerphone. Please leave a message'.

She started to lower the phone, but changed her mind at the last moment. She cleared her throat. 'Hi Noah, it's Chaya. I'm sorry to bother you again. I just wanted to tell you that I'm flying home this evening. At ten past seven.' She paused. What else was there to say? Realising the machine was still recording, she added, 'I'm... sorry if I upset you yesterday. I just had to know if there was any chance for us... but I know now that there isn't. I'm sorry again for... everything. That's all, really. Bye.' She hung up, feeling incredibly gauche.

Chaya wasn't sure why she told him when she was leaving. There wasn't any real chance of him rushing over to tell her he'd changed his mind; that he did want her after all. She stayed in the room, catching up on sleep, never too far from the phone. But it didn't ring.

Even at the boarding gate, she scanned the room, looking for a flash of red hair. Nothing. Disappointed, but not surprised, she turned and boarded the plane.

Chapter Eighty-Two

Chaya – London, 2013

Once the decision to separate was made, things moved quickly. Neither of them wanted a messy divorce. The first major shock was the realisation that it meant they had to actually separate.

Chaya stood in their kitchen, slicing a cucumber, the cold from the kitchen floor seeping into her socks, and contemplated where she wanted to live.

'I can move out,' said Gimhana. He was standing next to her, stirring. He picked up the small bowl of chillies that she'd sliced for him and stirred it in. The curry smelled amazing. 'One of the other houses is empty. I can move in there for a bit.' He owned four rental properties now. It made him a tidy income.

Chaya shook her head. 'I don't want to live here.' Although she'd lived in it for seven years, she couldn't think of the house as hers. It was his place. 'Before you ask, I don't want to move into your empty place either. I want somewhere for me.'

'I wouldn't charge you rent,' Gimhana said, sounding offended.

'Exactly. I need… to manage.'

Gimhana frowned. 'Like the place you used to have when we met? The bedsit?' He put the lid back on the saucepan and went to wash his hands.

'I'm hoping I can afford something a bit better than that.' She smiled. 'Even without the professorship.' She hadn't got the job, she had been told within a few days of getting back from Canada. Given everything else that was going on, it hadn't seemed as big a deal as she would have once thought. She had enough other stuff to deal with right now.

He returned and leaned against the work surface. 'Will you stay nearby?'

She intended to. There was no reason for them to completely sever ties. It wasn't like her feelings towards him had changed. He was still her friend. 'Of course,' she said.

'That's good,' he said. 'Can we still meet up? You know, hang out?'

'Obviously.'

The look of relief on his face was quite sweet, even more so because she knew how he felt. 'I'd miss you if we didn't,' she said.

'I'd miss you too.'

Without needing to be told, he passed her a handful of cherry tomatoes to go into her salad. It was strange how they'd fallen into these domestic habits. She would miss this companionship. She carefully sliced the tomatoes into quarters. It was all very well making plans to hang out, but that wouldn't last. If Gimhana found a new boyfriend, they wouldn't want her tagging along like the ultimate gooseberry. She would have to find her own social life. Maybe she could spend more time with Sara. Or take up a hobby or something.

Gimhana was looking at her again, with that mother hen expression on his face. It was nice that he worried about her, but really, she didn't need it anymore.

'How did you get on with contacting Zack?' she asked.

That distracted him. 'No luck,' he said. 'He's still not speaking to me.'

'Shall I try?'

Gimhana looked up. 'Would you?'

'I said I would, didn't I? I'll call him.'

'Or,' said Gimhana. 'We could go see him. He's in his old student house until the lease runs out. It might be better to talk to him face to face.'

His expression was so hopeful, she didn't have the heart to argue. Instead, she said, 'How do you know that he's there?'

Gim looked sheepish. 'He's blocked me from everything, but I can still see his friends' Facebook feeds. They're mostly public.'

She put the knife down. 'You really have got it bad,' she said, smiling.

Gimhana shrugged. 'Can't stop thinking about him. It's like... he's part of me. Does that make any sense?'

Chaya stilled. That was how she'd felt about Noah. How she still felt about him, if she was being honest. But he didn't want her, so that was that. The sadness gaped inside her chest, but she took a deep breath and rode it. She wasn't sure if this improvement was due to the drugs that she'd finally agreed to try, the counselling she had started again or the fact that she'd let go of something that was tying her in knots, but either way, she felt better now. Not happier, just more... normal.

'Okay,' she said. 'Let's go up there this weekend. If things go well, I'll grab a train back and you can drive back on Sunday.'

His eyes sparkled. 'Thank you.' His voice broke with emotion. He cleared his throat. 'You're a good friend.'

She smiled and sprinkled salt over the salad. 'It's the least I could do.'

–

Chaya looked out of the car window and said, 'Which house is it?'

They were in the street where Zack lived. Gimhana had pulled in awkwardly and stalled the car, which wasn't like him. Chaya looked across at him. He was staring at a house, his face taut and grey. Poor Gim.

'Is it the place with the blue door?' she asked, kindly.

He nodded.

'Okay.' She took a deep breath. 'Wish me luck.' Before he could reply, she got out of the car.

The person who answered the door wasn't Zack. 'Hi,' she said, smiling in what she hoped was a reassuring manner. 'I'm looking for Zack. I know he lives here.'

The young man looked at her. His gaze flicked up and down the street behind her.

'I just want to talk to him for a few minutes,' Chaya said. 'I'm happy to talk to him on the doorstep, if it helps.'

'One minute.' He disappeared, shutting the door behind him.

Chaya clasped her hands together. She wasn't entirely sure how she was going to persuade Zack, but it was important to Gim, so she had to try. She looked back at her friend, sitting in the car, his eyes wide as he watched. She gave him a tiny wave. He didn't respond.

The door opened again and Zack appeared. 'What do you want?'

'I need to talk to you,' she said. Afraid he would slam the door on her, she plunged on. 'I need to tell you that Gimhana loves you. He screwed up and he lied about a lot of things, but I don't think he lied about the way he feels. I've never seen him so upset about anything. And,' she said. 'We're getting a divorce.'

Zack peered past her at the car, where Gimhana was waiting.

'He's a complete mess without you,' said Chaya quietly. 'Give him another chance?'

Zack's expression was guarded when he looked at her. 'I suppose I should invite you in,' he said and stepped back.

When she entered, Zack said, 'Why should I believe you?' He stood, arms folded, at the bottom of the stairs. He had let her in the door, but not invited her any further into the house. Chaya stood in the cluttered hallway and tried not to mind the smell of old shoes and wet coats.

'Why wouldn't you?' she said, genuinely puzzled. 'I am his wife. Or was. Why would I come and talk to you about him if this wasn't true?'

He chewed the inside of his cheek. He was dressed in track-suit bottoms and a t-shirt, his hair sticking up on end, as though he'd just got up, which, given what Gimhana had said about his night shift, probably was the case. In the harsh light from the bare light bulb, he looked like he had shadows under his eyes. He was, Chaya thought, a good-looking guy. So that was Gimhana's taste.

'He's absolutely devastated about what happened,' she said. 'It was… a mistake. Not you. I mean, me. Gim and I… we should never have set off on this venture. It was a lie from start to finish and we should have known it wouldn't end well.' She shifted her weight. 'He loves you.'

Zack bent his head and put his palms to his temples, as though his head hurt. 'But he won't commit to me. He won't be seen with me. I'm just his… sordid secret.' He looked up. There were tears in his eyes. 'He doesn't respect me.'

She felt his pain. Was this how Noah felt too? That he wasn't enough? She stamped down the thought. It was too late for her and Noah, but Gimhana and this man still had a chance to be happy. She would do anything to make sure that happened.

'He does,' she said. 'The trouble is, that he… we… had so many conflicting things to keep in balance, that it was hard to do the right thing all the time.' She took a step closer. 'Look, Zack. I can't promise you that he's not going to hurt you again. I can only tell you that he's hurting too. I've known him for a long time and I've never seen him like this. Gimhana was always the strong one. The one who knew what to do. The upbeat one. I've never seen him beaten before. Losing you… it's broken him.'

He put his hands on his hips and looked down at her. 'This is so fucked up.'

She couldn't argue with that. 'It is.' She shrugged. 'Life is messy. We're all trying to get through it the best way we can.'

He glared at her, or through her, because he wasn't really seeing what was in front of him. After a second he sighed and sat down on the stairs behind him. 'It...' He rubbed his face. 'Why are you doing this? What's in it for you?'

She smiled. 'He's my friend. I love him too. Not like you do, obviously. But still. In my own way.'

He nodded. In the other room, his housemate turned the TV on. He glanced across into the living room, which Chaya couldn't see into. She shifted her weight and wondered if she'd persuaded him.

His gaze returned to her. 'I need to think about it,' he said. 'Tell him... tell him I'll think about it.'

That was the best she was going to get. 'Thank you.' She turned to go.

'Chaya,' he called after her.

'Where are you staying this evening?'

She looked over her shoulder at him. He was frowning, his expression intense. It seemed her answer would mean something.

'I'm not staying. I'm catching the train back later,' she said. 'Gimhana is staying overnight, though. In a hotel.'

His expression didn't change. He nodded. 'Okay.'

She hesitated, but he didn't seem to have anything further to say. She opened the door and stepped outside. The car was still there. Gimhana's head shot up from where he'd been resting it on the steering wheel. Poor man.

The door clicked firmly shut behind her. She hurried down to the car. Gim sprang out. 'How did it go?'

'He said he'll think about it,' she said. 'I'm sorry. It was the best I could do.'

His face fell. He looked older, and more tired than she'd ever seen him. He really did care about Zack.

'So what now?' he said.

'I don't know. Wait, I guess.' She opened the door to the car. He was staring at Zack's front door.

'Maybe you could take me to the train station?' she said.

'Huh? Oh. Yes. Of course.'

Chapter Eighty-Three

Gimhana – Manchester, 2013

Gimhana handed Chaya a latte and looked up at the departure board at the station. They were standing on the concourse at Manchester Piccadilly. Chaya's train was due to leave in about twenty minutes.

He was following her around because it was easier than trying to focus on anything. His brain seemed to be incapable of concentrating on anything for long.

The departures display refreshed itself. Still no platform number for her train.

'Gim,' said Chaya.

'Hmm.'

'Will you be okay?'

He looked down at her and felt a sudden urge to ask her to stay. Right now, he didn't know what Zack was going to say. Tomorrow could be brilliant or terrible and he didn't know which it would be. He felt raw and alone and exposed. And he really wanted to have some company. But he had already dragged her away from her work to come all this way. He should let her get on her train. She liked trains. She found them relaxing. Something about being in limbo from the real world.

'Yes, I'm sure I'll be fine,' he said.

She didn't look convinced. She drew a breath, as though she was about to say something. His phone rang.

He pulled it out. It was Zack. He looked at Chaya, whose eyes widened.

'Well, answer it,' she said.

Jolted into action, he accepted the call. 'Zack.'

'Is she still there?' he said.

'We're at the station,' Gimhana said. 'Her train—'

Chaya gave him a push. 'Go talk to him somewhere else. I'll see you tomorrow.'

'I'm going to walk out of the station now,' he said. 'Just a second.' He hurried out.

Outside, he found a railing to lean on.

'So,' said Zack. 'Has she gone?'

'Yes. I've dropped her off at the station.'

A pause. 'And you're staying?'

'Just tonight.' He gave him the name of the hotel.

'I'll meet you in the foyer at eight.' Zack hung up.

Gimhana stared at the phone, elated and frightened at the same time. It wasn't an unpleasant feeling. He just felt like he was reeling. He put his phone away and went back into the station. Chaya was gone. Gimhana ambled out of the station and walked back to the hotel, barely noticing life bustling around him.

–

Gimhana was in the foyer early. He still felt that odd sensation of being at the edge of a precipice. He had never prepared so carefully for a meeting. He had even re-ironed his already ironed shirt. He sat in one of the chairs in the foyer, a book open in his hand, trying not to look as nervous as he felt.

He saw Zack walk in and shot to his feet. Zack walked up to him and stopped a few feet away. He looked tired, poor love, and wary. So wary.

'Drink?'

Gimhana dropped his book into his satchel. 'Sure.'

They walked out together, not speaking. Not touching.

Zack took him to a pub and they found a quiet corner and sat, a small table with two pints of beer in between them.

'Zack...'

'You lied to me,' said Zack. 'How can I trust you again?'

'I'm so sorry,' said Gimhana. 'I don't know what I can do to prove that you can trust me. What can I do? I'll do it.'

Zack gave a wry sniff. 'Well, sending your wife to talk to me was a stroke of genius.'

'Almost ex-wife,' said Gimhana.

'Either way, she's pretty persuasive.'

Hope rose in his chest. 'She is?'

Zack smiled. 'Yeah.'

'So, you forgive me?' The feeling of being on the edge of something intensified. His heart raced.

Zack looked down and traced a line down the side of his glass. 'I... would like to try,' he said. 'You have to promise not to lie to me like that again.'

Relief popped like a firework in his chest. 'I promise,' Gimhana said.

'If we're going to be together, though,' said Zack. 'It has to be properly. No more hiding.'

Gimhana opened his mouth, then closed it again. 'I'm not sure how open I can be,' he said. 'If I'm being honest.'

'Then what's the point?' said Zack.

'The point is that I'm in love with you. I haven't felt like this about anyone in... actually, I've never felt like this about anyone.'

'I ... really like you,' said Zack. 'But I'm not built for subter-fuge. It took so much for me to come out. I'm not going back again. This is very important to me.'

Gimhana looked down at his hands. He wasn't wearing a wedding ring, he never had, but he could feel the symbolism of its absence now. He had tried fitting in. All it had brought was heartbreak. And he loved Zack. A life without him would be unbearable. He could try being out, even though the thought terrified him, if it meant another chance with Zack.

'How about...' he said, slowly. 'We meet in the middle? I will be more open, but you'll have to be patient with me.'

'Will you come out to your parents?'

'Already did that.' He took a sip of his drink, to hide his discomfort.

'Shit. How did they take it?'

Gimhana sighed. 'My mum's still talking to me. Just about. Dad... not so much.'

'Oh, that's harsh. I'm sorry,' said Zack. 'But... y'know, well done. You did it and that's amazing.'

The approval in his voice helped mitigate the pain. Gimhana muttered, 'Thanks.'

'And me?' Zack said. 'What do you expect from me?' He still looked wary, but not as much as he had done.

'Just... be discreet? A bit. Understand that it's a big change for me.'

Zack looked thoughtfully at him for a minute, then a slow smile grew on his face. 'That sounds fair.'

Gimhana's breath hitched. He wanted to kiss him so badly, it hurt. He looked round the pub, it was reasonably busy and he didn't know how friendly the neighbourhood was. So he reached across the table and squeezed Zack's hand instead. He let go and picked up his pint.

Zack grinned and moved his seat, until his knee was nestled next to Gimhana's.

He leaned forward. His knee moved against Gimhana's thigh. 'So,' he said. 'What happened since we last met?'

Gimhana tried to focus. 'Uh... well, I filed for divorce.'

Zack laughed. 'I meant in between those two events.'

They talked, but Gimhana couldn't really keep track of it all. Every time Zack moved, his knee rubbed against Gimhana's leg. Zack was teasing him and he knew it. He wouldn't exchange this for anything.

Finally, after what felt like an eternity, Zack said, 'Shall we head?'

Gimhana was only too happy to grab his bag and follow the younger man out.

'Hotel?' he said.

Zack grinned at him. 'Yeah.'

Gimhana felt a burst of happiness so intense, he was surprised he didn't explode.

Chapter Eighty-Four

Chaya – London, 2013 (One Month Later)

Chaya rummaged through the boxes to find the one with the bedding in it. Since neither of them wanted to stay in the house, she and Gimhana had put the house up for sale. Today he was helping her move into a one-bedroom flat in Swiss Cottage. It was an easy tube ride to work and it was closer to Sara and Jay than before.

'Where do you want this to go?' said Gimhana, looking at the bed that he and Jay had bolted together earlier in the day. Sara, Jay and their sons had been tramping around the little flat all afternoon, carrying boxes up from the van and putting together flat pack furniture. Now that they had left, the place seemed quiet and a little empty. The flat smelled of new furniture and fish and chips.

Gimhana had stayed behind to help finish off a few last things so that the place was habitable for her first night.

Chaya stood next to him. 'How about there? I get the sunshine in the morning, so if I open the curtain, I'll be able to step into the sunlight when I get up.'

They pushed the bed into position. Gimhana placed a cardboard box next to it to make a makeshift bedside table. 'We forgot to get you a bedside table.'

'I'll live,' said Chaya. 'Aha. Found it.' She threw a set of sheets on the bed and flapped out the fitted sheet.

Gimhana grabbed a corner and helped. 'Are you sure about all this?'

'Oh, yeah,' she said. She found the pillows and started pulling on pillow cases. 'I'll buy more furniture later. There's plenty of time to get things right.'

'No, I meant, everything,' he said. He waved a hand, encompassing the room and somehow the whole situation as well. 'The divorce, this place... everything. It's a lot of change. Are you sure you're okay?'

She straightened up and looked at him. He was standing surrounded by bags and boxes, his sleeves rolled up and there was a piece of polystyrene in his hair. She went up to him and removed the small white chip. 'Yes,' she said. 'I'm okay.'

'Good,' he said. "Cause I don't get crap in my hair for just anyone.'

She laughed and gave him a hug. 'I know. Thank you.'

He wrapped his arms around her and hugged her back. 'I'm sorry about how things worked out.'

'No you're not,' she said, stepping away. 'When's he coming down?'

'Next week.' Gimhana took one end of the duvet and handed her the other.

'Moving in together is a big step,' she said.

'It is.' He helped her stuff the duvet into its cover and gave it a shake. 'But it feels like the right thing to do.'

'Good. I'm glad. You look like a happier man.' She meant it. He really did look better now. In the weeks between now and their trip to Manchester to talk to Zack, Gimhana had accepted a new job and handed in his notice at his old firm. Between them, they'd told their families about their separation with varying results. Malini had been very supportive of Chaya getting a divorce. Amma had been distressed, but no more than she was on a normal 'bad' day. Gimhana's mother was speaking to him again, but his father was still refusing to.

'Pity it didn't work out for you,' said Gimhana, not looking at her.

She shrugged. 'It's probably for the best.' Curiously, she almost believed this. She still felt the lack of Noah in her life most days, but she was so used it, that she'd have missed it if the ache went away. In all other aspects of life, things were looking better. She was seeing a therapist, who was helping her unravel the knots she'd tied herself up in over the years. She didn't have to please anyone any more. She didn't know what she wanted for the future, but she had a feeling of *possibility*. She could do anything. Anything she wanted. If only she knew what that was.

'If you need anything,' said Gimhana. 'You know you can just call me.' The corners of his mouth twitched. Something was amusing him. Or perhaps he was just thinking of Zack. That must be it.

'I know.' She smiled, happy that he was so happy. 'You're a good friend, Gim.'

'Oh, you have no idea,' he said, grinning now.

Okay. He was up to something. She could feel it. 'What do you mean? What have you done?'

He twitched his eyebrows at her. 'I thought of a plan B,' he said.

'Plan B? What plan B? I thought this was plan B?'

His phone rang. Gimhana looked at the display. 'I have to get this,' he said, giving her another grin before threading his way between the boxes and out of the room.

She stared after him, wondering what he was up to. She cursed Zack's rotten timing, phoning just when he was about to tell her. He was talking softly in the kitchen. Chaya shook her head and finished making the bed.

Once the bed was done, she leaned against the window and surveyed the room. If you ignored the boxes and bags, it was quite homely. There was a built-in wardrobe, a sink attached to the wall and the chest of drawers that used to be in her old bedroom. After years of being rented out, the wallpaper and carpet in the flat looked faded and unloved, but the place was warm and cosy and just big enough for her.

The last time she'd rented, it had been a tiny bedsit where everything was within arm's reach. This flat was luxurious in comparison. Apart from the bedroom, she had a living room, a kitchen and a bathroom. The rent was twice as much as her bedsit, but it was worth it.

In the kitchen, she thought she heard Gimhana giving someone directions to the flat. It couldn't be Zack. He wasn't due to arrive until the following week. Gim was still sorting out various things for her, including her telephone and internet connection, perhaps the phone call was to do with one of them. Chaya stepped into the living room.

Gimhana turned. 'Okay,' he said, into the phone. 'I'll see you in a bit.'

He hung up. 'Is there anything else that needs to be done before I head off?' He was trying very hard not to grin.

'Not that I can think of,' she said. 'Gim, what's going on?'

He put on his most innocent expression. 'Nothing.'

Chaya's mobile phone, which was sitting on top of a box in the kitchen, started to ring. Gimhana looked delighted. 'Aren't you going to get that?' he said. When she picked up the phone, he said, 'Good luck.'

She didn't recognise the number on the display. Suspiciously, she said, 'Hello?'

'Chaya.' He didn't need to tell her who he was. She would always recognise his voice.

'Noah?'

'Yes. Hi.'

Her stomach flipped. She leaned against the kitchen counter, confused. 'What…?'

'I understand that this is a bit sudden,' said Noah. 'I… well, I got your message on my answer phone. I didn't want to risk being hurt again…'

'I remember.' A lump was starting to form in her throat. The mere sound of Noah's voice awakened the familiar pain inside. She had thought she would never hear it again. All her thoughts about freedom and coping on her own evaporated. Her pulse picked up pace. She had been doing so well and it was all undone in one phone call.

Noah cleared his throat. 'Well, the thing is, I really meant it, at the time. I convinced myself that it would be a bad idea to come to the airport to see you off.'

Surely, he hadn't phoned her just to tell her that. Her heart pumped furiously. She didn't say anything.

'The trouble was,' said Noah. 'I couldn't bring myself to erase your message. I kept listening to it, over and over and over. I woke up at night and played it, just to hear your voice again.'

She wanted to say something, but her mouth was dry and her mind had gone blank.

'Alex found out...' Noah's voice cracked. 'He asked about what I was doing and... and why. He made me see...' he sighed. 'I'm an idiot, Chaya. You asked me to leave, and I loved you so much, that I did. I thought that, if you love someone, you should set them free, even if it breaks your heart to do it.' His breath sounded ragged. 'I was wrong.'

Oh Noah. She had been wrong too. So wrong. She'd thought that by not seeing him, she could stop loving him. But all it did was hurt, hurt, hurt. *I was a fool,* she wanted to say. *A complete idiot. I'm sorry.* But none of it came out. 'I...'

Noah cleared his throat. 'So,' he said. 'I called your work. They said you were taking some time off. And I thought I'd lost you all over again. Then, a few days ago, your husband phoned me.'

Chaya whirled round, looking for Gimhana. He had disappeared into the other room. She took a few steps into the hallway, in a feeble attempt to find him. '*Ex* husband.'

'He explained about your arrangement We talked about a lot of things,' Noah continued.

Her heart pounded so loudly that she was afraid she wouldn't be able to hear what Noah was saying.

'Chaya?'

'Yes?'

'Chaya, I love you. I've always loved you. I never stopped. I spent all those years secretly dreaming about you coming back to me and when you did, I sent you away.'

Her heart beat louder and louder. Her chest constricted. It was like a panic attack, but instead of the walls closing in, they seemed to opening up, releasing her from a prison she'd built for herself.

The doorbell made her jump. She stared at the door and backed away from it. She wasn't sure what this phone call was all about, but she knew she didn't want it interrupted.

Gimhana appeared. Grateful, she stopped her retreat.

'I have never been as happy as I was when I was with you, Chaya,' Noah's voice wavered.

Gimhana slipped outside, leaving Chaya alone with Noah's voice. The door was left ajar. As she stepped forward to close it, someone pushed it open from the other side.

'I would like to get to know you again…' Noah stepped into the flat, a phone pressed to his ear. Slowly, he lowered his arm. '…if you'll have me,' he said. Behind him, the door clicked shut.

They stared at each other, both breathing hard. For a moment, the rest of the world ceased to exist. Time, the world, her heart, all stood still. All she could see was Noah. Only a few feet of carpet, a mere stride, separated them. But in it lay seventeen lost years. They had loved each other as teenagers and lost. Now, in middle age, she was being offered a second chance.

She couldn't believe that he was standing there, in her new hallway. His hair was windblown and falling into his eyes. Any moment now, he would push it back with that impatient flick. She knew without looking that there would be freckles on his arms, that he wore a t-shirt under his shirt, that his hair would feel soft under her fingers. All this time had passed and still she carried all these pieces of information inside. Pieces of dreams she'd tried not to have. Memories she'd tried not to relive. How foolish she had been to think that she could erase him from her life. To her surprise, tears rolled down her face.

A small frown of worry appeared on Noah's forehead. 'Say something,' he said.

Her chest felt like it was about to burst. She opened her fingers and her phone dropped to the ground.

The movement seemed to break the spell. They both moved forward at the same time. Noah pulled her close, an arm around her waist, a hand caressing her hair. She slid her arms around him, a movement so familiar she didn't even realise she was doing it. Her head rested in the space between his shoulder and chin and she breathed him in.

'I've missed you,' he whispered, his breath tickling her neck. 'I've missed you so much.' He hugged her so tightly that the air squeezed out of her lungs, making her gasp.

He released her and took her face in his hands. His thumbs gently wiped away the tears. 'You were crying when I met you,' he said, softly, echoing what he'd said when they'd parted all those years ago.

She leaned her cheek against his palm, just as she had done the last time. Noah smiled and leaned in, slowly, with the tiniest hesitation, as though he expected her to disappear any second.

Chaya rose on her tiptoes to meet him. When their lips met, she could feel the smile on his.

The last time she'd kissed him, it had been a kiss goodbye. This one was a whole new beginning.

On the floor, where she'd dropped it, Chaya's phone beeped. The next day she would find a text message from Gimhana saying:

Welcome to plan B.

A LETTER FROM JEEVANI

Thank you for reading *A Convenient Marriage*. I really hope you enjoyed the story!

If you enjoyed the story, please leave a review. It doesn't have to be long, just a sentence or two will do. Quite apart from making my day (thank you!), your review will help other readers work out whether this is the sort of book they'd like to read. If you know anyone who might like it, please tell them about it.

This was the first novel I wrote. I started sending it off to agents back in 2007 (by post, because this was the olden days!). You know how this goes – the rejections came in and some of them had notes written on the rejection slip. I was close, but not quite there yet.

In an attempt to work out how to make the book better, I joined the Romantic Novelists Association's NWS scheme. It's the best decision I ever made. My NWS report was detailed and told me where my book was weak. It also told me to try writing something funny, if only for fun. That's how I came to write as Rhoda Baxter. I found publishers for those books and kept on writing them, but in the background, there was always this book. The *first* book. I edited it. Then edited it again. And again. I think I've written about 300000 words in order to find the right ones to make this story work. I think (hope!) it's finally there now.

This book was inspired by 'what if's. My cultural upbringing was similar to Chaya's and Gimhana's. When I fell in love with a non-Sri Lankan, I was lucky enough that my family understood. But what if someone hadn't been so lucky? What if the person they loved was the same sex as them – something rarely discussed in Sri Lankan families? Gimhana remains one of my favourite characters. He first appeared in a fragment I wrote in creative writing class – he was hiding behind a pillar at a party. I think I was supposed to be focusing on setting, but he came along and stole the scene. He makes me smile whenever he shows up on the page.

Chaya is my answer to 'what if someone had a nervous breakdown and tried to carry on without help'? She changed a little with each rewrite of the book as I worked out why she was like she was. The more I learned about mental illness, the more she came into focus. With each iteration, her interactions with Noah changed too. It became more and more a story about the one that got away. The one thing that didn't change was Chaya's friendship with Gimhana. It was always the core of the story.

I would really love to hear what you think of the story, especially if it touched your life in any way. So, apart from writing a review (hint, hint!), if you want to talk to me, I'm usually hanging around on Twitter as @rhodabaxter (less frequently as @jeevanicharika) . Come say hello.

If you want to know what happened next to Chaya and Gimhana, I have a 'two years later' epilogue that you can get by joining my newsletter group at https://subscribe. jeevanicharika.com/Chaya

If you're reading it as part of a book club, then drop by my website where there's a list of questions for book clubs.

Happy reading

Jeevani

Website: www.jeevanicharika.com

ACKNOWLEDGMENTS

First of all, thanks to Jen Hicks and Joelle Tunning, without their ~~nagging~~ constant encouragement, this book wouldn't have got past chapter 3. A special nod to Jen who had read more than one version of it and given me feedback.

Thank you to the Romantic Novelists Association. This book was my first submission to the New Writers Scheme. My reader, it turned out, was Sue Moorcroft. Thank you for your invaluable input, Sue. I took your advice and thirteen years later, here it is!

Thank you to Federica Leonardis for helping me pummel the story into shape. Special thanks to Liam Livings, who beta read an earlier version and gave me lots of useful feedback about gay culture in the 90s. Thanks especially for giving me an excuse to talk about Jem and the Holograms.

Thank you to the fabulous ladies of the Naughty Kitchen for support and cheerleading and being a shoulder to cry on when things get too frustrating. Writer brain is very frustrating. You guys are the best.

Thank you also to Keshini and Lindsey at Hera for believing in this book and helping me polish it until it shone!

As always, thank you to my little family for putting up with me muttering bits of dialogue while I cook dinner and my total lack of a sense of humour after 8pm when it's my 'writing time'. Thank you to my big family for being supportive. It means a lot.

Last of all, thank you to *you*, the reader, for reading my books. Until the story goes from my head to yours via a book, it hasn't completed its journey. I literally couldn't do this without you.